HE ENCIRCLED her in his arms and she reached up to take his face in her hands. His lips brushed against hers, just the slightest whisper of a touch, and for the first time in her life, Carly understood what people meant when they said that *time stopped*. There was nothing in her world but Ford, and that delicious mouth, and the arms that pressed her to him. The sheer awareness of him spread through her, head to toe, and she felt her breathing go shallow and her heart pound. When his lips traced a trail from her mouth to her cheek, from her cheek to her neck, she thought either her head would explode or she'd faint, she wasn't sure which, and for the longest moment, she didn't care.

When his mouth made its way back to hers, she wrapped her arms around his neck and backed up against the table. His hands skimmed her back, then her hips, before settling momentarily on her waist. His body was hard against hers, pinning her against the table and his tongue teased the corners of her mouth until she felt dangerously close to losing control.

His hands grew still on her hips, and his mouth broke free from hers.

"Wow," he whispered. "For someone so small, you pack an enormous punch."

BY MARIAH STEWART

On Sunset Beach
At the River's Edge
The Long Way Home
Home for the Summer
Hometown Girl
Almost Home
Home Again
Coming Home

Acts of Mercy
Cry Mercy
Mercy Street

Last Breath
Last Words
Last Look

Final Truth
Dark Truth
Hard Truth
Cold Truth

Dead End
Dead Even
Dead Certain
Dead Wrong

Forgotten
Until Dark
The President's Daughter

ON SUNSET BEACH

The Chesapeake Diaries Book 8

MARIAH STEWART

BALLANTINE BOOKS • NEW YORK

A Ballantine Books Mass Market Original

Copyright © 2014 by Marti Robb

Published in the United States by Ballantine Books, an imprint of Random House, a division of Random House LLC, a Penguin Random House Company, New York.

BALLANTINE and the HOUSE colophon are registered trademarks of Random House LLC.

ISBN 978-0-345-53843-7
eBook ISBN 978-0-345-54675-3

Cover design: Scott Biel
Cover image: Kraig Scarbinsky/Photodisc/Getty Images

Printed in the United States of America

www.ballantinebooks.com

9 8 7 6 5 4 3 2 1

Ballantine Books mass market edition: July 2014

For Rebecca Jane Robb, Esq.

ACKNOWLEDGMENTS

Writing a novel—much like raising a child—takes a village. I will be eternally grateful to everyone at Ballantine Books for being my village—especially Gina Wachtel, Junessa Viloria, and most of all, Linda Marrow, who bought my first book lo those many years ago and started me on this incredible journey.

Heartfelt thanks to my agent, Loretta Barrett, for always representing me with honesty and integrity, and for the blessing of your friendship.

Thanks to Chery Griffin, Helen Egner, and Jo Ellen Grossman for unwavering friendship across the years and across the miles. I love you and appreciate the support you always offer.

And thanks to my beautiful, crazy, wonderful family—Bill, Becca, Kate, Mike, Cole, and Jack. You are my everything.

ON SUNSET BEACH

Diary ~

My baby boy is on his way home! Finally! Yes, at this very moment, Ford is making his way to Virginia, where he's to meet with someone . . . his explanation of this was somewhat murky but perhaps it was the poor connection that left me confused. In any event, he's back on our soil and on his way home, and isn't that what matters?

Certainly that matters more than the unrest that has been eating away at me since, well, since the day he left. I've always been able to "read" my children—though there were times, I must admit, I was unsure how to interpret that which I was picking up, times when their emotions somehow served to block the signal, so to speak. I've never really understood how that worked, frankly, especially when I tried so hard to see through that fog when I knew something was not right. I suppose some might say that type of prying is akin to reading one's child's diary, but since at those times I was unable to break through—well, no harm, no foul.

I suppose what I'm trying to say is that ever since Ford left, I've been unable to see through the fog. Right now the mist surrounding him is so deep I could barely breathe when I spoke to him. What I'm picking up are undefined emotions— a melancholy, a sadness, as if he's in mourning—but no clues as to their source. And I sense a deep conflict—wanting to come home yet wanting to stay to . . . what? There's a sense of unfinished business. Of course there could be a simple and logical explanation for his mixed feelings. After all, he has worked with the same group of people for several years, and I'm sure that leaving—leaving them behind, as it were—could well be the source of his conflict.

I try to convince myself this is all very benign, but then I sense something more. Something that is shrouded in darkness, something vengeful and frightening. Something I have never sensed in that boy before. When I try to decipher it, the fog turns to black smoke and drifts skyward as if it were smoke from a chimney. I have no idea what this means, but it fills me with an unholy dread.

I dreamed of a bleeding heart last night. Yes, the flower, but I know what this symbol means in that other world into which I so often glimpse. This is all I know for certain: my boy has a heartache, and that heartache is what has sent him home—and the closer he gets to St. Dennis, the farther away he seems to be.

As for the rest of it—the darkness, the fear—I have no clue.

Of course I've gone to my board seeking some clarity—

but you know, it's useful only if someone on the other side is listening. So far Alice—who's always so dependable in situations like this, don't you know—has been silent. My attempts to contact other friends who have gone before have been equally unsuccessful—but let's face it, Alice is my ace in the hole, so to speak. If she isn't talking . . . well, I can't begin to fathom what that might mean.

And that in itself is the most disconcerting of all.

~ *Grace* ~

Chapter 1 ⌁

I SPENT *much of today contemplating ways to kill my husband.*

"Whoa! Way to kick off a new year!" Carly Summit's eyebrows rose as she read the entry dated 1 January, 1905, in the journal she'd received in the mail that afternoon.

If James continues to deny me my artistic pursuits—as he so arrogantly professes he will do—I shall be forced to do something . . . well, something dire. While he voiced no such misgivings before we were married, suddenly he fears that the reputation of an up-and-coming banker (such as himself) would be tainted should his wife accept money for her work. Have I not promised to never use my married name on my work, that the RYDER name would remain pure and unsullied by my craft? Is the man really so simpleminded that he believes an ultimatum such as the one he issued at dinner would have me put down my brushes and destroy my canvases? Is his ego truly so fragile that he fears societal censure should I accept payment for my paintings? Can he really expect me to choose him over my work?

Had I suspected his narrow-mindedness before the wedding, I swear this marriage would never have happened. As it is, I shall simply ignore him.

Hmm. My work . . . his life.

Sometimes I think the choice is simple enough.

Carly sighed heavily and jotted the date and the sentiment in the notebook she kept by her side. As an art dealer and owner of upscale galleries in New York, Boston, and Chicago, and managing partner of several abroad, she was well familiar with stories of women who had been discouraged or even forbidden to pursue their art. But Carolina Ellis's story was more immediate and more intimate, partly because Carly was reading the story in its entirety in the artist's own words, partly because the artist was the great-great-grandmother of Carly's best friend, Ellie Ryder, and partly because Carly had recently discovered a cache of previously unknown works by this remarkable early-twentieth-century artist.

Carly had spent days examining each individual painting, but it had been through studying the collection as a whole that she was able to follow the artist's journey. Carolina's own words had opened a window into her very soul, a window through which Carly had been able to observe the artist's growth as she experimented with different media while seeking to gain her creative footing. Starting with pastels, Carolina moved on to charcoal (which she'd pronounced "too moody"), then to watercolor, to oils, then back to watercolor again, where, her journal proclaimed, she'd found her best, most expressive self. Using the journals and the paintings that were available to her, Carly had created an artistic time line that permitted her to trace the progression and development of Carolina's talent and ambitions. By putting the works in order—only some of the paintings had been dated—Carly felt as if she had been able to look over the artist's shoulder to watch as different methods, media, and techniques were tried and discarded, until Carolina's craft had been perfected.

Had there ever been such a find?

And the coolest part, as far as Carly was concerned, was that no one else knew the paintings—or the journals—existed.

Well, no one other than herself and Ellie. Okay, add Ellie's fiancé, Cameron O'Connor, but he wouldn't tell anyone. And Carly's parents—there was no way she'd be able to keep such momentous news from them, but she'd sworn them to secrecy. But no one else knew about the extraordinary find Carly had made while visiting the house Ellie inherited from her mother in St. Dennis, Maryland. There, Carolina had met and married James Ryder, raised their two children, John and Lilly, and scandalously defied her husband's wishes by setting up an artist's studio on the third floor of their home on the Chesapeake Bay, where she spent part of every day working at her easel.

Carly rested her elbows on the desk and continued reading.

"Amazing," she muttered as she read on. "That this woman was able to produce such works while under this sort of domestic strain . . ."

She reached for the phone somewhat absently when it rang.

"Yes?" she said.

"That's how you answer your phone now?" a familiar voice teased. "'Yes?'"

"Oh, Mom. Hi. Sorry. I was deep into one of Carolina's journals that just arrived this afternoon. Ellie found a box in the attic that held a few more and she sent them to me. My head is absolutely spinning."

"Lots of fodder for your book, I imagine." Roberta Summit was almost as fascinated by the Carolina Ellis story as her daughter. "I can't wait for you to finish Carolina's biography. Remember, you did promise that I could be your beta-reader."

"Yes, but I need you to be brutally honest."

"Not to worry. What kind of an editor would I be if I only told you what I thought you wanted to hear?"

Carly paused momentarily. Should she tell her mother that she'd hired a professional editor for her book, one who was already hard at work on the first half of the manuscript? Perhaps not. Roberta was so pleased at the opportunity to be helpful, to contribute to her daughter's work. Carly decided to keep that fact to herself.

"I can email you the first half and you can let me know what you think of it so far, if you like."

"Yes. Please. I can't wait to read it."

Carly opened her computer and attached the file to an email, which she addressed to her mother.

"It's on its way, Mom. I want this book to be fabulous and to generate a ton of interest in Carolina so that when I open my exhibit, people will stand in line for the opportunity to see her work." Carly straightened her spine to get the kinks out, then walked to the window. Outside all was dark. When, she wondered, had day turned to evening?

"The art world will be turned on its head when you announce what you've found. These paintings will create an absolutely deafening roar," Roberta assured her. "After all, no one has any idea that these works even exist."

"Every time I think about that, my brain threatens to explode. I can barely sit still long enough to write sometimes."

"I can only imagine what it's like to have made a find like this, and to have it all to yourself. Bless Ellie for trusting you enough to turn the entire project over to you, no strings. Of course, you were a good friend to her throughout all her troubles."

"We've been best friends since sixth grade," Carly reminded her mother. "The fact that her father was a crook is no reflection on her."

"I absolutely agree, and you know we love Ellie. But the fact of the matter is that you stood by her when everyone else she knew walked away."

"That's what best friends do. Ellie's at a very happy place in her life right now. Engaged to Cameron, living in that wonderful old house in St. Dennis—and she's learned a whole new skill set from Cameron. She can strip wallpaper and sling a hammer with the best of them now."

"Whoever would have thought that the daughter of a Wall Street giant and one of the world's first supermodels would end up working as a carpenter in some little bayside town on the Chesapeake?" Roberta mused.

"I know, right? But she's doing exactly what she

wants to do. If you could see how happy she is, you'd understand."

"I'd love to see her and meet this wonderful man of hers."

"Cam's the best. Maybe you can visit sometime when I go to St. Dennis. And not to worry about that little bayside town. It's quite the place. You should look it up on the Web," Carly suggested.

"I think I'll do exactly that. I don't know why I didn't think of it myself."

"So when will you be home?" Carly asked.

"Your father still has some business here in Portland," Roberta told her. "He's personally been supervising the design of the new plant Summit Industries is building. You know how he is about the safety of his employees."

"I do know. Everyone should be held to his standards." Patrick Summit was well known for his progressive efforts in plant safety and employee welfare.

"How's everything back in Connecticut?"

"Everything's good. I appreciate you letting me move all those paintings into your house."

"Don't be silly. It's your family home. You—and your paintings—are welcome anytime. Stay as long as you like."

"Normally I would stay at my own place, but your security here is so superior to what I have at the town house. I think the paintings are safer here."

"No need to explain. Though it does have me wondering just how good the security at your town house really is . . ."

They chatted for a few more minutes before Roberta said, "I should let you get back to your work.

I know you're eager to finish your book and start putting your exhibit together."

"I know exactly where every painting will go. Well, at least until I change my mind again."

"You're still planning on debuting the collection in your New York gallery?"

"Absolutely. New York is the hub of the art world. I can't imagine doing this anywhere else."

"What about the other galleries? Who's minding the store while you're so focused on this one artist?"

"You know I have great people working for me. Enrico is running New York, Helena is running Boston, and Colby has Chicago under control. London is still closed temporarily while they're making the repairs from that storm last month, but I'm seriously considering selling my interests in London and Istanbul. I've had long-standing offers on both, and I think it's time to divest."

"Are you sure that you want to close yourself off from the European market?" Ellie could hear the frown in her mother's voice.

"I won't be. Isabella is capable of handling London on her own. Though she's made me an offer for my half, and I'm strongly considering it."

"Do you need the money?"

"I need the time more than the money. As much as it pains me to admit it, I've realized that I've spread myself too thin. I'm finding that my focus is beginning to narrow—I'm more interested in providing a showcase for women artists. Besides, I don't feel that I need to prove myself anymore, not the way I did when I purchased those venues. I've made my name."

"That you have. I'm sure you'll make the right decision. Well, good luck with it all. I see your email is here. I'm hanging up so I can start reading immediately."

"Let me know what you think as soon as you've finished it. Love you. Love to Dad."

Carly stood and stretched after disconnecting the call. An unexpected yawn brought on an inner debate over whether or not to make a cup of coffee. Caffeine at this hour could keep her awake till dawn. On the other hand, she reasoned, she'd probably be reading till the wee hours anyway. She made the coffee and carried the mug back to her desk, then settled in and resumed reading.

She was halfway through one of Carolina's journals when she came across a loose piece of folded paper. Curious, she unfolded it, read it, then reread it, then read it again.

"Holy shit. Could this even be possible?"

Her heart beating faster, her hands shaking, she reached for the phone and speed-dialed Ellie's number.

"Ellie, there are more," she said breathlessly when her friend answered. "She says there are more."

Ellie laughed. "Who said there's more of what?"

"Carolina. She made a list—"

"Whoa. Slow down. Take a deep breath and start over."

Carly inhaled sharply, exhaled, then repeated the process.

"I'm reading one of the journals you just sent. She—Carolina—is talking about how her husband will not let her sell any of her paintings. At one point she was thinking maybe she should do away with him, but I digress. Anyway, she kept on painting and years later found herself with all of these canvases, so guess what she did?"

"She put them in the attic, where we found them."

"Wrong. Those were apparently the ones she kept for herself." Carly forced another breath. "When she found herself with stacks of paintings, she began giving them away."

"She gave her paintings away?"

"I thought that would get your attention."

"Seriously? *She gave them away?* Who'd she give them to?"

"I guess her family, her friends. She made a list. It fell out of the journal I was reading." Carly unfolded the paper. "Stop me if you recognize any of these names . . ."

She started reading the list aloud. Ellie stopped her only once.

"That last name was Sinclair? I know Grace Sinclair. You've met her, I think," Ellie said. "Actually, I've seen that painting—well, a painting—in the lobby at the Inn at Sinclair's Point."

"Carolina gave several paintings to someone with that last name. I can't read the first name, though."

"Could be someone related to Grace's husband. His family has been in St. Dennis for a really long time. I can ask her."

"Could you maybe ask her if she knows any of the other names? I can scan the list and email it to you."

"Sure."

"Great. I'd love to track down these paintings."

"And then what?"

"What?"

"What if you're able to track some of them down? What then?"

"Well, first I'll see if I can buy them. If not, I'll see if we can borrow them for the exhibit in my gallery. I think once people see how much Carolina's work can fetch, they might give serious consideration to selling."

"Maybe." Ellie sounded thoughtful. "But don't be surprised if some might want to hold on to them if the paintings have been in their family for a long time. Then again, don't be surprised if some of them have disappeared over the years. You know, if they were thought to be of no real value back then, some of those paintings might not still be around."

"I guess we'll just have to let that play out. First, we have to figure out who these people are and then determine if they still have the paintings."

"I'll do my best. I'll be seeing Grace soon. We're both on a committee to decide what to do about the Enright property."

"What's the Enright property?"

"Curtis Enright recently signed over the title of his home to the town, and everyone in St. Dennis is all abuzz about it. He set up a trust for maintenance and taxes, so it isn't going to cost the town anything. He wants it used as an arts center."

"Great idea. Every town should have one."

"It would be awesome," Ellie agreed. "I'll show Grace your list when I see her next Tuesday, see if she knows anyone on it or has any thoughts on where some of the paintings might be."

Carly felt a nip of disappointment. "Not till next week? I was hoping for something a little sooner."

"Can't do it. Grace's son is coming back from Africa tomorrow. Or maybe it was today." Ellie paused. "Anyway, he's been away for a couple of years and has quit the . . . I forget whether he was in the Peace Corps or something else. UN Peacekeeper maybe? Whatever. Grace has been over the moon about him coming home, so this week's meeting has been moved to next week. Besides, don't you have something else to do? A book to write? A gallery or four to run?"

"All of that, yes. Fortunately, I have very competent staffs in the galleries, and the exhibits that are currently running were set up before I got distracted by your great-great-grandmother and her glorious hidden stash of art. So I'm really concentrating on the book mostly. I'm almost finished, but I don't want to rush it. I want it to be good and I want it to be accurate. I want Carolina's spirit to show through."

"Sounds like you're getting to know the old girl quite well."

"I really feel as if I am. The more I read, the more I think she was a very modern woman trapped in an archaic world."

"Nice subtitle."

"Hmm." Carly wrote down her words in the margin of her notebook before she forgot them. "Maybe. Thanks for the idea."

"Don't mention it. Gotta run. Got an early date with the alarm clock. Send me your list whenever, and I'll see what I can dig up for you."

The ink on Carolina's list was faded and hard to read, so Carly photocopied it then scanned it into her computer. She enlarged and darkened the text before sending it to Ellie, who probably hadn't expected to receive it that quickly. But Carly was compelled to get that phase of the project moving, lest it weigh on her mind until it was in Ellie's hands. The job done, she sat back at her desk and picked up the journal.

"So, let's see what other surprises you have in store for me, Carolina." Carly rested her feet on the desk and crossed her ankles. "What other secrets have you been hiding for the past hundred or so years . . ."

Working on the effects of caffeine, Carly read for several more hours before falling asleep at the desk. When she finally awoke, every part of her body was cramped. Upon standing, she found her left leg numb from having sat with it under her for all that time. She stretched and flexed until she could walk without stumbling.

Through the French doors of the study, she could see the first pale colors of dawn. She unlocked the doors and stepped out onto the patio. The air was still, heavy with humidity, and saturated with the heady fragrance of honeysuckle mingled with rose. She inhaled deeply, then walked on bare feet to the edge of the stone wall that surrounded the patio. The only sound was the waterfall that overlooked the pool. She lowered herself onto one of the lounge chairs and leaned back to watch the stars as their last light flickered before disappearing with the dawn. Tired but still buzzed, in her mind she arranged, then rearranged Carolina's paintings on the walls of her Manhattan gallery for what was probably the fiftieth time.

While she'd earlier professed to her mother that she no longer felt a need to prove herself, in her heart, Carly knew that wasn't quite true. She was well aware that many in the art world considered her a lightweight, a wannabe player with deep pockets behind her. Armed with her degrees and her parents' money, she'd boldly opened the gallery in Tribeca when she was twenty-five years old, but she'd heard the talk then, and sometimes she still heard a whisper here and there. Her petite size and long blond hair had given rise to a host of snarky comments about "Alice in Wonderland using her daddy's money to take on the big boys."

It had taken several years before she'd been taken seriously, but these days, there didn't seem to be as much comment on her appearance as there once had been. She'd worked hard to establish relationships with artists whom she considered up-and-comers, treating them as important long before they became relevant, and, in doing so, had a long list of now-prominent artists who would deal only with her. She had not been unaware of the presence of other gallery owners at the last of her several openings. The word on the street was that Carly Summit had a knack for finding and cultivating the artists who would become the next big thing. Her reputation was flawless, yet she knew that more than one rival turned green with envy every time she announced a new showing for an artist they'd hoped to exhibit.

"Well, tough," she muttered. She'd earned her good name the hard way. Yes, her parents had fronted the money for her galleries—she'd never tried to deny that—but she'd paid them back in full. She was pretty sure that there were some who still believed that Patrick and Roberta still wrote the checks, but there was nothing Carly could do about that. Still, her success and her reputation aside, she sometimes felt that she had to work her butt off to prove that she was the real deal.

Which was why, she acknowledged, Carolina Ellis now dominated her days and nights. Once Carly announced her find and her plans to introduce the long-hidden paintings to the public, no one would ever again be able to question her legitimacy.

It had taken her a long time to admit that bankrolling the European galleries had been part of her efforts to be taken seriously—a longer time still to recognize that many in the international art world viewed her actions as those of an amateur, someone with more money than good sense, a desperate attempt to make a big splash in that very big pool. While she'd done well with those investments, it was time to focus on her real passion—American women artists of the past century. Carolina Ellis would be the first of what Carly hoped would be a long line of fine women painters whose works would be displayed and brought to prominence by Summit Galleries.

She yawned, closed her eyes, and with visions of long walls filled with glorious art dancing in her head, slept until midmorning.

Chapter 2 ~

FORD Sinclair eased his rental car onto the approach to the Chesapeake Bay Bridge-Tunnel in Virginia Beach and reduced his speed. It had been several years since he'd made this crossing, and he wanted to savor it. The bridge—named one of the Seven Engineering Marvels of the Modern World—had been a favorite destination when he was a young boy and his father was still alive. Some days, they would sneak away from the family's inn, just the two of them, and head south in the old Bay Rider down through Virginia's Pocomoke Sound. His father would drop anchor off Raccoon Island, where they'd sit for a while and watch the cars passing over the northbound span of the bridge-tunnel—which was still new back then, and attracted attention like a shiny new toy—then they'd head back into Maryland waters, where they'd spend the rest of the day fishing. They'd go home, more often than not sporting a farmer's tan along with a cooler of whatever had been running that day, rockfish or sea bass or croakers. Once his dad had helped him bring in a tuna that had given him—at ten—the fight of his life. The memory was so vivid that whenever Ford dreamed of that day, he still felt the rod biting into his hands as he struggled to hold it.

The bridge-tunnel itself was, in fact, a marvel. A little over seventeen miles long from shore to shore, it was exactly what the name implied: a series of bridges and tunnels that crossed the Chesapeake Bay where it joined the Atlantic Ocean, connecting Virginia Beach to Virginia's Eastern Shore.

Ford stopped at the first of the four bridges and pulled into the parking area. He walked to the rail that overlooked the water, and from there he could see for miles. Below, where the Chesapeake and the Atlantic met, the water was still dark and disturbed from last night's storm. In the distance, a large navy vessel headed into port at Virginia Beach, and far out in the ocean, another made its way toward the bridge. Noisy gulls circled overhead, hoping for a handout from the sightseers on the pier, while others swooped and soared over both sides of the bridge. Ford closed his eyes and inhaled the scent of salt water, and held it in his lungs for a few seconds before letting it out in a *whoosh*. Chesapeake born and bred, he hadn't realized how much he had missed the Bay's scent. In that moment, he couldn't wait to be home. He climbed back into the car and continued his trek north.

The radio reception was spotty along the back roads—some things, he thought, never changed—so he could only pick up a country station. He'd been away too long to know who was singing; he only caught enough to know it was a girl with a pretty voice singing about vandalizing the SUV that belonged to her cheating boyfriend. He turned it off when the static drowned her out, and drove in silence, the windows up and the air conditioner blasting against the heat and humidity of the late-summer afternoon.

Before he knew it, Ford was crossing the bridge over the Choptank River and was halfway to Trappe, where he and his high school buddies had proven their manhood by spending the night in the haunted White Marsh Cemetery and living to tell about it. Even now, memories of that night made him grin. They'd been so cocky, all five of them, until they heard the faint tinkling of a tiny bell borne on a breeze around three in the morning. They spent the rest of the night wide-awake, huddled in the car, windows closed and the doors locked, but still bragged that they'd lasted the night because they didn't drive back out through the cemetery gates until dawn.

Ford's smile faded when he recalled how far he'd come from that cheeky kid whose most terrifying moments had been spent in a dark cemetery with his friends telling ghost stories. Back then, he'd never imagined what real terrors the world held. The innocent boy— brash though he might have been—would never have understood the things he'd come to see. Even now, Ford was at a loss to really understand what motivated a man to commit atrocities such as those he'd witnessed over the past few years.

He was close to home now. One left turn off Route 50 and he was almost there. He cruised along just under the speed limit so he could take it all in.

If there hadn't been another car behind him, he'd have slowed even more as he passed the Madison farm. Ford had learned to ice-skate on the pond that lay beyond the cornfield. It had been Clay Madison—now married to Ford's sister, Lucy—who'd taught him to skate. Clay had always been sweet on Lucy—even as a small kid Ford had known that. An old pickup was parked near the back of the farmhouse, and he thought briefly about stopping to say hello, but he knew if his mother caught wind of him stopping somewhere other than home first, he'd be in for an earful. And somehow, his mother had always known what he was up to. He'd never really figured out how she knew things, but she did. He thought she must have had a pretty darned good spy network, though she never seemed to keep track of Dan or Lucy the way she'd kept track of him.

Ford hoped that hadn't held true these past few years. He hated to think she might have somehow picked up on exactly where he'd been and what he'd seen and done.

Though his mother's phone calls and letters had kept him abreast of the changes in St. Dennis, the development of the town's center still surprised him. He wasn't sure what he'd been expecting, but it wasn't the upscale shops he passed. The supermarket was still in the same place, but it's previously dingy facade had had a significant face-lift. When he left, most of the current storefronts had been boarded up or were still single-family homes. Now the shops he passed told a story of increased prosperity—Cupcake, Book 'Em, Bling, Sips, and on the opposite side of the street, Lola's Café, Cuppachino, Petals and Posies. Only Lola's and the flower shop had been there before he left.

A new sign at the corner of Kelly's Point Road pointed toward the bay and listed the attractions one would find by following the arrow: public parking, the municipal building, the marina, Walt's Seafood—

Ford was pleased to see that the St. Dennis landmark restaurant was still open—and something called One Scoop or Two.

His mother hadn't been kidding when she said there'd been a lot of changes in a very short period of time.

Farther down Charles Street he turned right, onto the drive that led to the inn, and stopped the car. A very large, handsome sign pointed the way to the Inn at Sinclair Point. The drive itself had been recently blacktopped, some of the trees on either side had been cut back, and it was now, he realized, two full lanes wide where, for as long as he remembered, it had been one.

What next? Ford wondered as he drove around the bend and got his first view of the inn that had been his family home and business for generations.

The large, sprawling main building had been painted since he left, the fading white walls now rejuvenated. The cabins that faced the bay had been painted as well, and he noted that the front of each sported a window box that overflowed with summer flowers. He parked his car in the very full visitors' lot and sat for a moment, trying to take it all in. There were new tennis courts, a fenced-in playground, and if he wasn't mistaken, jutting out into the bay was a new dock—longer and wider—at which several boats were tied. Kayaks and canoes lined the lush lawn that stretched toward the water like a carpet of smooth green Christmas velvet.

And everywhere, it seemed, people were engaged in one activity or another.

"Damn." Ford whistled under his breath. "Mom

wasn't kidding when she said they'd made a lot of changes since I left."

He got out of the car and looked around. While so much was different, the inn still somehow felt the same. Of course, he reminded himself as he gathered his bags out of the trunk of the car, it was still home.

Home. He stared at the building that loomed before him, where a seemingly endless stream of people came and went through the door to the back lobby. No amount of paint or landscaping or added features could change the way he felt when his feet touched ground at Sinclair's Point. The restlessness he'd felt when his plane landed that morning began to fade, but it was still there, under the surface. He knew that the sense of peace he felt would be fleeting, and could not be trusted.

He barely made it across the parking lot when his sister flew out the back door.

"You're late, you bugger! We've been waiting for hours!" Lucy threw her arms around his neck and hugged him.

"My plane was late." He dropped his bags and returned the hug for a moment, then held her at arm's length. "But look at you. You're all tan and your hair's long again." He tugged on her ponytail. "When I left, you had that short do and you were working your tail off out in L.A., and now you're—"

"Working my tail off in St. Dennis." She laughed.

"Business is good?"

"Business is great. If we were any busier, we'd be double-booking dates and holding weddings in the parking lot."

"Well, you must be doing something right, because

you look a million times better than you did the last time I saw you. I'm guessing marriage agrees with you."

"Totally. Work is good, home life is fantastic. I never thought I'd come back to St. Dennis to live—and me, live on a farm? Ha! But I guess it just goes to show, never say never."

"I'm glad you're happy, sis."

"Never happier." Lucy took his arm. "Let's go inside. Mom has been pacing like you wouldn't believe."

"I would believe. Mom never changes."

"I hope not. She's amazing, with all she does here at the inn, and still she keeps the newspaper going. Of course, that's her baby." Lucy chatted away as they walked to the inn. "She still does the features and most of the photographs—though sometimes someone in town will have a great shot of something or other and she'll use it. She did hire someone to do the ads, though, and someone to handle the books. And of course, the printing and mailing . . ."

Ford frowned. "Mailing? Since when has she mailed out the paper? Who's she mailing it to?"

"You *have* been gone awhile. Gone are the days when you could only pick up a copy at the grocery store or the gas station or Walt's." Lucy grinned. "The *St. Dennis Gazette* now has out-of-town subscribers, mostly summer people who want to keep up with what's going on so they'll know when to plan to come back. She mails the paper every week to places as far away as Maine, Illinois, Nebraska. In your absence, little brother, the family business has become the go-to spot on the Chesapeake. We're big doin's, kiddo."

He paused and looked around. "The place looks

amazing. And busy! I don't remember ever seeing so many people here, especially this late in the summer. And I see there's been a lot of work done on the grounds. I don't remember a gazebo there." He nodded toward the structure that sat between colorful flower beds and the water.

"We had a professional landscaper in last summer and he suggested the new gazebo and designed the new gardens at my request," Lucy explained. "I had a big-ticket wedding here and the bride wanted the ceremony out on the lawn overlooking the bay. Since she was dropping a bundle, we did what we had to do to make the area as gorgeous as we could."

"Well, you succeeded. It's really beautiful." He took one more look around before reaching for the door. "Who'd have ever thought the old place could look like this?"

"Dan, that's who. That brother of ours was determined to make the inn shine, and he did."

Ford opened the door and held it for his sister. Once inside, he gazed around the lobby, then whistled.

"Nice."

"Pretty cool, huh?" Lucy grinned. "Not fancy, but just . . . upscale and cool."

"Like me." Dan emerged from behind the reception desk. "Hey, buddy . . ."

Ford dropped his bags and hugged his older brother. "I can't believe what I've seen here so far. You've done a great job. Dad would be so proud."

"I like to think so." Dan gave Ford one last pat on the back before releasing him. "But the inn's old news to us. How are you? Glad to be home?"

"I'm dazzled by the changes, but yeah, glad to be here."

"I hope you can stay for a while." Dan picked up his brother's bags.

"I don't have any plans right now. I'm just glad to be back in the States, glad to see you guys again." Ford glanced around the lobby. "Where's Mom?"

"She's in her office. She's been pacing like an expectant father since dawn. Come on." Dan headed across the lobby, Ford and Lucy following behind.

"Mom has an office here?"

Lucy nodded. "She still has the newspaper office, but she likes to work here sometimes. Says she likes to keep an eye on things, likes to see the comings and goings."

"There sure seems to be a lot of that going on," Ford observed.

"Never been busier." Dan rapped his knuckles on a half-opened door, then pushed it open. "Mom, look who's here."

Grace was out of her chair, arms around her son, in the blink of an eye.

"Well, then," she said as she stepped back to hold him at arm's length, "let me have a good look at you."

Grace's eyes narrowed. "You've lost so much weight. Your face is so thin. Are you feeling all right?" She looked around him to address Dan. "Tell the chef he's going to be working overtime until we put a few pounds back on your brother."

Ford laughed. "Mom, I'm fine. I might have lost a few pounds, but you know, where I've been, fine dining was only a dim memory. A *very* dim memory."

"And where have you been?" Grace forced him to look into her eyes.

"Here and there," he told her. "Africa. Mostly."

"That covers a lot of ground, son," she said softly.

Ford nodded. He knew she was fishing for details, but right now he wanted nothing more than to savor the experience of being home. He knew there'd be questions to answer, but the longer he could leave the past behind him, the better off he'd be.

"Well, we can get the whole story from Ford over dinner." Dan stood in the doorway. "Right now let's get you settled in, then we can get together in the dining room and have a great dinner. We managed to snag a phenomenal chef from a fine D.C. restaurant last year. He's part of the reason we're such a hot destination venue for parties and weddings."

"Ahem." Lucy coughed.

"You didn't let me finish." Dan smiled at his sister. "Lucy's skills as an event planner are what really made our name, but the chef has turned out some pretty spectacular meals."

"We gave him the menu for tonight." Grace took Ford's arm as they walked into the lobby. "All of your favorites."

"That's great, Mom. Thanks."

"How 'bout you and I go out to your car and get the rest of your bags?" Dan offered.

Ford held up the two bags he'd brought with him. "This is it. Been living in tents or huts for the past six years, so I don't own very much."

Their expressions said it all.

"Really," he told them. "It wasn't always that bad."

They walked toward the stairwell in silence and Ford could only imagine what they were thinking. When they got to the bottom of the steps, his mother said, "Oh. Dan's son D.J.'s been using your old room, dear, so we had to move you into another suite. I hope it's all right."

"It's fine, Mom. Any room that has a bed and a bathroom with a working shower is more than fine," he assured her.

"There really isn't another room in the family wing, since Diana has Lucy's old room. We needed to keep Dan's children together, and—"

"Mom, don't worry about it."

"I saved a special room for you." Dan took Ford's bags from his brother's hands. "Overlooks the bay, has a sitting room and a bedroom. Nice fireplace, one of the few rooms that has its own balcony . . ."

"Captain Tom's old room?" Ford paused on the step.

"Yup."

Ford grinned. "I always wanted to sleep in that room."

"I thought you'd like it." Dan grinned back.

"Dan, don't you think the room just around the corner from the family suite might be more appropriate?" Grace frowned and gave her eldest son a look of clear disapproval.

"Nah. You heard Ford. He wants Captain Tom's room." Dan continued up the steps.

"Ford," Grace called from the bottom of the steps. When he turned, she said, "That room might have a few"—she cleared her throat—"cold spots. You might be more comfortable sleeping in a different room."

" 'Cold spots' is Mom's shorthand for 'uninvited guests,' if you get my drift," Dan whispered loud enough for their mother to hear.

"Daniel, you know there have been reports . . ." Grace threw her hands up in defeat. "Oh, never mind."

"Mom, you still think that the old captain is hanging around?" Ford laughed. "Dan used to try to scare me with that old tale about how the old man never left the building and how he haunts his old room." He winked at Grace. "I don't scare quite as easily anymore. But I'll tell you what. If Tom shows up, I'll be sure to get an interview for the *Gazette*. Can't promise a photo, though . . ."

He took the steps two at a time to catch up to Dan, who'd already reached the second-floor landing.

"You remember the way?" Dan asked.

"Sure. Down this hall, take a right, and go to the end. Last door on the left. I used to sneak in there every chance I got. Never did see the captain, though."

"I think that was something Mom made up to keep us from going out onto that balcony and falling off." Dan made the turn onto the side corridor and Ford followed.

"It wouldn't surprise me. She and Dad had any number of crazy stories about their ancestors. Tom was, what, Great-Granny Hunt's maternal grandfather?"

"Something like that. I know he went back about four generations." Dan handed one of the bags off to Ford so he could search his pockets for the key to the room.

Dan fitted the key into the lock and gave the doorknob a good twist. The door swung open silently.

The two men entered the suite through a short hall that led to a sitting room with a brick fireplace over which hung the ancestor in question.

"Ah, there's the old guy." Ford stood with his hands on his hips. "Good to see you again, old man."

The portrait's dark eyes seemed to be looking back at them as they entered the room.

"I'm sure he's happy to see you, too." Dan went past him into the bedroom. "There's only a light blanket on the bed, but if you need something else, just let house-keeping know. It's been pretty hot lately, and even though we have central air these days, this part of the building doesn't seem to cool off quite as well as some of the others."

"Central air, huh? So much for Mom's cold spots." Ford followed Dan into the bedroom, where an old poster bed stood directly opposite a pair of French doors. Ford crossed the room to open them, stepped out onto the balcony, and inhaled deeply. "Ah, the Chesapeake. Nothing smells quite like it."

"Be grateful we had the marsh dredged last year, or you'd be smelling something else entirely."

Ford laughed. "Hey, that marshy smell is a big part of one of my fondest childhood memories."

"Yeah, you and that buddy of yours . . ."

"Luke Boyer."

"Yeah, him. I remember the two of you used to spend hours out there and come home covered in mud and mosquito bites."

"Tracking nutrias. Never caught any—never really wanted to. The fun was all in the hunt."

"You'd find the hunting not as good these days. Nutrias have been mostly eradicated in this area. I'd like to get my hands on the guy who thought it would be a good idea to raise those nasty little critters." Dan stood in the doorway, his hands on his hips.

"I don't think anyone expected them to get loose. I think it was someone's get-rich-quick scheme. Raise the animals, sell them for their pelts. Just didn't turn out that way."

"They created chaos in the marsh here a few years ago before the town found a way to control them. Furry little bastards ate through large sections of the wetlands, cleared out whole areas of bulrush, cordgrass, cattails—you name it, they ate it. Big loss of habitat for a lot of wildlife. You take out the native grasses, the sediment erodes, and the native plant populations suffer."

Ford walked to the end of the balcony and looked across the vast lawn to the wetlands his brother was going on and on about. He knew all about the nutria and the damage the population had done in changing the face of the wetlands. He was well acquainted with the many ways that outside forces could change a place.

He could have told Dan how the long bloody wars had changed the face of emerging African nations, but what, he asked himself, would be the point? Besides, the last thing he wanted to do right at that moment was to look back at the devastation he'd left behind when he'd boarded the helicopter outside Bangui in the Central African Republic. Ford had witnessed the kind of horrors that were the stuff of nightmares. Being here, in this peaceful place, was almost jarring to his senses.

"So, you ready to head downstairs and see if we've exaggerated about our chef?" Dan asked from the doorway.

"Think I could grab a quick shower and change my

clothes first?" After having traveled nonstop for the past forty-eight hours, Ford was a little road-weary.

"Sure thing. Just come down to the lobby when you're ready." Dan started toward the door. He glanced back over his shoulder and said, "I guess it must be great to be back after all those years living in those foreign places."

"Yeah. It's great to be back."

"I'll see you downstairs." Dan closed the door behind him.

Ford stood in the middle of the small sitting room, taking in the papered walls that surrounded him and the cushy carpet under his feet, the comfortable-looking sofa and chairs. He went into the bathroom and stared at the clean white tiles and the gleaming glass shower. There were fluffy towels on a chrome shelf and a new bar of soap in a porcelain dish on the counter next to the sink. He picked up the soap and inhaled its light pine scent. The everyday things he'd once taken for granted were now luxuries that he'd only dreamed about. He turned on the hot water and let it run through his fingertips.

After where he'd been, home seemed like the most foreign place of all.

Chapter 3 ⌒

CARLY spent the next six days reading, making notes, sketching out the last half of Carolina's biography, and making changes to the order of the paintings as they'd appear in her exhibit. To show them in chronological order, arranged by subject, or by medium? She still couldn't decide. Any way they were shown would be fabulous, she knew. Chronological order might best show off the woman's incredible talent as she sampled the different media, searching for the best fit. Then again, the thought of hanging those dramatic land- and seascapes along the same wall made Carly's heart beat just a little faster. On the other hand, the oils would make such a statement, all those dark brooding colors lined up side by side along a stark white wall.

She made a note to have the gallery walls repainted a whiter white before she announced her exhibit.

Then again, it was difficult to completely plan the layout of the paintings when she wasn't sure what else was out there to be bought, or borrowed. More oils? Landscapes? Who knew what masterpieces Carolina had seen fit to give away to her friends and neighbors over the course of her lifetime? Had the list she'd left in her journal reflected the entirety of her gifts, or were there others that she had forgotten to include?

Carly shot off an email to Ellie inquiring on the status of her efforts to pin down Grace Sinclair to see if she knew any of the recipients of Carolina's largess as noted on the list, then waited expectantly for a response. When a full half hour had passed and no reply had been forthcoming, she dialed Ellie's number. Disappointed when the call went directly to voice mail, she left a brief message ("Call me") and disconnected the call. She tried to get back into the rhythm of reading, but was so distracted watching for an email or anticipating a call that she finally gave up. She'd no sooner closed her notebook and turned off the desk light than the phone rang.

"So what's going on?" she asked. "Please tell me you spoke with Grace."

"Yes, I did. As a matter of fact, I was with her when your call came through, but we were at a meeting and we're supposed to have our phones turned off. I left mine on vibrate because my sister was at her friend's house and was going to call me when it was time for me to pick her up. I'll be happy when that kid is old enough to drive." Ellie had been granted custody of Gabi, her fourteen-year-old half sister following the death of the girl's mother and the incarceration of their father.

"So what happened? Tell me already. I've been going crazy trying to put this exhibit together. I will need to integrate the new paintings—assuming we find them—into the collection of the ones I already have. And you know, I need to decide how they're going to show—"

"Carly . . ."

"I'm going to have the walls in the gallery painted stark white. You know, so there's no color to compete with, but any way I show them, it's going to be absolutely glorious. I can't wait to see—"

"Carly." Ellie interrupted Carly. "There's something you need to know."

Carly fell silent. Something about the tone of Ellie's voice made her stomach churn.

"I told you that Curtis Enright had given his home and property to the town, didn't I?"

"Yes, you did. Why?"

"Did you get the part where I told you that he was hoping that an arts center would be part of the plan?"

"Yes, I said I thought every town should have an art center. So what?" Carly fought an urge to bite a fingernail, a habit she'd ditched in seventh grade but one that always threatened to sneak back when she was under stress.

"I'm on the committee that was putting together some suggestions for the town council to review. The art center was voted on, as were several other proposals that we don't need to talk about right now."

"I'm not sure where this is going, but I have the feeling I'm not going to like it."

"Yes and no. Here's the deal: there will be an arts center in the mansion. But the council wants a grand opening that would include an exhibit of works by St. Dennis artists."

Carly's mouth went dry.

"Car? You there?"

"Shit, yes, I'm here." Carly sank into the nearest chair. "They want your paintings."

"Yes. They want my paintings."

"Wait. How did they even know about your paintings?"

"My great-aunt Lilly knew everyone in town, and at one time or another practically everyone she knew had paid her a visit. A lot of people saw the paintings hanging throughout the house, but they don't know about the ones from the attic. Then someone did a Google search for Carolina, and found out that two of her paintings have sold for big bucks over the past few years, and that two or three are hanging in big-time museums. Grace had written an article about the auction in New York where two of Carolina's paintings together fetched over two hundred thousand dollars. Grace said she even had several in the inn and that the town was welcome to borrow them as long as they could guarantee their security."

"So why can't they just show those paintings? The ones from the inn and the ones that everyone knows about?"

"For one thing, they're trying to make this as big as possible."

"So . . . ?"

"So when they asked me if I had any other paintings, or if I knew of any others . . ."

"You couldn't lie, could you."

"No. It just came out."

"Aren't there any other artists in St. Dennis?"

"Of course, and they're going to be invited to show their work as well. But once they latched on to the idea of showing Carolina's stuff, the idea exploded."

Ellie sighed. "It was like, 'Yes! An art center! Yes! An art center with a gallery! We'll have a grand opening! We'll do exhibits! We'll showcase St. Dennis artists.' Then Grace brought up Carolina's name and turned to me right there in the meeting room and asked if I'd be willing to let the town borrow whatever paintings I had for the grand ribbon-cutting dedication." Ellie's voice was glum.

"So now everyone in the world will know about the paintings before I even have a chance to show them. Swell." Carly blinked back tears. "So what did you tell them?"

"I said I'd have to think about it and that I'd get back to them."

"What's the worst thing that could happen if you say no?"

"If I say no, they will work on me. They'll all work me over until I cave."

"Grace didn't strike me as the brass-knuckles type," Carly muttered.

"You know what I mean. Everyone will be asking if I've changed my mind. Everyone I run into will want to talk about it. You know how small towns are. The next thing you know, people will be talking about how I have paintings by the only really famous artist to come out of St. Dennis and how I won't let the community see them."

Ellie's frustration was clear.

"You have to let them have the paintings," Carly said reluctantly.

"I feel so horrible even having this conversation with you. I know how happy you were—how excited you were the day we found them and how much you were looking forward to rocking the art world when you announced your find and your exhibit. I hate to take that from you. But you'll still be able to exhibit them after the showing here, you'll still be the exclusive broker when I'm ready to sell them," Ellie promised.

"I just won't be the one to spring it on the rest of the world."

"I'm really, really, sorry, sweetie."

"I know you are, and I appreciate that, El." Carly took a deep breath to push back against the huge lump that was forming in the middle of her throat. Ellie obviously felt terrible and the last thing Carly wanted was to make her friend feel even worse. But she had to be honest. "I'm not going to lie, El. I had that exhibit space planned out and have lived and breathed those paintings. I've studied them and I know every inch of Carolina's work by heart. I've imagined the articles in the *Times* and the *New Yorker* and the *Washington Post* and every influential art magazine that exists. But I understand the position you're in. I'm really disappointed, but I'll get over it."

"Not for a while, you won't. I know you."

"Yeah, it'll take a while," Carly admitted. "When do I have to have them back to St. Dennis?"

"I'm not sure. I'm hoping you'll continue to work on the biography."

"Of course. That will still be the prelude to the exhibit I'll have."

"I can't thank you enough for understanding. You don't know how much I hated making this phone call, but they want to include the gallery opening in the holiday tour this year."

"Wait, Ellie—they can't just slap these things up on a wall." Carly was appalled at the thought. "The temperature has to be regulated, the lighting has to be just right so that the works are shown to their best advantage, but also so that the paint isn't damaged. And they should be grouped a certain way. I've given a lot of thought to this over the past week." All of Carly's plans came out in a rush of concern. "I'm still trying to decide how best to display them, though I'm leaning toward grouping them chronologically, so that when you look at Carolina's entire body of work, you can see how she evolved and grew as an artist. And there should be a catalog—I was working on that. Title of the work, year she painted it, any comments she may have made in her journals about it. Like in her journals she talked about the process of specific paintings, what inspired her, what she was thinking . . ."

"There's been no consideration given to any of that," Ellie said, "but you're right. If they're going to do this, it's going to have to be done in a professional manner." She paused as if thinking. "Okay, here's the deal. I'm going to tell the council that the exhibit is a go but only if they agree to let you take over and that what you say is the way it's going to be."

"Wait. What?"

"You were already planning the perfect exhibit of these works. Why can't you do it here?"

"Because my gallery is in New York?"

"Carly, this way you can still be the one to introduce Carolina's works. When the exhibit here is over, you can move them to New York, but you'll still have been the one to present them first. Everyone will be happy." When Carly didn't respond, Ellie asked, "What are you thinking?"

"What if they say no, that they don't want an outsider involved?"

"Then they don't get the paintings. Carolina's work stays with you. They're too important."

"You could make some enemies there in town, you know."

"Blood is thicker than water."

"We're not related," Carly reminded her. "There is no 'blood.' It's all water."

"A technicality." Ellie laughed, as Carly had intended. "We might as well be blood. Look, they're my paintings and I can do whatever I want with them. But I have to be honest, I do love the idea of having them introduced to the world right here in St. Dennis. It's where Carolina lived and worked and raised her family. A lot of her subject matter was right here in town. Some things are gone—like the lighthouse— but other landmarks are still here. The town square, that tiny church on Old St. Mary's Church Road, some of the homes that she painted."

"Look, maybe you could approach them this way. Say that you aren't sure that the conditions in the mansion are suitable for a display of this size and importance, so you need to determine exactly what the conditions are. If there's too much moisture in the air, the paintings could be damaged. Too hot, too dry, too cold—"

"I get it," Ellie told her. "If I can get them to agree to hire you—"

"They can't afford me. Which is okay, I'll donate my time as long as the exhibit has my name on it."

Thoughts buzzed around inside her head and she began to think out loud. "Maybe it could work. Maybe. Understand that the way the art world perceives the exhibit will have a direct effect on the value of the paintings when you are ready to sell them."

"Okay, I'm hanging up now and I'm going to call the mayor and the president of the town council—"

"And security. There's going to have to be real security—"

"Really, I'm hanging up—"

"Ellie, wait. If I could make a suggestion."

"Certainly."

"If I were you," Carly began cautiously, "I'd ask them to call a special meeting to discuss this. Tell them you've thought it over and that you consulted with a pro. You know the paintings are very valuable and you are concerned about the security and the integrity of these works. If they are at all interested, tell them I'd like to make a trip down there to assess the conditions."

"They'll be interested when I tell them they don't get the paintings until you're on board."

"And tell them up front that if the conditions aren't right and the works can't be shown properly—"

"Then the paintings stay in New York. The more we've talked, the less comfortable I am with the thought of handing over a fortune in artwork to people who have no idea what they're doing."

"Probably not the best way to present your case to them."

Ellie laughed. "I'm hanging up now. I have calls to make. Thank you for your input. I knew you'd know what to do."

The call disconnected and Carly placed the phone on her desk. It made her crazy to think that Carolina's paintings would be shown anywhere other than Summit Galleries. This exhibit was all she'd thought about for weeks. Still . . . if she had control, if she were still calling the shots and debuting the works, did it matter where they were shown as long as her name was connected with the exhibit?

She grabbed her phone and sent Ellie a quick email:

Ellie, tell these people that you want to keep the existence of Carolina's paintings hush-hush until a big splashy announcement can be made. It's too much to hope that it could be kept a secret, but try to make them understand and appreciate the value of silence. Tell them that the greater the surprise, the bigger the news will be—that you want to bring as much positive attention to St. Dennis as possible. Then call me the minute you have something to tell!

She hit send and then sat back and prayed that the powers that be in St. Dennis had enough sense to know that what Ellie was proposing was the best way—the only way—to introduce the world to Carolina Ellis.

Over the next thirty-six hours, Carly jumped every time the phone rang or pinged with an incoming email. When Ellie finally called, she was bubbling over with news.

"You would have been so proud of me," Ellie told Carly. "I was so cool. So collected. So professional. So—"

"Right. I'm sure you were. Now what happened?"

"Well, first I went over the things we discussed. You know, temperature, moisture in the air, security, that stuff. No one knew anything about any of that. So I said that I'd already discussed the situation with the owner of a very prestigious New York gallery and that I couldn't possibly let my family's legacy be put in jeopardy unless the conditions in the mansion were right."

"Ah, that might have been piling it a little high."

"Who cares? They bought it. Long story short, they agreed that you should come to St. Dennis ASAP and go through the mansion and see if it would—or could—work for an exhibit such as this one. I pointed out that if we could get this exhibit off the ground, we could make it a huge event with tons of publicity, and it would bring in a lot of revenue for the merchants and the restaurants and the B&Bs."

"Nice touch."

"I thought so." Ellie sounded smug.

"So when should I come?"

"Oh, that's the other thing. I hope you don't have anything planned for the weekend, because I told them you'd be here on Saturday." Ellie paused. "I hope that works for you."

"It works. I'll be at your place on Friday, so make something really good for dinner."

"Will reservations do?"

"Of course. Oh, and Ellie? Tell Grace to please keep it all out of the paper . . ."

Chapter 4 ❧

CARLY stood in the foyer of the very impressive Enright home and marveled that anyone would give away such a treasure.

"This place is beautiful. It's hard to believe the man just gave it to the town." She doubted that she'd ever feel so philanthropic that she'd do the same.

"It is unless you know the man." Grace Sinclair, as a member of the committee that was to decide the fate of the proposed art gallery, met with Carly and Ellie at the property on Saturday morning.

"The Enrights have lived in St. Dennis for over a century," Ed Lassiter, who was there in his official capacity as president of the town council, explained. "I think Curtis wanted to make certain that the property was maintained and that it never fell into disrepair. That's the chance you take when you sell a property. You have no control over who buys it or what they'll do with it. But if you gift it with strings, as Curtis did, you can ensure that it will be properly cared for." He added, "At least until the money runs out."

"The word is that he provided quite handsomely

for the maintenance," Grace noted, "so that shouldn't be a problem."

"One hopes." Ellie took Carly's arm and steered her into the first room off the hall. "This was used as a living room, I believe. As you can see, there's quite a bit of wall space to display paintings."

Carly walked around the room, noting the abundance of windows.

"There's so much light in here. If this room were to be used as a gallery, the windows would have to be heavily draped or you'd run the risk of the colors in the paintings fading. Plus, with the light being uneven in the room, the paintings will be partially in shadow, which won't show them off well. Artificial lighting would have to be installed and carefully placed if this room were to be used." She paused in the center of the room. It was barely eleven in the morning, and already the temperature was in the eighties. "There's no air-conditioning?"

"Window units. The house was built long before duct work was in use," Grace explained. "Hence all the radiators."

Carly looked at Ellie almost apologetically. "If the temperature and humidity can't be controlled, you can't hang the paintings here for any length of time. They'll be damaged, some perhaps irrevocably."

Ellie nodded her head. "I understand."

The entourage followed Carly back into the hall and watched her climb the first few steps of the staircase.

"As grand as these stairs are, they really weren't designed for the type of foot traffic you're likely to have, especially during those first days of the exhibit.

You'll have people stumbling over each other, and bumping into each other, and the next thing you know, someone falls and there's—"

"A lawsuit against the town." Ed stated the obvious.

"Exactly. Also, there's no real gallery space here. These are important works of art and they will need to be displayed in a specific way, and that wouldn't be possible here." Carly turned to Ed, who had the fullest, whitest head of hair she had ever seen. She tried not to stare. "I don't really think this house is suitable, as magnificent as it is. I couldn't recommend it as being an appropriate venue to display your paintings, Ellie. I'm sorry. I know how much you wanted to share them with everyone."

Ellie nodded. "I understand."

"That's my assessment." Carly's voice reflected what she hoped would sound like the appropriate amount of apology. "And we still haven't discussed possible security."

"I know that Curtis has a system installed." Grace pointed to a keypad on the wall near the front door.

Carly came down the steps to inspect it. After a moment, she said, "This is a very common system for residential properties, and I'm sure it was adequate for Mr. Enright's needs. But when you're talking about hundreds of thousands of dollars—perhaps a million dollars or more worth of artwork, you need to be much more diligent. Any experienced thief could disable that system in seconds."

"We simply can't take that sort of risk," Grace told Ed. "We can't expose the town to that liability."

"Well, there's probably insurance that could be

purchased to cover the paintings for theft, right?" Ed asked.

"Insurance would cover the financial loss, but it couldn't replace the art." Grace's forehead creased with concern. "We certainly wouldn't want to see Ellie lose the life's work of her great-great-grandmother. Maybe this just wasn't meant to be."

"Which means our exhibit will consist of Elmer Dougherty's watercolors and Hazel Stevens's paintings of her cats," Ed said drily. "I'm sure those two will pack 'em in when the exhibit opens."

"I'm really sorry," Ellie said. "I was hoping we could work something out."

"I know you were, dear, but really, we can't be careless with Carolina's work." Grace patted Ellie on the hand.

"Well, I guess there's nothing more to say." Ed went out through the front door and the others followed. Once outside, he locked the door behind them and the four walked toward the driveway, where they'd parked their cars.

"It really is a beautiful property," Carly commented. "I love the way the gardens are filled with so much color and the way the beds are laid out."

"Jason Bowers designed them," Grace said.

"Sophie Enright's guy," Ellie told Carly. "You met him last year at Pirate Day." She glanced sheepishly at Grace and Ed. "I mean, First Families' Day. Mr. Enright hired Jason to re-create the gardens as they had been in the late 1800s."

"I remember Jason. He did a beautiful job here." Carly stood near the bumper of Ellie's car and gazed at the property as a whole. "This place would be fabulous for weddings and as a community center."

"All being considered," Grace told her.

The stone structure at the end of the driveway caught Carly's eye. She paused to study it. Two stories high, the building had small windows on the first floor and a single, simple door in front.

"What is that building?" Carly asked.

"Oh, that's the old carriage house. Mr. Enright hired us—that is, he hired Cameron's company—to restore it." Ellie smiled with pride. "We did a bang-up job inside and out, if I do say so myself."

"What's inside?" Carly asked.

"Not much. One big room—one floor, tall, open beamed ceiling." Ellie shrugged. "I don't know what Mr. Enright had in mind for it originally, but once he decided to give it to St. Dennis, he just had us finish the basic restoration. Walls, floor, roof, that sort of thing. Oh, and we had the exterior stone repointed."

Carly turned to Ed. "Would you happen to have the key?"

"I don't know." He fumbled with the ring of keys. "Maybe one of these . . ."

"Let's take a look inside," Carly suggested.

"What are you thinking?" Ellie whispered to Carly as their pace took them well ahead of their companions.

"I'm thinking that there are probably a lot of blank walls in here." Carly pointed to the side of the building. "And very few windows."

"Just one on each side in the front, two on the back."

They reached the door and waited for the others to catch up.

"I have a good feeling about this place," Carly told Ellie. "A really good feeling. It gives off great vibes."

"Wait. I can see where this is going." Ellie grabbed her arm and pulled her aside. "Wouldn't you rather display the paintings at your own gallery?"

"That was my first choice, yes, of course it was. But I have thought a lot about what you said, and I have to admit, the idea of displaying them in St. Dennis—right here, where Carolina painted many of the subjects that still exist—that really appeals to me. It's a unique concept. I can think of only a few galleries that display works by famous artists where you can actually go and see the subjects. The Brandywine River Museum in Pennsylvania with its collection of three generations of Wyeth paintings is the one that comes immediately to mind. It takes my breath away to think that we have an opportunity to do something similar here. And as much as I wanted this exhibit in my gallery, I want to be fair," she continued. "Which means we need to look at the spaces that could be available. Maybe this place won't be any more appropriate than the house, but like I said, I have a really good feeling about it."

"Let's see if any of these keys work." Ed tried first one, then another key in the big iron lock. The fourth key opened the door.

Inside the carriage house, the air was very still. Dust motes drifted in the light that spilled in from the few small windows and the opened door.

"There's a light switch on the wall." Ellie pointed

to it. "We had the electric brought up to code when we were working on the place."

She switched on the lights and at once the place came alive. "We had a lot of detail work to try to preserve the old floor, so we needed as much light as we could get."

Carly walked the entire length of the building, studying the height of the ceiling and the expanse of wall on each side.

"I wonder if it would be possible to install a sort of half wall right down the middle," she said to no one in particular.

"Like a partition?" Ellie asked.

"Exactly. Not to go all the way to the ceiling—the beams are gorgeous and it would be a shame to obscure them—but to divide the space." Carly appeared lost in thought.

"It's lovely," Grace said. "Nice and airy and spacious."

"I think this could work." Carly joined the others near the door, where they still stood. "Ellie, could Cam work up a floor plan if I gave him some specifications?"

"You're not thinking that this place could be the gallery?" Ed frowned.

"That's exactly what I'm thinking. The necessary elements for climate control could be installed here much more easily than in the main house, and at a fraction of the cost. The walls will need to be insulated— right now there's only the exterior stone wall between us and the great outdoors, but that's a simple fix. You can control the lighting and there's only one door." She frowned. "There should be another door. You can't have people coming and going through the same doorway."

"It's not a big deal to put another door in," Ellie told them.

Carly pointed to the side wall. "Right here. If there were partitions down the center of the room, the natural egress is right here." She walked to the wall and tapped on it for emphasis.

Grace followed Carly's gaze around the room. "I think Carly's right. I think this building could be perfect."

"I don't know." Ed put his president of council's hat back on. "We'd need to know what the cost would be."

"Cam can work up the numbers," Ellie assured him. "I feel certain that we can make this place work for way less money than it would cost to retrofit just the HVAC alone into the mansion. We'll crunch some numbers over the weekend so that we can have them ready for Tuesday night's meeting." She paused to defer to Ed. "That is, if you're okay with this idea."

"Get us some numbers and we'll see. I'm not sure how we could manage the expense." He clearly was concerned. "There's money for maintenance in the trust that Curtis set up, but not for improvements."

"How would you have paid for the changes that would be necessary at the mansion?" Carly asked him.

"I don't think anyone really considered that we'd be looking at huge expenses. I think we all just thought we'd hang up the paintings and charge people to come in and look at 'em." Ed shrugged. "But I understand why you made the suggestions you made, and I have to agree that we need to do this the right way, or we shouldn't do it at all. I'm just concerned about the money."

"Let's wait and see what Cam and I come up with. Maybe it won't be too bad."

"If we're going to charge for tickets to the exhibit, we could make up some of the money that way," Grace said.

"There is one other way the money might be raised," Carly offered. "I'm writing Carolina's biography—actually, it's almost completed. Perhaps I could share a portion of the proceeds from the book sales with St. Dennis."

"That would be very generous, dear." Grace was clearly taken with the idea.

"Do you have a publisher lined up? Have you sold it already?" Ed inquired. "Is the book finished?"

"No, but I don't expect I'll have much trouble selling it. Especially since the plan all along has been to put the book on sale in conjunction with the opening of a major exhibit."

"That's a bit optimistic, don't you think? You'll have to find a publisher and that will take time." Grace spoke up. "Then it'll have to be printed and so on. I don't know exactly what's involved, but I can't think it would be all that easy."

"I can publish it independently," Carly told them somewhat defensively. "I've already looked into it. I can do this."

"Well, without knowing what the renovations would cost, this is all academic," Ed said. "And keep in mind, even if the numbers are reasonable, we'll need council's approval. They may just vote to pass on the entire idea of a gallery, or they may go ahead with exhibiting those cat paintings of Hazel's and forget about Carolina's."

"I think they'll need to give a great deal of consideration to this," Grace said thoughtfully. "This is a once-in-a-lifetime opportunity to put St. Dennis on the map as a cultural destination. It would bring a new dimension to our little bay town, and would attract a different demographic. Art patrons, collectors of American artists, collectors of women artists—I would expect many would want to come to see such an important collection." She looked at Carly for confirmation.

"I think we could publicize this in a way that would make the movers and shakers in the art world sit up and take notice. I think they'll flock to St. Dennis if for no other reason than to say that they were here."

"And a good portion of them will want to stay for the weekend. Think of what that could mean for the restaurants and the B&Bs."

"Not to mention your family's inn," Ed said pointedly.

"The inn is always booked to capacity the week of the holiday tour." Grace ignored the implication. "But for others in town, this influx could make a real difference in their bottom line at the end of the year. Plus, I expect that Dallas's studio will bring in some VIPs. A trendy art gallery will give them just one more reason to stay."

"Dallas MacGregor has opened her own film studio in town. She's already cast her first movie and will be starting to shoot by early fall," Ellie explained to Carly. "As a huge movie star herself, Dallas has a lot of influence with a lot of people. I'll bet she'd be happy to invite some of her Hollywood friends to the grand opening of the gallery."

"I'm certain she would," Grace agreed. "Dallas loves St. Dennis and is always looking for ways to promote the town. She's been a steady patron of Sophie Enright's new restaurant out on River Road. Sophie tells me that the orders she has every day from Dallas's studio are keeping her in the black."

"I'll have to bring all of this up to the others on the council and see what they think." Ed turned to Ellie. "Let me know as soon as you have some numbers to go over. If the costs are reasonable in proportion to the expense, I'll back the project and see if I can bring the others in line."

"We'll do the best we can," Ellie assured him.

"Hopefully," Grace said, "it will be enough."

"Let's not get ahead of ourselves. I'll be waiting to hear from you and Cam," Ed said before turning to Carly. "I checked you out on the Internet and it looks to me like you know your stuff. This would be a big move for a small town like ours. I'm trusting that you'll be able to pull this off."

"Thank you. I'm confident that this could be a big moneymaker for St. Dennis, and as Grace pointed out, a windfall for the town's merchants as well."

"Let's hope you're right." Ed turned to the others. "Grace, Ellie, thanks for your time."

"We'll chat after we see the numbers, Ed." Grace gave a half wave as the man headed toward the end of the driveway and his car.

"That went well," Ellie said when he was out of earshot. "All things considered."

Grace nodded. "Better than I expected, particularly

after you said the old house wouldn't be suitable. Ed's a tough nut to crack, so I was encouraged when he said he'd sign on if the numbers are good." She tapped Ellie on the arm. "That's your part in all this."

"I can't see the cost being prohibitive, which it certainly would be if we were to try to turn that old house into a proper art gallery."

"Well, there may be some on the council who don't think the town needs an art gallery." Grace frowned.

"I can't wait to hear what they decide," Carly said as the three walked up the driveway.

"Grace, about that list of paintings that Carolina gave away . . ." Carly began.

"Yes, Ellie gave me a copy. I'm afraid I haven't had much time to study it. My son just recently arrived home and I'm trying to get this week's paper out."

"I understand." Carly forced a smile. "Whenever you get a minute, if you could go over it with me, I'd appreciate it." She reached into her bag and pulled out one of her business cards. "Just give me a call when you can. If there are other paintings out there, we should track them down. Who knows, someone in town might have a small fortune stashed in their attic or hanging on their guest bedroom wall."

"That's certainly a possibility. I'll bet a few folks will be in for the surprise of their lives." Grace chuckled as she put the card in her wallet. "Now, are you here for the week, Carly, or did you drive down only for the day?"

"I'll stay tonight and leave sometime tomorrow," Carly replied. "I hate to be away from the paintings for too long."

"Of course." Grace paused when they reached her

car, which was parked in front of Carly's. "If you have no other plans, try to stop over at the inn tonight. We're having a welcome-home party for my son Ford, and we'd love to have you both join us. Cam, too, of course."

"Cam did mention that Lucy had called with an invitation, so I think he's planning on it," Ellie said.

"Good. I know Ford would want to see him again. They were friends once upon a time." Grace turned to Carly. "And I hope you do come along."

"I don't know your son, so he might think it's odd." Carly made a face. Would it be awkward to attend the welcome-home party for someone you'd never met?

"I'm sure he'll be delighted to meet you." Grace patted Carly's hands. "In the meantime, we'll see if we can lobby more support for the gallery. I have the feeling that you're going to do great things in St. Dennis." Grace smiled. "Yes, I do believe there are great things waiting for you here . . ."

Carly and Ellie watched the older woman walk up the slight incline of the driveway to her car.

"Does she sometimes give you an odd feeling?" Carly asked under her breath.

Ellie shook her head. "Odd like how?"

"She just gave me this feeling that she . . ." Carly stopped. How to put into words, even to your best friend, that somehow something—something important—had just passed between her and Grace, and that she had no idea what it might have been.

"That she what?"

"I don't know. Nothing, I guess. I probably imagined it."

"The important thing is that Grace is behind us and

will advocate for turning this building into the gallery that you want."

"Does she have any influence with the council members?"

"I suspect she does," Ellie said thoughtfully. "Remember she owns the only newspaper in town. She can use that as a platform to get people behind the project. Plus, she knows everyone and is pretty much universally liked. I think she could help make it happen."

"Assuming your numbers are right," Carly reminded her.

"They will be."

"You sound so sure of yourself."

"I am." Ellie nodded. "I know this building. I don't carry prices in my head the way Cam does, but I think the cost will surprise everyone, and I mean that in a good way." She looped her arm through Carly's as they headed toward the car. "I've been hoping there'd be some way to bring you to St. Dennis to stay for a while. If you think I'm going to let this opportunity pass me by—"

"Who said anything about staying here?"

"Do you think you can oversee this"—Ellie waved a hand in the direction of the carriage house—"from New York? Uh-uh. We get the green light, toots, and you're looking at a couple of months between now and the time the exhibit would open."

"So . . . ?"

"So who do you think is going to be supervising the job, making sure everything is exactly the way you want it? Who's going to set up the partitions and place the lighting and the air vents and the paintings? Or are you going to delegate all that to someone else?"

"Good point." Carly opened the driver's-side door and got in.

"Your galleries are covered, right? You have good people working for you?" Ellie slid into the passenger seat and fastened her seat belt.

"The best."

"So you're covered there. Besides, you're less than a four-hour drive from New York. You can go back anytime you want."

"True enough. Still, I hadn't thought about staying here indefinitely."

"Of course, the other option would be for you to go back to New York and do your thing, and we'll find someone else to take care of the business here. We could probably find someone in Baltimore or DC who'd love to be involved with our little project."

Carly shot Ellie a withering gaze.

"Thought so," Ellie said smugly. "So I suggest you make a six-month plan for your directors and your managers, because I have the feeling you're going to be spending a lot more time here than there."

Chapter 5

THE kayak glided across the water's surface, following the gentle curve of the Chesapeake into Blue Heron Cove. Ford lifted the paddle and rested it across the hull, content to drift on the waves while they drew him closer to the pebbled beach. It had been years since he'd kayaked this far down the coast, but once upon a time, these waters had been as familiar to him as the paved roads of St. Dennis. Even as a young boy, he'd loved exploring the inlets and coves and rivers, loved the freedom, the solitude, the comfort of being alone on the water with nothing but his thoughts and the local wildlife for company. The stress and conflict he'd been feeling since he arrived at the inn were overbearing, and so he'd sought refuge in the only place where he knew for certain he'd find peace.

Ford closed his eyes and let the kayak drift closer to shore. He'd slept fitfully since he arrived at the inn, and he was nearing exhaustion. His first night home, he'd stood in the shower, the hot water beating down on him like a summer storm until his skin turned red, and even then he'd been reluctant to turn off the water.

He'd joined his family in the main dining room and had been treated to the kind of meal he'd only dreamed about: exquisite, delicate crab cakes, twice-baked potatoes, and grilled summer vegetables, all served with beer from Clay's own brewery. For dessert there'd been Ford's favorite blueberry cobbler topped with whipped cream. Before eleven o'clock, he'd crawled into bed between soft clean sheets the likes of which he hadn't seen in years and fully expected to pass out from the rigors of the last few weeks. He hadn't anticipated tossing and turning through the night.

At one point, he'd gone out onto the balcony and let the warm night breezes wrap around him. The sound of the water lapping against the shore was just as he'd remembered. Through the branches of the enormous pines that stood near the shore, he could see the Bay shining smooth as glass in the moonlight, and every once in a while, he'd hear something rustling in the trees or in the shrubs below his room. Whatever else in his life may have changed, the sights and sounds of the Bay had remained the same. The comfort he'd drawn from those few minutes had lured him back to his bed and finally lulled him to sleep.

He'd been awakened that first morning by a soft rap on the outer door, and thought he'd heard someone moving about in the sitting room. By the time he'd gotten out of bed, wrapped a towel around his waist, and opened the door, whoever had come in had left. Ford suspected that it had been his brother who'd popped in just long enough to leave a tray of goodies on the console table: a carafe of steaming-hot coffee, a plate of fresh fruit, a croissant flaky enough to have floated off the tray on its own. Ford downed two cups of coffee while he leaned on the balcony railing, nibbled on his breakfast, and watched the inn's grounds come alive. Even at an early hour, there were couples on the tennis courts, kids in the fenced play area, and sailboats out on the Bay. A lawn mower cranked along somewhere on the grounds, and down below, his sister greeted a smiling couple in the parking lot.

Ford dressed in a pair of khaki shorts and a short-sleeved tee and went downstairs. His mother had gone to a meeting, Lucy was still with her prospective clients, and Dan had the inn to run. Ford had slipped out of the inn and walked down to the waterline. Nearby, kayaks were lined up on the grass for the use of the inn's guests. He'd selected a twelve-footer, walked it into the water, dropped into the cockpit, and headed off into the Bay.

That first foray out onto the Chesapeake had been everything he'd remembered. He'd enjoyed it so much that he'd repeated the excursion every morning since. Being alone on the Bay was the only time his head was clear enough to think things through. How best, he wondered, to transition from where he'd been to where he was and where he was going? And where *was* he going? How to make sense of the life he'd led in contrast to the life he now found himself in? How to adjust to the peace and quiet of this beautiful place when in his mind he still lived amid the chaos of the past few years?

And ultimately, where did he really belong? Here, or there?

It didn't help that everyone Ford saw had asked some variation of the same questions: where had he been, how long was he staying, and had he come back to help his brother run the inn?

To the latter, he'd responded that Dan was doing a great job on his own and didn't need help from anyone, but inside he was starting to wonder if maybe Dan resented the fact that Ford hadn't been around to help, that he'd been off trying to "save the world," as Dan had once quipped, instead of helping his family to save their business. As he looked around the grounds now, it was hard to imagine that there had been lean years following their father's death, years when the future of the inn had been in question and there'd been the real possibility that it might pass from Sinclair hands for the first time in its long history. Only hard work on the part of his mother and his brother had ensured that the inn would remain in the family. Had Dan resented that the burden had fallen on his shoulders, and that neither Ford nor Lucy had stepped up?

Still in high school when their father passed away, Ford had worked at the inn with the rest of the family on the weekends, while Dan, who was seven years older, had taken on the bulk of the responsibility. Grace—and Dan—had been insistent that Ford go to college, as Dan and Lucy had done, but the only way they could afford for him to do so was through the ROTC program. Four paid years of college had obligated Ford to four years of military service, and so he'd gone into the army after graduation, eventually going on to Ranger training. His last assignment had been part of a small, newly formed covert force intended to help protect civilians from al Qaeda–backed rebels in a central African nation that was in the throes of civil war.

"Be our eyes and ears on the ground," his superior had said, "and try to keep the rebels from taking over the country and wiping out the civilian population while you're at it."

Once on the ground, however, he and his cohorts had found that providing security to the small villages against the ravages of the well-armed, well-trained rebels was pretty much a full-time job. There'd been no words to describe the horrors they'd witnessed, no way to assure his family that he, too, would not become a victim of the same forces, and so he'd permitted his mother to believe that he was part of a UN Peacekeeping Mission, which was sort of a truth, though a very thinly stretched one. There *were* UN Peacekeeping Forces in the area, and his unit had been instructed to have their backs. He knew that if his mother had known the full truth, she wouldn't have had a day unmarked by worry, and he'd wanted to save Grace from six years of sleepless nights, so he'd stuck to his original story.

Had several members of his own unit not been massacred along with two UN Peacekeepers in a bloody ambush six weeks ago, Ford might still be there. But when U.S. forces took a hit—as they had on previous missions, such as the slaughter in Mogadishu—the remaining troops were withdrawn and brought home, the unit disbanded as quietly as it had been formed. Upon his return to the States, Ford had opted for a discharge and had headed for home . . . yes, to see his family, but also because he couldn't think of anywhere else to go.

The last thing he wanted was to have people asking where he'd been, what he'd been doing, and what his plans were. He was getting tired of saying, "Here and there," "This and that," and "I don't know."

All of which was why his stomach had clenched into one great big knot when his mother had announced at dinner on Thursday that she'd invited a few friends to the inn for a little welcome-home party for him on Saturday night. For one thing, Grace's idea of a few friends and his were two very different things. She'd probably invited half the town, which meant he'd be repeating himself over and over and over all night without once having told the truth. He'd wanted to tell her right then and there that a party was out of the question, but the look on her face was so joyful that he didn't have the heart. He knew she'd missed him—of course she did; after all, she *was* his mother—but he hadn't realized just how much pain his absence had caused her. Now that he was home, he'd do anything to try to make it up to her, even if that meant enduring an evening spent with well-meaning friends and neighbors where he'd be forced to repeat his lies to everyone in town.

Well, at least they'd all hear the same story.

And now it was Saturday, and he was thinking that maybe he should have asked his mother to cancel the party. He'd taken the kayak out early hoping to start the day in a serene state of mind after an hour or so paddling on the Bay. But he'd been out for almost most of the morning and he still wasn't feeling much better. At Sunset Beach he turned the kayak and paddled in toward the shore.

This had been his go-to place when he was a kid.

This was where he'd come to lick the wounds of having lost a school-yard fight or the affection of a girl who decided that he wasn't so interesting after all. Later that year, his opponent in the fight—which had mostly consisted of rolling around in the dirt—had become his best friend, but the girl, well, he could no longer remember her name. He'd come to this narrow stretch of sand to replay the ball he'd failed to catch in that day's baseball game or the touchdown pass he'd caught the day before. The beach had witnessed his tears of grief when his beloved retriever, Barney, died, and his heartbreak sophomore year in college when the girl he'd been sure was "the one" had dumped him for a senior.

This was where he'd fled, too overcome with shock and pain to even cry, when he'd learned that his father had died.

What had happened, he wondered, to that boy who'd wanted nothing more than to play sports, to ace a test, to fish with his dad and crab with his friends, to kiss a pretty girl in the backseat of his buddy's car after a high school dance?

He sat in the kayak, ten feet from shore, and watched the waves break so gently onto the beach that they hardly made a sound. If any part of that boy still existed, Ford was pretty sure he'd find him here—but not today. Some other day, he'd come back and he'd sit on the sand and think about all the things that had mattered to the boy he used to be, and all the things that had brought him to this place in his life, and maybe—just maybe—he'd be able to figure out where to go from here.

* * *

"Are you sure you think I should go?" Carly joined Cam and Ellie in the kitchen of their home at the end of Bay View Road. "I mean, I hardly know Grace, and I wouldn't know her son if he fell over me."

"You'll know lots of other people," Ellie assured her. "If I know Grace, half the town will be there. Besides, she specifically invited you, so I think you should go."

"Ellie's right. You've already met a lot of people here in town. You're bound to know some of the other guests," Cam added.

"And what better opportunity to talk up our hopes for the art exhibit." Ellie put her arm through Carly's and led her to the front door. "It's a perfect setup for us to try to garner support for the project."

"I guess as the owner of the bulk of Carolina's work, you're the right person to drum up interest." Carly waited on the front steps while Cameron locked the door behind them. "But I think you should do most of the talking. I don't want anyone to think I'm trying to push my own agenda. I think the push needs to come from St. Dennis residents."

"You have a point." Ellie paused. "Are we walking? Driving?"

"Driving. It's too hot to walk." Cam tossed his keys up and down in his hand. "My pickup or Carly's Benz?"

"Since the truck is behind my car, I say we take the pickup," Carly replied.

"Fine with me." Ellie opened the passenger door and she and Carly got in.

"Cam, do you think you'll have some time in the

morning to go over the carriage-house renovations Ellie and I talked about?" Carly asked as they turned onto Charles Street.

"Ellie's already filled me in on what you two have in mind and I have a few ideas for the project. It isn't going to take much, since we're not going to have to take anything down and we've already installed new electric. I will have to talk to my HVAC guy, but it's a pretty straightforward project. Curtis already paid for the big-ticket items when he had us renovate the place from the ground up, so all the heavy lifting's been done and paid for." Cam headed up the lane toward the inn. "But to answer your question, sure, we'll work on it first thing tomorrow and see if we can put together something Ed and the others on the council can live with."

Every space in the inn's guest parking lot was filled, so Cam drove around to the back of the building and parked in the employees' lot.

"Wow, they really have a full house tonight," Carly noted as they walked to the well-lit inn. "I don't suppose all these people are here for Grace's party."

"The inn is always full this time of the year," Cam told her. "But I did recognize a few cars while I was looking for a spot to park. Let's go on in and see who's here . . ."

Carly trailed a few steps behind Ellie and Cam, feeling just a little out of place. She reminded herself that she'd been wanting to visit the inn. Hadn't Grace said that one of Carolina's works hung in the lobby? Carly was itching to take a look.

The party for Grace's son was in what Grace had

referred to as the drawing room near the front of the building, and was already in full swing when Carly, Ellie, and Cam arrived.

"You weren't kidding, Ellie," Carly said from the corner of her mouth. "I'll bet half the town *is* here."

"Ford grew up in St. Dennis," Cam reminded her. "Everyone in town knows him. I guess a lot of people wanted to stop by and say hi."

"Which one is the welcome-home guy?" Carly asked.

"I don't know," Ellie said. "I've never met him either. Cam?"

Cameron looked around the room. "I don't see him, but he's got to be here somewhere. There's Grace . . . and I see Lucy and Clay . . . and Dan and his kids." He nodded. "Yeah, Ford must be around since his entire family is here."

Carly did recognize some of Ellie's friends she'd met before. Dallas MacGregor and her husband, Grant Wyler, gestured for the newly arrived threesome to join them. Carly had been secretly pleased that the movie star had remembered her and greeted her by name.

"Dallas, I heard about your new venture," Carly said. Everyone had heard about the new studio and film production company Dallas had started in St. Dennis. It had been the talk of Hollywood—and therefore the magazines—for months. "I wish you much success with your film. *Pretty Maids,* right? From the book?"

Dallas nodded. "We plan to start shooting in two weeks. I can hardly wait."

"You're filming locally?" Carly asked, though she knew the answer. That, too, had been in the news. Everyone in town knew that Dallas was more at home in St. Dennis than she was in Hollywood.

"Yes. We're looking for extras, if you'd like to make your film debut. We need people on the street, that sort of thing." Dallas put a hand on Carly's arm. "Though I'm sure you have better things to do. I heard about the plan you have for the carriage house at the Enright place, and I think it's a brilliant idea to put it to good use. There are very few stone buildings in St. Dennis and that one is a beauty."

"How'd you hear about it so fast?" Carly laughed. "We only met and discussed it this morning."

"Ed brought his cat in for shots this afternoon," Dallas explained. "Besides being the only veterinarian in town, Grant's also on the town council this year."

"So does your husband think the idea is brilliant, too?" Carly couldn't help but ask.

"He does, but like Ed, he wants to see what Cameron comes up with. I have total confidence in Cam. I'm sure he'll do a fabulous job. He and his crew just finished some renovations on our house and everything they did was perfection." Dallas leaned a little closer to Carly. "Ed also said you were writing a book about one of the local artists you'd be highlighting at the gallery. An ancestor of Ellie's?"

"Yes, Carolina Ellis was Ellie's great-great-grandmother. Ellie was kind enough to loan me Carolina's journals and diaries as references. Since so little is known about her as an artist and as a woman, I thought her biography would be a nice introduction to her work."

"Could I impose on you for an early copy of your work? I'm looking ahead for my next project, and I'd love to do a film about a woman artist." Dallas added,

"A woman artist from St. Dennis would be even better."

It was all Carly could do to keep her composure. "I'll send you the manuscript when I'm finished. I hope I can do her justice. Carolina was quite the girl. She was crazy talented and made the most of it while raising two children and dealing with a husband who hated that she painted and did everything he could do to discourage her. The gallery show—assuming the town council will approve it—would be spectacular."

"Now I know I have to read that manuscript." Dallas's legendary lavender eyes began to twinkle. "Yes, please send it to me as soon as you've finished. I can't wait to read it." She opened her bag and took out a card which she handed to Carly. "My email's on the back."

"Thanks. I'd just ask that you keep it to yourself right now. I'm hoping Ed and the others will keep it under wraps as well. I'd like to make a splashy announcement."

"You can count on me," Dallas assured her, "and I'll make sure to tell Grant to remind the others that we don't want the story getting old before its time."

"Thanks, Dallas. I'd appreciate that."

They were joined by Steffie Wyler and her husband, Wade MacGregor, who was Dallas's brother. The talk immediately changed to the news that Steffie and Wade were expecting their first child, and Steffie's attempts to avoid eating the ice cream she made for her shop, One Scoop or Two. Feeling like a fifth wheel, Carly drifted away into the crowd. She glanced around for Ellie and Cameron, but somehow had lost track of them. There were several small bars set up at different points in the room, and Carly headed for one, where she ordered a glass of wine. Once she'd been served, she made a beeline for the door that led into the lobby. On the way, she was stopped several times, once by Ed, who wanted to introduce her to another member of the town council, once by Ellie's friend Sophie Enright, who'd also heard about the proposed plan for her grandfather's carriage house ("Fabulous idea. I couldn't be more excited. If it ever went to a referendum, you'd have my vote"), and once by Lucy, who wanted to introduce Carly to her brother, who was nowhere to be found at the moment.

Finally escaping into the lobby, Carly sipped her wine as she strolled around the room, glancing at the walls in search of the painting Grace had mentioned and trying to appear calm and collected. Had Dallas MacGregor really just asked to read her book once it was completed? Did she really say she might be interested in a film about Carolina, a film that could conceivably be based on Carly's book?

Carly took another sip of wine and forced her feet to stay on the floor. The urge to jump up and down was hard to suppress.

Then she saw it. Across the room, on the wall behind the reception desk, hung an oil painting in a style Carly recognized from thirty feet away. She drew closer for a better look.

The subject was a grand white house with tall columns that rose to the second floor, where a balcony graced the front of the building. In the background, pine trees bent by wind stood their ground against the moonlit Bay, where choppy waters crashed over a wooden dock.

Carly knew the painting, though she'd never seen it before. Carolina had written about it in one of her journals. She stepped closer.

"Excuse me." The woman behind the counter reached out to touch Carly's arm. "Guests aren't permitted behind the reception desk."

"Oh, I just wanted to get a better look at that painting," Carly explained.

"I'm sorry," the desk clerk said. "It's house rules."

Carly sighed and stepped to the side of the desk, craning her neck to get as close as she could.

"Will you slap me if I help you up?" a male voice said from behind her.

Carly straightened up, a frown on her face. "What?"

"You were leaning over so far, I thought you were about to fall over."

She turned and looked up into eyes that were as gray as a stormy summer sky set in a deeply tanned face too rugged to be classically handsome. For a moment, she forgot where she was and what she'd been doing.

"Are you okay?" he asked.

"Oh. I was trying to get a closer look at that painting." Embarrassed by how she must have looked, she needed a moment before she found her voice.

"Just go on over and look." He gestured to the space behind the desk.

"I tried that and got my hand slapped." Carly lowered her voice. " 'Guests aren't permitted behind the reception desk. It's house rules.' "

Carly supposed his smile must have dazzled the desk clerk as much as it dazzled her, because before she knew it, he was standing in front of her, the painting in his hands.

"I'll put it right back. Promise," he hastily told the desk clerk. "We won't move from this spot, right?"

"Right." Carly nodded.

He held the painting at his chest level. "How's this?"

"It's . . . thank you." She moved toward the painting to study the colors, the brushstrokes, the mood. Definitely one of Carolina's late oils, she told herself. For a moment, she forgot everything except the canvas—even the man who held it for her.

"It's the inn," Carly heard him say, "seen from the front."

"I wouldn't have recognized it. I've only seen the back of the building," she said. "Are the columns still there?"

"Sure. The columns, the porch, the balcony—nothing's changed, architecturally speaking—in about two hundred years."

"That's remarkable." Carly was engrossed in the painting, but felt obligated to comment. To ignore him would have been rude, especially after he'd made it possible for her to see the painting up close.

"It looks like a storm's moving in, doesn't it?" He peered over the top of the frame.

Carly nodded. "The water's churned up—see how it's swirling around the dock there? And how she—the artist—used all these shades of gray in both the sky and the water?" *Gray like your eyes*, she could have added, but she'd cut her tongue out before she said something that sounded so intimate to a stranger.

"I'm picking up some anxious vibes from . . ." He turned with the painting in his arms to the woman behind the desk and read from her name tag. "Marjorie. So I'd better hang this back here before she gets upset."

He flashed his smile again—he had the sexiest mouth—and Marjorie merely stepped aside to permit him to return the painting to its place.

"Did you see whatever it was you were looking for?" He came back around the desk and stood in front of Carly, his hands on his hips, his gaze on her face.

"I did, thank you so much." Carly's heart thumped inside her chest under his scrutiny. She wished he'd stop looking at her.

"How 'bout a refill on that wine?" He gestured toward the empty glass in her hands.

"Oh. I'm good. But thanks . . ."

She started to walk away, and he fell in step with her.

"Maybe you should take a look at the front of the inn," he suggested. "See those columns and the balcony for yourself."

Having just seen Carolina's interpretation of the inn, she found the idea appealing.

"I think I will, thanks. And thanks for the painting." Carly shook her head. "I'd never have had the nerve to grab that off the wall the way you did. I'm surprised she let you get that close."

"Must be my charm," he said drily.

"Do you know which way is the front?" Carly stopped in the middle of the room.

"It's this way." He gestured toward the room where the party was being held. "Through the double doors . . ."

He held the doors for her, and lightly touched her arm when they encountered a small crowd walking in their direction. Her skin tingled under his fingertips and she thought he must have felt it, too, because he instantly pulled his hand away.

"Hey, people are looking for you." Someone called to him as they neared the party.

"The door right ahead there goes out to the front of the building," Carly heard him say just before he suddenly turned and vanished into the party crowd. "Enjoy the rest of the night."

Just that quickly, he was gone.

Trying to pretend that she hadn't been taken aback by his abrupt disappearance, Carly continued to the front door on her own. She stepped outside and went directly to the grassy circle formed by the curved driveway. She crossed her arms over her chest and stared at the old inn that had been depicted in the painting she'd seen in the lobby, and wondered if Carolina had ever painted it as it appeared on a night like this. Tonight clouds drifted like soft mist across the face of the moon and the breeze whistled through the cattails in the marshy area on the other side of the driveway. Music floated from inside the inn and she could hear laughter from a gazebo off to the left of the building. There were lights in all the front windows and the inn looked alive. She could—probably should—go back inside and rejoin the party, but she wasn't in a party mood. Besides, she still felt awkward, never having met the guest of honor. She walked up to the front porch and took a seat on one of the wicker rocking chairs. She'd wait until she heard the party start to break up before going back in to find Ellie and Cam.

Carly sat and rocked and watched the moon emerge

from the clouds only to be hidden again minutes later. Eventually her fingers went to the spot on her elbow where the man with eyes the color of a stormy sky had touched her, and she wondered if she'd see him again.

Chapter 6 ⤳

"Here are the numbers I've come up with." Cameron passed a spreadsheet across the table at an angle so that Ellie and Carly could see it at the same time. "What do you think?"

Both women leaned forward to look it over.

"I think it's a little low." Ellie studied the bottom line.

"I don't see costs for too much other than the heating and air-conditioning."

"I thought I'd eat a little of the cost here and there. Like the drywall." He shrugged. "I can't cut the number for my HVAC guy unless he agrees to do that on his own. Which he might be willing to do if we ask him nicely. He's relatively new in town and a bit shaved off the top here would go a long way to endear him to the community."

"In that case, I think the town council will love it," Ellie replied. "Of course it's hard to say, not knowing what their budget might be."

"There's no number for security," Carly noted. "Security is going to be big, Cam."

"I didn't have any specs for that, and besides, that's

not a cost that I can estimate," he told her. "You're going to need a security expert to help you out there, since you said it would have to be a really sophisticated system."

"I think the council needs to decide first if they want to use this building as a gallery," Ellie said. "If yes, then they'll have to decide if they want to go with the additional costs to secure Carolina's work."

"I think you're right," Carly agreed. "If the town doesn't have the funds for the right kind of security—"

"We'll deal with that if and when we have to. Right now I'm going to drop this off to Ed and see what he thinks." Cam put the spreadsheet into a folder and stood.

"You might mention to him that a lot of people were talking about the proposed gallery last night and were really excited about it. Since he'll be running for reelection in a few months, he might be interested," Ellie said.

"I don't know that the opinions of a few people at a party would sway him one way or another," Cam replied, "but it can't hurt to let him know that people are talking favorably about it. Though he probably heard some of that talk himself last night." Cam leaned down to kiss the top of Ellie's head. "What do the two of you have planned for the afternoon?"

"Just some sightseeing." Ellie grabbed the front of his shirt and pulled him closer to kiss him, then let him go. "We'll meet up with you back here for dinner."

"See you then." Cam disappeared into the hall, and seconds later, Ellie and Carly heard the front door open, then close.

"So what did you think of Grace's wandering boy?" Ellie got up from the table and began to fill the dishwasher.

"Who?" Carly frowned. "Oh. Right. The guy the party was for. I never did meet him."

"Actually, you did."

"No, I didn't."

"Yes, you did. I saw you talking to him when I went to the ladies' room." Ellie turned and added, "In the lobby."

"I met some guy in the lobby but . . ." Carly paused. "That was him? Grace's son?"

Ellie grinned. "Some hunk, huh?"

"I didn't notice."

"Liar." Ellie laughed.

"Okay, yeah, I noticed. He didn't introduce himself. He just walked over and . . ." Carly blew out a long breath. "Yeah. He was pretty hot."

"So what were you guys talking about?" Ellie leaned back against the counter.

"Mostly just the painting. I'd wanted to see it up close but the desk clerk wouldn't allow me to go behind the counter. Then he came along and just walked back there and took it off the wall . . ." Carly sighed. "I should have figured out right then that he wasn't just another guest at the inn. At the time, I guess I thought he'd charmed her into letting him hold it."

"That's it? You just talked about the painting?"

"Pretty much." Carly got up and refilled her water glass. "Why no interrogation last night? Why wait till now?"

"I didn't think you'd come clean with Cam in the room, since he and Ford are old friends."

"There's nothing to come clean about." Carly shrugged. "We had one brief conversation, then the next thing I knew, someone was calling him from the room where the party was being held and he disappeared."

"So, what? No impression?" Ellie persisted.

"I didn't talk to him long enough to form an impression. Other than his previously established hotness. Why the interest?"

"As we were leaving, Grace mentioned that she was disappointed that she hadn't had an opportunity to introduce you to Ford, that's all. Apparently she hadn't seen the two of you in the lobby."

"I don't know why that would have disappointed her." Carly took a long drink of water. "So, did you actually meet him?"

Ellie nodded. "Sure."

"So how did he impress you?"

"As not wanting to be there." Ellie appeared to choose her words carefully. "As someone not comfortable with the spotlight on him."

"Maybe he's not a party guy," Carly suggested.

"The party was clearly Grace's idea, and it seemed as if everyone there was happy to see Ford, but it didn't seem that he really engaged with anyone. He didn't show much emotion."

"What do you mean?"

"I mean that you'd think that if you'd been away from your friends for a long time, when you finally saw them again, you'd look happy to see them."

"Well, yeah, if they were really your friends, you would be. Are you saying he seemed unhappy?"

" 'Unhappy' isn't the right word. I think maybe 'distant' is a better term. Or 'detached.'" Ellie appeared to weigh the word. "Yes, detached is the best way to describe him."

"Funny. I didn't have that impression of him at all. At least, not at first." Carly rinsed her glass and sat it on the counter. "In the lobby, he was friendly and talkative. We were going to go out front to look at the porch columns, but—"

"Wait. What?"

"He was talking about the painting, how it was the front of the inn. I mentioned that I hadn't seen the front, so he said I should probably take a look, that I could go out through the double doors, and we started walking in that direction. That's when someone came out from the party room and told him that people were looking for him." Carly paused again. "I suppose it should have occurred to me right then who he was, if people were looking for him."

"Not necessarily. But go on."

"There's not much more to tell. Just that when his friend said that, his demeanor changed from friendly to . . . I don't know, disinterested, maybe." She mulled over Ellie's words. "Maybe detached, yeah. And then he just went into the room where the party was and I went outside by myself. A little while later the party was over and we came back here. End of story."

"Too bad."

"What's that supposed to mean?"

"I could see the two of you—"

"Stop. No. No, you cannot see anything. I'm not here to get fixed up or to find a guy. I'm here because of your great-great-grandmother's work and that's all."

"Not even to visit with your bestie?" Ellie had adopted a faux-injured expression.

"Okay, yes. Of course I wanted to visit with my bestie." Carly laughed. "I always love to visit with you. I love your company and your house and your town. But I'm not looking for any other kind of love. Just not interested."

"Pity." Ellie shook her head. "Well, if not love, then how 'bout ice cream?"

"I'm always interested in ice cream."

"Last night Stephie said she's made some new coconut cashew mango something or other and it sounded heavenly."

"Of course." Carly could only imagine what Steph's latest concoction might taste like. Whatever it was, she knew it would be delicious. "What's a visit to St. Dennis without a stop at Scoop? Just give me a minute to grab my bag . . ."

"Did you enjoy the party, son?"

Grace had come into the inn's dining room shortly after Ford arrived. This morning there'd been no tray of coffee and goodies left in his room, so he assumed that meant he was to eat where everyone else ate: in the dining room.

"It was a very nice party, Mom. Thanks for putting it together on such short notice." He stood as she approached the table and held a chair for her before reseating himself.

"I detect a note of formality that belies your words." Grace signaled a waiter for coffee. "I don't think you enjoyed yourself as much as you pretended to. It's all right. You can be honest."

"I guess I'm not used to large gatherings," he said carefully. "And I'm not much for small talk. It was nice to see old friends, though."

"I realized after the fact that I should have asked you first. I'm just so accustomed to doing my thing and not asking for anyone else's opinion." Grace shook her head. "I just thought it would be so nice for you—"

"Mom, it's fine. Perfectly fine. The party was really nice and I survived in spite of myself." He tried to make a joke but she barely smiled. "Look, I know that you were only thinking of me and I appreciate it. Really, I do. It was very thoughtful. So no harm, no foul, as you always say."

"All right, then. It's done and behind us and you've become reacquainted with old friends and neighbors and that's that." She shook her napkin and placed it on her lap. "I'm having a crab omelet this morning. How does that sound?"

"Sounds great."

The waiter served their coffee and Ford gave him their orders.

"So who all *did* you talk to last night?" Grace asked.

"Mostly people I knew from school. Cam O'Connor, that crowd. Met a lot of new people, too. Two of Curtis Enright's grandkids . . ."

Grace nodded. "Jesse and Sophie. Jesse is married to Clay's sister, Brooke."

"Right. And Sophie owns a new restaurant out on River Road—I do remember that."

"A lovely place. Blossoms, it's called. Who else?"

He mentioned a few other people as he added a swipe of cream to his coffee and savored the flavor.

He'd been drinking bad black coffee—bad instant coffee, at that—for so long that every cup now seemed like a tiny miracle.

"Did Cam introduce you to his fiancée? Ellie?" His mother pressed on.

"He did. She seems nice." Ford figured that was the expected response.

"She's lovely. Her father is Clifford Chapman, did you know?"

"Who's Clifford Chapman?" The name meant nothing to him.

"The King of Fraud?"

Ford shook his head. "Sorry."

"I guess the scandal broke while you were away. He was an investment broker who defrauded his clients of billions of dollars. He was arrested, pled guilty, and is serving a life sentence." Grace leaned forward to add softly, "Along with Ellie's former fiancé, can you imagine? Lucky for her that she had to move here and in the process met Cameron."

"Why did she *have* to move here?"

"The poor thing had nowhere else to go. The government confiscated everything she owned because she worked for her father, and therefore everything she purchased with money she earned was considered 'fruit of the poisoned tree,' as they say."

"If she worked for her father, why wasn't she arrested, too?"

"She wasn't involved in investing. She handled their PR."

"That doesn't explain why she had to come here."

"She inherited a house in St. Dennis from her mother. Do you remember Lilly Cavanaugh?"

"Sure. She lived down at the end of Bay View. Mr. Cavanaugh carved duck decoys and they always had the best Halloween candy." Ford's eyebrows knitted together. "Wait, how could Lilly have been her mother? Lilly was ancient."

"Not Lilly, dear. Lilly's grandniece, Lynley Sebastian." Grace tapped him on the arm. "And be careful when throwing around words like 'ancient.'"

"I definitely remember Lynley." Ford grinned. "Every guy in town was madly in love with Lynley."

Grace sipped her coffee, then, as if an afterthought, added, "Oh, did you happen to meet Ellie's friend Carly?"

Ford frowned. "Whose friend?"

"Ellie's. Carly Summit."

"Maybe. I don't know." He shrugged. "I don't think so. The name isn't ringing a bell, but I met a lot of people last night." He hesitated, then asked, "Should I have?"

"I was just wondering because she came with Cam and Ellie. I invited her because she was staying with them this weekend, and I didn't want them to decide not to come because she was a houseguest."

"Here's breakfast." Ford dismissed all thoughts of the party and whom he met or didn't meet. None of that mattered. The party was behind them, he *had* survived it, and there was no point in rehashing it any further, as far as he was concerned. He was just happy that it was over and that with any luck he wouldn't have to deal with a crowd like that again. Ever.

He'd been right all along, of course. His mother *had* invited half the town. Everyone from his graduating class who still lived in or around St. Dennis, and everyone he'd known while growing up. At least when there were that many people to greet, there wasn't time to get into any real discussion with any one person, so every conversation was pretty much superficial. He'd spent most of the night saying things like "It's good to see you again, too" and "Yes, my mom is still going strong. Yeah, she looks great for her age" and "Yes, peacekeeping *is* a tough business, that's for sure."

So all in all, he did okay. The evening passed by pretty quickly, and the only time he felt the need to duck out was when Ed what's-his-name started asking him where in Africa he'd been and had he been close to any of those villages that they were always talking about on TV—"You know, the ones where they took all the little boys to make them into soldiers and then raped and killed everyone else."

Ford had made some lame response and excused himself, making his way through the lobby for the side door and some fresh air. It was on his way back that he'd seen the petite woman standing near the desk, her body at a near forty-five degree angle to the floor. His curiosity had drawn him to her, but when she'd turned around and looked up at him, he'd felt as if he'd been sucker punched. She was pretty—very pretty—and he'd liked the way her blond hair fell around her face. But there was something else about her that had pulled him closer—something he couldn't put his finger on. Whatever the attraction, she held much more appeal than going back to the party, so he'd been happy to fetch and hold the painting she'd been trying to study from ten feet away. He'd convinced her to take a look at the front of the building, and had been thinking how nice it might be to share the history of the inn with her. Maybe they'd grab another glass of wine on their way out and they could spend some time having a conversation that wasn't about him and his life. But two things had happened on their way toward the front door. The first was when some of his old buddies spied him passing the room where the party was being held and had made a big deal of how he needed to go back inside.

The second was when he'd touched her arm, and a jolt of something had traveled from his fingertip straight up his arm. Static electricity, he'd told himself at the time, even though he knew that made no sense at all under the circumstances. Whatever it had been, it had startled him and caused him to back off. He'd dropped her like a hot potato, and had immediately regretted it. He'd watched as she continued toward the front door as if she'd taken no notice that he was no longer with her— and that she couldn't have cared less.

He knew that last part didn't feel right.

He should have gone outside, but the party had already started to break up, and by the time he was able to get free of the crowd again, she was gone. The thought that she might be a guest at the inn was the only thing that had brought him to the dining room for breakfast. He'd been there for twenty minutes before his mother showed up, and the blonde was nowhere to be seen.

Maybe she plays tennis, he thought. Maybe she was down there at the tennis courts right at that moment.

But wait, that would mean she had a partner . . .

"Ford." His mother was waving a hand in front of his face.

"What?"

"Have you heard anything I said?"

"Sure." He dug into his omelet to avoid making eye contact.

"What did I say?"

"You said . . . ah, something about . . . ah . . . the party, and, ah . . ."

Grace laughed. "You never were good at fudging things. If you're going to drift away when someone is speaking to you, at least nod your head from time to time or toss out an occasional 'uh-huh.' "

"Sorry, Mom. What were you saying?"

"I was just bringing you up-to-date on what we're doing with the newspaper."

"Ah, the *St. Dennis Gazette*. I can't believe you're still—"

"Stop right there, mister." Grace put down her fork and slapped his arm. "I do not want to hear one disparaging word about my newspaper." She shook her head. "Don't even get me started on what that paper means to this community. And to me."

"I'm sorry. I was only going to say that I was surprised to hear you were still running it."

"Why? Because I'm old?" Grace did not look pleased.

"Ma, you're not that old. What I meant was . . ." He cleared his throat, not certain what he'd meant. "I guess because the inn is doing so well, it just hadn't occurred to me that you'd still need the income from the paper."

There. That was good, wasn't it?

She gave him a withering look.

"It has nothing to do with money, Ford. The *Gazette* is as much a family business as the inn. Only difference is that the *Gazette* was my family's and the inn was your father's. St. Dennis wouldn't be the same without either of them."

"Okay, I get that. But I'd think you'd have wanted to retire by now, have some time to yourself."

"And do what with all that time?" No, she clearly wasn't pleased.

"Mom, people do retire, you know. It's not so terrible to take things easy for a while. Enjoy life. Do something for yourself."

"I enjoy every day of my life. The paper *is* what I do for myself. Do you not understand that?"

"Apparently not." He'd never had a conversation like this with his mother, but he knew this was one of those times when he'd learn something really important if he asked the right questions and listened—really listened—to the answers. "Why do you keep it going?"

"At first, it was for my father after he passed away. I'd taken over for him when he fell ill, temporarily, I thought, but then he died, and I felt obligated to honor his memory by keeping the paper alive. He'd loved it, as his father had loved it, and his grandfather, who'd founded it, had loved it. There was no one else to carry on with it."

"What about Uncle Pete?" Ford asked.

"My brother had been the heir apparent all along, but as it turned out, he had neither interest nor aptitude for it. He'd have run it into the ground. I felt my father—and my family name—deserved better than that, so I kept it afloat. And, might I say, I've done a damn good job of it."

"No question about that, Mom. But you know, you could have sold it. You had your hands full when the three of us kids were younger." He remembered having to sit in the office of the newspaper waiting until his mother finished that week's edition on days when Lucy and Dan had after-school activities and no one was around to watch him.

"I'd thought about that from time to time," she surprised him by admitting. "But then Daniel—your father—died so suddenly, and it shook me to the core. Shattered my world completely." Tears formed in the corners of her eyes but did not fall. "Your brother was already out of college, so he stepped into your dad's shoes, and to give him credit, over the years he's made the inn more than anyone ever dreamed it could be. I held on to the paper then for my own sake. It gave me something to do, gave meaning to the hours, hours I couldn't bear to spend at the inn. Watching your brother do all those things your father used to do . . ." Her gaze was far away, her jaw set squarely, as she remembered painful times. Ford took his mother's hand and squeezed it, and was surprised by its delicacy. He didn't recall that his mother's fingers were so tiny.

"Danny had learned the business well," she continued. "Things ran so smoothly, it was almost as if your father were still here. Of course he wasn't, and that was unbearable. So I clung to the newspaper like it was my lifeline, and in many ways, it was."

"But maybe now—"

She held up a hand to stop him. "Now I keep the paper going for the town, for the community." Her eyes narrowed. "That better not be a smirk, Ford Sinclair." Without giving him a chance to respond, she said, "I'll have you know that people depend on the *Gazette* to tell them what's going on in St. Dennis and who's having a sale on what. At the beginning of every month, I give them a general overview of what's coming up. Then every week, I give them a list of all the events and all the particulars—what, where, when."

He nodded. "I can see where that would be helpful to the residents."

"Not just the residents." She stared at him for a moment. "I suppose I should cut you some slack since you've been away for a long time and may not be aware that St. Dennis has become the 'in' place on the Eastern Shore."

"I wasn't aware of that. When did that happen?"

"It's been gradual, over the past ten years or so. People from all over the country come here for vacation. Much of the inn is booked a year in advance—we have families who come every year for the same week. Most of the B&Bs are booked ahead as well. The restaurants are written up in magazines and newspapers from all over the East Coast, and the inn has been declared the number one spot on the Eastern Shore for destination weddings."

"Lucy mentioned that."

"Oh, that's Lucy's doing, make no mistake. Our event business has tripled since she brought her business back from California. But I digress." She paused to take a sip of water. "People plan their vacations around certain events—First Families' Day is always big, the regatta, the Waterman Festival, the Christmas Tour, always big draws for tourists. Think of what that means to the community, to the merchants, to have all these people coming into town twelve months of the year, booking rooms and shopping on Charles Street and eating at our restaurants. And every week I have a feature, something about the history of the town or an upcoming event, or an interview with one of our residents that might be interesting. For example, I did a lovely feature on Dallas MacGregor when she first moved back here and another when she married Grant. As a follow-up, I did an article on Grant's veterinary clinic and his efforts to rescue dogs from high-kill shelters and to find good, loving homes for them. A few months ago, I interviewed Dallas again about the film studio she's built here and her plans to make movies right here in St. Dennis."

He nodded. He got it.

"People like those features, Ford. They look forward every week to see who or what is on the front page. Of course, we cover the elections and the police blotter and new businesses, that sort of thing, but it's the stories about the people and the events that have made the paper relevant again. And for the first time in its hundred and some-odd years in existence, the *Gazette* has paid subscriptions from out-of-towners, summer people and people who want to be summer people. Day-trippers. Friends of friends. We've never taken in as much advertising revenue as we do now. Every business in town—and some not in town— advertises with us because they know that this paper is read by the people who are or who will be their customers."

"So in other words, you couldn't stop if you wanted to."

She laughed. "Why, I'd be burned at the stake if I tried. The merchants would never forgive me. I'd never be able to show my face in public again."

"But you could still sell it, if you ever wanted to retire."

"I won't be wanting to retire, but I admit that I do worry about what will happen to the paper when I'm gone."

"Mom . . ."

"Oh, don't give me that face. Everyone dies, son. Every single one of us. It's the only sure thing in this life. If you were born, you *will* die."

He'd learned enough about this particular topic to know she spoke the truth. Still, the last thing he wanted to think about was life without his mother.

"I don't worry about the inn. Danny *is* the Inn at Sinclair's Point now, so your father's family business is secured. It's my family's legacy I worry about." She shook her head. "I thought perhaps your cousin Andrew might be interested—for a time, he seemed to be—but apparently that was just a passing fancy." She blew out a long breath laden with sad thoughts. "But that's a problem for another day, right? Today I'm happy because you're home and you're happy because the party is behind you, so let's just finish our breakfast and get on with our day, shall we?"

"I agree." He leaned over and kissed his mother on the cheek. "I'm sorry that I wasn't aware of how deeply you care about the paper and what it means to you. I'm glad you kept it going all these years, Mom. I'm happy that there's something in your life that gives you so much satisfaction."

"Thank you, dear. You know the old recipe for happiness—I'd say I have all the ingredients."

He shook his head. "I don't know that one."

"Someone to love, something to do, something to

look forward to. I'm such a lucky woman to still have all those things in my life." She was smiling but her eyes grew wary as she added, "Now tell me, what are you looking forward to?"

"Right now I'm looking forward to finishing this delicious breakfast and taking out a kayak and making it all the way down to Cambridge and back before lunch."

He returned her smile but knew that the answer he gave wasn't the one she was hoping to hear, but he couldn't have answered any other way. Someone to love? The woman he'd once loved was dead. Something to do? At the moment, he had no idea what he wanted to do with the rest of his life—and seriously, what did he have to look forward to now?

It was sobering to think that his mother, who was well into her seventies, had a life that was much more fulfilling and complete than his.

And what, he wondered, did that say about him?

Diary ~

Happy me! I've been waiting forever, it seems, to have all three of my children under the same roof. What a joy to see my wandering boy's face again!

Now truth be told, my boy's face is thinner than it should be—actually, all of him is too thin. And there are things inside him—dark things—that I cannot read. I'd thought the fog I'd sensed would lift once he was home, but it hasn't. He's here physically, but sometimes it's as if he's somewhere else. I know that something is hurting him deeply but I can't read him the way I did when he was a child.

Which is probably a good thing, now that I think about it—after all, he is a grown man, for all I think of him as my boy.

But on to other things—the welcome-home party should have been a happy night for Ford, but he seemed so on edge that it saddened my heart. I could feel his unease from across the room. He did, however, remember his good manners and was cordial if not pleasant to everyone.

I just don't know what to make of it. Dan says it's just that Ford's been away so long that he has to acclimate himself to being home, but somehow, that seems too simple an answer. There is a restlessness in Ford that worries me—

it's as if he might take off at any moment and disappear again. And of course, now that he's home, I want him to stay—though I doubt the company of his mother and his siblings alone would be enough to keep him in St. Dennis.

My secret dream, of course, is that he'll want to stay and take over the _Gazette_ for me. I know! I know! A snowball's chance and all that. We actually chatted about the paper and he gave me no indication that he had any interest in it at all.

But there is nothing I wouldn't do to make that happen.

Oh, sure, I suppose I could resort to a spell but I hate to interfere in that manner. I mean, what if his fate really lies elsewhere?

So I guess there is something I wouldn't do after all. But don't think it hasn't occurred to me!

In other news, I met with Ellie and her friend Carly Summit—the New York art dealer and gallery owner— on Saturday at Curtis's place to discuss the proposed art gallery. I must say, Carly has some wonderful ideas for the old carriage house. I've already decided to do a series of interviews with her as part of a feature about the gallery. I figure if the town council starts dragging their feet, perhaps public pressure will move them along. I think the whole idea of turning the Enright mansion into a cultural center is a wonderful idea, one that will only further St. Dennis's reputation as a bright spot on the Eastern Shore. I cannot imagine anyone not seeing this as a good thing, but you never know when you're dealing with the public. Here's where I confess that my motives aren't exactly pure. I'd invited Carly to the party hoping Ford would meet her and take a fancy to her, but he claims not to have met her. There is something about that girl . . . I sense she will be important in our lives in some way.

Yes, of course I've asked, but the spirits haven't been speaking to me this past week. As a matter of fact, the silence has been deafening. I do hate to whine, but what good are spirit guides if they aren't there when you need them?

Even Alice—who used to be so reliable at times such as this—seems to have taken the summer off.

~ Grace ~

Chapter 7 ~

"Ford," Dan called from the hallway after having rapped on the door once. "You in there?"

"Yeah." Ford put down the newspaper he'd been reading and went to the door and opened it. "What's up?"

"Nothing, really. I was just taking a short break and thought I'd check in with you, see what you were up to."

"Come on in." Ford stepped aside and his brother entered the room.

"Everything okay here?" Dan stood halfway between the sofa and the fireplace, and gestured with a nod of the head in the direction of the captain's portrait. "He giving you any trouble?"

"Haven't heard a peep out of him. He's been on his best behavior."

"Maybe he only likes to toy with the ladies."

"Sit down." Ford folded the newspaper and tossed it onto the table.

"Ah, I see Mom's got you reading her *Gazette.*" Dan grinned and picked up the paper at the same time that he sat on the arm of the sofa.

"We were talking about it at breakfast the other day and she seemed so proud of it, I thought I'd take a look."

"It's actually pretty good, for a small-town newspaper. This week's cover article about Curtis Enright's gift to St. Dennis is great."

"I just read about that. It's the house down at the end of Old St. Mary's Church Road, right?"

Dan nodded. "That big place with all the trees on the one side and the carriage house in the back."

"Imagine owning a place like that and just giving it away." Ford sat on the chair next to the fireplace. "Did his family have a problem with that?"

"Apparently not. Enrights have been in St. Dennis forever. Curtis has two sons—Craig, who he hasn't spoken to in years, and Mike, who I know isn't interested in the house. His wife is really ill and they just moved to Florida. There are a bunch of grandkids, I'm not sure how many, and from what I hear, they've all been taken care of in Curtis's will, but he didn't want to show favoritism by leaving the property to one and not the others. At the same time, he wanted to ensure that the house would always be kept up and maintained. Mom said he's put money into a trust for that purpose, so the town couldn't refuse to accept the property on the grounds it couldn't afford the upkeep." Dan stretched his legs and leaned back. "Someone else suggested that he did it so that no one who wasn't an Enright could ever own it or live there, but I don't know about that."

"The article said he wanted them to turn the main house into some sort of community center."

"That's old news. They want an art center, and an art gallery, and a place to hold community events. Artsy stuff. Mom met with someone on Saturday who doesn't think the house is suitable for a gallery, though. She said the old carriage house would be better." Dan shrugged. "What do I know? Either way, if it's good for St. Dennis and brings people into town, I'm for it."

"From what I'm hearing, you don't need to worry about bringing people to the inn."

"We're lucky, full every weekend."

"I think it's more than luck. Mom says you've made the place what it is."

Dan shrugged. "It's always going to be a work in progress. We try to update or bring in something new every year."

"You've obviously done a great job. I can't imagine anyone doing better." Ford hesitated before adding, "I wish I'd been around more to give you a hand."

"You have your own thing to do. Everyone isn't cut out for innkeeping, but me, well, it suits me to a tee. There's nothing else I ever wanted to do. Even when I was a kid, I knew that someday I'd run this place."

"Win-win," Ford said.

"Pretty much. So what about you? What's your thing?" Dan turned to look at his brother full in the face. "I mean, now that you've saved the world."

"I'm afraid I didn't save much of anything," Ford said.

"Want to talk about it?"

"Thanks, but not really." Ford sighed. "It's complicated."

"Does it have anything to do with the fact that you

were not working with the UN as a Peacekeeper?" Dan asked.

Ford tilted his head to one side and studied his brother's face. "You knew?"

"A few years ago, D.J. had a report to do for school, and he chose the Peacekeepers as his topic since you were purportedly one of them. He did some research and brought it to me to ask how come you'd been away for so long if Peacekeepers were only supposed to serve for one year."

"Under most circumstances, that's true." Ford chewed on his lower lip. "He didn't say anything to Mom . . ."

"No. We told him to keep that information under his hat, that Gram would be upset if she knew that you weren't where you said you were. He got it." Dan laughed. "But now my son is convinced that you're working for the CIA."

Ford smiled weakly. "Who's 'we'?"

"Me and Lucy. She said she figured it out a long time ago after she saw something on TV about the UN."

"You think Mom figured it out, too?"

Dan shook his head. "No. I think she'd have said something if she had. She was worried enough when she thought you were on Peacekeeping Missions. She'd have been nuts if she'd known you were . . ." He paused. "What were you doing, anyway?"

Ford got up and walked to the window. There was no way he could tell even his brother everything— every place he'd been and everything he'd done.

Finally, "I was with a special forces group that served various functions." He chose his words very carefully.

"Most recently, we were to provide backup—security— for a group of Peacekeepers who were in Central Africa. I didn't tell Mom 'cause I knew it would worry her."

"And if you hadn't come back at all?"

Ford shrugged. "Let's just say it wasn't my call to make, and leave it at that."

"So who else was in this backup group in Africa?"

"Just some other special ops guys."

"Sounds very shadowy and covert." When Ford didn't respond, Dan added, "Sounds like a lot of muscle to protect a couple of folks on a Peacekeeping Mission."

"It was a dicey area." Ford cleared his throat. "Much of Central Africa is pretty dicey these days."

"So who were you supposed to be protecting these people from?"

"Even the answer isn't simple. There are so many different factions fighting each other, it's hard to tell the good guys from the bad. There are rebel troops with ties to al Qaeda. There are tribesmen who have traditionally fought with other tribes, destroyed their villages, and made off with the women and kids, and there are rebel forces that are doing the exact same thing. Then you have the legitimate government that isn't equipped to handle all the chaos—villages being burned, women and children stolen, raped, and/or murdered, boys of nine and ten being taken to serve as soldiers. The UN had Peacekeepers on the ground, but many of them were caught in the cross fire. Getting them safely out of the country was part of our mission."

"How'd that go?"

"Not so good," was all Ford said.

"I'm sorry." Dan moved from the arm of the sofa to

one of the seats. "I can see this isn't something you want to talk about, and I'm sorry for pushing you. I had no idea . . ."

Ford could tell his brother was rattled.

"Look, it's okay. You had no way of knowing since I hadn't shared much of anything with you over the past few years. It isn't something that I like to talk about . . . so much went wrong in so short a time." Ford shrugged. "I think it was a mission set up to fail in the first place."

"What do you mean?"

"You have a situation where people who want to do good are sent into all this chaos and you expect them to work miracles. To be a calming influence on a bunch of hotheaded egotists who are all out for their own gain. You put them in the middle of a civil war that is complicated by having outside forces—namely al Qaeda—trying to manipulate the population." Ford shook his head. "It had disaster written all over it."

"Why are so many factions so eager to be in control?"

"Oil," Ford said simply. "Huge resources as yet untapped. The government hasn't had the means to extract, refine, and move it. There are lots of folks who'd like to help them do just that."

"So how did you manage to get out?"

"We were heavily armed and had helo support. I never figured us being in danger."

"All of your people got out alive?"

"Unfortunately, no."

"So, what's your status now? Are you out? In?"

"I've been discharged."

"What are your options now?"

Ford shrugged. "I don't know. I went into the army

right from college, then volunteered for the Rangers. Got recruited for this unit. Frankly, I haven't been trained to do much more than . . ." He hesitated.

"Dangerous stuff." Dan filled in the rest. "I guess someone has to."

Ford could have debated that point, but he let it ride.

"I thought I'd take some time while I was home to think over where I go from here."

"You can always help me run the inn," Dan offered.

"Thanks, but I think you have that covered."

"Always room for another pair of hands around here. Just keep it in mind while you're mulling things over." Dan stood. "Consider it an option."

"Will do." Ford rose as well. "Just don't say anything to Mom. She seems so happy that I'm here that I don't want her to start worrying prematurely."

"My lips are sealed."

Ford walked his brother to the door. "But while we're on the subject . . . does Mom seem, I don't know, *older* to you?"

"No older than she seemed last week, or the week before. Why?"

"She just seems . . . well, older than I remember."

"Ford, she *is* older than she was the last time you were home. That was six years ago. She's midway through her seventies now." Dan opened the door, then leaned against the jamb. "Frankly, for a woman her age, she's remarkable. She's totally independent, goes where and when she pleases, puts a newspaper together mostly on her own every single week, and she's in perfect health. She's a bit of a legend around St. Dennis, you know. Everyone says they want to be just like Grace Sinclair when they get to be her age. She's a role model for a lot of people."

"I guess in my mind she was still in her sixties and walking five miles every day . . ."

"She still does that, pal. Don't ever underestimate that woman. And for the love of all that's holy, do not let her know that you think she's aging," Dan cautioned. "She will eat you up and spit you out before you know what's happened."

Ford laughed. "That's the mother I remember."

"She hasn't changed. God willing, she never will. She's ageless." Dan stepped out into the hall. "See you at dinner. Oh, and a heads-up: D.J.'s going to ask if he can kayak with you on Saturday morning. He's been itching to go out beyond Cannonball Island and I won't let him go past the point alone. If you don't want to be bothered, it's okay."

"It's fine. I'd love to have him come with me."

"Thanks. I'd go but we have a wedding on Saturday morning and a second one at night. Besides, I still don't really like kayaks."

"Still got that old sailboat of yours?"

"The Sunfish? Yeah. She's been painted a couple of times and has had a little work done here and there over the years. I had to replace the sail again before I took her out this summer, but she's still my number one ride when it comes to the Bay. And it's still the most popular sailboat ever made." Dan grinned. "Moves a lot quicker across the water than that old kayak of yours."

"Speed only matters if you're in a hurry. When I'm

on the water, I like to take my time. Chill. Enjoy the scenery."

"Smell the roses."

"Something like that."

Ford watched his brother set out down the hall and disappear around the first corner, then closed the door and went back into the sitting room. Funny, it had never occurred to him that anyone would have guessed that he hadn't been part of a UN unit. That it had been his eleven-year-old nephew who'd figured it out put a smile on Ford's face. Smart kid. Even though he appreciated his time alone, he'd enjoy being with his brother's son and getting to know him. Everything he'd seen of the boy had been thumbs-up. Considering that Dan was raising D.J. and Diana on his own, Ford had to give him credit. It couldn't be easy, being a single parent.

Of course, Dan wasn't exactly alone. He'd always had Mom around to help out with the kids, even before his wife, Doreen, died. And that had been how many years ago? Ford was hard-pressed to remember for sure, but he thought it was around eight years. D.J. had been really little when his mother died, maybe three or so. Ford thought it might have been the year Diana started kindergarten. He'd only been in the army for a few years and hadn't been able to secure a leave to come home for Doreen's funeral, which had pissed him off mightily. He was certain his brother would never forgive him for not being there, but when he'd told his mother this, Grace had assured him that Dan had barely noticed who'd been there and who hadn't.

Apparently that was true. Dan had never brought it

up, so if in fact he'd been aware that Ford wasn't there the day they buried Doreen, it must not have bothered him.

"The thing that mattered," Grace had told Ford, "was that Doreen was gone. Who was there in the church or who was there at the cemetery was immaterial. His wife was gone. When you grieve the way your brother grieved, not much else gets your attention."

Ford wondered what it was like to love someone so much that when they were gone, you were blind and deaf to everything going on around you. Knowing firsthand how fragile life could be, how uncertain, he wasn't sure it was worth it.

Ford had never really known Doreen all that well. He'd met her several times, had been his brother's best man at the wedding, but he'd never gotten to really know her. He knew that she'd been a huge help to both Dan and Grace in running the inn, that she'd agreed to put off having her children until Dan felt that he had the inn under control and in the black, that she'd been a terrific mother to her daughter and her son. He'd have been embarrassed if he'd had to admit it, but he'd had to look at her photo on the mantel in the family suite to recall what she looked like.

And all he knew of her passing was that she'd drowned somewhere out in the sound, alone.

Which explained why Dan wouldn't allow D.J. to go out past the point by himself.

Well, it might be fun to have the company, he thought, and probably as close as he might ever come to knowing what his father felt when he kayaked with Ford. The chances of him settling down here and having a son were about as slim as . . . Ford thought for a moment of a proper analogy, then smiled. *About as slim as his mother slowing down.*

The thought cheered him. He wanted to think of his mother as eternal, even though he knew that she was mortal and would eventually pass on. That, of course, wouldn't happen for a long time. That pink bunny he saw on TV had nothing on Grace Sinclair.

He went to the side window and looked out. From there he could see the children's playground, the tennis courts, and in the background, the blue-gray of the Chesapeake. Maybe he'd take a stroll around the grounds, check out a kayak that might be suitable for a young boy, make sure it's in proper condition for a trip around Cannonball Island, maybe even beyond, depending on how good the kid is. Maybe he'd take the long way round to the dock, the path that looped around the courts. He wondered if the pretty blonde was still at the inn, if right now she might be one of those women outfitted in white shorts lobbing balls back and forth across the clay court.

It wouldn't hurt to look.

Chapter 8 ⌒

CARLY propped up the painting—one of her
favorites—on the counter in her parents' kitchen
where the lighting was best. Carolina must have painted
it from memory, she thought, unless she'd managed
somehow to paint it from a boat, as the perspective was
one of looking inward from the water at a small cove
and its narrow stretch of beach.

The sand had a yellowish cast and the loblolly pines
that stretched along the left side were pale green in
what looked to be the fading light of afternoon. On
the beach, a couple sat upon a blanket that had been
spread on the sand. A basket was placed on one corner of the blanket and a bottle of wine and two glasses
topped the basket. Obviously a picnic on the beach,
but it was clear that neither the man nor the woman
had any interest in food or wine as they gazed at each
other with such intensity. The woman was dressed in
the style popular in the 1920s, the skirt fanned around
her legs. Her dark hair was loose and fell in thick curls
onto her shoulders, and her wide-brimmed hat lay
forgotten on the sand as she gazed into the eyes of . . .
whom? Her husband? Lover?

The title of the work had been written in a clear hand on the back of the painting: *Stolen Moments*.

A tickle went up Carly's spine every time she looked at it. She couldn't shake the feeling that those stolen moments had been Carolina's. Could it be possible, she mused, that her artist had had an affair, and that the painting might be the evidence? It was highly unlikely that the man in the painting was James Ryder, Carolina's husband, who'd made her life so miserable. For one thing, Carly couldn't imagine Carolina would have looked at him the way she was looking into the eyes of the man in the painting with complete and total adoration. For another, the date on the back of the painting was 1927, and Carly knew from Carolina's journal entries that James Ryder had died in 1924. And while the work lacked the kinetic energy of so many of Carolina's works, there was a vibrancy surrounding the subjects that was impossible to ignore. She hadn't mentioned it to Ellie, thinking that in this case, showing was definitely better than telling.

She was wondering if it might be provocative to use this painting for the cover of the exhibit catalog when the phone rang.

Carly's heart beat a little faster when she read the caller ID.

"So what do you know?" she immediately asked. "What have you heard?"

"That the town council likes the idea of being the ones to introduce the art world to the body of Carolina Ellis's work. They like the idea of you sharing revenue from the book proceeds with them to help pay for the work on the carriage house," Ellie replied. "They especially liked that part."

"Too bad you can't see me. I'm pumping my fist in triumph," Carly told her. "So what happens now?"

"One thing at a time." Ellie laughed. "Don't you want to know how the voting went, or what Grace said to convince the members of the council?"

"Nope. I want to know when we get started." She corrected herself. "When you get started. You and Cam."

"You were right the first time. As you and I discussed before, they definitely want you to be here to oversee it. Cam will, of course, take full responsibility for the work, but as someone pointed out, if it wasn't done to your specifications, you could conceivably come back and make us do it over. So they want you here while the work is being done, and then they want you to prepare a timetable of when you expect to be able to open the exhibit. There's a great deal of interest in making a big announcement about Carolina's work. Grace mentioned it would bring in lots of additional foot traffic to town, and since everyone on the council has a business of some sort . . ."

"They're all seeing dollar signs," Carly completed the sentence.

"Pretty much."

"I thought they wanted the exhibit to open in conjunction with some sort of holiday tour in St. Dennis."

"That was *before* they started seeing the dollar signs. Now it's 'How soon can we get this off the ground?'"

"What did you tell them?"

"I told them it would depend on how soon you could put the exhibit together."

"I don't have a quick answer for that."

"Of course you don't. I didn't expect you would. But I think it's safe to say that you'll be hearing from Ed at some point today. I just wanted to give you a heads-up. What you tell him is your business."

"How soon can Cam line up an HVAC guy?"

"The guy he has in mind is new to the area and eager for work. He'll be available to start as soon as Cam gives him the go-ahead."

"I appreciate the heads-up. Hopefully by the time Ed calls, I'll have some sort of timetable in mind."

"Oh, who are you kidding?" Ellie teased. "You know how much time you'll need."

Carly laughed. "Sort of. What I won't know until we get working on the building is how much exhibition space I'll have, which translates into how many works I can include. Once I know how many of what size, I may have to start to cull the herd, so to speak."

"Maybe you won't have to. Maybe there'll be room to hang them all."

"Doubtful, but we'll see. I don't like to crowd the work. If they aren't spaced properly, you won't really be able to appreciate each one. You need to be able to see each painting as a work apart as well as part of the whole."

"Car, you know that if you were a glass-half-empty person, you'd be totally bummed at having the chance to introduce Carolina's work from your own gallery snatched away."

"The way I look at it, the only thing that's changing is the venue. I still have control and I still get to have my name on the exhibit. So what's to be bummed about?"

"I thought you'd be more disappointed, that's all."

"Oh, I was at first, but I'm excited to put this together here, where Carolina lived and worked. I am determined that Carolina will make a huge splash. This is about her, you know, not about me."

"You're being very gracious."

"I'm a realist. And besides, I am going to have a damn good time doing this." Carly tapped a pen on the kitchen counter. "Now I'll have to work out something with my galleries. I'd planned on going in to New York tomorrow anyway."

"Well, just let me know when you're coming to St. Dennis, and I'll have the guest room ready."

"Don't you think you have your hands full already? I mean, with your sister and her friends, and the dog . . ."

"Gabi will adjust, and happily. She just loves having you around. And as for the dog, you know that Dune loves her aunt Carly."

"I admit to being a big favorite of kids and dogs everywhere."

"So get your ducks in a row there, pack a bag or two, and head south."

"Will do. I'll give you a call back after I hear from Ed."

Carly hung up and did a little dance across the kitchen floor. She was still dancing when the phone rang again, and Ed gave her the good news.

"I'm delighted to hear this, Ed. St. Dennis will not regret the decision, I promise you."

"We're hoping you can start immediately. We'd like to move forward with publicizing the exhibit as soon as possible."

"I'll be down there by the beginning of next week to go over the job with Cameron," she told him. "Ed, I'm requesting that you permit me to handle all the promotions and any announcements that are to be made in connection with the gallery in general and this exhibit in particular. I think we have to build expectations in the proper manner. I have a lot of experience in building a buzz for a showing."

"I agree. I'm leaving it all in your hands. I trust you'll be in touch once you and Cameron have worked out a timetable?"

"Absolutely. You should hear from us next week."

"Excellent. I'll let the other members of the council know. Oh, and one more thing. We're thinking that there should be some sort of contract between us—the town—and you relative to your services, expectations of renumeration."

"I've already told you that I'll be donating my time, Ed, as well as some of the proceeds from the book, once it goes on sale."

"And that's all very generous of you, don't think we don't appreciate it. We just feel it should all be set out in writing so it's all legal and so that everyone involved is on the same page."

"It's fine with me. Have the town's attorney write it up and I'll look it over."

"Jesse Enright is working on it right now."

"That's fine. I'll look forward to discussing it with him once he's finished."

Their business completed, Carly ended the call and began to work out her schedule for the rest of the week. She'd go in to New York tomorrow, as she'd planned, and hit Boston on Thursday. She'd fly back to Connecticut that same day and spend the weekend packing, making an inventory of the dozen paintings she had with her—size, subject, medium, and where in the course of Carolina's career they fell—and preparing them for transport. Fortunately none of the paintings were overly large, so she should be able to fit most of them in the new Escalade she brought home on Monday. She'd also take Carolina's journals, her notes for the book, and her laptop.

She'd just started going through the paintings when the title for her book came to her: *Stolen Moments*. It reflected not only that one painting and whatever story it told—would she ever find out?—but the time Carolina had to steal from her everyday life in order to paint. Pleased with the title and with herself, Carly went online to make a reservation for the train the following day and the flight on Thursday, then happily went about the task of measuring every painting.

The train into Grand Central on Wednesday morning was delayed twice, and accordingly took way longer than it should have. It was almost noon by the time Carly paid the cab she'd taken from the train station and walked into the gallery she'd opened eight years earlier.

Carly loved the renovated town house she'd bought in Tribeca, where she started her professional career as an art dealer and gallery owner. Over the years, she'd cultivated a number of young talents in the neighborhood, artists she met at street fairs and in the co-ops in and around the gallery. It was Carly who offered gallery space—however small—to artists who showed promise long before anyone else recognized their potential. Several of her early finds had gone on to become names in the art world, and they all remembered who gave them the thrill of seeing their work hang in a real gallery for the first time, or who brokered their first sale. For these early sales, Carly often waived her fee when she sensed an artist was about to break bigtime, or if their financial situation was precarious. She offered advice and sometimes dinner or cab fare when it was needed, and never asked to be paid back. She gained the reputation of being a friend to struggling artists, of being totally honest, ethical, and generous. It was a testament to her that once-struggling artists who'd gained notoriety in the art world would still deal only with her—a fact that did not endear her to much of her competition, gallery owners and art brokers who resented that she somehow, uncannily, always seemed to know which artists would be the next big thing.

The bell over the door had rung lightly when she entered, but no one had greeted her. She could see into the next room, where a tall, dark-haired woman chatted with a short bald man. Where, she wondered, was Enrico, her gallery manager?

Carly couldn't help but beam with pride as she gazed upon the sidewall to the right of the front door, where Elvira Chesko's work was displayed. The watercolors were gorgeous, every one of them, and it pleased Carly enormously that the young woman had fulfilled the promise she'd seen in her early works. Carly's sixth sense had paid off in a big way when it came to Elvira, and Enrico had done a fabulous job placing the works.

An exhibit of works Carly couldn't place hung opposite Elvira's, and she crossed the floor to get a better look. A small white card affixed to the wall under the first of the works identified the artist as Peter Stillman, a name she didn't recognize. Carly stepped back and studied the exhibit overall. The third and fourth paintings needed to be switched with the sixth and seventh, she decided. She dropped her bag on a chair and lifted the first of the four, standing it up against the wall while she removed another.

"Miss, please!" The dark-haired woman Carly had seen when she entered the gallery now flew into the room, alarm on her face and in her voice. "You can't touch the paintings! You can't just take them down! I'm sorry, but I'm going to have to ask you to just put it down or I'll . . . I'll call the police."

"Well, I . . ." Carly stood up and turned to face the woman, who, close up, didn't appear as young as she had at first glance.

"Carly! My sweet!" Enrico swept in through the front door, a bag from the trendy take-out establishment across the street in one hand. "You naughty girl! You didn't tell me you were coming in today." He turned to the woman who'd seconds earlier had chastised Carly. "I see you've met the boss."

"Ah . . ." The woman flushed scarlet.

"Carly Summit." Carly offered her hand. "You are . . . ?"

"Ava." The woman's voice was barely above a squeak. "Ava Miles. I'm so sorry, Ms. Summit, I had no idea . . ."

"It's Carly. And please don't apologize for doing your job. I should have introduced myself, but you seemed to be involved with the gentleman . . ."

"Oh, my goodness. Mr. Lentz! I left him in the middle of a sentence."

"Yours or his?" Enrico asked, but before she could respond, Carly shooed her back into the other room.

"You scared the living crap out of her, you know." Enrico took Carly's arm and tried to steer her toward his office, but she wasn't finished in the gallery.

"Who is this artist?" she asked. "Peter Stillman."

"He belongs to the co-op around the corner. Do you like?" Enrico gestured at the wall.

"I don't know yet. Maybe."

"The paintings haven't come in yet from Georgina Jeffers and you know how I hate a blank wall. I hope you're okay with it?"

"I'm okay, yes, but if I could . . ." Carly resumed shuffling paintings around until she was satisfied.

"I have to admit, this is better. I hadn't considered hanging the streetscape next to the one with the tall trees, but side by side, the trees seem to echo the streetlights. I like it."

"Good. Let's go into the office, where we can chat." She grabbed her bag from the chair where she'd tossed it. "What's for lunch?"

"Lentil, pear, and walnut salad, a little blue cheese sprinkled over top. Turkey, avocado, and tomato on a croissant. One very large brownie. I'm happy to share."

"I'm happy to hear it. Grab two forks and a couple of plates from the kitchen and meet me in my office." She grabbed the bag out of his hands. "I'll hang on to this."

Carly turned on the light in her office and went straight to her desk, where she placed Enrico's lunch next to her handbag. There was mail to be read and phone calls to return—those calls Enrico didn't feel important enough to send to her cell phone. She could hear him in the hall, talking to Stephen, the gallery's operations man, and she smiled. After she'd spent so much time alone with Carolina's paintings, it was a joy to be back in this place that she loved with people she enjoyed.

Enrico appeared in the doorway, plates and knives and forks in one hand, two bottles of Perrier in the other.

"I thought you might like some bubbly water," he told her as he lined everything up on her desk.

"That's great, thank you." She sat back in her chair and watched as he placed half of the sandwich on a plate, next to which he piled half of the salad, careful to divide the walnuts and pears evenly.

There were days when everything Enrico did made her smile. Thirty-eight years ago he'd been christened Richard but declared it lacked flair when he was nine and changed it to something that he felt better reflected who he was. Everything he did, Carly had learned shortly after hiring him, had flair. He passed a plate across the table to her, then followed it with a bottle.

"There aren't any clean glasses right now," he told her. "The dishwasher is still running. If I'd known you were coming, I'd have washed up a bit. On the other hand, I know you're not above drinking out of a bottle now and then."

Carly laughed. Next to Ellie, Enrico was her best friend. He'd been her first hire when she opened the gallery, and she'd missed his company for the week she'd been home with her nose in Carolina's journals.

They chatted and gossiped over their food, but when

they'd finished and Enrico had cleared away the remains, Carly rolled her chair closer to the desk, rested her arms on the top, and asked, "So tell me about Ava."

"I did tell you about Ava. I emailed her résumé to you and told you that I thought she was the best candidate for the new receptionist and you emailed back and said 'fine.'"

"I did?" Carly frowned. "When was this?"

He took out his iPhone and scrolled through emails, then turned the phone around so she could see the message and the date. The Saturday she'd been in St. Dennis. No wonder she didn't remember.

"How's she working out?" Carly decided not to try to explain why she'd been distracted.

"She's doing great."

"Any word from Jackie?" Their previous receptionist had simply failed to show one day.

"No. I did manage to catch her sister at her home one night last week. She said that Jackie's having a hard time since breaking up with the guy she'd been dating and then wrecking her car." He leaned a little closer and lowered his voice. "It sounded like a breakdown to me."

"Have you tried her apartment again? Is there anything we can do for her?"

"She's gone back to Illinois to stay with her parents. The sister seemed very embarrassed and surprised that Jackie had left without a damn word. Frankly, I was surprised, but you never know about people."

"I was surprised, too," Carly admitted. "If you hear from her, let me know. And give her sister a call in a few weeks, see if there's anything we can do for her, then give me a call."

"Give you a call?" Enrico narrowed his eyes. "Where are you going? Back to London?"

"No. This time, I'm going . . ." She hesitated. It wasn't that she didn't trust Enrico, but she hadn't really thought about discussing her plans with anyone just yet. "I'm going to be at my friend Ellie's for a while. I don't know how long."

"Oh my God, tell me she isn't sick." Enrico's hand flew to his heart.

"She isn't sick. I'm just going to be lying low for a bit, working on a very sensitive project that I'm not announcing yet."

"Oh, do tell," Enrico whispered.

"You have to promise not to breathe a word, Enrico. Not to anyone."

"Cross my heart." He did.

"Ellie's great-great-grandmother was Carolina Ellis."

"No. The Carolina Ellis whose paintings of that old church we had here for, like, a week before they both went to auction last year for megabucks?"

"The same. Ellie inherited the house Carolina lived in, the house where she painted—and all of Carolina's paintings that were hanging there and stashed in the attic."

"For real?" His eyes widened. "Like, an entire cache of paintings . . ."

Carly nodded. "An entire cache of hitherto unknown paintings."

"And she's going to let you exhibit them. Here."

"You're half right. She has agreed to let me handle the exhibit—and the subsequent sale of any she decides to sell. I can see you're already thinking about the commissions and the raise you're going to ask for."

"You know me all too well. But what part was half right?"

"The exhibit isn't going to be here. It's going to be in St. Dennis." She explained everything that had gone on, from Curtis Enright's bequest to the decision to renovate the carriage house.

"Still, that's . . . well, is 'once-in-a-lifetime opportunity' overstating the importance?"

"Not at all. That's exactly how I feel about it. It's a once-in-a-lifetime chance to introduce the works of an artist who'd been thought to have only produced a handful of works."

"How many paintings are we talking about?" he asked.

"Right now there are thirty-two that I've seen, and that doesn't include the ones that Ellie doesn't own. Apparently there are others in St. Dennis that I haven't seen. I know they exist, because Carolina wrote about them in her journals, but she gave away quite a few, and sold a few on her own. We will be trying to track those down."

"How generous of her to give away her work. Family and friends, I'm assuming?"

"Well, yes, but I also think she didn't want her husband to know exactly how many works she was producing. He didn't approve of her painting, thought it was beneath the wife of a bank officer to take money for her little hobby."

"The bastard."

"Exactly."

"So you're going to be setting up this exhibit in St. Dennis. Preparing for the big reveal, as it were.

Something splashy, well publicized and well attended, and very posh."

Carly nodded. "Which means I'm going to be spending a great deal of time there. I'm going to need you to be totally in charge here." She hastily added, "Not that you aren't."

"I understand completely. Your energies are going to be focused elsewhere. Not to worry," he assured her. "I won't let you down."

"I know you won't. And I'll be available twenty-four/seven. Phone, email—"

"Skype. I love Skype."

Carly laughed. "Anytime. We already have several showings on the schedule, so we're set for a while. I can come back for the openings of the new exhibits here. Otherwise . . ."

"Otherwise, I'm in charge."

"You are in charge, Enrico."

"So then there are only two things left to discuss." Enrico sat back in his chair and smiled confidently. "My raise, and whether or not I get to come to your grand opening."

Chapter 9 ☙

IT had cost Carly an extra day, but making the trip to Boston had been worth it. It had been several months since she and her managing partner, Helena Ramsey, had had time to sit and talk. Lately, it seemed Carly had done little more than make appearances to confer about upcoming exhibits and discuss staffing issues. She'd advised Helena ahead of time to block off a few hours to go over their projected exhibit schedule for the next six months, and to bring her up-to-date on anything she felt Carly should know, however small or petty it might seem.

Helena did small and petty very well. By the time their meeting ended, Carly knew more than she really wanted to know about their staff and several of their artists, but she did have a better feel for the gallery when she left on Friday night. Where the New York gallery was all Carly, Boston was more like 70 percent Helena and 30 percent Carly, who'd bought into it when she decided to expand her horizons. She'd met Helena on a buying trip three years ago, and they'd hit it off well enough that Carly agreed to provide some financial backing when Helena expressed an interest in buying some South End gallery space on Harrison Street before the subtle shifting of the Back Bay art scene from Newbury Street had begun. The artists who exhibited at Ramsey-Summit were younger, hipper, more avant-garde than those whose works hung in the New York gallery, which suited Carly just fine. Helena was the one who had the Midas touch when it came to New England's contemporary artists, and Carly was just as happy to let her run that show.

Satisfied that the Boston gallery was in the very best of hands and would not suffer from Carly's lack of attention over the next several months—she thought optimistically that perhaps two might be all she'd need in St. Dennis—Carly returned to her parents' home and carefully finished packing the paintings she'd spent the last three nights wrapping securely. On Sunday morning, she loaded up her car with her belongings and headed south. For a moment or two, she'd questioned whether or not traveling alone on I-95 with a small fortune in artworks had been a smart idea, but her course had already been set. She breathed easier once she'd gone over the Delaware Memorial Bridge. She took Route 213 all the way to Route 50, and from there it was an easy drop to her destination. The thought of driving through all those pretty Eastern Shore towns along the way—Chesapeake City and Chestertown, Centreville and Wye Mills—had given her spirits a lift. As much as she loved the hustle and bustle of New York, she loved the ease of those small towns just as much. There was something soothing about stopping for lunch in a waterfront eatery, like the lovely place on the Chester River where she'd watched sailboats drift past on their way to the Chesapeake while she ate a fabulous crab salad. This time around, she'd skipped that stop. Best to drive straight through and deliver her cargo of paintings to their destination, which for now, once again, was Ellie's attic.

She was famished by the time she arrived at Ellie's house on Bay View Drive, and was disappointed to find no cars in the driveway and no one at home, not even Dune, the little dog Ellie had found on the beach the year before and had adopted. Had Ellie not gotten Carly's voice mail? Carly sat on the steps of the front porch and dialed Ellie's cell.

"Hey, where is everyone?" she asked when Ellie answered.

"Gabi has a tennis match," Ellie replied. "I thought we'd be home by the time you got here, but she won her first match and now we're sitting through the second." Ellie lowered her voice. "Right now I'm supposed to be with Cam, finishing up a kitchen for Hal Garrity. His renters are arriving tomorrow, and we still have a few more hours of work to complete. I told Cam I'd be there by two, and it's past that already and he's called twice. But I can't just walk out on Gabi."

"Where are you?"

"At the courts at Sinclair's Inn."

"How 'bout I come over and stay with Gabi and you go on and finish what you have to do."

"Are you sure you wouldn't mind?"

"Of course I'm sure. But the thing is, I have all the paintings in the back of the car. I'm not so sure I want to leave them there in the inn's parking lot. Not that I'm looking for trouble, but you never know."

"There's a house key taped to the bottom of the

gnome on the back porch. Leave the paintings in the house and come on over. I'll wait for you."

"Okay. See you soon."

"Really? Under the gnome?" Carly muttered as she retrieved the key. " 'Cause no one would ever think to look there."

Key in hand, she proceeded to empty the car, carrying the paintings two at a time into the house and up the steps to the third floor, where she stood them against the wall. By the time she was finished, the packages completely lined the attic's perimeter, and several more were propped up against a trunk that sat near the top of the steps. Carly ran downstairs, pausing only long enough to grab a bottle of chilled water from the refrigerator. Locking the front door behind her, she got back into the SUV and headed for the inn.

Once again, the inn's parking lot was filled with cars. Carly had to park in the farthest corner, then walked to the end of the lot to look for the tennis courts. Spotted on the other side of a fenced-in playground, the courts were reached by following a path of crushed shells. Ellie was seated on one of a number of folding chairs to the right of the court on which Gabi lobbed the ball back and forth with a girl who appeared several years older. Not wanting to distract Gabi, Carly took the long way around to the seating area.

"Hey, she's looking really good," she whispered in Ellie's ear.

At the sound of Carly's voice, Dune sprang up from under Ellie's chair and into Carly's arms.

"She's great. Way better than I have ever been." Ellie turned in her seat and handed the dog's leash to

Carly. She stood so they could switch places, and when Carly was seated in the chair Ellie had occupied, the dog jumped into her lap. "Can you keep Dune with you? That way I can go right over to the job."

"Of course. She's always happy to be with Aunt Carly, aren't you, Dune?" The little light gray dog's pink tongue licked Carly's chin, her tail wagging merrily.

"I'm afraid I don't know how much longer you'll be here. This match should be over very soon, and if Gabi wins, she'll play the winner of the first match, so you might be a while."

"Not to worry. It's a beautiful day, and anytime I get to sit in the sun and relax is a good day as far as I'm concerned."

"Thanks. I'll see you back at the house."

Hunched over in an effort to cause as little distraction as possible, Ellie made her way around the court.

"It's just you and me now, Dune," Carly whispered. "We're going to have to cheer on Gabi . . . oh, that was a nice shot!"

Carly watched as Gabi won her match, then stood and applauded when the girl raised her racket in the air in triumph. Gabi scanned the crowd for her sister and, when she saw Carly in Ellie's place, made a beeline for the sidelines.

"Hey, you got here." Gabi greeted Carly with a hug.

"Just in time to see you take the match. Good job, kiddo."

"Thanks." Gabi looked around. "Did Ellie leave?"

"She stayed as long as she could, but Cam needed her on a job. Actually, she just left a few minutes ago."

"I told her it was okay if she had to leave. I know they need to have that job done today." Gabi grinned and scooped up the dog from Carly's lap. "She didn't have to rope you into staying with me. I could walk home when it's over."

"No roping was necessary. I enjoyed watching you play."

"Seriously? You don't mind sitting here alone?"

"Who's alone? I've got Dune." At the sound of her name, the dog's bottom wagged furiously.

"If you're sure you don't mind . . ."

"I'm happy to be here. Really."

"Great." Gabi glanced over her shoulder at the court. "I guess I'm up in a few minutes." She took a long drink from the bottle, finished it, and looked around unsuccessfully for a recycling container. "See you when it's over."

"Good luck." Carly put out her hand for the empty bottle.

"I'll need it." Gabi handed over the bottle with a thanks, and added, "This girl is freakin' *good*."

"So are you."

Gabi went off toward the court, and Carly leaned back in her chair, her face held up to the sun. When the match began, she leaned forward slightly to watch. It was clear that Gabi was overmatched by her opponent, who was older and stronger, but she made a good effort, which was exactly what Carly told her when the match ended.

"I did okay," Gabi admitted, "but she's the best right now, so I didn't expect to beat her. I just didn't want to look lame playing against her."

Before Carly could assure her that she'd looked

anything but lame, Gabi's eyes lit up and she waved to someone behind Carly.

"My friend Diana is here. Can I go talk to her for a minute?"

"Sure, but . . ."

"I'll be right back." Gabi grabbed Dune's leash and took off.

Abandoned and now alone in the spectator area, Carly stood to stretch her legs. She drank from the water bottle she'd brought with her, then tucked it back into her bag. While she waited for Gabi to return, she checked email on her phone and was about to respond to one when a shadow crossed over her. She looked up into gray eyes she'd seen once before, and hadn't forgotten.

"Hi," he said. "I thought that was you."

"Oh, hi." She couldn't help but smile. "Were you here for the match?"

"No. Just out and about, and I saw you, thought I'd stop and say hello." He nodded to the court. "You play or just spectating today?"

"Spectating. My friend's sister had a few matches and my friend couldn't stay, so I offered to." She noticed his wet shorts and partially wet T-shirt. "Out and about in the Bay?"

He glanced down at his wet clothing. "Just a little kayaking excursion with my nephew."

"Did you tip over?"

He laughed. "No. We took a break and stopped at a beach so he could rest for a few minutes."

"So that *he* could rest?" she teased.

"Hey, I can paddle from here to Smith Island and not get winded."

"I guess that would impress me more if I knew where Smith Island was."

"Ah, you're not from around here, are you." It wasn't really a question.

"No, but I do enjoy my visits."

"Come here often?"

"Not as often as I'd like."

"Are you staying here at the inn?"

"No, I'm staying with my friend. She and her fiancé live in town."

"You on vacation? How long are you here for?"

"I'm not really sure." She should probably introduce herself. *After all, I know who he is,* she thought, *and I should let him know why I'm here.* "I was asked to—"

An out-of-breath Gabi, Dune by her side, seemed to appear out of nowhere. "Can we go now?" She seemed surprised when she realized that Carly was engaged in conversation. "Oh. Sorry. I didn't know—"

"Apology accepted. Now, where's the fire?" Carly asked.

"Paige just called me. Her dad got a van full of rescued dogs from someplace and Paige has to walk them and she said I could help. But they're already unloading the van . . ."

"Okay, got it," Carly said. She turned to Ford and explained. "Gabi's friend's dad is the town vet, and runs a shelter for rescued dogs."

"Nice," was all he said.

"Well, it was good to see you again. Maybe we'll run into each other again sometime."

"I hope so."

For a moment, Carly thought he was about to say

something else, but instead he merely stepped out of the path so that she and Gabi could get around him.

Carly could feel his gaze on her back almost as far as the parking lot. She'd just reached her car when she heard her name.

"Carly." Grace was waving from several cars away. "I saw you from the window in my office, and I said to myself, she's just the person I wanted to see."

"How are you, Grace?"

"I'm very well." Grace turned to Gabi. "How'd your match go?"

"Won two, lost the last one." Gabi shrugged, and then sighed softly, as if she knew her trip to the shelter would be delayed and there was nothing she could do about it.

"Good for you. I heard you were doing very well with your lessons." Grace turned to Carly. "Our coach here speaks very highly of Gabi. He thinks she shows a great deal of promise."

"I'll be sure to pass that on to Ellie." Sensing Gabi's impatience, Carly unlocked the car doors. "Was there something you wanted to tell me?"

"I'm almost through with the list of people on Carolina's list. You know, the list of—"

"People she gave paintings to." Carly leaned back against the car and gave Grace her undivided attention. "I was going to call you about that."

"I have a few more names to trace. You know, all of the people on Carolina's list are deceased, so it's their descendants we have to identify. I may not be able to trace them all, so I'll need a few more days. In the meantime, I think I mentioned that I'd like to do a series of articles on you and the proposed gallery. Sort of follow your progress from week to week. We want to play this up as much as possible, you know. Of course, it really is a big deal, but if we can . . ."

"Yes, certainly. That's a great idea. I'm going to be meeting with Cameron and Ellie and their subcontractors at the carriage house this week. I expect I'll be there in the mornings, at the very least. Give me a day or two, then stop over. Say maybe Wednesday or Thursday? By then I should have a good idea of exactly what the work will entail."

"Wednesday will be perfect. I'll try to have the list completed by then. But I think once we have everyone identified, you might want to consider letting me make the contacts. Where some folks might hesitate to talk to a stranger . . ."

"I totally agree, Grace. I certainly wouldn't tell a stranger what I've inherited from someone in my family, let alone let that stranger into my home. It makes much more sense if you make the initial contacts and break the ice." Carly nodded. "I appreciate your offer to help."

"Well, then. I'll bring my list along on Wednesday and we'll go over what all still has to be done." Grace stepped back from the car. "I'll see you then."

"Thanks, Grace. I'm looking forward to it."

Carly started the car, and backed out of the parking space. She'd just begun to accelerate when she saw Ford jog up toward the inn. She rolled down her window and waved as she pulled away. He slowed down and returned the wave, a smile on his face.

"Who's that?" Gabi turned in her seat to look.

"That's Grace's son, Ford."

"The guy they had the party for?"

Carly nodded.

"Then he's Diana's uncle. She said her grandmother's all upset and worried 'cause he spends all his time alone kayaking or reading. Diana heard her grandmother telling her father. She said he should be going out or doing something with people and not acting like a recluse." Gabi remained turned around until they reached the driveway. "But wow. He is *hot*." The teenager glanced at Carly and grinned. "But you probably noticed that."

Carly slowed to allow another car to pass her before making the turn onto Charles Street.

"Probably . . ."

Grace rarely cursed, but was in the mood to do so now. When she'd seen Carly standing alone near the tennis courts at the same time Ford was carrying his kayak onto the dock, she realized this was her chance to introduce them. She'd sprung up from her chair and started across the lobby, but she was stopped twice before she could get to the door. By the time she made it outside, Carly was getting into her car and Ford was nowhere to be seen.

"Damn." Back in her office, she slumped into her chair, glad that no one could hear her behind the closed door.

She'd been wanting Ford and Carly to meet in the worst way. There was some sort of connection there, she felt it. Every time she looked at the young woman, she could almost, but not quite, read it. She was going to be important somehow. Grace wished she knew more, but her spirits having apparently deserted her, there was no help coming from that quarter.

"Thanks, Alice," she said drily. "Thanks for nothing. Honestly, I don't know what your problem is these days, but I wish you'd get over it."

Grace had been at her Ouija board every night since she'd first sensed something dark around her son. She asked and cajoled and all but begged, but the usually reliable Alice, her old friend and sometimes spirit guide, had seemingly abandoned her. Grace's own *sensitivity,* as she liked to think of it, was generally spot-on, but she was having some difficulty understanding what she'd been picking up, both from her son, and more recently from Carly. How, Grace asked herself, could Carly matter if she and Ford never met? She'd been hoping to introduce them at the welcome-home party, but it seemed Ford was either talking to someone on the opposite side of the room, or he'd disappeared.

"Kids can be so frustrating." She sighed heavily. "Doesn't matter how old they get, they can still frustrate the devil out of you."

She opened her laptop and began to lay the groundwork for the article she'd write following her meeting later this week with Carly. She already knew how to begin, so all she'd need would be a few quotes from Carly and a few photos, and she'd be good to go. If she worked quickly enough, she'd have the article to the printer in time for next week's edition of the *Gazette.* The following week's article would be longer, and she'd need to spend more time with Carly so that her readers could get the sense of being there as the gallery came to life.

She finished as much of the article as she could, leaving room for her quotes, and turned off her computer.

"Alice, I know you're around," she said aloud. "I could use a little help here, you know? My boy's back but I don't know for how long. I don't want him to leave again. I know, I know, selfish of me. But he's such a restless soul right now . . ."

She sighed again and got up from her desk. "I'd do anything, you know," she said as she turned off the office light. "Anything to have him stay. Anything at all . . ."

Before she closed the door behind her, she added, "Be a friend, would you, and see what you can arrange."

Chapter 10 ⌒

CARLY couldn't have been more pleased by the way the carriage house was shaping up. The walls were now the right shade of white ("*White* white, not cream or screaming white," she'd told Cameron, and he'd delivered) and the partition bisecting the room was almost complete. She'd spent time measuring every painting, cutting out paper templates for each to pin to the partition to determine spacing so that she wouldn't have to haul the actual works back and forth from Ellie's house. Evenings she spent working on the last part of her book, but it was becoming more and more difficult to concentrate. With school out for the summer, it seemed that every night a small crowd of Gabi's friends gathered at Ellie's to hang out. Some nights they watched movies in the living room, sometimes they sat on the back porch and played music to which they'd sing along. Other nights, the group might consist only of Gabi's girlfriends, and they'd congregate in her bedroom, where there'd be much laughing and talking and yes, playing of music. Loud music, accompanied by group sing-alongs.

Carly couldn't bring herself to complain—she was

merely a guest in Ellie's home. Gabi lived there and, as an almost fifteen-year-old, was certainly entitled to have her friends over. But more and more it became apparent to Carly that she needed a quiet place to work if the book was to be completed on time for the gallery opening. She made a mental note to talk to Ellie about the possibility of finding a short-term rental in town for the duration of her stay. After all, she couldn't expect Ellie and Cam to put her up for the entire summer any more than she could expect Gabi to forgo entertaining her friends.

On Wednesday morning, she was pinning the last of the templates on the left side of the partition while Cam's crew nailed up the right. They'd designed it so that there would be a space between the two sides to accommodate the electrical wires to the lighting that Carly wanted over several of the paintings. She was busy moving one template a few inches to the left when she heard the door open. She leaned around the partition in time to see Grace close the door behind her.

"My, this is different," Grace exclaimed.

"This is the partition I talked about. Cam's guys have done a terrific job putting it together." Carly stepped back to admire the layout of the paper cutouts.

Grace came closer and walked the length of the left side of the room.

"I see. Very nice layout." She smiled. "Assuming, of course, that these paper squares and rectangles represent the actual paintings."

Carly nodded. "The exhibit will begin here"—she pointed to a section of white wall on the left side of the room—"and continue around here to this side of the partition, then around to other side."

"Where were you planning on hanging the other artists' paintings, dear?" Grace asked.

"What other artists? What other paintings?"

"There have been other artists from St. Dennis, you know. A number of them have stepped forward since the word got out that there would be a gallery to display local works. Didn't Ed tell you?"

"I hope you don't mean someone's paintings of her cats."

"Sadly, yes, I do." Grace glanced around the room. "I can't even begin to imagine them hanging here. I've seen Hazel Stevens's work." She added drily, "I use the term loosely."

"I'm going to have to speak to Ed. He can't be promising people that their work will hang here with Carolina's." She blew out a long breath. One look at Grace's face reminded her that Ed could do pretty much whatever he and the others on the council wanted.

"Perhaps we could suggest that the other works be hung in the mansion," Grace said thoughtfully. "You know, the living artists of St. Dennis will have the *privilege* of displaying their work in the mansion itself."

"That's brilliant." Carly took a long drink of water from a bottle she'd left on the floor near the door. "I'd never have come up with that."

Grace's hand fluttered to indicate the insignificance of her suggestion. "You might have if you knew Hazel's ego. She'll be delighted to be able to brag that her paintings were chosen to hang in those venerable halls."

"You're so clever. I love it. I'll do it. I'll call Ed tonight."

"Now, what else needs to be done here?"

"The new heating and cooling system needs to be installed and the electrician needs to finish up. As you can see, the painting is done. Cam's working on the new door over on the other sidewall, and we still have to meet with the security people to see who can do what. Other than that"—Carly shrugged—"we should be good to go by the fall."

"And your book?"

"The book is this close to being finished." Carly held up her thumb and her index finger, a fraction of an inch separating the two. "I'm thinking I might get more work done if I were by myself somewhere. I'm used to living alone."

"A lot going on at Ellie's, I suspect, with Gabi home for the summer."

"How did you guess?"

"A teenage girl is bound to have friends in and an iPod with a playlist of all sorts of music on it." Grace smiled knowingly. "My granddaughter, Diana, is one of the girls who gathers nightly with Gabi and Paige Wyler and several others. I know they spend a lot of time at Ellie's."

"Which is great for Ellie because she knows where Gabi is and who her friends are. Important, I know. But at the same time . . ."

"You don't have to say it. I've shooed them from the lobby at the inn on more than one occasion. They just get a little loud at times."

"If you hear of any apartments or small houses for rent on a short-term basis, please let me know."

"I might be able to find a small suite for you at the inn. I can check with Danny and see if we have any vacancies that might fit your needs." Grace frowned. "But of course, there are always kids at the inn, and sometimes they will run up and down the halls when their parents aren't paying attention. Though we do have a few cottages . . ." She appeared to be thinking. "Most are just one bedroom, one bath, and a sitting room. We use them for staff, and sometimes for our interns. I could ask . . ."

"That's really nice of you, Grace, but I think I'd like something with a kitchen."

"I'll ask around and see if anyone knows of . . ." She stopped in midsentence. "You know, Lucy mentioned that Sophie Enright will be moving into the apartment over her restaurant sometime soon. I wish I'd paid closer attention to exactly what she said, but I had my mind on something else at the time and it went right past me." Once again, Grace's hands fluttered.

"Where's Sophie living now?"

"She's in a little rented house right off of Cherry Street. Actually, Jesse—her brother—had rented it, but when he got married, he moved into Brooke's house. When Sophie moved to St. Dennis, she sublet it from Jesse. Apparently, there's still some time left on the lease, so I imagine that he could sublet to you, now that Sophie's moving." She appeared to pause in thought for a moment. "I'm pretty sure that place belongs to Hal Garrity. I can look into its status, if you'd like."

"I'd really appreciate it."

"I'll let you know what I find out. Now. Let's talk

about the articles I want to write. I thought this first one would be a sort of here's-what's-going-on-at-the-Enright-mansion. There are so many rumors flying around town, don't you know. So I thought we'd just put it out there, and briefly introduce you. Then next week's article will be more of a 'meet Carly' piece. You know, your background, your work. You can talk about your long-standing friendship with Ellie, your galleries, particularly the one in New York, where you displayed Carolina's work in the past."

"That was a very brief showing prior to the auction," Carly interjected. "We only had two paintings for a couple of days. We put them on a very limited exhibit as a favor to the owner, who was a good client of ours and who wanted to sell them. She wanted them shown in a prominent gallery to drum up more interest. That's how Carolina first came to my attention."

"You can certainly go into that, though I did a brief piece that year on the auctioning of those two paintings. I read about the sale in the *New York Times*, and of course recognized Carolina's name right away. I didn't have any information other than what was in the *Times*, though. I did call the auction house for some details, but they gave me the run-around, so I never did expand on the sale and what it meant for a St. Dennis artist to be recognized."

"We can go more into that if you'd like."

"I would. I think people should understand just how important Carolina's work is."

"There is a problem, though, in that I was trying to keep a lid on the fact that we've found a treasure trove of Carolina's works."

"Perhaps you could just mention her name along with several others."

"You mean, like Hazel Stevens?"

Grace laughed. "Oh, yes. You can even use the interview to declare that you'll be looking over the works to decide who goes into the mansion and who will be relegated to the old carriage house."

"I like it." Carly hoped the ploy would work. The thought of Carolina's exquisite paintings hanging next to some amateur portrait of the artist's pet was just not going to happen. "Speaking of Carolina's work . . ."

"Oh, yes. Dear me, I almost forgot." Grace opened her sizable bag and took out a small notebook. She flipped through it until she found what she was looking for. "Here we go. These are the folks who are descended from the friends of Carolina who received paintings from her as gifts." She handed the notebook to Carly, who skimmed it.

"I don't know any of these people," she murmured.

"Of course not, dear, but I do." Grace leaned over Carly's shoulder. "Look here. Susan Lane is the wife of the late Reverend Lane. His grandfather lived on Bay View Road, a few houses away from Carolina. And this name—Ariel Peters. She's the great-granddaughter of Larinda Peters, who was the librarian in St. Dennis for more years than anyone remembers. Now, Lawrence Ash, I doubt he'd let us exhibit whatever painting he might have. He's pretty much an old sourpuss. Always has been."

"But the others—they're still around?"

"Most, I'm afraid, are long gone and I have no idea how to trace their descendants. But I can set up a date to visit with Susan and Ariel. You just let me know when you're ready, and I'll make the calls." Grace was all but beaming. "I'm really tickled to be involved in something as big as this, something that could be so good for the town. It does give me a happy lift."

Carly laughed at the expression. "I'm happy that you're happy. Let's hope your enthusiasm rubs off on the rest of the town."

"Now, how about we plan on getting together on, say, Saturday for the first real interview."

"Saturday is fine. Whatever works best for you."

"Let's try for eleven, shall we?" Grace removed a glass case from her purse and took out a pair of oversize sunglasses. "And I'll check up on that house for you."

"Where is it again?" Carly walked Grace to the door.

"It's on Hudson, right around the corner from Cherry. The house is a small brick two-story, if I remember correctly. Three houses from the corner, if you're planning a drive-by. It's a nice neighborhood. Vanessa Keating—I'm sure you've met her, she owns Bling—"

"One of my favorite shops."

"She lives on Cherry Street, around the middle of the block, I think. Anyway, it's a nice part of St. Dennis."

"I haven't seen a part of St. Dennis that isn't nice, Grace." Carly opened the door, held it for Grace, then followed her out into the driveway.

"Yes, well, we do our best to keep things up. See you soon." Grace put on the large glasses that covered a good part of her face and smiled. "I just love the Jackie Kennedy look, don't you?"

Grace gave a little half wave, then took off for the street where she'd left her car. Carly waited until Grace pulled away before turning back to the carriage house. She knew she needed to make some final decisions about what to hang on that first finished section of the partition, but she kept thinking about the house that Grace described. Finally, she told the guys working inside that she had to step out for a few minutes but she'd be back well before they finished for the day.

The house was exactly where and as Grace had described it: a small two-story brick three from the corner. There was a small bit of lawn out front, a strip of a garden bed between the driveway and the house next door, and a fence around the backyard. There were flowers in colorful swaths on either side of the front walk, and some rosebushes around the small front porch. If the inside was as appealing as the outside, it could be perfect.

Carly tapped her fingers on the steering wheel and tried to recall everything she knew about Sophie Enright. All she could come up with was that she was a friend of Ellie's and that she'd recently opened a new restaurant somewhere in St. Dennis. Satisfied that between Grace and Ellie she'd get the scoop on the little house, she turned the car around and headed back to work.

She'd have to find just the right time to talk to Ellie. She'd hate for Ellie to be insulted that Carly didn't want to stay with her family.

She found her chance that evening while she and Ellie were in the kitchen, Ellie rinsing the dinner dishes and handing them off to Carly to load into the dishwasher.

"El, I've been thinking," Carly began.

"About what?"

The words stuck in her throat.

"Car?" Ellie turned to her. "What's up?"

"You know, these projects—the gallery and the paintings and the book and the catalog for the exhibit—they're all really time-consuming."

"I know. So what did you want to talk about?"

"Just that I've been thinking . . ."

"You said that." Ellie dried her hands on a towel.

"I love staying here with you and Cam and Gabi, and of course Dune. I love having a dog around. I had one when I was little but it's been a long time . . ."

"You're hedging. Get on with it."

Carly took a deep breath. "I think I need to find a place. Like, a place to myself. You know, these last few years I've been living by myself, and I . . ."

"And it's driving you nuts having a barking dog and ringing phones and teenagers inside, outside, everywhere." Ellie laughed. "I wondered how long you were going to last."

"You did?" Carly frowned. "Am I that transparent?"

"No, but I know you. You're used to being in a quiet place. You don't work well with noise, any kind of noise. You never did. Not back in school, not when we were in grad school and we shared that apartment in Boston, remember?"

"The guys next door who had parties twice a week." Carly grimaced.

"The girls upstairs who had parties every night," Ellie reminded her. "The point is, you're a person who likes her space. And right now you're trying to complete several important tasks at the same time. So what are you thinking? One of the B&Bs?"

"Actually, I was speaking with Grace today—she stopped by the carriage house—and the topic came up. She mentioned that Sophie Enright had been renting this house over on Hudson Street and that Sophie would be moving out sometime soon."

Ellie nodded. "Like this weekend soon. She and Jason have been working their butts off to fix up the apartment over her restaurant. I don't know where she gets the energy. She works at the restaurant from five in the morning till two in the afternoon, then she goes into the law office and works until she's finished whatever she has to do there. Then she goes back to the restaurant to work on the apartment. Though I think Jason did most of the painting, and Cam helped him with the plumbing, which wasn't in great shape." Ellie paused. "Is this your way of saying that you're interested in renting the house?"

"Grace said she knows the person who owns it. She was going to find out when it might be available."

"I'd say by early next week, but I can call Sophie if you'd like, find out when she expects to have her stuff out."

"You don't mind? I don't want you to think . . ."

Ellie waved an impatient hand. "Stop. I understand. You're not hurting my feelings. I want you to have the time you need to work. And really, I was wondering how long you were going to be able to deal with the kids being here all the time. This isn't a quiet place." She smiled. "I mean, Gabi believes that my great-aunt Lilly—who's been dead and buried for years—visits her sometimes at night, so what does that tell you?"

Carly stared at her blankly. "I dunno, what does it tell me?"

"That the kid—on her own or with a crowd—can make enough noise to raise the dead."

Chapter 11 ❧

FORD dragged the kayak onto the grass, then carried it into the small boathouse where Dan stored the canoes and the kayaks for the use of the inn's guests. Ford kept this particular kayak separate because it was his favorite and he didn't want someone else taking off in it when he wanted to use it, which was all too often this past week. He knew he needed to do something besides paddle and read, but being on the water gave him time to think. He just wasn't sure if that was a good idea or a bad one.

It wasn't that he hadn't made an effort to fill his hours in other ways. Every day this week, he'd walked down to the tennis courts, Dan's racket in hand. He'd told himself that it was exercise he was after, but he couldn't kid himself into believing that he hadn't been hoping to catch a glimpse of the pretty blonde. So far, the only game he'd been able to scare up was one against Hal Garrity, the retired chief of police who had to be closing in on seventy, and who, as a friend of the family, had court privileges even though he wasn't staying at the inn.

Hal had beaten the pants off him.

Ford had gone with D.J. to soccer tryout yesterday morning, and he'd sat on the bleachers and watched a bunch of twelve-year-olds show off their dribbling and kicking skills. It held his interest for all of the twenty minutes that his nephew was on the field, and after that, his mind wandered all over the place.

Twice in the past week he'd walked into town. He'd had coffee one morning at Cuppachino with his mother, Lucy, Clay, and a bunch of St. Dennis residents he didn't really know. The talk had been about a new restaurant that had just opened out on River Road. Sophie Enright was the owner and there was much chatter about how great the food was and how everyone would meet there for lunch at noon. Everyone except Ford had agreed. Instead he'd stopped at Book 'Em and picked up a few new books, the reading of which had served to give him another excuse to spend time alone in his room.

There'd never been a time when Ford had been inactive, when he'd had to look for things to occupy his time. He'd always been in a structured environment of one sort or another—he'd gone from school into the military—and having no set schedule was driving him crazy—crazy enough that he'd all but decided to ask Dan to find a job for him at the inn. He had an open offer of employment from an old buddy who'd started up a security firm, but that was in Virginia, and Ford didn't think that his mother would ever speak to him again if he left so soon after having been home for a whopping ten days.

For the first time in his life, he had no real focus,

and it was making him flat-out nuts. Something was going to have to change.

He held the door open for a trio of middle-aged women who were deep in conversation and he went into the cool of the lobby. His clothes were wet and uncomfortably sticking to his skin, and he couldn't wait to change. As he started across the lobby floor, he looked up toward the staircase that bisected the lobby. His mother was on the landing, just about to descend. Seeing him, she smiled broadly and raised her hand to wave to him, and before Ford could register what had happened, she'd stumbled somehow and was falling . . . falling . . .

"Mom!"

Ford reached the staircase in less than a heartbeat, but already Grace had landed at the bottom of the stairs, her head on the last step and her body on the floor. A bone protruded from her right forearm, and her left leg lay at an odd angle to her body.

"Call 911!" he shouted across the lobby to the reception desk as he felt for a pulse. "Someone get Dan!"

His brother was there in a flash.

"Dear God, what happened?" Dan knelt next to their mother.

"She fell." Ford couldn't believe it even though he'd seen it. "It happened so fast. One second she was on the landing, the next she was falling and I couldn't get there in time to break her fall."

Dan reached out to Grace as if to pick her up, but Ford brushed his hand away.

"Don't touch her, don't try to move her," he said. "You could end up doing more damage."

"Is she still breathing?" Dan wanted to know.

"She is. She—"

"What happened to Mom?" Lucy demanded as she, too, fell to her knees next to the still form.

"She fell from the landing." Ford repeated what he'd told Dan.

"Oh my God, is that her bone?" Lucy pointed to her mother's arm and began to cry.

"Let's hope that's the only break she has." Ford didn't like the way Grace's leg was bent, but didn't want to get his siblings more upset than they were. He was grateful to hear the shriek of the ambulance's siren as the vehicle sped up the drive.

Seconds later, there were four EMTs rushing across the lobby with a gurney, and Ford, Dan, and Lucy were all forced to back away while their mother's condition was assessed. After what seemed like an eternity, the medics lifted Grace very carefully onto the gurney and headed toward the door.

"Wait! I'm going with you!" Lucy rushed after them.

"Come on, Ford." Dan tapped him on the arm. "I'll drive."

"Where are they going to take her?" Ford jogged to keep up with his brother.

"I'll ask but I'm pretty sure it'll be Eastern Memorial out on the highway. It's the closest." Dan stopped at the ambulance to confirm the destination and found his sister in an argument with the EMTs.

"I need to go with her," Lucy insisted as Dan took her by the arm and tried to steer her away from the vehicle.

"Ma'am, we can't let you do that. We'll take good care of her," the medic told her firmly. "You can follow us—"

"I want to . . ." Lucy tried to shake off Dan.

"Stop it, Lu. Use your head. Let them do their jobs. You can ride with Ford and me and we'll meet the ambulance there." Dan nodded to the EMT who mouthed, *"Thank you,"* before closing the ambulance doors.

"Someone should be with her." Lucy began to cry again as they ran to Dan's car.

"Someone *is* with her," Ford said. "Several someones who know what they're doing. They're the ones she needs right now."

The ride to the hospital seemed to take forever, but by the time they'd arrived, Grace was already in triage.

"They're going to take her for X-rays," the physician's assistant told them. "Why don't you all go into the lobby until we get things settled back here. We'll keep you updated, I promise."

"I never saw Mom like that." Lucy buried her face in her hands.

"None of us have." It was clear that Dan was rattled, too. "Come on, Lu. Let's go sit down and try to calm ourselves. It won't do Mom any good to see the three of us this upset."

They pushed three chairs together and sat in silence for several moments.

"Her arm was broken." Lucy stated the obvious.

"Broken bones can be fixed," Ford, who'd seen more than his share of broken bones, reminded her.

"I hate thinking that she's in pain." Lucy's face was white, her eyes rimmed in red.

The simple statement hit Ford hard. He'd seen so much pain over the past few years that in some ways he'd become immune to thinking about what others felt. But when it came to his mother—his indomitable, invincible mother—he, too, hated the thought. She was the epitome of strength to him, the standard by which he'd judged women, and the reason, he knew, why the helpless type had never appealed to him. After their father died, Grace had kept the inn going while running the newspaper and raising three kids. She was loved and respected by everyone who knew her for her gentle nature as well as her can-do attitude. She was deeply involved in community affairs and a staunch defender of St. Dennis's history. He could not think of one person who'd ever had an unkind word to say about her.

The fact that he'd given her years' worth of sadness by his absence pained him now more than he could say.

Hang in there, Mom, and I promise I'll stick around for as long as you need me.

He cocked his head to one side. Funny, he thought, but for a mere instant, it was almost as if he heard his mother whisper: "Don't think I won't hold you to that, son."

Over the next several days, Grace was watched over and kept company by at least one of her children at all times. By Thursday afternoon, though the pain medications kept her a bit groggy and her brain somewhat fuzzy, she was awake almost as much as she slept.

"What's this?" she'd demanded of Ford upon opening her eyes for the first time.

"What's what, Mom?" Ford dropped his magazine on the floor and hurried to his mother's bedside.

"This thing. What is this thing?"

"It's a cast," Ford explained. "Your arm was broken when you fell. You have one on your leg, too, don't you remember?"

"I fell . . . ?" Grace had scrunched up her face in confusion, and Ford had had to explain the events of the last several days.

"Oh, for Pete's sake," Grace had grumbled before closing her eyes and falling back to sleep.

Ford took the Saturday-morning shift, since both Lucy and Dan had a wedding at the inn to set up.

"She's been awake several times," Lucy told him as she scanned the emails on her phone. "Each time she seems to be a bit stronger, though she's still a little confused about what happened." She paused. "You said you saw her fall?"

Ford nodded.

"Was there someone behind her on the steps?" she asked. "Someone with her? A woman?"

"No. Mom was the only person on the stairs when she fell. Why?"

"It must be the drugs, then."

"What must be the drugs?"

"Oh, last night she was muttering something in her sleep, something about someone named Alice having pushed her or somehow had caused her to fall down the steps."

Ford shook his head. "She was dreaming. She was alone at the time."

"Funny." Lucy appeared thoughtful. "I remember hearing about someone named Alice who Mom knew when she was younger . . ."

"What about her?"

"Nothing." Lucy shook off whatever she'd been thinking. "In any event, she's been a little more lucid each time she wakes."

Lucy paused at the door. "I hate to leave."

"You go. I've got this."

"You've had, what, six hours of sleep since Wednesday?"

He'd stayed from the time they'd admitted Grace until Friday morning, when Dan and Lucy insisted that he go back to the inn with Dan and get some sleep.

"More than that. Go ahead, do what you have to do. We'll be fine." Ford picked up the book he'd brought with him and moved a chair closer to the window, where the light was best, and sat down and tried to read the spy novel he'd picked up earlier in the week, but he couldn't concentrate. All he could think of was the woman in the bed, and how her life was going to change, at least for a while.

When he'd wished for something to happen, this wasn't exactly what he'd had in mind.

"Mom? You're awake." He closed the book and switched to the chair next to the bed in one smooth movement. "How are you feeling?"

"Like I've been hit by a truck." She hesitated before asking, "Was I hit by a truck?"

"You fell down the main staircase at the inn."

"Ah, yes, I do remember now that you mention it.

Sorry. I seem to be a bit forgetful. I think Lucy told me . . . Is Lucy here?" Grace's head moved slowly from one side of the room to the other.

"She was here last night and earlier this morning, but she and Dan have a wedding to deal with and—"

"Of course. The McGonigal wedding. Lovely people." She grimaced as she tried to move.

"What can I do for you, Mom?" Ford was on his feet. "Do you want to sit up a little more?"

"Yes, and I'd like some water."

"Let's see if we can get you upright a little without causing you any pain." He reached for the bed controls and raised the back by inches at a time.

"Oh, for crying out loud, Ford, just get me up," she said impatiently.

"I'm trying to go easy."

"Well, I'm fine."

Ford paused. "You want to rethink that last one?"

"All right. I'm not fine. Just move this contraption a little faster."

He maintained the slow speed on the controls, watching her face to see if she showed any signs of pain.

"There. That's good. Thank you." She nodded. "Now if I could have a drink . . ."

He held the large tumbler to her lips, but as soon as she had the straw in her mouth, she snatched the cup with her good hand and drank. When she finished, she handed the cup back to him.

"Nothing wrong with my left hand, Ford."

"I can see that." He set the cup on the tray next to the bed and pulled the chair closer to the bed. "Now, how are you really feeling?" he asked as he sat.

"My left leg hurts like the dickens," she admitted, "and my right arm isn't feeling too good either, and I have the headache to end all headaches. Other than that, I'm fine and ready to go home."

"Do you want me to ring for the nurse and see if it's time for your pain meds?"

"She'll bring it when it's time. I hate to take that stuff, you know. It makes me groggy. And it's addictive. Why, I've read any number of stories of how people have become addicted to prescription medications."

"We'll make sure they cut off your supply before that happens," he said drily.

"Oh, you." Her left hand reached out for his and he took it. "I'm so glad you're here, Ford."

"I'm glad, too. I'm happy that I was here when . . ." He gestured to her casts. "Of course, I'd be happier if we could have skipped this part."

"It is what it is. Into each life a little rain must fall, and all that." Grace sighed heavily, and Ford knew that she was in pain. She closed her eyes and winced.

"Mom, what can I do for you?"

"Nothing, dear." She winced again, her hand squeezing his. "It's enough to know that you're here."

She closed her eyes, and Ford thought she was drifting back to sleep, but a few moments later, her eyes still closed, she asked sleepily, "What day is it, anyway?"

"It's Saturday."

"Saturday?" Her eyes flew open. "But it can't be Saturday."

"Yesterday was Friday, Saturday usually comes next."

"Well, then, they're just going to have to let me out of here. Give me that damned thing so I can call for the nurse." She sat up and reached for the buzzer.

"Whoa. Hold on, Mom. What's the big deal about Saturday?"

"I have an interview this morning. An important one. It's for the paper and I—"

"So we'll call whoever you're supposed to talk to and explain what happened." If they didn't already know, he added to himself. He was pretty sure that everyone in St. Dennis knew by now that Grace had taken a tumble. There were almost a dozen flower arrangements lined up on the windowsill. "I'm sure whoever you're supposed to meet will understand. We can reschedule and—"

"No. *You* don't understand." Her eyes filled with tears and she began to cry. "I wanted to write a series. The articles are supposed to spread out over the next weeks. It's important. I have it all planned . . ."

Ford couldn't remember seeing his mother cry since his father died. A few tears now and then, but she was really *crying*.

"Mom . . . Mom . . . it'll be okay." He tried to soothe her.

"I've never, ever failed to get the paper out on time. Not one time, in all the years since my father passed it on to me. Not even when your father died. I've always gotten the paper out on time." She began to cry harder, and Ford thought for sure her heart was breaking.

He ran a hand through his hair. He couldn't stand to see his mother so upset. It almost seemed that this realization—that her beloved *Gazette* might have to go on hiatus—was more devastating to her than the physical pain of her injuries. "Mom . . . look, tell me what to do and I'll do it. I'll do whatever you need."

"You would?" With her good arm, she reached for the tissues on the tray next to her bed. Ford handed her the box and she pulled a tissue free. "You'll help me get the paper out?"

"Of course, Mom. Whatever you want me to do." He patted her left shoulder reassuringly.

She pulled another tissue from the box and wiped her eyes. "I'm afraid it's more complex than you might think."

"So you'll walk me through it."

"You'd really do this for me?"

"Mom, I'd do anything for you." The lump in his throat cautioned him not to say more.

She rested her head back against the pillows. "You've taken a huge weight off my mind, Ford. I don't know what I'd do if we couldn't . . ."

"Don't even think about it. The paper is going to be out on time, Mom. Just give it to me in steps."

"Well, the first thing you have to do is this interview." She paused. "Have you ever done an interview, son?"

"Sort of." He wondered if *interrogations* might count as roughly the same thing but thought better of asking. "What's the interview about?"

Grace told him about Curtis Enright's handing over his property to St. Dennis and the new art center in detail, and her plan to do a series of articles about the proposed gallery in Enright's newly renovated carriage house. She yawned, the effort to explain having exhausted her. She rested her head again and closed her eyes.

"The appointment this morning at the carriage house is to interview the person setting up the gallery and the exhibits. Today's just the first interview, like I told you. It's just to introduce her to St. Dennis. Take some pictures. Make sure there's a good one for above the fold. There's a file on my laptop that has a good deal of background material on it along with my notes for the interview. There's also a little notebook on my desk that you should probably read before you go."

"Okay. Not a problem." He leaned over to kiss her forehead. "Don't worry about a thing."

She sighed happily and began to drift off to sleep.

"Mom." He shook her gently. "You didn't tell me who I'm supposed to be interviewing."

"Carly," she whispered. "Carly Summit . . ."

Carly Summit. Ford frowned. Where had he heard that name before? It sounded familiar, and yet he couldn't put a face to that name, something he was usually very good at.

He hurried through to the parking garage, located the car he'd borrowed from Dan, and drove straight to the inn. On his way to his mother's office, several people stopped him to ask about Grace. He realized then he didn't have a key to the office and couldn't find Dan. The grandfather clock in the lobby chimed twelve noon. Frustrated, he stood outside his mother's office door, wondering if it would be inappropriate to kick it down. He was seriously considering doing just that when Dan showed up and unlocked the door. Ford went straight to Grace's desk. Her laptop sat in the middle, but once he turned it on, he realized he didn't know her passwords. He groaned, then spotted the notebook she'd mentioned. He picked up and flipped through it. Just as she'd said, there were lots of notes about the carriage house renovations and a list of questions she wanted to ask during what she referred to as "Interview #1." He didn't have time to read through it now, but he could skim the outline as the interview progressed. How hard could it be?

He pocketed the notebook, turned off the light, and headed for the lobby door and the car he'd left right outside the door in front of the "No Parking at Any Time" sign.

The drive to Enright's took exactly seven minutes, due mostly to traffic in the center of town. Summer Saturdays in St. Dennis, he was learning, were swell for the merchants and the restaurants because of the weekenders and the day-trippers, but they were murder on the residents. He took backstreets all the way down to Old St. Mary's Church Road, all the while wondering what he'd gotten himself into.

He almost wished he'd kept his mouth shut. In one way, he did wish exactly that. He knew nothing about real interviewing. Oh, he'd taken a course or two in journalism back in college, but that was years and another life ago. Even he had to admit that interrogating terrorists wasn't the same thing. But his mother had looked so despondent, had been in such a state of despair—well, there was no way he could not have stepped up.

In his mind's eye, Ford kept reliving over and over

that terrible moment, watching Grace fall. He could see himself moving as if in slow motion to reach the bottom of the stairs before she did, hoping to catch her, to break her fall—and failing. He couldn't help but think if he'd been just a few steps quicker, she might have been spared the pain of those broken bones. The doctors said it was a miracle that she hadn't fractured her hip. Actually, what they'd said was they couldn't understand how she hadn't.

Grace had been a great mom—the absolute best—and if what she needed was someone to take her place at the paper, he'd be her man. He wouldn't fail her in this.

The Enright place looked pretty much as Ford remembered it. Big and stately, the graceful brick house in the Georgian style stood surrounded by tall trees on the biggest single parcel of land that still remained in St. Dennis. He parked in the wide driveway behind a big, shiny, expensive-looking SUV with Connecticut plates and a battered old pickup with more than its share of nicks and dents. He paused once on his walk down the driveway to admire the gardens behind the house that were in full and glorious bloom.

He still thought it sounded crazy that anyone would just hand over a place like this, just give it away, since it must be worth a fortune. Mr. Enright must have a philanthropic streak as wide as the Chesapeake, Ford was thinking as he approached the door.

He'd just reached for the handle when the door opened.

"Hey, man. What's up?" Cameron stepped out into the bright sunlight, the door closing quietly behind him.

"Not much. You working here?"

Cam nodded. "Just finishing up a few details. Hey, sorry to hear about your mom. How's she doing?"

"A little better each day. We're hoping she'll be home by Monday or Tuesday."

"Knowing her, I'm sure she's getting antsy to get out."

"I'm sure she will be once she isn't sleeping as much. They have her on some pretty heavy meds right now for the pain."

"Poor Grace." Cam shook his head. "Give her our best, will you? Let her know we're thinking about her."

"Will do."

"So what are you up to? Curious about what we've done inside?" Cam gestured toward the building behind him.

"My mom had an interview set up for this morning with the woman who's running the gallery, and she was so upset to miss it . . . you know, afraid the paper wouldn't get out, that sort of thing. Anyway, I said I'd do the interview for her."

"Nice of you." Cam grinned. "Your mom is going to make a newspaperman out of you yet."

"Not likely." Ford snorted. "This is just temporary, till she's back on her feet."

"Well, let's hope that's soon, for both your sakes." Cam glanced at his watch. "I'm late. Ellie's going to kill me. I promised I'd be back at the house by eleven." He hoisted the toolbox he held under his arm. "Carly's inside. I'll see you around . . ."

"Right." Ford opened the door and stepped inside

and out of the heat and humidity. The cool air surrounded him and he closed the door quickly.

"Cam, did you forget some . . ." The woman stepped out from behind a partition that divided the room into two equal parts, and Ford's breath caught in his chest.

He blinked to make sure the heat hadn't brought on a hallucination.

But no. It was her.

"Can I help you?" she asked.

"I'm Ford Sinclair," he somehow managed to say.

"Yes, I know."

"You do?" He frowned. "How do you know?"

"I was at your welcome-home party." She leaned back against the end of the partition.

"You were?"

"Yes, don't you remember? We met in the lobby. I was looking at—"

"A painting, the one behind the receptionist's desk, yes, of course I remember that part." He could have added that he'd been kicking himself in the butt ever since for letting her get away that night without finding out more about her. Like her name. "But I thought you were a guest at the inn."

"I was staying with Cam and Ellie, and I think your mother probably invited me to the party because she was afraid they wouldn't come if they had to leave me home alone. I went into the lobby because I felt awkward, since I hardly knew anyone, including the guest of honor."

"You weren't the only one who felt out of place."

"What, you? The party was for you."

"I'm afraid I'm not much of a party guy," was all the explanation he offered.

"By the way, I'm Carly Summit."

"I was hoping you were." And he had been, ever since he opened the door and saw her standing there. He should have put it together right away—the pretty blonde who'd shown such intense interest in the painting in the lobby would, naturally, be the art dealer. For days, he'd been wondering if he'd ever see her again, and now here she was, compliments of his mother.

Apparently, it was true: no good deed goes unrewarded.

"I'm so sorry about your mother's fall," Carly was saying. "I think it must have happened right after she left here."

"She was here on Wednesday?"

Carly nodded. "She stopped by to go over a list that she was working on for me."

"A list?" Grace hadn't mentioned a list that morning.

"People who may have inherited paintings by a local artist. The same artist, incidentally, who painted the picture I wanted to look at in the inn."

"Just say the word, anytime you want a closer look."

Carly smiled. "So, Ford Sinclair, what can I do for you this morning?"

"You can give me those few minutes you were going to spend with Mom." When Carly raised an eyebrow, he explained, "My mother asked me to interview you in her place. She was really worried about the series of articles she wanted to do for the paper not getting done, so I told her I'd take over until she's recovered enough to do her thing."

"That's nice of you. You've done this before?"

"Not really," he admitted. "But she did tell me what she wanted and she gave me the questions she'd planned on asking . . ."

Carly nodded. "I see. Well, then, where would you like to begin?"

Ford took the notebook out of his back pocket and opened it.

"She thought we should start with introducing the community to you. You know, where you're from, where you went to school, that sort of thing."

"I'm from Connecticut—I still live there—and I went to Rushton-Graves Prep in Massachusetts from sixth grade on. Grad school at Penn, some art-history courses at the Sorbonne, art conservation internship at Winterthur, that sort of thing."

"So you'd categorize yourself as an art historian . . . conservationist . . . dealer? What?"

"All of those things, actually, and I own galleries in New York, Boston, and Chicago. I also have invested in one in London and another in Istanbul . . ."

"You have art galleries in all those places?"

Carly nodded.

"You get around."

She shrugged. "It's business."

"Which is your favorite?"

"My favorite gallery? After New York, the one in Istanbul, I suppose, although I'm thinking of selling my interest in it. I don't really get there often enough to justify holding on to it, and the woman who runs it really wants to buy me out." She grinned. "She promised me visitation rights, though."

"What do you like about it?"

"I love the city. The architecture. The views from the rooftop restaurants. The history. The artists. And of course, the food."

"The *doner kebab*." He nodded knowingly. "The *manti*."

She shook her head. "I don't eat lamb."

"How do you eat in Turkey if you don't eat lamb?" He frowned.

"Oh, please." She laughed. *"Patlican dolmasi. Biber dolmasi. Hamsili pilav."*

"Let's see, that would be stuffed eggplant, stuffed peppers, and you're going to have to help me with that last one."

"It's a rice dish with small fish." She was grinning.

"You're a vegetarian?"

"No. I just don't eat baby animals." Before he could comment, she said, "So you've been to Turkey. Vacation?"

He shook his head. "It was just a stopover from one place to another."

"You should go back when you can spend some time there. The city—Istanbul—is one of the most remarkable places in the world. A friend of mine described it once as being the perfect convergence of the old and the new. That's certainly true of the art scene there. The museums and the galleries are packed with vibrant contemporary works. They're world class, really."

"Including your own, of course."

"Of course. But I can't take credit for its success. My associate there, Elvan Kazma, is responsible for the exhibits. She has an amazing eye for talent." Carly pointed to the paper squares and rectangles that hung on the wall and on the partition. "But it's this exhibit you're here to talk about, right?"

"Right. I think the residents of St. Dennis might want to know how you came to be interested in working here. You know, why someone who owns galleries in all those places would want to spend time working— unpaid, if I understand correctly—in a little place like St. Dennis."

"I've been friends with Ellie since sixth grade, so when she moved here, of course I came to visit. I am falling in love with the town, I don't mind saying it. It certainly has its charm, and it's a place where people seem to care about each other. I've met some terrific people here." She hesitated. "What exactly did your mother tell you? About the artwork, I mean."

"She didn't really have much time to tell me much," he admitted.

Carly seemed to be debating with herself. "There are some things you should probably know that you can't put into the article. At least, not this article. Not yet."

"O-kay," he said.

"Let me tell you about a St. Dennis artist named Carolina Ellis." Carly told him everything, about how Carolina was Ellie's great-great-grandmother, how her husband had tried to stifle her talent, how she'd painted so many works that had been stored in Ellie's house and had even given some away to friends and family members. How a few of Carolina's works had made their way into regional museums before Carolina had been recognized as a great talent, and how, eventually, a few of her paintings had gone to auction and fetched some hefty dollars, enough that the art world began to take serious notice.

"So few of her works were available, and so little was known about her," Carly told him, "but her paintings were so strong, and her talent so incredible, that the few pieces that were available were prized."

"I'm afraid I've never heard of her. Then again, I don't know a lot about art."

"There are a lot of people who haven't heard of her, but that is going to change, once this exhibit opens. The paintings we found in Ellie's house . . ." She shook her head as if she still couldn't believe what they'd found. "You have to see them to believe it. Once this exhibit opens and the art world sees what we have here, Carolina Ellis will be recognized for the great artist she was." Carly smiled, somewhat ruefully, and added, "I had hoped to be able to introduce her—and her work—at my gallery in New York. Manhattan's the hub of the art world—well, one of the hubs, anyway—and the thought of being the one to bring this woman's work out of the shadows—or more accurately, the attic—was the sort of thing everyone dreams of doing. You know, like an athlete hopes to play that game that people will talk about forever, or a writer hopes to write that one book that shakes the literary world. That's how I felt when I thought about being the one who would . . ." She shook her head again.

"So what happened?" he asked. "How did it go from you showing the paintings in your place in New York, to setting up this place here?" His gesture encompassed the carriage house.

Carly explained how the vision of the gallery had

grown, and how the town council wanted to use Curtis Enright's gift. "And then someone—your mom, I think—remembered that Carolina was a St. Dennis girl, and that some of her paintings had been auctioned in New York. It was no secret that Ellie had inherited the house Carolina had lived in with her family, and that some of her paintings were hanging on the walls."

"So they asked Ellie if they could borrow them."

Carly nodded.

"And they wanted all of Carolina's paintings, the ones from the attic as well, I'm guessing."

"They don't know about those. Actually, no one except Ellie and Cam—and your mother—knows about those. That's the part I'd like you to leave out of your article, if you don't mind." That rueful smile again. "They know that Ellie has a number of paintings hanging throughout her house, and they believe that's what they're getting.

"I'd wanted to make such a splash at my gallery with these paintings," she explained. "Something the entire art world would sit up and notice."

He nodded. He got it. "So if you can't do that there, you want to do that here."

"Exactly. But we don't want anyone to know just yet what we're planning."

"Doesn't that piss you off? That you had something spectacular planned that would draw big-time attention to your gallery, and it was snatched away from you?"

"Oh, I don't look at it that way. I'm still getting to introduce the world to Carolina's work, and that's the important thing."

"That sounds like rationalization, if you don't mind my saying."

"I don't mind. I admit that at first I was really disappointed when I had to cancel my plans." She looked momentarily wistful, then her face brightened. "But I still have the pleasure of setting up this new gallery, and bringing the attention of the art world to this lovely town, and that's a good thing, so what's to be angry about? I mean, Carolina's paintings being shown are what's important here, and the exhibit's going to be great, no matter where we hold it."

"Are you going to tell me there's no resentment at all?"

She shook her head. "None whatsoever."

"Okay, then." He pretended to jot something in the notebook, but what he really was doing was trying to wrap his head around the fact that she was cool with the fact that her gallery wasn't going to get to do the exhibit. He was pretty sure if he'd been in her shoes, he wouldn't have been as easygoing.

She glanced at her watch. "Do you think you have enough for the first article? I promised Ellie's sister I'd drive her to her field-hockey tryout this afternoon, since Ellie's working."

"Oh. Sure." He tried to tuck the notebook into his back pocket but it was just slightly too big to fit. He tried to fold it, but the cover was too hard. The effort left him feeling just a little foolish and he hoped she hadn't noticed.

"Do you want to schedule next week's interview now?" she asked as she gathered her purse and her iPad and her phone, which she'd left on a nearby stool.

"What's a good day for you?"

"I'm here every day, so whenever you need to write next the article . . ."

"I'm not sure. I don't know the schedule for the paper." He hesitated. "How 'bout early in the week . . . say maybe Tuesday? That way, we can be sure to meet the deadline."

"Sounds great. I'll be here."

She was obviously leaving, having turned off the air-conditioning and the lights, so Ford had no choice but to follow her out the door.

"So I guess I'll see you on Tuesday. Same time?" he asked.

"Great." She stopped next to the big SUV and opened the driver's-side door and slid in behind the wheel. "I'll see you then."

He would have liked to have just stood there until she'd gone, just to look at her, but he was parked behind her. He walked back to the car and got in and backed out of the driveway far enough to let her pull out in front of him. She waved as she drove off.

The last thing Ford had expected was what—who— he'd found when he stepped inside the carriage house. Carly Summit had all but knocked him off his feet. She was not only very easy to look at, but she was interesting in a way a lot of women in his experience had not been, and he was drawn to her in a way he hadn't been attracted to anyone since Anna. Anna of the golden hair and the brilliant blue eyes and the heart and soul of a pacifist, a woman who was totally devoted to the job that she did, a woman who truly believed in the good of everyone she met. Apparently, the rebel soldiers she and the others had met up with hadn't gotten the memo on that last part.

He had no idea how much time had passed, but a glance at his watch told him he'd been there for almost two hours.

So it was true, he thought as he made the turn onto Hudson Street. Time really did fly when you were having a good time—and the two hours he'd spent in Carly Summit's company had been the best two hours he'd had in a very long time.

Chapter 12 ⤳

THE bleachers at the high school field were just a few feet too far from the tree line to have offered any shade before late afternoon, and Carly was lamenting the lack of sunscreen. Gabi had yet to run through the drill that was a required part of the tryout for the varsity field-hockey team, so Carly thought it would be rude for her to leave her seat and go back into the air-conditioned comfort of her car, so she stayed where she was. Some things, she reminded herself, you just had to suck up, and this was one of them. Early July on the Eastern Shore could be hot and muggy, and today was all that and more. She brushed sweat from her forehead and tried to find something positive in the experience, but it was tough with the inside of her head about to boil over like a cauldron of bubbling soup. She tried to distract herself by thinking cool thoughts, but the image of Ford Sinclair standing in the doorway of the carriage house left her anything but cooled off.

Ford had been wearing a dark blue polo shirt that deepened the storm-cloud gray of his eyes, and khaki shorts, and looked more like the adventurer he was supposed to be than he had the first time they'd met. His sunglasses had hung from the V of the shirt placket and his hair was a few weeks past needing a trim. Her heart had all but stopped when he walked in. She tried to remember the last time she'd had such a reaction to a man, and sadly had to admit it had been probably never, unless the first time they'd met counted. Or the day he'd turned up at the tennis court . . .

"Carly." Gabi stood on the step two rows down, waving a hand. "I said I'm finished."

"Oh. Of course." The image in her mind began to fade away. "How'd you do?"

Gabi laughed. "I did fine, but none of us will know if we made varsity or junior varsity until next week. So are you ready to go?"

Carly picked up her bag and walked down the bleacher steps till she reached the ground.

"Think we could stop at Scoop for ice cream on the way home?" Gabi leaned heavily against Carly as they walked toward the car.

"Absolutely, but stop leaning. I'm already so hot from sitting in the sun I'm about to spontaneously combust."

"Why didn't you move into the shade? Or go sit in the car?"

"I thought it would be rude."

"Rude to who? Whom?"

"To you."

"You're kidding, right? I didn't expect you to sit and watch. I thought you were going to just drop me off and I'd get a ride home with someone else."

They'd reached the car and Carly unlocked it with the remote. "Now you tell me," she grumbled.

It seemed that half the town—and most of its visitors—had the same desire for ice cream as Carly and Gabi. The line into One Scoop or Two stretched down the wooden boardwalk almost to the marina.

"Wow. Looks like Steffie is having an exceptionally good day," Carly commented when she parked in the only spot she could find in the municipal lot. "I wonder if it's been like this all day."

"Pretty much. Paige was at tryouts and she had to leave as soon as she was finished to get back here to work. She said weekends are the worst, when all the tourists are in town. She said sometimes they even run out of ice cream 'cause Steffie makes it all herself and sometimes she underestimates how many people there will be." Gabi paused. "Are you coming?"

Carly looked at the length of the line.

"We can go in the back door," Gabi told her. "Steffie lets us."

"That's when you're with Paige," Carly pointed out.

"Yeah, mostly."

"I don't think those people who have been waiting out there in line would appreciate the two of us sneaking in the back door ahead of them."

"Probably not." Gabi thought for a moment. "But if you wait here, I can go in by myself and no one will notice."

Before Carly could respond, Gabi was out of the car and yelling that she'd be right back.

Just as well, Carly thought. *The last thing I feel like doing is going back into that heat.*

She turned on the radio, searching for a station that was playing something she could sing along with, when her phone rang.

"Ellie, hi," she said after glancing at the caller-ID screen.

"Hey, where are you?"

"Sitting in the municipal parking lot waiting for your sister to emerge from the back door of Scoop, ice cream in hand. The line stretches halfway to the marina, so she decided she'd use her friends-and-family pass to go in, get the goods, and slip back out before anyone notices that she cut the line."

"She's a slick one," Ellie admitted. "But it's better than waiting an hour for a ice cream cone that'll take you less than five minutes to eat."

"True."

"The reason I'm calling . . . you mentioned you might want to take a look at the house that Sophie Enright was renting."

"Yes."

"I'm sitting outside of it right now, key in hand, if you want to come by."

"Of course I do, but how did you manage that?"

"The job Cam had lined up this morning was to help Jason finish painting the apartment on the second floor of Sophie's restaurant. They're pretty much done, and since Sophie brought very little of her own furniture with her—she only had some pieces in the bedroom—she doesn't have much to move other than her clothes and personal items. The lease is still in Jesse's name, but he'll sublet to you until it runs out in November. By then, you'll most likely be back in New York, right?"

"That's the plan, yes."

"So come over now and take a look."

"As soon as Gabi gets back, I will."

Carly tapped her fingers impatiently on the steering wheel, wishing Gabi would hurry. Now that she knew she'd be in St. Dennis for at least a few months, she was eager to get into a place of her own, a place where she could work at night without being disturbed. She had to admit that were it not for work required to finish Carolina's book and design the catalog for the exhibit, she'd love the bustle of life in Ellie and Cam's house. But right now, with so much to be done in so little time, she needed the evening hours to read, and to write.

Finally, she saw Gabi's head bobbing along between the cars in the lot. When she drew closer, Carly could see she was carrying only one dish of ice cream.

"What, you ate yours while you were on the way to the car?" Carly asked when Gabi opened the door.

"No, Steffie wanted me to work with Paige for a while this afternoon, so I'm going to stay."

"Are you old enough to do that?" Carly reached for the bowl.

"I guess." Gabi shrugged. "I've helped out before when they got real busy, and Paige does it all the time and she's the same age as me."

"Paige is Steffie's niece, though, right?"

Gabi nodded. "It'll be okay. I just have to let Ellie know."

"I'm going to see her in two minutes. I'll tell her."

"Great. Thanks. And thanks for coming to tryouts with me." Gabi blew her a kiss from the open door. "And for staying, even though you didn't have to."

"We're even. Thanks for the ice cream. Now close the door before it melts."

"It's blueberry cobbler crunch. Steffie just made it

this morning." Gabi slammed the car door and waved, then ran back toward Scoop.

Carly took two spoonfuls of ice cream and all but sighed. It was cold and delicious and tasted of fresh blueberries, and if she hadn't been in a hurry, she'd have finished it right then and there. But she was anxious to see the house, so she placed the ice cream container on the console and prayed it wouldn't tip over.

The drive to Hudson Street took exactly four minutes, most of it spent at the light at the corner of Charles Street and Kelly's Point Road due to the number of visitors to the town. But once she turned onto Cherry, it was a quick hop around the corner. An SUV sat in the driveway, the back hatch up, and Ellie's car was parked on the street out front. Carly parked behind Ellie and went up to the side door, which stood open.

"Hello," she called.

"Carly, in here," Ellie called back.

The door led into a small room off the kitchen. Carly followed Ellie's voice into the living room, which, like the rest of the rooms, was on the small side, but neatly furnished.

"I'll be out of here in a few minutes." Sophie Enright poked her head out from a door at the end of a hallway. "I'm on my last load. I think . . ."

"Take your time," Carly told her.

"It's cute, right?" Ellie whispered.

"So cute." Carly looked around. "She's not taking the furniture in the living room?"

Ellie shook her head. "Whatever is still here belongs to Jesse, who doesn't need it and doesn't know what to do with it. He took the few pieces he wanted when he and Brooke got married and he moved in with her. The stuff from Sophie's bedroom has already been moved out, but the living room and the dining room stuff stays. Oh, and there's nothing in the kitchen. That all belonged to Sophie and she's taken it, so you will need some dishes and pots and flatware and all that stuff."

Carly walked from the living room through the small dining room that had space only for a trestle table, two chairs, and a bench. Perfect for spreading out her work, she thought as she passed into the kitchen. There was a big window in the middle of the back wall, from which she could see the yard, which was enclosed by a picket fence. There was a brick patio off the back door and several flower beds in which perennials fought weeds for growing space. There were hedges of something thick and green, and clumps of some flowering thing here and there.

"It's perfect," Carly told Ellie when she heard her enter the kitchen.

"You haven't seen the bedrooms or the bathroom," Ellie reminded her.

"They're fine, I'm sure."

"You're really anxious to move, aren't you?" Ellie laughed.

"No, it isn't that . . . well, yes, in a way, it is," Carly admitted. "I just can't wait to spread out all those notes and start putting the book together. I can leave everything—notes, photos, journals—on the table in order and not have to put it all away every night."

"I totally understand."

Sophie came into the room carrying two large tote bags, a garment bag over one arm.

"I think I have it all," she told them. "If you find anything that looks like it might be mine, just put it aside and drop it off at the restaurant or the law office when you get the chance."

"Thanks for letting me come in and look around," Carly told her.

"Hey, it's yours if you want it." Sophie started for the door, and the garment bag slipped. Ellie caught it.

"I'll take it out for you," Ellie told Sophie. To Carly, she said, "I'll be back in a few. I have some things in my car to drive over to the apartment for Sophie."

"Take your time," Carly told her. "I'll be here."

"Give Jesse a call when you make up your mind. Or you can stop in at the law office on Monday morning . . ." Sophie's voice trailed away.

"I've made up my mind," Carly called to her, but she heard the side door open, then close, heard the engines of the two vehicles start up, then fade as both Ellie and Sophie drove off.

Suddenly the house was very quiet. Carly's footfalls echoed in the hall as she checked out the downstairs bedrooms. There were two, with a small bathroom between. The bedroom in the back was the larger but had windows on two sides and overlooked the backyard.

She took the steps to the second floor, where there were two more bedrooms and another bath. She could use one as an office, the other for storage.

This will be fine, Carly thought as she went back downstairs. *Better than fine.* She could buy a bed and a dresser and a small kitchen set from that furniture place out on the highway—the one that had a sign promising next-day delivery—and be completely moved in before the end of the week, assuming that Jesse agreed to sublet to her, and it appeared that he already had. She poked her head into the bathroom, and found it, too, to be satisfactory. The tiles were pale yellow and very 1990s, but the sink and vanity top appeared relatively new.

She could see herself in this house, she thought as she walked back through all the rooms, could see her papers on the dining room table and could see herself cooking in the kitchen and eating at a small table near the back door, and waking up every morning in that back bedroom.

She went out into the yard and looked around. She could pick up a small table and a few chairs, maybe a lounge, for the patio, so she could sit out here on mornings when it wasn't too hot, and drink her coffee before heading over to the carriage house. She walked across the yard to the flower bed that grew along the back fence, recalling how her mother had enjoyed gardening in the yard of the house she grew up in. Roberta had prided herself on her roses and her irises, had babied her annuals and doted on her peonies. There didn't look to be much in these beds, other than the tall weeds, a few rosebushes, and some Shasta daisies. Carly wondered if it was too late to toss some seeds into the soil and see if she could get any annuals to grow. She could call her mother and ask for her suggestions.

She went back into the house and locked the door behind her. All in all, the little house was more than suitable. She would call Jesse as soon as possible.

When Carly heard Ellie's car pull up out front, she walked out to meet her.

"So you think this"—Ellie gestured toward the house—
"will work for you?"

"Totally. I love it." Carly stepped back to admire its
facade. "It's a little plain, but it's nice."

"You can get some flowers for that front porch and
it will completely change how the place looks. The
market in town is selling big pots of petunias. They're
asking an arm and a leg for them, but you'd only need
two."

"I'll stop and see what they have. After I speak with
Jesse, that is."

"You can call him right now, if you're sure." Ellie
pulled her phone from her pocket and scrolled through
her contact list. She handed the phone to Carly to copy
the number into her own phone.

"Thanks." Carly saved the number. "I'm positive.
I'll call him now."

"I'll see you back at the house, then. Right now I'm
going to lock up." Ellie started toward the house,
then stopped and turned back to say, "I'm glad you
found a place. I know how important this project is,
not just to you, but to everyone in St. Dennis, too."

"Thanks, El." Carly gave her a quick hug. "Oh, I
nearly forgot. I left Gabi at Scoop. Steffie needed an
extra pair of hands and asked her to stay and work
for a while. Gabi said it would be okay with you."

"Of course. Thanks for letting me know." Ellie
went into the house, keys in hand, to lock the doors.

Carly got into her car and immediately rolled down
the windows so that the stifling air could escape. She
called what turned out to be Jesse's cell phone, and
was disappointed to have to leave a voice mail. She
turned on the air-conditioning full blast and reached

for the dish of ice cream. Steffie's delicious concoction had melted into a dark blue, almost purple soup in which whole blueberries floated.

"Bummer," she muttered as she got out to dump the mess into the trash can that stood there. She'd just lifted the lid when she heard the phone ringing in the car. She made it back in time to answer it before it went to voice mail.

"Carly, Jesse Enright returning your call. I understand you're interested in subletting the house on Hudson Street from me."

"I am. Thanks for getting back to me so quickly."

"I'm on my way into the office to pick up a file. Do you have time now to—"

"Yes," she said before he finished, and they both laughed.

"Do you know where the office is?"

"I do. I was there last year with Ellie during that Pirate Day thing."

"I'll see you there in a few."

"I am on my way." She turned the car around in the driveway and headed for the law offices of Enright and Enright.

All in all, it had been one heck of a day.

When she woke up that morning, Carly hadn't expected to have found her place before the day was over, but she was delighted that she had. She couldn't wait to move her things into the little house on Hudson Street and get to work. The gallery partition was almost finished and she'd found a home for herself for however long she'd need it—not to mention that she'd spent almost two unexpected hours with Ford Sinclair, who was the first guy she'd been interested in since she'd broken things off with Todd the year before. There was something about Ford that seemed dark and mysterious—so different from Todd's cool bearing—something that had drawn her the first night she met him, before she even knew his name—and she'd see him again on Tuesday for more of the interview.

Carly could hardly wait.

Chapter 13 ⌒

"WHAT I want is for you to write your article and print it out for me," Grace replied after Ford called to ask her what she wanted him to do with the notes from his interview with Carly. "And use fourteen-point font so that I can read it. And I want two copies. One single spaced, the other triple spaced."

"Why—"

"So that I have enough room to correct your grammar."

"What makes you think I don't know how to write using correct grammar?"

"Well, since I hardly ever saw a letter from you, I don't have much to judge by, do I?"

She's on her way back, Ford mused as he hung up the phone. *Almost herself again.*

He wrote the article and printed it out as she had instructed, and took both copies to her in her hospital room. He was feeling pretty good about it, thinking he'd done a bang-up job on the article. It wasn't something he'd particularly enjoyed doing—he wasn't the

writer in the family, and he'd never had any aspira-
tions to follow in his mother's footsteps, but still, he
was pretty sure she'd be delighted with his effort. After
all, he'd had a pretty special subject to write about. So
he was unprepared for his mother's reaction.

"Try again," she said, waving the sheets of paper at
him with her left hand.

"What's wrong with it?"

"Well, for one thing, it reads with as much verve as
a phone book. For another, you need to learn how to
properly use commas." She sniffed. "We still use the
Oxford comma at the paper, dear. Some feel it's passé,
but I prefer it."

"What's the Oxford comma?" He frowned.

"There's a book on proper usage on the shelf in my
office at the paper. Strunk and White's *Elements of
Style*."

"Anything else?" He folded his arms and tried not
to appear petulant, though he was feeling much like a
chastised child at that moment. He couldn't believe
she was criticizing his work because she didn't like
the way he used *commas*.

"Yes, as a matter of fact, there is." She adjusted her
glasses on the bridge of her nose and glared at him
through the lenses. "You say very little about Carly,
and what you do say, well, you could be talking about
anyone."

"The article is *about* Carly."

"Supposedly. But we get to the end and we don't
know her, and that's the whole point of the article.
We want the people in St. Dennis—the intended readers of the piece—to feel as if they know her."

He stared at her blankly. "I'm sorry. I don't get it."

"I read your article three times. I don't know what she looks like, I don't know what her voice sounds like. I don't know how she feels about the project. Is she enthused, or is she just going through the motions? You did give me some facts, but you didn't give me Carly Summit. You didn't even give me a photo. Try again."

"Mom . . ."

"Oh, you can do this, Ford. Don't look at me like that. If I thought you were incapable of writing the article we need the readers to see, I'd take your facts and I'd write the damned thing myself. But I don't feel up to it, and you are capable, so I suggest you go back to the office and put this thing into shape. You have to get it to Mel in production by tomorrow afternoon, no later. There are a few pictures on my camera if you need to poach one of those. In the future, however, I suggest you take your own."

He returned to the *Gazette* office on the second floor of the building on Charles Street—grateful that the paper had its own small parking lot, because the center of town was crawling with tourists—and sat at his mother's desk. He pulled the article up on the computer screen and reread what he'd earlier written.

"You want more Carly, you'll get more Carly," he muttered, and started over again.

He read over the second draft and, trying to be objective, found it lacking something. He tried again.

Did his mother go through this process—this write, rewrite, write, rewrite—every time? He doubted it. She'd been writing for this paper for most of her adult life. She was a professional. Surely once you got the hang of it, the words would flow like water through your hands, wouldn't they?

At this rate, he'd never get the hang of it. But that was okay, he reminded himself, because this was only a temporary thing. As soon as Grace was up and about, she could have her notebook, laptop, and office back, and he'd never have to go through this tedious exercise again.

He deleted the entire page, and started over. Again.

This time, instead of measuring his every word, he tossed out all his preconceived ideas of how newspaper people wrote and went with his gut. He wrote off the top of his head, his impressions of Carly, the way her eyes lit when she talked about the proposed gallery, and her plans to bring an important exhibit to St. Dennis. He described the gallery itself, the renovations being made to the carriage house, and the largesse of the man who'd donated the property to the community. He reread the piece several times, making minor changes each time, until he felt it was as right as he was going to get it. He scrolled through the photos on his mother's camera and selected one that he thought might work.

He hit print, and while the copies were being made, he compared the way he'd described Carly in the article—"a cool, competent, petite blonde with ice-blue eyes and the sure confidence born of experience and education"—to the way he really saw her: a smoking-hot blonde with a killer body and the face of an angel. He'd been tempted to slip that in as a joke, but, well, his beta-reader was his mother and he wasn't sure it would be wise, especially if she didn't like this version any better than she'd liked the first.

But she did.

"Excellent." Grace nodded her head when he delivered the finished product later that evening. "Yes, this is it exactly what I wanted." She looked up at Ford and smiled. "Well done, son. I knew you could do it."

"Thanks, Mom." He was more pleased by her praise and more gratified by her smile than he would have expected.

Funny, he thought as he drove back to the *Gazette*'s office for the second time that day, *but you never really outgrow your inner need for that pat on the back from your mom.* He'd been away from his home for so long, he'd forgotten how good it felt to have your family—especially a parent—offer you praise and approval. He was whistling as he set up the file as she'd directed, and sent it off to the production department.

His first assignment, and he was a day early.

Before locking up the office and leaving for the inn, Ford printed out his mother's notes relative to the gallery, the local artists, and the woman to whom St. Dennis was entrusting its art treasures. He'd study up for Tuesday's interview, and by then, he'd know everything his mother knew about Carly Summit, but somehow, his instincts told him, that wouldn't be quite enough. Whatever else he wanted to know, he'd have to discover on his own.

∽∽

Carly couldn't believe her good fortune. On Monday morning, she'd gone shopping for a bed, mattress and box spring, and one dresser, and ended up buying those pieces plus a sweet love seat that was on sale and would look great in the downstairs bedroom that she planned to use as a study, and a pair of leather club chairs to complement the living room sofa. She figured there was a good chance she could sell them to the next person who rented the house, but if not, there was always the newspaper and its classified ads.

She wondered what the *Gazette* charged for classified ads.

Thinking about the *Gazette* felt like license to think about Ford, which led her to thinking about her meeting with him on Saturday, which naturally made her think ahead to their appointment on the following morning.

She'd been so busy packing her things and driving back and forth between the two houses that she'd given little thought to what they'd talk about. She wondered if he was getting direction from Grace or if he was flying by the seat of his pants. A little of both, she suspected.

When she arrived at the carriage house on Tuesday morning, Carly found the HVAC crew already on the job. There was noise and dust and loud music playing, and several workers moving around the area where she normally worked. Ford appeared earlier than she'd anticipated, and he'd looked around at the chaos before trying to speak over the din. "We should probably go somewhere else to talk."

She motioned for him to follow her outside.

"It is a little loud in there," she agreed. "Sorry. I'd forgotten the heating and air-conditioning guys were going to be working here today."

"We could go to the inn, though it's probably not real quiet there right about now either, since it's getting close to lunchtime and they've had all sorts of kiddie things going on this morning." He paused as if considering the options. "Have you been to the new restaurant out on River Road? Blossoms? Sophie Enright's place?"

She shook her head. "Ellie's mentioned it, said it's pretty terrific. She said it was named for her great-aunt Lilly, Curtis Enright's late wife, Rose, and Violet Finneran, who worked for the Enright law firm. Blossoms, get it? Lilly, Rose, Violet?"

"Got it. Mom wrote an article when the place first opened, and she did mention that. How about we move the interview over there, kill two birds with one stone," he suggested.

"Great. I haven't had anything but coffee this morning since I overslept, so I'm famished. Anyplace that serves food sounds appealing. And besides, I'd like to support Sophie's business, since she kindly arranged for me to take over her sublease."

"You're going to lease a place in St. Dennis?" he asked as they walked toward the driveway.

"I already did." She stopped in front of her car. "Should I follow you?"

"Why don't you ride with me? I have to move my car out of the drive anyway."

"Okay. I'll just let the guys inside know . . ."

She went back into the carriage house, grabbed her bag, and shouted over the whine of the power tools that she'd be back in a while. The foreman nodded and waved—message received—and Carly went back outside into the warm late morning.

"It's almost impossible for me to work in there right now, but we really do need the climate inside the building controlled," she told Ford as she hopped into the passenger seat of his car. "Heat and humidity are not the friends of fine art."

"Damaging?" Ford watched in the rearview mirror for the last of three cars to pass before pulling out onto the street.

"You betcha. If we weren't able to have this work done, there's no way we could exhibit Carolina's paintings in that building."

"Good thing the town coughed up the money for it, then."

"The town council did set some money aside for renovations, but I don't know how much will be left when this stage has been completed."

"It looks to me to be pretty much finished inside. What else has to be done?"

"We are going to need a top-notch security system, and that's going to be a big ticket. So far, all of the security firms I've spoken with have admitted they aren't set up to deliver a system as sophisticated as the one that's needed here."

"I might be able to help you with that."

"Oh?" She turned in her seat to face him. "Are you a security expert?"

"Sort of." A small smile played at the corner of his lips. "Actually, a friend of mine owns a security firm in Virginia. He specializes in custom work. Maybe you could give him a call."

"I'll do that. Thanks. I need to get an estimate quickly so I can get the shock over and done with as early as possible."

"What shock?"

"The shock the town council is going to feel when they see what proper security is going to cost."

"Did they give you a budget?"

"Not really. Cam worked up estimates for pretty much everything except the security, and they okayed the scope of the work, understanding that there would be additional costs to secure the building. I did try to explain to Ed that it was going to be expensive, but I guess it's all relative. I've had top-notch security installed in all of my galleries, so I know it's pricey. The cut-rate services that I've talked to just aren't sufficient."

"So what are you going to do if you get what you feel is an adequate number and the council won't or can't authorize the funds?"

"Then it comes out of the proceeds from the book I'm writing on Carolina Ellis. And if that isn't going to be enough, I suppose it will come out of my pocket. Actually, I'll probably have to front the costs and then repay myself what I can from what the book makes. I already told Ed I'd donate a portion of the sales to the art center."

"You can take a hit that big?"

She merely nodded without elaborating on her financial situation.

The car turned onto the River Road, and Carly got her first glance of the New River as it flowed behind the houses built on its banks and toward the Chesapeake.

"It's smaller than I'd thought it would be," she commented. "More narrow."

"What is?"

"The river. I guess I was expecting something bigger, more important-looking." She turned to him and smiled. "After all, they did name a road after it."

"Around here, they named roads after a lot of things that may or may not seem significant now." He turned in to the parking lot next to a small stone building and parked. "The river had its place in St. Dennis history, even if it's lost some of its muscle over the years."

They both opened their car doors and got out at the same time.

"Now, you know you're going to have to tell me more," Carly said.

Ford opened the door to the restaurant and held it aside for her to enter.

"Wow, it's really pretty in here." Carly leaned closer to him to whisper. "So different. Look at that wall of old photos . . ."

The perky hostess met them just inside the door. "Will there be just the two of you?"

When Ford nodded, she asked, "Is a table near the window all right?"

"Could we maybe have the table closer to the photo wall?" Carly asked. "I'd love to get a closer look."

"Of course." The hostess smiled and led the way.

"Mom had great things to say about the food here," Ford said as he and Carly were seated. "The place hasn't been open very long, but apparently with Dallas MacGregor's new film studio opening down the road recently, it's a good place to celebrity-watch if you're into that sort of thing."

"I'm not," Carly said, "but I can't wait any longer. I have to look at those photos."

She rose just as the hostess—who was apparently going to be their waitress—brought menus and a bowl of small tan-colored beads to the table.

"Roasted chickpeas," she said as she placed the bowl in the center of the table. "What can I bring you to drink?"

"Unsweetened iced tea for me, please," Carly replied.

Ford nodded. "Same for me."

"All right, then, let's look at these pictures." Carly stood before the wall, her arms folded over her chest. "I wish I knew which one was Ellie's great-great-grandmother." She scanned the photos.

Ford stood behind, almost but not quite close enough to touch her, close enough that she could hear—but not feel—him breathing. She stood midway between the wall and his body, and she had to force herself to focus on the pictures in front of her.

"I can help you there." Sophie emerged from the kitchen, a white apron tied around her waist and at her neck.

"Hey, Sophie." Carly turned and smiled. "We were just admiring your decor. I love this idea." She pointed to the photos. "It's so different and so charming."

"Thanks. The idea was to bring St. Dennis into the room without overplaying the whole Chesapeake Bay thing. You know, the blue claw crabs, the oysters, the crab pots. The stuff that half the restaurants on the Eastern Shore have done. I wanted the place to be more personal to the people who live here."

"Have you met Ford Sinclair?" Carly asked.

"We have not." Sophie extended a hand to him.

"But I know the rest of the family." She smiled. "My brother had his wedding at the inn and I'm happy to count your mother among my friends."

"Well, then, any friend of my family, and all that." Ford shook her hand briefly. "Now, can you point out who's who here?"

"This is my grandma Rose Enright, Lilly Cavanaugh, and Violet Finneran." Sophie pointed to several faces in turn.

"The Blossoms," Carly said.

"Right." Sophie pointed out several other residents— some living, some not. "Oh, and here's Ellie's great-great-grandmother Carolina, the one you're writing the book about."

Carly grinned and stretched her neck to better see the photograph. Carolina was dressed in tennis whites and held a racket in both hands. At her elbow was a handsome man who appeared to be several years younger than she.

"I wonder who the man is," Carly thought out loud.

"I have no clue. Someone else in town might know, though."

"Is that a picture of my parents?" Ford pointed to a photo on the left side of the wall.

"On their wedding day, yes." Sophie removed it from the wall and handed it to him.

"I've seen this one before. My mom gave this to you?" he asked.

"Your sister did. I'd asked Lucy for one so we could surprise Grace on opening night. She seemed very pleased to have it included. Look how beautiful your mother was at that young age. Not that she isn't beautiful now," she hastened to add. "Your parents look so happy together, don't they?"

"They always were." Ford handed the photo back to Sophie, who returned it to its place on the wall.

"So have you had a chance to look at the menu yet?" Sophie asked, and Ford and Carly both shook their heads.

"You might want to get your order in sometime in the next"—Sophie glanced at her watch—"five minutes or so. It's almost time for the studio folks," she explained. "They usually start to roll in around twelve thirty. I thought they'd be big on takeout but it seems they like the atmosphere here, so we get a crowd every day right around now."

"I'm surprised the tourist crowd hasn't caught on to that." Carly looked around at the empty tables.

"It's a little early for them." Sophie grinned. "In another half hour, there will be a line out the door. Go ahead and look at the menus. Make sure you don't miss the specials. Mariel—that's your waitress—will take your order."

"Look, Ford, even the menus are unique." Carly held up the folded light blue paper. "There are little anecdotes about different early residents of St. Dennis." She looked over the names. "There's a Daniel Sinclair here . . ."

"My great-great-however-many-greats grandfather. He built the inn." Ford appeared to be more interested in the food.

Guess he skipped breakfast, too, Carly thought, and turned her attention to the specials. When it came time to order, Ford went with the burger, and Carly ordered a grilled vegetable wrap.

"Can I get a small, side version of the strawberry, goat cheese, and walnut salad with that?" she asked.

"Of course." Mariel smiled agreeably, took their menus, and disappeared into the kitchen.

"Did you say you were or you were not a vegetarian?" Ford asked.

"I am not, but I love vegetables when they're done creatively, and I'm willing to bet that Sophie's are terrific. I take it you're a meatasaurus?" She sampled the chickpeas. "These are yummy. Crunchy and spicy."

She passed the bowl over to him, and he popped a few into the palm of his hand.

"I'll eat just about anything." He held up the bowl. "Even these."

Carly laughed. "Oh, please. They're not that exotic."

He popped a few into his mouth. "You're right. They're spicy. I like them."

"I'm glad to see you're adventurous about food."

"Are you kidding?" He scoffed. "Where I've been, you eat what's available and you don't think too much of it. These"—he held up the small bowl—"would have been a delicacy."

"Where have you been?"

For a moment, he looked as if he didn't understand the question, as if he'd spoken without thinking. "Oh. Africa, mostly."

"Where in Africa?"

"Central African Republic. Sudan. The Democratic Republic of the Congo. The Southern Nile Republic."

"Why were you there?" She added sweetener to her iced tea and took a sip, added a little more.

"Who's interviewing who here?" he asked.

"Sorry. Just curious. I don't know too many people who have spent time in Africa lately." She paused, then added, "Actually, I don't know anyone who's been there in the past five years."

"There are a lot of hot spots, to be sure." He glanced at the door as it opened, and a group of five or six came in. "Looks like the place is starting to fill up." He turned his wrist to look at his watch. "Right on time, too."

Carly's curiosity was piqued, but she sensed that Ford had already said more about himself than he'd intended. "So. The article for next week's paper."

"Right. Well, last time we talked a little about you and your plans for the gallery space. Want to elaborate on that a little?" he asked.

"Sure. Our focus is going to be on artists from St. Dennis. Once the gallery is finished, we're going to ask residents who'd like to exhibit their work to bring them in so we can take a look, see what we have. We know there's a lot of artistic talent in St. Dennis, so obviously we're not going to be able to show every work by every artist, but I'll do my best to make sure that the exhibit is representative of the best the town has to offer."

"So in other words, you'll be picking and choosing what paintings you want to use."

"Yes, but we can't word it that way." She lowered her voice. "I have it on good authority—that would be your mother—that there are some pretty poor specimens out there. Only a crazy person would set aside works from someone like Carolina Ellis to exhibit someone else's paint-by-numbers. Or worse."

"So how do we want to word that?"

"Exactly the way I said it." She looked beyond the plate the waitress had just placed in front of her to glare at him. "You weren't taking notes," she said accusingly.

"I didn't know I was supposed to." He leaned back to let Mariel serve his burger.

"You're a reporter." Carly picked up her fork and prepared to attack her salad. "Reporters take notes."

"I'm new at this."

She put down the fork and reached out her hand. "Give me your notebook." She paused. "You did bring your notebook."

"I left it in the car."

"I'll wait."

"Now?" Ford looked longingly at the burger on his plate.

"Now. I'm having furniture delivered this afternoon, so I have to be there on time. I don't want to be sleeping on the floor this week because no one was there to let the deliverymen in with my bed." She picked up her wrap and took a bite.

Ford sighed but got up and went out to the car. He came back empty-handed.

"I must have left it at the office. I could have sworn . . ."

Carly stared at him for a long moment, then started to laugh. "What kind of a reporter . . . oh, never mind." She picked up her bag and rummaged through it until she found the long, thin notepaper she always carried with her.

"Pen?" she asked.

"I'll ask Mariel if we can borrow one." Ford got up again, walked to the counter, then back again, a pen in hand. He placed it in front of Carly before he returned to his seat, picked up his burger, and took a bite.

Carly proceeded to write for several minutes, then ripped the sheet of paper and handed it to Ford.

"Write it that way," she told him, then turned her attention back to her lunch.

He skimmed the few paragraphs she'd written.

"I could have written this, you know."

"Maybe. If you had notes to work from," she said between bites.

"Sorry. I was in a hurry to get out this morning and I forgot the necessary tools. I'm not used to wielding a pen, you know? It's not my usual weapon of choice."

She wanted to ask him what *was,* but she could tell he was feeling really foolish, so she let it pass. She slid her notepaper and the pen over to his side of the table.

"So what else do you want to know?" she asked.

"Do you want to say anything about how many of Carolina's works you're planning on showing?"

"Uh-uh." She shook her head. "Did Grace forget to tell you that we're holding back the fact that the gallery showing is going to be all Carolina, and that the other St. Dennis artists are going to be exhibited in the mansion?"

"She didn't mention anything about whose works would be shown where."

"Because the conditions in the main house are unsuitable for showing works as valuable as Carolina's, we're going to make a big deal out of the fact that only selected works will be chosen to hang in the mansion."

"Got it. But you want me to hold up on that part."

"Please. In another few weeks, I will have a better feel for how many paintings I'm actually going to show, and I'll have the book ready to go to the printer and I'll have the catalog all worked out. Then we can throw it all out there. Right now I want people in town to be looking in their attics for works by local artists. We could find some real gems, who knows? And if we find more of Carolina's works, so much the better. Actually, your mother was trying to help me with that—that's the list she was working on—but it looks like she's going to be tied up for a while."

"Is that important to you?"

She nodded.

"I'll talk to her about it, see what we can work out. In the meantime, we'll use only what you've given me." He held up the sheet of paper she'd written on. "How 'bout we go back to the carriage house and get some pictures, show the progress of the work there. Mom said each week she wanted to run updated photos so everyone in town can see how the gallery's coming together."

She looked at her watch. "We'll have to do that pretty quickly. My furniture's supposed to be delivered between two and five." She looked up at him. "You do have a camera, don't you?"

"It's in the car." When she raised a skeptical eyebrow, he laughed. "I just saw it."

She finished her salad and started in on her veggie wrap.

"How is it?" he asked.

"It's fabulous. I'm loving every bite."

"As good as *patlican dolmasi* in old city Istanbul?"

"Almost as good as *my patlican dolmasi*."

"Now you're going to tell me you cook Turkish like a native."

"Not quite like a native, but I am damned good."

"That sounded slightly overconfident."

"You can be my first guest when I get settled in my new kitchen, and you can judge for yourself. I can't promise that lamb will be on the menu, though."

"Eggplant and greens?"

"Maybe something a little more substantial. We'll see."

"I'll bring the wine." He looked pleased at the prospect, and her heart did a little flip.

"It'll be fun. I love to cook for other people, and I am an excellent cook. Just ask Ellie or Cameron. I almost always cook when I stay with them." She whispered conspiratorially, "Ellie never did get the hang of it, but you didn't hear that from me."

"My lips are sealed."

"How are we doing here?" Mariel appeared at Carly's elbow.

"Everything is wonderful. The salad, the wrap . . . delicious. I'll definitely be back," Carly told her.

"I'll let Sophie know. I'm sure she'll be pleased." She removed the empty plates. "Dessert?"

"None for me. Ford?" Carly asked.

"No, I'm fine. Just the check, please."

"I'll be right back with that."

Carly reached for her bag and took out her wallet, but Ford waved her away. "Business expense," he told her.

"Thanks. And thank Grace for me."

"I'll do that. Just don't tell her what a poor excuse of a reporter I was today." He took the check that Mariel handed him. "I don't know what I was thinking, leaving the notebook on the desk."

"I'll bet you don't do that again."

"I bet you're right." Ford rose, left the required cash on the table, then held Carly's chair for her. "Looks like we're leaving none too soon. There's already a line for tables."

They stepped out into the heat of midday, and drove back to the carriage house with the windows down to let the Bay breeze in.

"Let's get some shots inside the mansion," she told him when he parked behind her car. "Oh, snap. I don't have the key. I'll have to get it from Ed."

"Look, it's already one forty. Why don't you go back to your house, call around for the key while you wait for your furniture to be delivered. Let me know when you find it, and I'll meet you back here and we'll get a few shots."

"That's perfect. Thanks for being so understanding."

"Please." He laughed self-consciously. "You're talking to the reporter who showed up for an interview with nothing to write with and nothing to write on."

"Good point." Carly gestured in the direction of the carriage house. "I need to check on the guys' progress from this morning."

"Wait. Let me give you my number." He read it off to her while she tapped the numbers into her phone.

"Great. Thanks. And thanks for lunch. I'll give you

a call after the furniture guys leave and we'll see if you're free."

"I'll be free. Call me anytime."

Will do. She smiled as she slipped her phone into the pocket of her jeans. *You can count on it.*

Chapter 14 ⌒

HAD it been physically possible, Ford would have kicked himself in the ass all the way back to Grace's office at the inn. Showing up at an interview with nothing to write on—or with—was about as dumb as showing up at a kayak race without a paddle. What the hell had he been thinking?

Apparently, he hadn't been thinking at all.

There was more to this reporting thing than he'd thought there'd be. He'd gone to the carriage house expecting—well, he wasn't sure what or who he'd been expecting, only that it would be a bit of a dry exercise, not very interesting but necessary, and no more difficult than remembering a few details, a quote or two, and finishing up with a little yada yada yada. All of which had proved to be wishful thinking on his part.

Ford searched his pockets for the blurb Carly had written for him to use. He unfolded the paper and read it over several times. Her handwriting was much like the woman herself, he decided, clear and straight-forward, as easy to read as she was to talk to, as easy as she was to look at. He looked at his own scrawled notes. What, he wondered, did his half print, half script say about him?

Probably that he was easily distracted by a pretty face and a gentle laugh.

Carly was definitely a distraction. The pretty face aside, she made him not only smile, but laugh out loud. And she was passionate about her work. Ford had a weakness for women who were passionate about what they did.

Anna, again, he thought.

But why look for trouble? Carly didn't strike him as the short-term type. The last thing he wanted was a reason to stick around St. Dennis, which seemed to hold few prospects beyond the *Gazette* and the inn, neither of which he saw in his future. Besides, as much as he admired passion in others, he was a man who was passionate about what he did in his own life, wasn't he, and he just didn't see any reason for passion when it came to running an old inn or writing for a small-town newspaper.

He opened the laptop he'd picked up at the *Gazette* office on his way back from the carriage house, and typed up his notes. Where to begin, he wondered once he had all his thoughts—and Carly's notes—on one page. He read and reread until a suitable starting point occurred to him, and he began to write. He incorporated everything they'd talked about that morning, but once he'd started to proofread the article, he found his mind beginning to wander again, this time to the photos on the wall at Blossoms.

There were scenes from his childhood that he remembered, like the way the park had looked before the baseball diamond had been built the year he turned nine, and the old wooden boardwalk that ran from the parking lot at the end of Kelly's Point Road all the way to Captain Walt's. The original boardwalk had been installed by Walt himself, when his wife, Rexana, had complained that, in rain or snow, she couldn't walk to their own restaurant without ruining her shoes. There'd been no marina then, only a very long dock that stretched out into the Bay. One Scoop or Two was still an old crabber's shack back then, and had belonged to Steffie Wyler's uncle Fritz, who had been, in fact, an old crabber.

There was a picture of the old lighthouse that had once stood a stone's throw from Ellie's house. It had been taken down by a storm sometime in the 1940s, so Ford had never really seen it. For a long time, he'd thought it was just local legend, though as a kid he had played on the stone base that remained on the beach not far from the end of Bay View Road.

And there'd been that photo of his parents on their wedding day. The unexpected sight of the two of them looking so young and happy, captured on that day when their life together was just beginning and held so much promise, had caught him off guard and brought a lump to his throat. The simple truth was that Ford missed his father every day he'd been gone. He'd known that his father was sick, but as a fourteen-year-old boy, Ford hadn't had a true appreciation for what that really meant. Thinking back to all the opportunities he'd had to spend time with his dad when he was sick—opportunities he'd missed—made him wish that life came with a reset button. He'd do over the entire year he was fourteen, and maybe a few after that as well.

He couldn't remember a time when his parents had been angry with each other. Oh, little disagreements, sure. That was part of life. But real arguments . . . not really. They had been happy together—his mother had reminded them so many times that Ford knew it was the truth. It was so wrong on so many levels that his father had died. He should still be here with Grace, the two of them living each day together. He should have been there for Ford, who'd been so lost without him. For Lucy, who'd seemed so full of conflict. For Dan, who'd had to grow up too fast, who'd had to take over the inn before he'd even graduated from college. He should have been there for Grace, who'd never stopped loving the man who'd won her heart when she was just a girl.

But that was life, right? Bad things happen and there was nothing you could do about it. There were no happy endings. Everyone dies in the end. No one gets out alive, and all that.

The ringing of his phone brought Ford back from his dark musings.

"Ford, it's Carly. I'm back at the Enright property and I have the key, if you have time to come back over for pictures of the house."

"I'll be there in ten minutes." He hung up, saved his work on the laptop, and grabbed the camera. He was halfway out the door when he stopped, returned to the desk, and picked up the notebook. He tucked it into his back pocket, along with a pen he found in the top desk drawer, turned off the light, and closed the door behind him.

*   *   *

"There's the grand stairwell. You might want to take a few pictures of it." Carly pointed straight ahead from inside the front door of what had been the Enright family home for more than a hundred years.

"Why don't you stand there on the bottom step." Ford held the camera in his right hand.

"I look like a bag lady." She glared at him. "I've just spent the last two hours lugging stuff around in a house that has no air-conditioning." She pulled at the front of her T-shirt. "Dirty and sweaty. Not quite the image I want to project to St. Dennis."

"I thought you were just having furniture delivered."

"I did. But after they got the bedroom furniture in, I decided I didn't like where they put it, so I had to move everything." She stood with her hands on her hips, looking more tired than bedraggled.

"You could have called, you know. I would have helped you." Ford lined up a shot and took it.

"I'll remember that if I decide to rearrange things again."

"The house has no air-conditioning?"

"It does, but apparently something happened to the main switch, or whatever it is that makes cool air. I called Cam and he's looking at it right now."

"Might be the compressor." Ford took one more shot of the stairwell, then several of the wall at the landing.

"That's good." Carly pointed to the shadows on the wall where paintings, now gone, had once hanged. "You see the marks on the wall where Mr. Enright's paintings were removed, and the local artists can all imagine their work hanging in the space."

"Good caption," Ford agreed. " 'Picture your work here.' "

"I like it." She nodded. "I don't know if the second floor is being made available or not, but let's look at this big front room. I think Mr. Enright used it as a living room or sitting room."

She moved across the hall and turned on the overhead light.

"Lots of wall space in here." She folded her arms across her chest and wandered around the room. "Very nice. Yes, I think we can easily sell this as the place you'd most want to see your work displayed."

" 'Here's your chance to see your work hanging in a historic mansion.' "

"You're good at this." Carly smiled.

"I'm a quick study." He returned the smile. "Maybe I'll toss in a little local history, you know, about the house and the original owners, and how the Enrights came to own it."

"How did they come to own it?"

"Bought it from the widow of a Confederate officer who died at Gettysburg. I think I remember hearing something about this place being a stop on the Underground Railroad."

"That would make sense, with the river running right along the back of the property."

"And I could add something about how the idea for the gallery grew out of Curtis's desire to have an art center in town."

"You really are a quick study."

"Well, that, and my mom did mention that that's what started the ball rolling."

"You can say that I'm looking forward to seeing

works of our local living artists hanging here in this grand hallway. We need to play up that angle. I think people will relate more to the house than to the carriage house, because so many of them knew the family that lived here. And I think we should put my email address in the article, tell people if they'd like to have their works considered for exhibit to contact me and we'll make arrangements for me to look at their paintings."

"You'll get all kinds of crazies wanting to show you their etchings, you know." A half smile played on his lips, and it was all she could do to look away from that sexy mouth.

"What's that old saying about kissing a lot of frogs before you find a prince?" She laughed. "I don't mind looking at amateur works because there's always the possibility that I'll discover something wonderful."

"And if all you find are a bunch of frogs?"

"That's okay, too. I'm expecting most of it to be bad. But even bad artists like to show off their stuff, and you can almost always find something positive to say." She held up her hand and began to count off. "You can say, 'Oh, I love the way you use color.' Or, 'That's an interesting perspective.' Or, 'How original. I wouldn't have thought to have painted the sky brown.'"

"Are you always this positive?"

"Sure."

"Why?" he asked bluntly.

"Why not? Life is too short. Why surround yourself with negative energy when you can be positive?"

"When life gives you lemons, and all that."

"Exactly. I mean, what's the alternative? Suck on the lemons?"

Ford frowned. "You sound like my mother."

"Your mother is a very wise and sensitive woman, a positive force in her own right. I'm surprised that you're not more like her."

"Yeah, well, it's been my experience that if shit is going to happen, it's going to happen, good vibes or not."

"You're very cynical, aren't you." It wasn't a question.

"Just logical. You can't control whether good things or bad things happen just because you think good thoughts." He paused. "I remember there was some kids' book where one of the characters told the others to think good thoughts . . ."

"Peter Pan." Carly nodded. "When he was teaching the Darling children to fly."

"Right. And we all know what happened to them, don't we? Caught by pirates and tied up. Made to walk the plank."

Carly laughed, turned off the lights, and gestured toward the front door. "I think you have all the pictures you need."

"I do." He followed her outside and waited while she locked the door. "Oh, before I forget . . ." He removed a slip of paper from his shirt pocket and handed it to her. "Here's the name and phone number of the security guy I was telling you about. He's expecting your call."

"Thanks. I'll definitely get in touch with him. I really haven't liked any of the proposals I've seen so far."

"Let me know before you call him, and I'll give him a heads-up."

"I'd appreciate that."

"How 'bout I drop off a copy of the article before it goes to the printer? You know, in case you want to add something, or change something."

"That would be great. Either way, just give me a call. By the way, how's Grace doing? Is she home yet?"

"She's doing great. They're springing her tomorrow."

"Please tell her I've been thinking about her and I'll stop over one day after she gets settled."

"I'll do that." He slid his phone back into his pocket. "So where's home this week?"

"The house I'm renting is on Hudson Street. Right around the corner from Cherry. It's a really cute place, but it's going to take me a few days to settle in."

"Hey, if you need help with anything, just let me know."

"I might take you up on that. Thanks." Carly opened the driver's-side door of her car.

"So I'll give you a call when the article is finished." Ford closed the door for her after she'd slid in behind the wheel.

"Great. I'll talk to you then."

Carly started the engine, waited for Ford to back out of the driveway. He hit his horn one time as he drove away, and she waved in return. She drove straight across Old St. Mary's Church onto Hudson, where she made a left turn. A few blocks down, she pulled into her driveway and sat in the car for a moment, studying the little house that so quickly and unexpectedly had become her home. Smiling, she went inside and dropped her bag on the dining room table on her way to the kitchen. She opened and closed the cabinet doors, then the drawers. It was all so woefully empty, especially for someone who loved to cook. Her kitchen at home was well stocked with just about everything she could ever need, and there was no point in replacing everything here, but there were staples that she just had to have. Driving back to Connecticut to pick up some household things was out of the question. She didn't have a few days to waste. She made a list of her absolute necessities, then weighed the pros and cons of running out to find a store nearby that carried everything she wanted, or ordering online.

Online, with overnight delivery, won out. She could pick up some takeout for dinner and have a simple breakfast in the morning, and by this time tomorrow night, all of her purchases would have arrived. Satisfied with her decision, she opened her laptop and began to order her must-haves. When she finished, she drove into town and picked up dinner from the Thai restaurant on Charles Street, then went back to her house to eat and finish unpacking her clothes. A summer storm was brewing and the temperature was beginning to drop, so she opened all the windows to let out the warm air of the day and turned on the ceiling fans in the bedroom and the living room.

By ten P.M., she was exhausted, but the only thing left on her to-do list was to grab a quick shower before she fell into her new bed in her new bedroom. She stretched her legs and sighed, listening to the drum of raindrops on the roof, so pleased to have accomplished so much in so short a time. She was well on her way to falling asleep when it occurred to her that Ford could have offered to email his article to her instead of bringing it over himself. Smiling into her pillow at the thought of seeing him again so soon, she turned over and went to sleep.

Chapter 15 ❧

"WELL, now I know how Cleopatra felt, riding on one of those litters, being carried by handsome young men." Grace forced a smile as the two EMTs lifted her and carried her from the bottom of the steps to the top of the staircase, where Dan and Lucy waited with a wheelchair. "Without the canopy, of course."

After she'd been deposited into the chair and the footrests adjusted to accommodate her broken leg, Grace wrinkled her nose and frowned. "A wheelchair. I never thought I'd see the day when I'd be forced into using one of these."

"It's only temporary, Mom." Ford came up the steps carrying some of his mother's belongings that they'd gathered from her hospital room. "Where do you want your stack of get-well cards?"

"It depends on where you're going to hole me up, doesn't it?" she grumbled as Lucy began to wheel her down the hall to the family's living quarters.

"Thanks, guys." Ford saluted the EMTs before following the chair.

"Good luck," one of the guys tossed over his shoulder as he headed for the lobby.

"No kidding," Ford muttered under his breath.

"You got this?" Dan asked.

"Oh, sure." Ford continued down the hallway. "You've got work to do. Go do it."

"Thanks. Let me know if Mom needs anything." Dan turned and went down the steps.

"Mom," Ford called when he reached the open door of the family suite.

"In here," Lucy returned the call.

Ford went into the living room and found his mother staring out the window.

"I'm trapped," she told him. "Trapped in an aging body and a cast that weighs more than the rest of me."

"Mom, it's only—" he began.

She cut him off. "Temporary. Thank you. You don't need to keep telling me that. But how would you feel if you were stuck someplace and couldn't go where you wanted to go, or do what you wanted to do?" She glowered at him.

He could have replied that he was starting to feel a bit of that himself, stuck in St. Dennis, playing Jimmy Olsen when he'd rather be out on the Bay, but he knew better than to even hint at the comparison.

"I understand, Mom, but right now it can't be helped. So we do what we have to do to get past this, right?" He could have been talking to himself. "Isn't that what you always told us?"

Grace sighed deeply. "I'm sorry to take it out on you. I'm just so frustrated. I've never had a broken bone, never been dependent on anyone to do a damned thing for me, and yet, here I sit. Even need someone to get my tea for me."

"I know it's tough on you. I do understand." He leaned over and kissed her on the forehead. "But we're all here to help you, and none of us mind fetching your tea."

"Am I going to be stuck up here on the second floor until this cast is off?" Tears welled in her eyes.

"You want to go downstairs, outside, to Cuppachino for coffee in the morning, you let me know. I'll make sure you get to wherever you want to be, Mom."

"You're a good boy, Ford." She reached out to take his hand. "There are no words to tell you how happy I am that you are here right now."

"I'm happy to be here," he said, surprising himself when he realized how much he meant it.

"Here's your tea, Mom." Lucy came into the room carrying a tray with a carafe, a cup, and a plate piled high with scones and croissants. "Franca baked these this morning. She thought you might want a snack."

Lucy set the tray on a small side table on the left side of the wheelchair, within reach of her mother's good hand.

"Oh, for the love of Pete," Grace muttered. "Who does she think is going to eat all of that?"

"I'm sure she was thinking you'd be sharing with your son. Your *favorite* son." Ford reached for a scone. "Oh, boy. Chocolate."

"You're just like you were when you were a kid." Graced smiled for the first time that morning.

Ford pulled over a side chair and straddled it.

"Careful," Grace warned. "That chair's an antique. Queen Anne. Been in—"

"—the family for years. Same as it was when I was a kid." He grinned at her, took a bite of the scone, and she laughed.

"I may have to marry Franca," he said before taking another bite. "We should keep her in the family."

"Every family should have a great pastry chef," Lucy agreed. "However, Franca's already married."

"A technicality." He finished the scone and reached for one of the napkins on the tray.

"You got crumbs on the floor," Lucy pointed out.

"We have housekeeping service here, right?" he asked, only half kidding.

Under his mother's glare, he got up and picked up the crumbs and dumped them into a nearby trash can.

"Mom, can I get you anything else?" Lucy asked.

"No, dear. Now go on to your meeting or you'll be late. Not the best first impression for a potential client."

Lucy started for the door. "If you're sure . . ."

"Luce, I'm here. I can handle it," Ford reminded her. After his sister closed the door behind her, he asked Grace, "Want to read my latest article for the *Gazette*?"

"You have next week's article finished already?" Grace set her cup down on the wheelchair's tray, the crumbs already forgotten.

"I do. Complete with photos."

"Yes, of course I want to see it."

"It's in my room." He got up and headed for the door. "Back in a minute."

It actually took him seven, but he'd have thought it was an hour judging by his mother's impatience.

"What took you so long?" She held out her left hand and he gave her the pages he'd printed out.

He started to say something, but she shushed him. She'd already started to read.

When she finished, she looked up over the frame of her glasses.

"This is a better first draft than the last one."

"First draft?" Ford frowned. "That's, like, the twentieth draft."

"Then permit me to help you out with number twenty-one."

He might have been more annoyed than he was if not for the fact he could tell, for at least that little slice of time, his mother seemed to forget she was in a wheelchair and had no use of her right hand.

"I can't write a thing with my left hand, so you're going to have to make the revisions as I read them to you. Now scoot that chair closer so you can see." She swung the wheelchair tray to the left so he could lean on it to write.

For the next hour, Grace revised and Ford wrote. At first, it was an exercise to be tolerated, but before long, he found himself asking, "Why write it that way?" and "Why'd you take out that part?" and "Why'd you change that word?" and "Why'd you move this photo to this spot?"

"Why, why, why," Grace said at one point. "You didn't ask this many 'whys' as a three-year-old."

But he could tell she was pleased by his interest, so he sat with her until they'd completed the piece.

"Well, that's quite a repair job, Mom."

"I hope you're not insulted, dear."

"Not really. I guess this is the sort of stuff I should

know if I'm going to be doing this for another week or so." It was on the tip of his tongue to ask how much longer she thought she might be laid up, but he knew better than to ask. She'd assume—correctly—that he was wanting out of the assignment.

Then again, with his reporting duties no longer necessary, he'd lose his excuse to spend time with Carly.

He wasn't quite ready to examine that thought too closely.

"I'll call Lucy back upstairs so she can sit with you while I go down to the office and type this up." Ford stood and returned the chair to its place next to the table under the window.

"No need, dear. I think I'll take a catnap." She closed her eyes and rested her head.

"I don't think you should sleep in the chair," he told her. "What if you fall out? I think you should sleep on your own bed."

"And I think you should mind your own business," she replied, but he could tell by the way the corners of her mouth turned up slightly that she wasn't offended. "I'll be fine. Don't bother Lucy. She has work to do. And so," she added without opening her eyes, "do you."

He stood in the doorway. "Do you want me to—"

"The only thing I want you to do is rewrite that article."

"Right."

Ford closed the door behind him softly and went one flight down to his mother's office. He turned on the laptop, pulled up the file, and began to make the changes Grace had suggested.

Suggested, he mused. Probably not the right word

for the way his mother had sliced and diced through his article.

By the time he finished and read the article over one last time, he had to admit that it was, in fact, better than it had been originally. He made a mental note of the changes Grace had made and her reasons for doing so, so he'd remember next time. It was late afternoon by the time he finished, and he debated whether to call Carly and drop off a copy right then, when he knew she'd be at the carriage house, or to wait for a few hours so he could stop by the place she rented on Hudson Street.

Hudson Street, definitely.

That would give him time to spend an hour or so on the Bay, something he hadn't done in several days, and he was itching for not only the solitude but the exercise. He turned off the laptop, left the article on the desk, and headed out to the boathouse.

Carly arrived home to find boxes stacked on her side porch from the door clear down to the driveway. It took her twenty minutes to get it all inside, then another thirty to unpack everything, and yet another to wash and dry the dishes, flatware, pots, pans, and kitchen utensils. She washed the inside of the cupboards and the utility drawers, wishing the air-conditioning repairs had been completed, but once she'd found places for everything, she felt her life taking a turn toward normalcy. Normal, to Carly, who'd lived alone for so long, wasn't bunking in someone else's guest room indefinitely, even if that someone was your BFF.

She'd just finished drying the flatware when she

Carly laughed. "Hey, I just moved in. Give me a few days to load it up."

"Well, at least you have the staples. Apples and a bottle of wine." That sexy mouth curved into a smile and Carly felt the temperature in the room rise about ten degrees.

"Do you think it's cooler outside? The air-conditioning guy doesn't come until tomorrow."

"I think it's probably about the same as in here but with mosquitoes . . . and those green-headed flies are swarming today."

"What?" She frowned. "Why?"

"Why are they swarming?" Ford shrugged. "Just that time of year, I guess. And there's a land breeze, so they're coming this way from the marshes."

"So we'll eat in here. Have a seat." She unscrewed the lid of one of the water bottles he'd set on the table and took a long cool drink. "Thanks for thinking to pick up water. Wine with pizza is generally an unbeatable combination, but in this heat . . ."

"Water. Right."

She grabbed some paper napkins from the counter and took the other chair. "The pizza smells wonderful."

He opened the lid and turned the box in her direction. She lifted out a piece and immediately took a bite. "Oh my God, whoever told you this was good was not lying."

"Best I've had in a long time. There wasn't pizza like this where I've been."

Before she took another bite, she asked, "You know, that's at least the second time you referred to having been 'someplace.' Where were you?" She smiled. "Or is that a state secret?"

He chewed slowly, as if deciding how to answer. Finally, he said, "I think I mentioned that I'd been in Africa."

Carly nodded. "Right. You did. So the question should have been, why were you there and what were you really doing?"

"I was part of group that was sent there to back up the Peacekeepers, who are, for the most part, under-armed at best, totally unarmed at worst."

"So was it part of your military service?"

"Yes."

"And are you out of the service now?"

"Yes."

"You don't like talking about it, do you?"

"Not so much. It was a job, and that job is done."

"Would you go back?"

He hesitated longer than she'd expected. "I guess it would depend on the circumstances."

"What were the circumstances that sent you there in the first place?"

He set the pizza on the plate, his expression dark, his voice weary and grave, his words direct. "People were being slaughtered in their homes, villages being burned to the ground. Little boys were being kidnapped and made into soldiers. Little girls were being forced into prostitution." He shrugged. "There are places in this world that are very ugly right now, where ugly things happen to very good, beautiful people. Even to the people who go in to try to help . . ."

A sadness washed over his face momentarily. Something in his expression made Carly feel like crying, and she didn't know why.

"Anyway, you do the best you can to keep the killing at a minimum. Or at the very least, to keep the bad guys aiming only at each other."

"That was the short version, wasn't it."

"More or less."

Mostly less, she thought, but she let it go. They ate in silence for a few moments before he looked at the stack of cardboard boxes and asked, "What are all those boxes from?"

"The stuff I ordered online. Everything came today and had to be unpacked and washed and put away. That's what I was doing when you called."

He looked her over. "You don't look so sweaty to me."

"I jumped in the shower the second I got off the phone," she admitted.

"That bad, huh?"

"You have no idea."

Ford laughed, the dark moment having passed. "You wouldn't believe how long a person can go without a hot shower. But if you're out of polite society long enough, it's not as much of an issue."

They'd finished the pizza and tossed the napkins into the empty box. Carly carried their plates to the sink and rinsed them before setting them on the counter.

"No dishwasher?" Ford asked.

"You're looking at 'er. But it won't be too bad. Most of the time, it'll just be me here by myself."

"Now, that doesn't sound like much fun."

"It's okay. I have a lot of work to do in a very short period of time. When the idea of the gallery was first proposed, the town council was thinking of combining the opening with the house tour they do at Christmas each year, which would have given me months to get this thing organized." A strand of hair slipped out of the elastic to hang into her face. She pulled off the elastic, smoothed back her hair, and redid the ponytail. "When I spoke with Ed the other day, he made an offhand remark about some people on the council wanting it sooner, possibly for some town holiday at the end of the summer, but I'm trying not to think about it because I'll panic. One month is simply not enough time."

"Well, the carriage house is just about finished, right?"

"Aside from the HVAC work—which should be done by Friday—the only thing left is the security system. I meant to call your friend today, but I got distracted with moving. I'll call him tomorrow."

"Assuming he can do what you need, at the right price, within a few weeks' time, you could be ready by the end of the summer. I'm guessing the town holiday is Discover St. Dennis. It's a full weekend, Friday through Sunday. It's actually a festival the town started about ten years ago to bring new faces into town—you know, drum up the tourist trade, attract the day-trippers. I haven't been around for it the past few years, but they used to have sailboat races and a big picnic down in the park and a footrace for charity early in the morning, that sort of thing."

"I can see where someone would think that would be a good opportunity to unveil the exhibit, but I need more time."

"I thought we just walked through what still needed to be done."

"That's just the building. There's still the exhibit catalog. Thank God the book is finished. That's a huge weight off me."

"Tell me about it."

"It's about Carolina the woman as well as Carolina the artist. I wanted it ready to go a week or two before the exhibit. I thought if I could get some high-profile publicity, it would spur on sales of the book, which would in turn generate interest in the exhibit. I'll have to call in a few favors, but I know some people in PR who I think I can count on to give me a hand where the promo is concerned."

"So what still has to be done?"

"The catalog of paintings for the exhibit."

"What's involved in that?"

"I've read through the journals and made notes on all the paintings Carolina described as she was doing them. I have to match up the notes with the actual works, so that next to the photos of the paintings in the catalog, I can quote Carolina, what she said about each. And then I have to write a coherent narrative for the introduction."

"I feel your pain there," he muttered.

"What?" She stared at him before laughing. "And speaking of your temporary career, weren't you going to show me the latest article?"

"Right." Ford stood and retrieved the folder from its place on the counter. He opened it, and handed Carly the several pages it contained.

She skimmed each page before going back to the first and reading through to the end.

"It's really good. You hit every point we'd wanted to make. You could have a future in this, you know."

She handed the folder back to him.

"For the love of God, please don't let my mother hear you say that." He pretended to look horrified. "I wouldn't be surprised if she broke another leg if she thought it would get me to take over the paper."

"You don't really think your mother fell on purpose?"

"Of course not." He dismissed the thought. "But you have to admit, it was awfully convenient."

"If she'd fallen while you were away, would you have come home?"

"Good question. I hadn't thought about that. I'd like to think I would." He seemed to be thinking about it now. "Yeah, I'm pretty sure I would have. If I didn't come back, the responsibility for the paper would fall on Dan and Lucy. Dan has his hands full with running the inn and raising his kids. Lucy has a really full event schedule, so I have to think I'd have come home. Besides, my mom never asked much of any of us, so if she needed me here, I'd be here."

"Even if it meant leaving behind whatever it was that you left?"

"There wasn't anything left to leave, Carly."

"Oh. I'm sorry. I didn't mean . . ."

"It's okay." He smiled sadly. "But that's a story for another time."

"Will I hear it?"

"I think you will. But we'll drop it for now."

She could sense that he was ready to leave—wanted to leave—so she stood.

"Oh. Your wine." She started to open the refrigerator door, but he reached out for her hand and held it.

"Save it for next time."

"Okay." She'd been hoping there'd be a next time.

"What do you do on the weekends for fun?"

"Fun?" She pretended to not understand. "Weekends?"

Ford laughed and drew her to him. "I was thinking maybe a real dinner out, you know, a Saturday-night thing. We could work on the plot of your catalog."

She laughed. "It has no plot." Her heart began to race as his arms closed around her. "It's a *catalog*."

"Still, there are things you might want to discuss."

"Actually, there is something I'm not sure about, something I discovered about Carolina." Her mind flashed back to *Stolen Moments,* and the story it told.

"What?"

"I think I'll save that for Saturday." She smiled and tugged on the collar of his cotton shirt, drawing down his face until that sexy mouth was hers. She kissed him, holding on until he began to kiss her back. His lips were soft and oh so sweet, just as somehow she'd known they'd be, and something inside her wished the kiss would go on until they couldn't breathe. His arms tightened around her and pressed her against him until she swore she could hear his heart beating.

As a first kiss, it was a bell ringer.

Then it was over, and those lips were whispering in her ear. "Thanks for dinner."

Carly leaned back and laughed. "You brought dinner."

"Right. Well, then, thanks for sharing it with me." He kissed the side of her face. "Looking forward to Saturday."

"Me, too."

"Call tomorrow about the security system."

She nodded and unlocked the front door. "Will do."

"I'll let him know."

"Thanks."

He leaned back in for one more kiss, then he was out the door. Carly leaned against the jamb and watched until the lights from his car disappeared at the end of the street.

Well . . . She exhaled as she closed the door and locked it. She'd been wondering what it would be like to kiss him, and now that she knew, she couldn't wait to kiss him again. She went into her room, opened the closet, and looked over the clothes she'd brought with her. She wanted to knock 'em dead on Saturday night, and nothing in the closet fit the bill. She made a mental note to hit Bling between now and their dinner date. Vanessa always had something killer in stock, and killer was exactly what Carly had in mind.

Diary ~

Well, this is certainly a fine kettle of fish I find myself in.
Note to self: When asking Alice to intervene, be more specific. Giving her carte blanche—i.e., "I'd do anything . . ."—
should come with a caveat. And I know Alice's hand was
in this—literally. I swear that I saw her right before I
took that tumble, felt a little nudge right between the shoulder
blades. Which is interesting because in her life here on earth,
Alice never set foot in the inn. An agoraphobic, she rarely
went into her own backyard except to tend to her herbs, and
then only because there was no one else to do that for her.
Nice to see she's getting out more these days.

When I said I'd do anything, had I said, "I'd give an
arm and a leg . . . ?" I can't recall.

I suppose I shouldn't complain too much, since the end
result is what I was looking for. Ford has taken over for me
at the paper. Of course, I'm going to have to milk this thing
for all it's worth. If he finds out I have voice-recognition
software on my laptop, he'll be wanting to drop off his notes
so I can write the articles myself, and that simply won't do.
I need him to work on his skills so he can feel confident in his
ability to take over for me permanently. Between you and
me, his first two attempts were far better than I let on—but

I know my boy, and I know how he reacts to challenges. If he has to work at something, he puts his whole heart into it, but if it comes easily to him, he loses interest. He'll make a fine newspaperman, as fine as his grandfather and great-grandfather in their day. The <u>St. Dennis Gazette</u> is his destiny, as the Inn at Sinclair's Point is Dan's. I just need to find a way to make that as clear to him as it is to me. I know this is where he's supposed to be just as surely as I know that Carly Summit is the one for him. Stubborn boy! He's been to interview her twice already and he's barely even mentioned her name beyond the article.

But something is going on with him. The light surrounding him isn't as dark as it was when he arrived home. Perhaps he's finding some peace. He's spent a lot of time out on the Bay, and when I ask him, he says he's revisiting places he used to go. I suspect he means places he used to go with his father. Daniel always made a point to do things with Ford, who, as the youngest, seemed to be left behind by his older brother and sister. They had a special bond, and I believe that he, of the three children, suffered the most when Daniel died.

Whatever it is that is haunting him now, whatever the cause of the darkness, I sense the same sort of grief that emanated from him when his father passed. I have tried to rely upon my own powers to see into his heart, but as always, my powers fail me when it comes to Ford. I'm hoping that he'll find a way to put that sadness aside. I would hate for him to go through life carrying so great a burden.

~ Grace ~

Chapter 16 ⌒

A T ten minutes after eight on Thursday morning, Carly's phone began to ring. From her own experience, she knew that nothing good ever came from a call before nine A.M. or after midnight.

"Carly, Ed Lassiter here. Sorry for the early call, but I wanted to get in touch with you as soon as I could, give you the news before someone else did."

"What's that, Ed?" Carly's stomach began to knot with dread. She had a feeling she already knew where this call was headed.

"The council met last night to discuss how to proceed with the Enright property, and the vote was unanimous. We'd like to dedicate the new community art center on the Saturday of the town's three-day Discover St. Dennis weekend."

"That's August," she said flatly.

"Right. The end of August." Then, as if to tell her something she didn't already know, he added, "That's next month."

When she did not respond, he went on as if he hadn't just dropped a bomb in her lap.

"We know how hard you're working and we know you can make it happen."

"Thanks for the heads-up." She hung up without protesting. What good would it do? The decision had been made, and made without her input.

Her emotions veered wildly between anger and panic.

As if she didn't have enough to stress about. How could she accomplish everything in less than a month?

Breathe, she demanded. One long breath followed by another until her head cleared and rational thought returned. She had a to-do list. She'd follow it and somehow she'd find a way. There was no choice in the matter. The building had to be ready and the book had to go on sale in two weeks.

The book. How was she going to get it into the marketplace to make the kind of splash she'd envisioned? That was the purpose of the book, wasn't it? To introduce the art world to Carolina, to make everyone who was anyone flock to St. Dennis for the opening of the exhibit? Without the book, what were her chances of doing justice to Carolina's work? In her New York gallery, this wouldn't be as much of a problem. Many of the people she wanted to draw to the exhibit were in New York—well, those who hadn't left the city for the summer, anyway. But here, in this tiny town on the Eastern Shore, she wasn't as certain that even if the book went on sale tomorrow, she could generate the kind of interest in the gallery that she'd been hoping for. She'd have to call in a lot of favors.

And she needed to talk to her editor . . . now.

Before she could make that call, the phone rang again.

This time it was Cam, calling to let her know the HVAC guys were on the job and expected to finish by tomorrow. Okay, she told herself after she hung up. There's something big to check off that list. That was good, right?

The third call was from her mother, who wanted to let Carly know that her parents had returned home and ask when she would be coming back to Connecticut. "And by the way, I loved the book. I'm so proud of you, Carly."

"Thanks, Mom. But it's going to be a while before I can leave St. Dennis," Carly told her. "Let me bring you up-to-date . . ."

"Oh," Roberta exclaimed when Carly had finished. "Let us know when you get a firm date, and we'll make every effort to be there."

The fourth was from Tony Rosetti, Ford's friend, returning her earlier call. She explained what she was doing and what she needed. He already had a system in mind based on what Ford had told him, he said, and offered to drive to St. Dennis the following day to meet with her and look over the carriage house. They agreed on an eleven o'clock meeting. Carly hung up the phone and sighed with relief. If they could get the security installed on time, she had a good chance of meeting the deadline Ed had given her that morning.

One other big item would be checked off the list.

Actually, soon there would be three items, she reminded herself. With the heating and cooling and the painting completed, the interior of the building would be ready. Get the security up and running, and she could move the paintings from Ellie's to the gallery. She began to calm a little. Unless something unforeseen happened, at the very least, the building would be ready.

Now, if she could only finish the catalog . . .

She went back to the dining room table to assess her progress. In Carly's mind, that project was already done. She knew exactly how she wanted it to look, and now that she had the order of the paintings worked out in her head—if not on paper—she needed only to photograph each of the works. She had finished rereading the last of the journals the night before, but found nothing really new that would change the narrative Carly had already begun. She'd used index cards for the salient points that she wanted to make, then put the cards in order of how the paintings would be listed in the catalog. She already had quotes from Carolina to correspond with the paintings, so she found herself further along than she'd thought. Good news, with the opening now painfully close. She gave herself until Sunday to finish the catalog so that on Monday, she could take it to the graphic designer she'd contacted in Annapolis.

Next on her list of things to do was a call to the freelance editor she'd hired, Gail McAfee, whose service included formatting the manuscript. Gail assured her that she was on top of the project and that she'd meet the deadline with time to spare. With luck and hard work, the book would be available—albeit in electronic form only—the week before the opening. A print edition could come later if she decided to go in that direction, Gail had pointed out, and while Carly wished she could have sent both formats into the marketplace simultaneously, now that the town council had changed the timetable, there simply wasn't time.

With any luck, Gail told her, the book would generate enough interest that a print publisher would come looking for her instead of the other way around. In a perfect world, Carly might have followed a more traditional publishing route—submitting the manuscript to an agent to shop to publishers for her—but in *her* world, time was ridiculously short.

And one more big item on that list would be checked off.

Now, how best to call the attention of all the right people in the art world to the exhibit?

Invite them. She could have invitations made to send out ... something that would catch the eye. Maybe if she could design something quickly and get it to a printer ...

The ringing phone brought her back to reality. She glared at it before reaching for it, but once she saw the name on the caller ID, she smiled.

"Enrico, I was just thinking about calling you."

"You're not going to believe what just happened." Enrico was on the verge of hyperventilating. "Barely ten in the morning, and my day—my week, my *month,* perhaps my entire year—has been made."

"Calm down." It could be anything, Carly knew. Enrico wasn't one to hide his enthusiasm. Ever. "What's going on?"

"Well, you remember Taylor Radell? The dealer from West Chester who brought us those lovely Michael Jarrett charcoals a few years ago?"

"Of course. What about her?"

"She just brought in two . . . oh my God, I still can't believe it . . ."

"Enrico! Focus!"

"Right." He took a deep breath. "She brought us two Lewis Mitchells. Two! Two that haven't been on the market since, like, the seventies."

"Really?" Carly frowned. "How did she . . . ?"

"Provenance is all I know. I already told her we needed to see the paper trail. She promised to messenger everything to me today if you're interested."

"Have you seen the works?"

"OMG, have I ever. Did I leave out that part?" Enrico sounded close to hyperventilating again. "Gorgeous, truly, Carly. Two of the best I've ever seen. Early watercolors. Muted colors, very romantic. Almost Monet-ish."

"What do you think?"

"You're kidding, right? It's *Lewis Mitchell,* Carly."

"I'd like to know where they came from."

"Taylor said the owner is a longtime client of hers. He bought them years ago from Dunbower Galleries. She has copies of the receipts."

Carly chewed a fingernail that was weeks overdue for a manicure. Over the past fifteen years, Lewis Mitchell had become a Very Important Artist of the twentieth century. Carly had only ever had one of his paintings in her gallery, and that one had sold within twenty-four hours of her hanging it on the wall.

"I want to see them, but I can't leave St. Dennis." Carly told Enrico about the timing of the exhibit being moved. "Okay, send me a text with the photos so I can at least see what we're getting into, and send me the paper trail so I can sleep at night."

"So we can take them?" Carly heard Enrico's voice catch in his throat.

"Assuming we can follow the trail, yes. Congratulations."

"You want Taylor's number?"

"No. I want you to call her. This is your gig, Enrico. Now start working on the announcement that you're going to run in all the papers and online sites to let the art world know what you have."

"Oh, yay! I'm calling Taylor right now. I'll send you everything you asked for the second I get it."

"Oh, and email me any recent updates to the list of our contacts. Press, critics, customers, dealers, other gallery owners. Art bloggers, columnists, anyone whose name and information I might not have on my list."

"I'm on it. Now you go do your Carolina Ellis thing," he said happily, "and I'll tend to Miss Taylor. Oh my, but Summit Galleries is hot hot hot right now."

Laughing, Carly disconnected the call but tucked the phone into her pocket.

She was almost as excited as Enrico had been at the prospect of adding two Mitchells to her inventory. If the past was any indication, they wouldn't be there long, and she'd have a nice commission to share with Enrico. She generally didn't delegate transactions as big as this, but she trusted Enrico, knew that he'd do his homework and would let her know if something didn't feel right. Besides, given the current circumstances that were keeping her in St. Dennis, he was going to have to step up. It wasn't easy for her to give up control to anyone, but she was going to have to do it, and now was the time.

Put it aside, she told herself, *and get back to the task at hand.*

To that end, she gathered the index cards from the table and began to sort through them, putting the paintings into their final order.

Ford dipped the paddle into the calm water of the Bay and glided over the surface toward the Choptank River. When he was a boy, he'd heard the stories of how the native people had built villages all along the banks, and how vestiges of those villages could be found, if you looked hard enough. As a kid, he had looked plenty hard, but he'd never found a trace. It had been years since he'd searched, and today, when the winds were easy and the sun not quite as blazing hot as it had been, seemed like a good day to take up the hunt.

He turned into the river and raised a hand to shield his eyes from the sun while he scanned the shoreline. When he found the place he was looking for, he turned the kayak to the right and beached it on the rough sand. He pulled the craft almost to the where the grasses began and laid the paddle across the bow. He walked up a slight embankment to the clearing he remembered from when he and his buddies used to haunt these shores and the woods that lay beyond. After twenty minutes of searching for something that would let him know he was at least in the right ballpark, Ford sat on the thick trunk of a fallen tree.

The excursion this morning wasn't as much about finding an ancient settlement as it was about getting his head straight. He'd spent a good portion of last night and again this morning trying to talk himself out of pursuing any sort of relationship with Carly, other than, of course, a professional one. Reporter to reportee, so to speak.

He'd thought up any number of rationalizations. They were both in St. Dennis temporarily, so why start something that obviously had no future? She was definitely an uptown girl and he was more the survivalist type. And maybe he was only interested in her because she was one of the few people in St. Dennis with whom he had no history, his thinking being that, unlike just about everyone else in town who'd known him his entire life, Carly had no expectations of him, no preconceived ideas of who he was or who he should be, and didn't compare him to his father or his brother.

Even he knew it all sounded like so much BS.

And besides, if he wanted to be around someone who always looked for the upside of things, he could talk to his mother, who even his father had once referred to as Pollyanna. Her own brother used to call her "Silver Lining Gracie," because no matter how hard things were, his mom could always find something good to focus on. Carly was like that, too. Being Grace's son, he figured he had enough positive energy floating around him to last the rest of his life.

He knew the way the world really worked. He knew that people often acted inhumanly. He'd seen grown men who didn't bat an eye at shooting a woman so heavily pregnant she couldn't even run away. He'd seen families burned in their homes, the exits blocked so that none could escape. He'd seen just about everything that man could do to man, so he knew damned well the world wasn't always quite as skippy as people like his mother—and Carly—believed it to be. He'd never be able to convince either of them of that, though. People like that were just not wired for reality, that's all. It wasn't their fault, no more than it was his fault that he always expected the other shoe to drop.

And in his experience, hadn't it?

Had he always been the cynic that Carly had called him out to be? He couldn't remember.

Maybe it had started on his fourteenth birthday, when he and his dad had planned a trip to Smith Island in his uncle's skipjack. He'd been promised a Smith Island cake—thirteen microlayers of amazingness—but a storm had been brewing and the wind had been judged too much for a sail, so the trip was postponed for the following week. But Dan had come home from college to recover from a kick to the head he'd gotten in a soccer game, and it wouldn't have seemed right to have gone off without him. So they looked to the next week, but his dad had gotten sick, and that had pretty much taken care of the trip to Smith Island.

If he were to be honest with himself—and he was trying to be—he'd admit that to have your entire life's view colored by something that happened when you were a kid wasn't real mature.

More likely, it started on the day he'd watched helplessly as Anna and three others were shot and left to die by a band of rebels led by a man who was now coming dangerously close to overthrowing the legitimate government. Seeing the woman you once loved shot in the back will go a long way to play with your head. Somehow, Ford knew, he was going to have to move past that. Not forget—he'd never forget—but move past. Ford was pretty sure that wasn't going to happen as long as Raymond Nakimbe still was free to murder and spread his evil brand of terror among the very people he wanted to govern.

Ford had a feeling that if he wanted any kind of relationship with Carly—even one of friendship, which was probably not his first choice after kissing her last night—he was going to have to let in a little more light to push out some of the darkness. And he knew he was going to kiss her again, at the very next opportunity. He'd been about to kiss her when she'd kissed him, taking him totally by surprise. It had been a pleasant surprise, but a surprise all the same. He was used to being the pursuer, but he was all right with the way things worked out.

It had been a long time since he'd kissed someone for real. Oh, he'd kissed women after Anna, but his heart hadn't always been in it. Last night, his heart had been there, all the way, and he supposed that simple fact was what had him in a turmoil today. He'd come to St. Dennis looking for some time with his family, a time to heal a little maybe, a time to get reacquainted with himself, nothing more. The last thing he'd expected to find there was a woman who carried so much light within her, she lit up a room when she entered.

None of his attempts at rationalizing could explain the effect that light had on him. He only knew it was true, and that light had touched him, and he was unable to look away. Where it was going to lead was anyone's guess.

Chapter 17 ⌒

CARLY had barely gotten to the carriage house on Friday morning for her appointment with Tony Rosetti when she heard a firm rap on the door a mere second before it opened.

"Miss Summit?" A tall, somewhat gangly woman somewhere between fifty and seventy stood in the doorway, a large leather portfolio in her left hand.

"Yes, I'm Carly Summit." She inwardly groaned. Somehow she knew what was coming.

"I'm Hazel Stevens. I was told I'd find you here." The woman walked into the room, leaving the door to bang shut behind her. "Ed Lassiter's wife told me I could bring my paintings down here for you to look at and you'd hang 'em in the great hall over there in the mansion."

The entire time she was talking, Hazel was taking in the carriage house from the roof to the floor. She appeared unimpressed.

"Yes, we are looking for some works by local artists for the exhibit, yes," Carly told her. "There will be a piece in the *Gazette* this week inviting people to bring there work down for me to—"

"I heard all that from Shelly—Ed's wife—but I thought, why wait and take the chance that all the spots will be filled up?" She looked around for a flat surface and, finding none, moved two sawhorses close together and laid the portfolio open across them. "Now, I don't know how many of these you're going to want, but I know you'll want at least three of them."

She held up the first one, then another, then a third watercolor painting of—Grace had called it correctly—cats. Carly had nothing against cats. She liked cats. Hazel's cats were scary, with large yellow eyes that leaped off the paper.

"Ah . . ." Carly searched for something to say, but no words came out.

"You're speechless, right?" Hazel beamed. "I knew it. I knew you weren't expecting to find talent like this in St. Dennis."

Carly cleared her throat and took each painting in turn in her hands and held it up as if studying it critically.

"That's Bitsy, that one there with the black face," Hazel pointed out. "She's my baby doll."

Bitsy was perhaps the scariest of all. Surely the cat herself was a sweet animal. It was her owner's portrayal that was eerie. Carly put the painting back on the open portfolio and turned the same critical eye onto the next one.

"Now this would be . . . ?"

"Fancy Nancy. I called her that because I always thought calicos looked like they were all dressed up in fancy clothes."

"I see. Yes." Carly nodded. "I can see where you'd think that."

Fancy Nancy was less scary than Bitsy but not by much. It was a shame Hazel wasn't more of an artist, Carly thought. Her cats were probably very beautiful.

"Tiger, Tiger, Burning Bright," Hazel said.

"Excuse me?"

"That's the tiger cat in that last picture. That's her name."

"Oh. Of course. I get it." No, she didn't really. "Do you mind if I look at whatever else you have in your portfolio?"

"Oh, help yourself." Hazel reached for her painting of her tiger cat and watched over Carly's shoulder as the contents of the folder were viewed. She ran a commentary the entire time. "That there's Milton, and that next one, Sherlock . . ."

"How many cats do you have?" Carly couldn't help but ask.

"Oh, only the three right now, the first three I showed you. These others, they've all gone over the Rainbow Bridge."

"The Rainbow Bridge?" Carly asked.

"Kitty heaven," Hazel whispered.

"Oh. I'm sorry for your loss." Carly corrected herself. "Losses."

"Thank you, dear." While Carly looked through the rest of the paintings, Hazel chatted away.

"You know, when we heard that the town was bringing in some New York art dealer to show our paintings and run our exhibit, well, we all thought for sure you'd be some stuck-up art snob. But Grace Sinclair said you were lovely, and she was right. You're a very nice young woman."

"Well, thank you, Hazel." Carly went back and forth between several of the paintings, trying to decide which one was least likely to frighten small children. "You know, your work is very . . . unique, Hazel. I can honestly say I've never seen anything quite like it. But space in the mansion is very limited, and I did want to save what space we have there for living artists from St. Dennis, so you'd certainly qualify. But in all fairness to others who might want to bring in works for the show, I really can only accept one painting from each artist. I'm sure you understand."

"Well, I was hoping . . ." Hazel frowned.

"Of course you were. And I don't blame you. Your work has a certain . . . energy, and we'd certainly be privileged to show it. But I can only choose one . . ." Carly went back through the portfolio a second time, hoping that she might have missed something that was better than what she'd seen. Finally, she pulled one out at random. "I think this one, Hazel."

"Kitty Bright." Hazel sighed. "She was my first."

"Then it's appropriate that we choose her, don't you think?" She handed the painting to Hazel. "Now, I'm going to ask you to have this framed, and to hold on to it until we're ready to start arranging the exhibit in the mansion."

"All right." Hazel put the selected work on top of the others in the portfolio and closed it. "I hope you'll remember that I was the first person to bring in a painting and that *Kitty Bright* will have a prominent place in the hall."

"I promise I'll find the appropriate place." With a hand on Hazel's back, Carly guided the woman to the door, opened it, held it for her, then, with a final wave good-bye, closed the door and slumped against it.

She ran a hand over her face, wondering how many more such viewings she'd have to endure.

"Cam, your work has a certain energy." The voice floated from the other side of the partition.

"I know, Ford. I bet you didn't expect to find anyone with talent like mine. You're speechless, right?"

"I sure am. Your work is so . . . unique."

Carly peered around the side of the partition and found Cam and Ford leaning against the wall.

"You two think you're so funny." Carly crossed her arms across her chest.

Ford walked toward her, laughing. "If you'd heard that conversation from back here, you'd think it was funny, too."

"Actually, it *was* pretty funny," she admitted, "in a macabre sort of way. Those cats were scary. It's the only word that I can think of to describe them. But I had to pick one."

"That's pretty much what you're going to get from the locals," Cam told her. "We had an art fair about four years ago and you wouldn't believe what people brought out."

"After seeing Hazel's cats, I'm afraid I would." She grimaced at the thought of an entire exhibit filled with Hazel's frightening felines.

"I think you handled her really well," Ford told her. "I know I couldn't have kept a straight face."

Still laughing, Cam headed toward the door. "I'll be back in an hour or so to finish up," he told them. "Thanks for the entertainment."

"So what brings you out this morning?" Carly asked after Cam left.

"I was hoping to catch Tony. I tried to call him this morning to see if he could grab a quick lunch before he heads back, but he didn't pick up. It's been a long time since we've gotten together, so I thought this would be a good opportunity to catch up. I hope you don't mind. I wasn't intending to hang around for your meeting."

"I don't mind at all, and you're welcome to stay while he's here."

"So what does *Kitty Bright* look like?" Ford put first one, then his other arm around Carly.

"All white, huge yellow eyes." Carly pretended to shudder. "All of Hazel's cats have huge yellow eyes totally out of proportion. That's what makes them so scary."

"But you'll include it in the exhibit and Hazel will be happy."

"What's the point in making her feel bad? She obviously enjoys doing it. There must have been thirty watercolors in that portfolio."

The door opened and a dark-haired man stuck his head in. "Hello?"

"Yes?" Carly broke out of the circle of Ford's arms to see who was there.

"Tony Rosetti." The dark-haired man entered the room. When he saw Ford, he grinned, his arm outstretched. "Hey, buddy. Long time . . ."

Ford nodded and took the hand that reached for his. "Tony. You're looking good," he said as they exchanged a man-hug.

"You, too. Thinner maybe, but good." Tony patted

Ford on the back, then turned to Carly. "Sorry. We used to . . . work together. It's been a while."

"It's quite all right. I'm Carly."

Tony nodded and looked around and got right to the point. "So is this the place?"

Carly nodded.

"You're planning on displaying a fortune in art *here*?"

"I am. Assuming, of course, that you can secure it."

"I can secure anything." He walked around the room, mostly looking up.

"Take all the time you need," Carly told him.

Tony took some measurements—walls, ceiling height, length and width of the room—with an implement he removed from his back pocket. He studied the doors and the windows, then, without a word, went outside.

Ten minutes later, Carly looked out front and saw him get into his car.

She frowned and turned to Ford. "You don't suppose he's leaving?"

"He wouldn't leave without saying something. Maybe he's making a phone call. Give him a few minutes. He'll be back."

Several minutes later, Tony came through the door.

"Okay, this is how I see it." He walked Carly through his proposed system, where he would install cameras and sensors.

"How soon can you do this?" she asked.

"I can have this up and running in . . ." He appeared to be calculating. "A week. Ten days. No more. I'll have to order a few things that aren't normally available."

"What does that mean?"

"He means stuff you don't find in the average home security store," Ford told her.

"Okay, then. How much do you think a system like this would cost?"

He gave her a number, and she almost passed out.

"Tony," Ford said before Carly could find her voice, "I think you can do better."

Tony scratched his head. "I don't know, man, the kind of sensors we're talking about are really pricey."

Ford continued to stare at him.

"All right." Tony tossed out a revised number. "That's the best I can do."

Carly thought over the other systems that had been proposed, none of which were nearly as sophisticated as the one Tony had in mind. Of course, none of them cost as much either. After all the renovations on the carriage house, there wasn't much left in the budget. She'd have to go back to Ed and see what the town council was willing to contribute. The rest of it would have to come from the book sales.

"All right. Get me a written proposal, outlining exactly what you're doing."

"Uh-uh." Tony shook his head. "If I outline what I'm doing and circulate that, then what's the point? Someone could possibly figure out how to get around the system. Not real likely, but it could conceivably happen."

"You have to give me an estimate for me to take to the town council."

He nodded. "I'll get you something you can use. It just won't spell out all the bells and whistles."

"Can you get it to me by Monday?"

"Sooner, if I can."

Carly gave him her email address. "I really can't thank you enough for coming all the way out here on such short notice."

"Hey, anything for an old comrade-in-arms, right?" He bumped his fist on Ford's arm. "Got time for a quick lunch before I head back?"

"I was just about to ask you the same thing. I know a great place just about a mile from here." Ford turned to Carly. "You're welcome to join us, of course."

"Very nice of you, but no thank you. I have to get back to work." She turned off the lights and followed the two men out the door, then locked up. "Thanks again, Tony."

"My pleasure. Any friend of Ford's, and all that." Tony walked toward his car at the end of the drive.

"Where's your car?" she asked Ford, who'd held back.

"I felt like a little exercise, so I walked over."

"Thanks for whatever it was that you did to get him here so quickly."

"You needed something really good, really fast. Tony's the best, and I figured he'd do a favor if he could."

"I appreciate it."

He leaned over and kissed her. "We're still on for tomorrow night, right?"

"Absolutely."

"I'll pick you up at seven."

"See you then . . ."

She watched him sprint to the end of the driveway and hop into the passenger side of Tony's Jeep. Then, remembering there was one more thing she needed to do before she went home to work on the catalog, she got into her car and headed straight to Bling. There was a dress in the window just that morning that might be exactly what she was looking for.

Chapter 18 ⌒

THE dress in Bling's window turned out to not work on Carly the way she'd hoped it would, but Vanessa had something else in mind.

"This one." Vanessa brought a blue sheath with a squared neckline, front and back, into the dressing room and held it up in front of Carly. "The blue is almost the exact shade of your eyes and there's just enough spandex in it to . . . well, you'll see. You have to try it."

Always happy to try on pretty things, Carly pulled the dress over her head, then smoothed it over her hips.

"There. What did I tell you?" Vanessa beamed. "It's so close to perfection I can barely stand it." She adjusted the neckline slightly. "Just tight enough, just short enough, and just low enough in front to give you a little cleavage without being, you know, slutty. I take it this is for something special?"

"I have a date for dinner tomorrow night." Carly turned in the mirror to check the side view. Vanessa was dead-on about the fit.

"And you want to wow." Vanessa nodded knowingly. "This is definitely the dress." She slipped off the hair tie from Carly's ponytail and pulled all of her hair to one side. "That's the look you want. Sexy but ladylike. No man with a pulse could resist you."

"Well then, I suppose I have no choice." Carly grinned and Vanessa helped her out of the dress. "I'll take it."

Vanessa put the dress on a hanger and took it with her while Carly dressed in the clothes she'd worn into the shop. She was putting her hair back up as she walked out front.

"Do you need anything to go with the dress?" Vanessa asked as Carly approached the counter. "Earrings? Killer shoes? A bag?"

"Actually, I could probably use some of each. I didn't expect to be going out, so I left all of my good clothes back home."

Vanessa held up several pairs of earrings, and Carly reached for the dangly ones with the blue stones.

"I'd go with them, too." Vanessa nodded and returned the other two pairs to the case. Her phone rang, but before she answered it, she told Carly, "Shoes are toward the back, and bags are on the right side of the shop. I'll be with you in a minute."

Carly went straight to the shoes, and gravitated toward the highest pair of heels in the shop.

"When I said 'killer,' those were the ones I had in mind." Vanessa leaned against a display. "What size?"

"Seven, please." Carly couldn't wait to put them on her feet. Metallic leather sandals that fastened at the ankle on the thinnest straps imaginable, the shoes were, in fact, killers.

Vanessa found the right size and handed Carly the box and stood by while she sat on a nearby stool and tried them on.

"I love them." Carly stood and walked a few steps to make sure she could, in fact, walk in them. "They're gorgeous."

"Here's a bag that works with them." Vanessa handed her a clutch of soft, silvery leather.

"I'll take it." Carly took off the shoes and returned them to their box. "And the shoes and the earrings and the dress."

She smiled all the way to the cash register. "Vanessa, your shop is amazing. There are places in New York that don't have what you have here."

"Thank you. Just for that, I'm giving you ten percent off." Vanessa laughed. "Another ten if you tell me who the lucky guy is. If, of course, that isn't too personal a question."

"For twenty percent . . . sure." Carly leaned on the counter and watched Vanessa tally up the damage. "It's Ford Sinclair."

Vanessa's hand stopped moving and she glanced up at Carly.

"Grace's son? Tall, rugged-looking guy? Dark eyes?" she asked.

Carly nodded.

"I don't blame you for going all out." Vanessa grinned. "I was wondering how long it would be before someone snagged his attention. I'm attracted to men like that myself." She hastened to add, "Not that I'm attracted to Ford, per se, but my husband, Grady, is cut from that cloth, too. Too rugged to be classically handsome, maybe, but irresistible. And *hot*." She wrapped the earrings in tissue. "Pretty boys have never really done it for me."

Carly thought back to her last boyfriend. Todd could

be categorized as a pretty boy, she supposed, though she wasn't sure if he was as pretty as he thought he was. Everything about Todd had seemed . . . precise. From head to toe, he had always been perfectly un-wrinkled, perfectly coiffed, and very *GQ*. What, she asked herself now, had she seen in him?

"You're going to kill him in this dress, you know," Vanessa said as she swiped Carly's credit card. "I wish I could be around to see it. I love it when a big guy crashes to his knees . . ."

"So I made reservations at Lola's." Ford stood in Carly's foyer, his eyes on her face as if he was afraid to look past her chin.

"Oh, great. I've been wanting to try it. I've heard it's wonderful." Carly leaned across the dining room table, searching for her phone amid the piles of paper. She could feel Ford's stare, and it was all she could do not to smile. Vanessa had been spot-on. The man had looked gobsmacked when she opened the front door.

"Here it is." She held up her phone, then tucked it into her bag. "All ready?"

She took two steps toward the door, then stopped in midstride and snapped her fingers. "I almost for-got . . . just one second."

She pivoted on her ridiculously high heels and headed to the kitchen to lock the back door.

"You look really beautiful," he said when she re-turned to the foyer. "I like your dress."

"Thanks. I got it at Bling yesterday when I realized I didn't have any clothes with me that might be appro-priate for dining out." She laughed, then added, "Who am I kidding? I felt like shopping. It was my reward for working so hard all these weeks without taking a break."

"Well, whatever inspired the purchase, I definitely approve."

He held the door for her, and she heard his breath catch as she brushed past him. He closed the door behind them and waited while she locked it. It seemed like the most natural thing in the world to link her arm through his as they walked to the car, to walk arm in arm with him on a beautiful summer Saturday night.

"So how was your lunch with Tony?" she asked.

"It was good. Great, actually. It's been a long time since we've seen each other."

"I gathered that from the conversation. Where do you know each other from?"

"Oh, we worked together, on and off." He opened the car door for her and she slid into her seat.

By the time he'd gotten behind the wheel, she had her seat belt on. He fastened his as well and started the car.

"I haven't been to Lola's in so many years, I don't even remember what it's like," he said as he started the engine.

"I've never been, but I know that Cam and Ellie like it. They've mentioned it several times."

The restaurant was only a few blocks away, but every available parking spot on Charles Street was taken, and they were forced to park in the big municipal lot on Kelly's Point Road.

"Lots of tourists in town this weekend because of the sailboat races," Ford explained after he pulled into one of the lone remaining spots.

"Are you racing?" Carly asked as she got out of the car and waited for him.

"No. Dan always loved to sail, but I've always preferred kayaking."

"Oh, I love to kayak. I used to go with my dad when I was younger."

"I'll take you out one of these days, and we'll paddle around some of the little inlets around the Bay."

The lower part of the lot had yet to be paved, and she had to pick her way carefully in those tall strappy shoes until they reached the macadam. He held her arm to help her across the stones, but once they reached the road, he took her hand and held it until they arrived at the restaurant.

The sidewalks in the center of town were alive with people in all manner of dress. A few, like Carly and Ford, were well dressed and obviously headed for one of the fine dining establishments, but most were in shorts and tank tops. There was a line out the door across the street at Sips—which sold mostly cold drinks—and Cuppachino, the coffee shop, was filled to capacity. Ford had to lead Carly through the throng gathered on the sidewalk to get to Lola's door.

"I can't believe this is St. Dennis," he told her while they waited for their table. "I never would have imagined this town could attract crowds like this."

"The inn is filled all summer long, though, right?"

"I'm still getting used to that, too."

The hostess led them to a table, and soon after they were seated, a server arrived to pour water and offer menus, and describe the specials.

"They serve crab all over the world," Ford noted

after they'd both ordered, "but none as good as what we have right here on the Eastern Shore."

"I have to agree." Carly nodded. "I can't wait to try the crab-mac-and-five-cheese side dish we ordered. I've had lobster mac and cheese, but not crab."

"The chef at the inn makes it. I had it at dinner a few nights ago."

"Do you eat all your meals in the dining room?"

He nodded. "I can't remember a time when my mother cooked anything. We've always lived there, and there's always been someone downstairs in the kitchen to cook, so my mother always deferred to the chefs, as she liked to say." He smiled. "I think she was just happy to have someone else take over those chores. She always had so many other things to do, God knows when we kids would have eaten if dinner had been left to her. We always ate together in the dining room at the same time every night, but it was only because she didn't have to cook."

"I guess she helped your father run the inn?"

"Not really. I mean, she did help out from time to time when someone called in sick, and she often took over the reception desk and handled reservations at night. But most of her time was spent at the paper. That's always been her thing." He fell silent as their salads were served. "My mother loves it. She's never wanted to do anything else. But she's a controlling son of a gun, never delegated much to anyone else, which is why she's in such a pickle now."

"So you've taken over for her?"

"Temporarily. I'd agreed to write the feature articles, but it seems the community calendar has to be up-dated, so I worked with her on that today. And then there are the ads from the merchants that have to be placed, and the spotlight on local businesses that she likes to run every week. Oh, and there's her new pet project, interviewing random people on the street, asking them about their visit to St. Dennis." He laughed and lowered his voice, mimicking a TV reporter. "Is this your first visit to St. Dennis? No? So what keeps you coming back? What's your favorite place for dining out? Antiques shopping?" He laughed again. "She's decided she wants to run three of these mini-interviews every week from now until Labor Day."

"And she wants you to be the roving reporter."

"Of course. But it's not bad, really. I did my three this afternoon down at the marina." He paused. "It was actually quite interesting, you know? Seeing my hometown through the eyes of other people?"

"It sounds to me like Grace knew what she was doing when she tapped you to take over for her."

"It's her way of trying to keep me in St. Dennis. I think she thought if she made me take over for her, I'd find that I liked it enough to stay and run things for her."

"Is it working?"

"I don't hate it," Ford admitted, "but I never thought about the *Gazette* as my life's work."

"Why not?"

He shrugged. "It just wasn't something I was interested in. I was always more the outdoor type. Spent most of my spare time on the water. Still do."

The waiter brought their entrées—a duet of pan-seared scallops in an orange glaze and grilled tuna—and served the wine Carly selected and the beer Ford ordered to go with their meals.

"My brother-in-law brewed the beer," he explained. "Drinking wine makes me feel like a traitor."

"I won't tell Clay," Carly promised. She tasted the scallops and sighed. "Perfect. It's no wonder Lola's is reputed to be the best in the area."

"Lola herself—the first Lola—was quite a girl, if I remember correctly. She's gotta be well into her nineties now, and if all the stories about her that I heard when I was growing up are true, she must have had some life."

"She's still alive?"

Ford nodded. "She stopped at the inn yesterday to see how Mom's doing."

"Seems like a shame for you to be wasting your interview time on me," Carly said. "I would think Lola would make a much more interesting subject. It sounds like she'd have plenty to talk about."

The hand holding his fork paused midway between his plate and his mouth. "I hadn't thought about it, but you're right. She's very outspoken—some might say blunt—and very opinionated. I don't know that I could do her justice, though."

"I don't know why you'd say that. The two pieces you've done so far have been really good." She cut a scallop in half and added, "I think you sell yourself short. You're a good writer." Carly was beginning to suspect that Ford liked being a journalist more than he wanted to admit.

"Speaking of writing, how are your projects coming along?"

"Great. I'm actually further ahead than I'd realized. Once I started putting my notes together, I realized I have the bones of the catalog already written. All that's left to do is match up the paintings with Carolina's comments. I should be finished by Monday."

"And once you finish it, then what?"

"Then I send it off to the graphic designer I found to format it and turn it into a printed catalog."

"So do you make a cover . . . ?"

"I photographed one of Carolina's paintings for the cover. It's so perfect. I'm using the same one for the cover of the catalog, the book, and for the invitations to the opening that I'm sending out."

She put down her fork and opened her bag, took out her phone, and scrolled until she found what she was looking for. She passed the phone to Ford, saying, "This is the painting. Carolina called it *Stolen Moments*. It might be the most romantic thing I've ever seen."

He took the phone and turned it to the light.

"It looks like two people on a picnic, but I can't see it well enough to get a feel for it." He handed back the phone.

"It is a little dark in here, and the image is small," she conceded. "I'll show you the real thing when we get home. Well, not the real thing, but a larger copy of it."

"Where are they now?" he asked. "The paintings."

"In Ellie's attic."

He put his fork down and leaned across the table slightly.

"You are concerned about having a high-tech, state-of-the-art security system at the carriage house to protect paintings that are currently sitting in Ellie's *attic*?"

"That's where we found them. Those paintings have

been there for most of the last century," she explained. "No one knew they were there then, and no one knows they're there now. Once we move them into the carriage house, everyone will know where they are. That's when the security will matter."

"You don't think you're taking a chance . . ."

She shook her head. "None."

"I hope you're right."

"I think next week might be time to drop the C-bomb." Carly had finished her meal, and took the last sip of her wine.

"The C-bomb?"

She laughed. "The Carolina bomb. The announcement that we have Carolina's lost works and that they will be on display for the first time ever at the carriage house at the end of August."

"You sure you want to do that before Tony gets the security system up and running?"

"He said he only needed a few days, right? By the time the article runs next week, he'll have the installation completed."

"True. I'll just have to stay on him to make sure he keeps his word."

"Thank you again for arranging that. Once the exhibit is in place, it has to be secure."

The waiter came by to ask about dessert, which neither Carly nor Ford wanted, so Ford took the check, paid it, and stood to take Carly's hand.

They took their time walking back to the car. The sun had set over the Bay, the last pale touch of light a mere sliver of coral on the horizon, and the moon was beginning to rise in the sky. The night was warm, but not humid or cloying, and there was the faintest bit of breeze off the water.

"It's such a beautiful night. Look how pretty the light is on the water. Could we walk down to the Bay?" Carly asked.

"Sure." He pointed toward the marina. "When I was a kid, there weren't as many boats docked here, and those that were, mostly belonged to the watermen from town. There were hardly any tourists back then. Oh, we had some summer people, but not like now. Everything changed so much in the years I was gone."

"I didn't know the town then, but I really like what I see now. There's a different vibe here than there is in any other place I've been. I can't put my finger on it, but I always feel welcome here. Besides, I really like the little house I'm renting."

They stopped near a lamppost and watched a whaler back into the dock. Ford stood behind Carly, his arms around her, and she leaned back into him. She tried to remember if she'd ever felt so right about being with anyone before. Todd? She almost laughed at the comparison.

"Want to come back to the house for coffee?" she asked.

"Sure." He turned her around and lifted her chin with his hand, then kissed her. If she'd thought the first kiss had been a winner, this one was a gold medal. She was crushed against his chest and had to stand on tiptoe, even in those high heels, but she hardly noticed. Kissing Ford took her breath away, and everything about him—his lips, his tongue, that tiny bit of five o'clock shadow that grazed her skin—sent her senses reeling.

When he relaxed his hold on her and her feet hit the ground again, she made an attempt to speak, then thought better of it. All she could think of to say was "Um . . ."

"So we'll head back to your place, and you can show me your progress on the catalog." He took her hand as if he hadn't just totally tuned her up and they walked to the car.

The drive back to Carly's house took less than five minutes. At her suggestion, Ford parked in the driveway, and they walked hand in hand to the side door. She unlocked it and they went through the small back hall into the kitchen. Carly dropped her bag and keys onto the table.

"Coffee?" she asked because she knew she had to say something.

"Let's break out that bottle of wine I left here the other night. Unless, of course, you went on a binge and polished it off yourself."

"Who has time for a binge?" She got the wine from the cupboard and handed it to Ford to open while she looked for glasses.

"Corkscrew?" he asked.

"Oh. The first drawer next to the sink." She looked over the glassware in the cupboard. "I didn't order wineglasses, so I guess we'll have to go with these." She took down two fat pale green glasses and placed them on the table.

"They'll do just fine." He pulled out the cork, then poured wine into each glass. When he finished, he tucked the cork back into the mouth of the bottle and handed her a glass. "Here's to your book and your gallery and your exhibit, and to the success of all your projects."

"And to the *St. Dennis Gazette* and your budding journalism career." She tilted her glass to touch the rim of his. "And if that doesn't work for you, then we'll drink to your heart's desire."

He smiled, his eyes locked on hers, then raised the glass and took a sip, and she did the same.

"So you were going to show me the picture that you're using for the cover of the book and the catalog," he said, his eyes still on hers.

"Yes, I was. I mean, I am." She put her glass on the table and gestured for him to follow her. "It's in the dining room. That's this way." She was sounding uncharacteristically like an idiot, which she attributed to Ford's proximity more than to the wine.

"Mind if I take off my jacket?"

"Of course not." She held out her hand and took his jacket when he removed it. The scent of his aftershave clung to it, and she held it against her body as they walked into the dining room.

"I'm afraid I don't have any hangers in the closet out here," she said as she draped the sport jacket over the back of a chair. The scent was still with her, and she cleared her throat. "The photo I took of the painting is here . . . somewhere . . ."

She searched the table for the right pile.

"Oh, here." She held it out to him, but instead of taking it from her hand, he moved next to her so that he was looking over her shoulder. His breath was warm against her cheek and it was all she could do not to take his face in her hands and kiss that mouth.

"Where did you say this was painted?" He took the photo and turned it to the light.

"I don't know where. I'm assuming it's someplace around St. Dennis. At least, I think it's a real place, and I think it's a real scene. I think that's Carolina in the painting. Doesn't she look like the photograph of Carolina that we saw in Blossoms?" She pointed first to the woman on the sand, then to the man seated next to her. "And this man—he's the same man who was in the photo. My gut tells me that she painted this from memory, a very special memory." Carly sighed. "*Stolen Moments*. It's very romantic, don't you think? It makes me wonder who the man was, and where they were."

"I don't know who, but I think I know where."

"What?"

"It's Sunset Beach. It looks different now, after all these years, but I'm pretty sure that's where this scene took place."

"How can you tell?" She frowned.

"Those trees in the background—they're loblolly pines. The only beach in St. Dennis where those trees grow is Sunset Beach."

"It's real, then." She stared at the photo. "It's just as I thought. Carolina and her mystery man stealing away on a summer day . . ."

Ford laughed and put the photo on the table. "I can see I'm going to have to take you on that kayak trip sooner rather than later. You can only get there by water."

He encircled her in his arms and she reached up to take his face in her hands. His lips brushed against hers, just the slightest whisper of a touch, and for the first time in her life, Carly understood what people meant when they said that *time stopped*. There was nothing in her world but Ford, and that delicious mouth, and the arms that pressed her to him. The sheer awareness of him spread through her, head to toe, and she felt her breathing go shallow and her heart pound. When his lips traced a trail from her mouth to her cheek, from her cheek to her neck, she thought either her head would explode or she'd faint, she wasn't sure which, and for the longest moment, she didn't care.

When his mouth made its way back to hers, she wrapped her arms around his neck and backed up against the table. His hands skimmed her back, then her hips, before settling momentarily on her waist. His body was hard against hers, pinning her against the table and his tongue teased the corners of her mouth until she felt dangerously close to losing control.

His hands grew still on her hips, and his mouth broke free from hers.

"Wow," he whispered. "For someone so small, you pack an enormous punch."

She held him to her for a moment longer, then felt him disengage slowly.

"I think maybe I should be going," he said, leaving unspoken the implied *before things go too much further*.

Carly nodded. She wasn't really sure where she wanted this relationship to go, and apparently Ford wasn't either. Slow seemed the way to go right about now.

"So when do I get my Turkish dinner?" he asked, that five o'clock shadow just a tickle on the side of her face.

"What's your schedule this week?"

"My schedule is more flexible than yours." He leaned forward to touch his forehead to hers and rested it there for a moment. "What do you have lined up?"

"A bunch of residents who want to show me their paintings. You?"

"I have a couple of interviews."

"I can make dinner and you can interview me while we eat," she suggested.

"I like it. That works. How 'bout Wednesday?"

"Wednesday works for me, too. I should have the invitations to the exhibit sketched out by then."

"It's a date."

His arms were slow to let her go. Carly walked with him to the door, her emotions conflicted, not wanting him to leave, but not yet ready for him to stay.

She stepped out onto the side porch and inhaled deeply. Flowers from the neighbor's yard perfumed the air, and the night sky was clear as could be. Ford went down the two steps to the ground, then came back up to kiss her good night.

"Talk to you soon."

She nodded, her arms folded across her chest, and watched him get into the car. He waved as he backed out of the driveway, and she raised a hand to wave back, though she knew he wouldn't see her from the road. She went inside and changed out of her killer dress into shorts and a T-shirt, and unstrapped her killer shoes.

She took her glass outside onto the little patio. She sat on one of the folding chairs she'd borrowed from Ellie and set the glass on the small table—also Ellie's—and leaned back to watch the stars and thought about how life sometimes throws you curves when you least expect them. She'd come to St. Dennis to set up an art gallery and show off some paintings she believed should be seen. Romance was the last thing on her mind, and yet, there he was, and he seemed so *right*.

So right, actually, that she wasn't sure if she should be running to him, or away from him.

Chapter 19 ~

"DID you have a nice dinner, dear?" Grace asked Ford when he brought her the Sunday newspapers: the *Baltimore Sun*, the *Capital Gazette*, and last week's *Bay Times*, without which Grace swore she could not begin her day.

She patted the table next to her, indicating he should place them there. "How did Carly like Lola's?"

"She liked it just fine." He stared at his mother suspiciously.

"Your father and I went there frequently when we were courting. Of course, Lola herself was just a sassy young thing then." Grace glanced up at Ford and smiled. "She's still pretty sassy. Talking about running off with one of the busboys." She laughed and shook her head.

"How did you know . . . ?"

"That you and Carly had dinner there last night?" She peered at him over the rim of her glasses. "This is St. Dennis, Ford. Everyone knows you, and thanks to your articles, everyone knows Carly. Barbara from the bookstore stopped in this morning and brought me one of the new bestsellers. She and her niece just happened to be dining there last night as well. She said Carly looked stunning." She looked up at Ford expectantly.

"She looked pretty good."

Grace smiled that infuriatingly knowing smile, and he knew she could see right through him. Well, he'd make her work for it.

"How is the carriage house coming along, did she say?"

"She did." He took a seat on a rectangular ottoman that stood near her feet.

"Well?"

"Well what?"

"How is the place progressing? What's been done? What still has to be done?" She swatted at him and he laughed.

For the next fifteen minutes, he fielded her questions and brought her up-to-date. There was no such thing as an abbreviated version where Grace was concerned.

"Well, then, it sounds as if she'll be ready to open on time. That's good. I knew she could pull it off."

"She's got a lot on her plate right now, but she's determined."

"I do hope you'll offer to help her where she needs a hand, Ford."

"Sure." He nodded. "Well, enjoy your reading. Do you need anything else right now?"

"No, dear. Dan's had the staff waiting on me hand and foot." She smiled. "It's nice for a change, but I wouldn't want to get used to it. I'd rather do for my-self."

He kissed the top of her head and started for the door. He stopped halfway and, snapping his fingers, turned back. "I almost forgot. What would you think of an article about Lola? She is, as you've said, quite the character, and just about everyone who spends any amount of time in St. Dennis ends up at her restaurant."

"Why, that's a fine idea. I don't know why I never thought of it."

"Actually, it was Carly's idea, but I thought—"

"Clever girl. And wouldn't it be nice to follow up with an article about Captain Walt and Rexana. Yes, I could see a whole series of articles about the faces behind the restaurants." Grace tapped her fingers on the arms of her wheelchair. "Excellent idea, Ford. Give Lola a call this afternoon and see what you can set up before she takes off on her next jaunt. She made some mention of seeing the south of France . . ."

"Well, I didn't mean for me to do it." He stood in the doorway, his hands on his hips. "I wasn't volunteering."

"Who were you thinking of?"

"Well, I thought you could do it once you got back on your feet."

"Who knows how long that will be? So no, I cannot. But since I am still editor in chief, I give out the assignments. So I'm tossing this one back at you."

"Wait a minute, I thought the deal was that I was standing in for you on the Carly articles . . ."

She gave him The Look, the one that had turned each of her children to stone on many an occasion while they were growing up.

"All right." He knew when he was defeated. "I'll see if I can fit it in."

"Thank you. Oh, and leave the door open just a

crack, would you? Housekeeping should be on their way up sometime soon . . ."

Ford did as she requested, leaving the door to the family quarters slightly open, then went back to his room for his running shoes. He was getting soft sitting around, with no exercise other than paddling the kayak every couple of days, and he needed to move. He tied on the shoes and went down the back steps to the door used by staff to come and go through the kitchen, then started out on his run.

St. Dennis was a quiet town most mornings, but Sunday mornings were pretty much dead, even in the summer. The churches were full, and the restaurants that served breakfast or brunch were gearing up for the crowds that would show up later in the morning. It was the perfect time for a run, not too hot yet, the breeze was just right, and he didn't have to share the roadway with many others.

He started out on Charles Street, but without planning to, he found himself making the right onto Cherry and running the one block to Hudson. His feet slowed as he passed Carly's house, but the shades were still drawn on the side of the house that took the early-morning sun. At some point, he'd have to pick up that jacket he'd left in her dining room last night, but it wouldn't be now.

Was she sleeping in, he wondered, or had she gotten up early to work?

Had she lain awake last night as long as he had, wondering where, if anyplace, they were headed? Had she wished he'd stayed?

There was no question of where they could have ended up if he hadn't put the lid on it, a move that had come at considerable personal sacrifice. There'd been nothing he wanted more than to take her to bed. There was no denying that she brought him to the boiling point, but at the same time, he had to recognize certain basic facts. Carly was a forever woman, if, of course, you were looking for such a woman, which he was not.

The problem wasn't that she could take him from zero to sixty faster than just about any woman he'd ever met. The problem was that the more time he spent with her, the more he really liked her. What would he do with a woman like that at this point in his life, when he didn't know where he was headed or what his next move would be? It disturbed him that he'd passed his thirtieth birthday without having a clue about who or what he wanted to be for the rest of his life. He'd been a soldier for so long—a highly specialized one, to be sure, but a soldier all the same. The skills he'd been taught, the areas in which he excelled, were hardly translatable to the real world in which his family lived, in which Carly lived.

He supposed he could go into law enforcement like some of his friends had done. He'd heard that Beck was looking to add to the police force, but that didn't seem like a good fit to him. Dan would jump at the chance to bring him on board at the inn, but he'd already thought that through and dismissed it. He had no desire to run the inn, especially since Dan was so good at it, and Ford didn't have a clue. It was good that someone in the family shared their father's love for the old place, though. He appreciated the sense of history there, felt the presence of his ancestors in every one of the rooms. There was something about being part of an unbroken chain that went back so many generations in this town that made you feel grounded, whether or not you wanted to be. In the past, he hadn't felt the pull quite as much as he did this time around. Of course, he hadn't been home in a long time, and maybe being a little older he might be more aware of such things.

His feet took him all the way to the end of Hudson, where it dead-ended on Old St. Mary's Church Road. The carriage house on the Enright property was closed and still, the workmen—and Carly—gone for the weekend, the driveway empty of the cars and pickups that filled it every weekday. He jogged past the house, the mansion that old Curtis had signed over to the town, and kept going until he reached the town square. He stopped for a moment, recalling holidays that had been celebrated there: First Families' Day, Memorial Day, Veterans Day. Halloween parades that had wound through the center of town and ended right here, where prizes for best costume had been given out and photos taken of the winners for the front page of the *St. Dennis Gazette*. He recalled one year when his mother had dressed the three of them as cowboys in matching outfits, and how Lucy had squawked at having to wear chaps like her brothers and a hat that made her hair go flat on top.

Their grandfather had been alive then, and had taken their picture in front of an old live oak that stood behind the library. Ford walked around the building to see if the tree was still there, and found himself surprisingly disappointed when he realized it had been taken down. He wondered what had happened to that photo.

He resumed jogging, and went straight back onto Charles Street and turned right. He ran past houses he'd known well when he was a child, houses where friends had lived, and he wondered what had happened to them all, where they were now. His best buddy through eighth grade, John-Luc, had lived in the gray clapboard house on the corner—it had been white back then—and Amy Weathers, the class brain, had lived next door. The last time Ford came home, his mother mentioned pointedly and on several occasions that Amy and John-Luc had married, had two children, and were living happily over on Fifth Street in the house they bought from the estate of Mr. Davis, who at one time or another had taught piano to just about every kid in St. Dennis.

There was that chain again. So many people who lived in St. Dennis had families that went back several generations, so your parents knew theirs. Their grandparents had danced at your grandparents' wedding. Their family albums held photos of some of the people you were descended from, and yours held theirs. It wasn't something he thought about while he was away, but now that he was here, steeped in it all, he realized he was finding comfort in his own history, and that of his family.

Farther out on Charles Street, the shoulder became more narrow, and the houses farther and farther apart. Up around the big bend was the Madison farm, where Lucy lived with her husband, where they'd raised their family. He felt a stab of something that took him a moment to recognize as envy, which made no sense to him at all.

He crossed the road and took a left onto River Road and ran past Blossoms, where he'd had lunch with Carly, and past the old warehouses that Dallas MacGregor had bought and turned into a film studio. Well below the studio, the lanes narrowed again and the properties were larger and more stately. He ran past several large Victorian homes, the largest of which belonged to Dallas's great-aunt Berry Eberle, known on the silver screen as Beryl Townsend, who was as colorful a character as any she'd played in films. Still he ran, back toward the center of town, past St. Mark's Episcopal Church and the First Baptist of St. Dennis, where cars overflowed the parking lots on this Sunday morning. His route took him past the cafés and the shops, past the building that had once belonged to his grandfather, the building that housed the *Gazette*. There was a light burning on the second floor, and Ford paused before crossing the street. The first-floor door on the side of the building was open, so he trotted up the steps, wondering who had forgotten to turn off the lights and lock the door.

"Hello?" he called from the top of the steps.

There was a shuffling noise coming from the hall, and he rounded the corner to find Ray Shelton, the production manager, coming out of his office.

"Oh, Ford." The older man smiled with relief. "I couldn't imagine who . . . and then I realized I'd left the door . . . but come in, come in." He gestured for Ford to follow him. "Have a seat there. Just put those things on the floor . . ."

Ford leaned against the doorjamb. "I don't mean to interrupt anything you're doing, Ray. I just saw a light on and wasn't sure if it had been left on by mistake, so I thought I'd check."

"I come in most Sundays." Ray lowered himself into

his worn leather chair. "Oh, heck, I come in every morning. Gives me something to do. I hate to admit that I'm slowing down, but I am. Now it takes me seven days to do what used to take me four. Not complaining, mind you. I understand the alternative to getting old." He grinned. "How's your mother doing this week? She driving everyone at the inn crazy?"

"I don't know about everyone else, but she'd doing a number on me."

Ray laughed. "She's something else, that Gracie. I know how happy she is that you came home to take over for her. I have to admit, I was worried."

"Oh, I'm not taking—"

"You know, this paper's been around for somethin' like a hundred and fifty years, give or take. Yes, sir, it's the voice of St. Dennis. People depend on it for their hard news and their gossip. Folks need both, you know. You can see the history of the entire town played out, right there on the wall of the old conference room. If it happened and was worth talking about, there was a photo on the front page of the *Gazette*. Don't know what we'd have done if you hadn't stepped in to take 'er over, Ford." Ray leaned back in his chair. "Maybe one of these days I'll have time to show you what we do here in production. I won't be around forever, you know."

"I thought you had an assistant."

"I did. He went back to college in the spring, decided he'd rather be an engineer. Heard there was more money in it. Not too many people get rich putting out a weekly newspaper."

"Maybe you should run an ad, see if you can find someone to give you a hand." Ford tried to calculate how old Ray must be by now, surely well past retirement age. He had to be almost as old as Grace.

The thought gave him a start. It was still hard to acknowledge that she was aging.

"I'll run it past your mother when I get a chance, see if she's all right with bringing in someone."

Ford made a mental note to mention it when he got back to the inn.

"In the meantime, I have some ads to get ready." Ray stood.

"Right. Well, I guess I'll see you later in the week. I'll have another article for you."

"Good, good. You're doing a fine job with those. I know how proud Gracie is. I have to say, I'm looking forward to St. Dennis having a real art center. Yessir, it's going to be good for the town to have a fine art gallery. There was some talk a few years ago about someone opening one up the street here, but then Clay Madison's mother bought the storefront and opened that shop that sold sweaters for dogs . . ." Ray's voice trailed down the hall.

Ford was almost to the bottom of the steps when he remembered what Ray said about the walls of the old conference room displaying the history of the town. He went back up the steps and walked straight to the front room and opened the door. The air was musty and the layer of dust on the top of the table was clear evidence that it had been a long time since any sort of conference had been held there.

There on the four walls, in dusty frames, hung the front pages of editions long past. There were pages that spoke of national history—from the *Hindenburg* disaster to Pearl Harbor to the assassination of John

Kennedy and the horror of the World Trade Center on 9/11, and natural disasters like Katrina and Sandy—as well as stories that were big local news. There were photos of winners of the Fourth of July sailboat races and of local pageants, and of returning servicemen from World War II. He smiled at the pictures of Brooke in her beauty queen days (LOCAL BEAUTY CROWNED MISS EASTERN SHORE!) and Dallas MacGregor winning her first Academy Award. Ah, and there were the three amigos in their cowboy clothes, he and Dan grinning like fools while a scowling Lucy sat on the ground in front of them, her hat pulled down over her eyes.

He'd gone halfway around the room when he came to a photo of a once-familiar face. He leaned closer to read the caption: *Future editor in chief? William T. Ellison, the current editor in chief and owner of the* St. Dennis Gazette, *shows off his newest grandson, Ford Winston Sinclair, the third child of Mr. and Mrs. Daniel Sinclair. "You mark my words, he's going to follow in my footsteps someday," Mr. Ellison predicted.*

Ford felt as if the wind had been knocked out of him. He remembered his grandfather with great affection, recalled sitting on his lap in this very room while grown-up talk about the newspaper swirled about him like the smoke from his grandfather's cigar.

"I get it, Gramps," he said aloud.

He did get it. He understood what the paper had meant to his grandfather, and what it meant to Grace. She hadn't been the one her father had expected to pass the paper on to, but she took on the job and kept the family legacy alive when neither of her brothers would. He understood what the *Gazette* represented to the community, but more, what it meant to his family. It was as much a part of them as the Inn at Sinclair Point. He felt its pull as much as he'd fought against it.

He closed the door softly and went down the steps and out onto the street.

Don't know what we'd have done if you hadn't stepped in to take 'er over . . .

No pressure there, he thought, and with a sinking heart, he jogged back to the inn, wondering if he was capable of carrying on that legacy—if he could live up to the standard set by old William T—even if he wanted to.

There was, he supposed, only one way to find out. Whether or not he was ready to take that step remained to be seen.

Chapter 20 ⟅

CARLY awoke on the living room sofa, a light throw over her legs and a crick in her neck. She sat and stretched, yawned, stood, then stretched again. She found her phone and checked the time: 7:39. A trip into the bathroom was followed by a trip into the kitchen, where she made coffee on her newly purchased one-cup-at-a-time machine. She stepped outside onto the patio and found the morning cooler and less humid than she'd expected. The neighborhood was quiet at this hour, the only sound she heard was the pounding of feet as a jogger passed by out front.

She went back inside and fixed her coffee, then into the dining room, where she'd left her work from the night before spread out around the table. After Ford left, she'd tried to focus on the catalog, but finally gave up. He was too much in her head. More troubling, he was inching his way into her heart, and that, she told herself, was a no-no. She'd learned a long time ago to stay away from men who didn't know who they were. And if ever a man needed to have a stern talk with himself to figure it out, it was Ford

Sinclair. As far as she could see, he was suffering from a major case of denial.

He could protest all he wanted, but it was pretty clear to Carly that he was adapting to his reporter gig much better than he admitted. He seemed more comfortable with each of their meetings, not only with her, but with his role. Maybe he'd never accept that the *St. Dennis Gazette* was a good fit for him, which would be a shame, because he sure didn't seem comfortable with the role he'd been playing these past few years, but it wasn't her place to point that out to him since their relationship was so vague and undefined.

Not that she wanted to put a label on it, of course, she reminded herself quickly. And yet last night . . . last night . . .

She sighed and took a sip of coffee, which had grown cold while she played back most of the evening in her mind. The glint of approval in his eyes when she opened the door. The sweet way he'd held her hand while they walked to Lola's. The look on his face when they talked over dinner, as if he listened to every word and cared about what she was saying.

That interest in her—that ability he had to make her feel like what she had to say mattered—was something she'd been missing in her last two relationships. She'd always made a point to care about what other people said and felt and wanted—but she'd rarely found the favor returned when it came time to talk about her goals, her galleries, her wants. Especially with Todd. Todd, who became so enamored of his own success that after a while, he couldn't talk about anything else. She'd actually been relieved when he told her he'd found someone else. Two years of her life down the tubes with that one, and she'd been glad to wave good-bye.

Well, that's how it went with relationships sometimes, she thought. You pay your money and you take your chances, as her grandmother used to say. There just weren't any guarantees. Carly knew that, but why was it so hard to find the right one? And why had the one who *seemed* like the one turned out to be a dud, and why did you have to invest two years of your life before you realized that he *wasn't* the one after all?

She was still pondering these weighty matters when Ellie called.

"What are you doing?" Ellie asked.

"Staring at the mess on my dining room table and wondering why it's so hard for me to toss out all my notes."

"How 'bout we get together for pancakes?"

"What, you're making pancakes? Seriously? You're going to cook?"

"Well, no. Actually, Gabi and I were hoping you were. Cam's sailing this morning, so we thought it was a good time for a girls' breakfast."

Carly laughed. "Sure. Come on over and we'll christen my frying pan. Bring eggs. Oh, and maple syrup."

"You got it. See you in fifteen."

So, there goes the morning, Carly mused, and headed toward the bedroom to change, then back into the kitchen, where she made a second cup of coffee and began to get out the ingredients she needed for pancakes. Despite the fact that her family had always had a cook, she had learned early on that she had a talent for cooking. Ellie—not so much, although her family also had had the luxury of wealth and a professional cook.

"We're here, Carly!" Gabi announced from the side door.

"Come on in." Carly had just finished setting the table for three. "Oh, you brought Dune! Hi, pup!" Carly knelt to pet the little dog, who gleefully danced around her feet.

"We picked up blueberries." Ellie held up a bag. "And syrup."

"Thanks. You can put it all right on the counter." Carly stood.

"Your house is so cute, Carly." Gabi wandered into the living room. "What's upstairs?"

"Two rooms and a bath. You can go look, if you'd like," Carly told her, and the teenager took off up the steps, the dog at her heels.

"I hope you don't mind that we brought Dune," Ellie said. "As soon as she heard your name, she went right to the door, wagging her tail. Gabi swears she understood 'Carly,' 'pancakes,' and 'girls' breakfast,' and she assumed she was included."

"Of course I don't mind. If I could, I'd have a dog."

"Why can't you have a dog, Carly?" Gabi came back down the steps and into the kitchen.

"Because I don't have time to take care of one when I'm home. I travel a lot, I'm gone sometimes days at a time."

"You could leave it with us. We could take care of it when you go away."

"That would be a pain, driving the dog from Connecticut to St. Dennis every time I had a trip," Carly told her.

"Oh. I thought this was your house. That you were living here." Gabi frowned.

"Only till the exhibit is over, honey. Then I'll go back to my old life."

"I like this life better," Gabi said. "I like it when you're here."

"I like being here," Carly admitted.

"I love your little house." Gabi went to the back door. "Oh, your yard is fenced in. Can Dune and I go out and look around?"

"Of course."

Gabi opened the door and Dune shot out. "Hey, wait for me . . ."

"Make sure you clean up after her if she makes a mess," Ellie called to her sister as the girl ran out after the dog.

"Is there something I can do?" Ellie asked.

"No, I'm good, thanks." Carly rinsed the berries and set them aside to drain while she made the batter. "So how's the book?"

"Done and on its way to being formatted. It actually came together quite nicely."

"Why do you sound surprised?"

"Because I've never written a book before."

"You've been writing about art and artists for years, Car."

"But not a book. I wanted to do Carolina justice."

"So do you have a copy of it that I could read?"

"Help yourself. She's your great-great-grandmother. See what you think. It's that stack of papers on the left side of the dining room table."

Ellie left the room and Carly began making pancakes, pouring the batter into the hot pan and watching for just the right moment to flip them over.

Ellie came into the room holding Ford's jacket. "Whose jacket is this?"

Carly turned to look. "Oh. That." She turned back to the frying pan. "That's Ford's."

"Ford was here? Wearing a nice sport jacket?" Ellie grinned. "A nice sport jacket that he apparently then removed?"

"We went to dinner last night."

"Do tell." Ellie leaned against the doorway.

"Not much to tell. We went to Lola's. Have you had their scallops? They're—"

"Yeah, yeah, I've had the scallops. I don't care what you ate. I want to know about your date and why you didn't tell me you were going out with him."

"I meant to as soon as I had an opportunity."

Ellie took her phone from her bag and held it up. "Hello? Phone? Text? Email?"

"Okay, I know. I should have called but I've been so immersed in trying to get the gallery ready to open. We finally got the HVAC straightened out, and the interior drywalled and painted . . ."

Ellie wiggled her left hand so Carly could see the ring on her third finger. "Engaged to the contractor, so you can skip all that. Go straight to the good stuff."

"Oh. The good stuff." Carly nodded. "That was pretty good."

"Hold that thought." Ellie returned the jacket to the dining room and was back in the kitchen in a blink.

"Spill."

Carly leaned against the counter, spatula in hand.

"Best date I've had in . . . damn, I can't remember when. The night was beautiful, the restaurant was beautiful, the food was perfect." She sighed.

"What did you wear?" Ellie leaned forward and rested her arms on the table.

"Only the most perfect dress I ever owned. I got it at Bling on Friday."

"Vanessa has the most uncanny knack for picking out the most fabulous things, but we digress." Ellie gestured for Carly to get on with it.

"So we walked down to the Bay after dinner, and we talked. We talked a lot, did I mention it?"

"No, you did not." Ellie made a face. "I hope that's not the 'good stuff' you were referring to."

Carly laughed. "Well, it was really nice to talk to a guy who listened, who conversed."

"That's important, of course it is, but right now what I'm interested in is what came after all the chatting."

"Best kisser on the planet. Hands down," Carly told her solemnly.

"Do tell."

"I hated to see him leave."

"Wait, he left?"

"Yes. Things were starting to get a little heated, and I guess we both thought it wasn't the right time to let them get out of hand."

"So, will there be a right time?"

"I've been thinking about that. I don't want to get in over my head with him if it's just the grown-up equivalent of a summer fling. But you know, I've had this feeling about him since the first time I met him."

"How do you think he feels about you?"

"I don't think he knows what he wants or where he wants to be." She thought for a moment, then added, "And then there's me. I travel so much. I have businesses everywhere but here, or so it seems. I'm only in St. Dennis temporarily, remember."

"On loan, as it were."

"More or less."

"I think he's sort of temporary, too."

Gabi came through the back door, Dune in hot pursuit. She stared in horror at the stove.

"Are you trying to burn the pancakes?" She pointed to the pan. " 'Cause if you are . . ."

"Oh, crap." Carly turned off the flame. "I forgot." She dumped the burned pancakes into the trash and started over.

"Sorry, sweetie. We started talking and I forgot what I was doing."

"That's okay. Can I watch your TV?" Gabi asked.

"Sure. I'll call you when the pancakes are ready, and this time, I promise to pay attention." Carly made the cross-your-heart sign on her chest.

"Cool." Gabi headed toward the living room. "Maybe I can catch the last few minutes of *Meet the Press*."

"Our budding pundit." Ellie rolled her eyes. "She starts every day with *Morning Joe* and ends it with Jon Stewart."

"She's a smart girl. She likes to be well informed."

Carly added blueberries to the mixture and poured batter into the pan. This time she positioned herself next to the stove.

"Don't distract me," she warned Ellie. "I don't have any more milk."

"I will say nothing more than this: If you really like

him, and it appears to me that you do, and you feel that he cares about you just as much, you need to decide whether or not to go for it." When it appeared Carly was about to reply, Ellie held up a hand to stop her. "You're overthinking things. You need to stop it and go with your gut."

"What if my gut is wrong?"

"What's the worst that can happen?"

When Carly didn't respond, Ellie said, "Everything else—where you live, where he lives—all that stuff can be worked out. That can all change. But how you feel inside—that's not going to change no matter where you are. So." Ellie smiled brightly. "Do we get to eat now?"

Chapter 21 ✎

Fɪʀsᴛ thing on Monday morning, Carly checked in with her galleries. Enrico was all abuzz because there were not one, not two, but three buyers interested in the Lewis Mitchells, but other than that, things were relatively quiet, because "you know that everyone leaves New York on Thursday night in the summer."

She called Helena at Summit/Boston and found that the showing of Mindy Mason's pottery they'd planned for November was finally contracted—signed, sealed, and delivered. Helena also was in discussions to exhibit some new artists she'd met at a street fair in South Boston and thought they might plan a sort of indoor street fair over the winter to showcase the best of them. Colby in Chicago had nothing on the calendar that she didn't already know about, but he reiterated his offer to buy her out. This time, instead of flat-out rejecting him, she surprised even herself by telling him she'd think about it.

And she would. As soon as she had time to devote some serious attention to what she could live without, and what she couldn't. If she wanted to explore in-depth her interest in discovering and promoting women artists, she needed to face the fact that something had to give. She couldn't possibly devote the amount of time and attention necessary to do justice to everything. She'd already pretty much decided to sell her holdings in the London gallery to Isabella, and that would free up some time. The others—well, she would have to make some choices. She knew she couldn't give up New York—though she could give more responsibility to Enrico, who'd proven himself over and over to be totally reliable and worthy of a big promotion. Chicago . . . maybe she could come to terms with Colby, and Boston . . . she'd have to think about that.

The next and last call was to Elvan Kazma in Istanbul.

Elvan brought Carly up-to-date on the most recent sales and acquisitions—and of course, the latest gossip—and promised to email copies of the previous months' ledgers. Their business concluded, Carly had one more thing on her mind.

"Elvan, that recipe you have for *manti* . . . do you think you could share that with me?" Carly asked.

"Since when do you have a taste for lamb?"

"I don't, but someone I know . . . well, he likes Turkish lamb dishes and that's the only one I can think of that you don't put on kebabs and grill," she explained. "I don't have a grill here, so I thought maybe—"

"Oh, a man, eh?" Elvan laughed again. "I'll send you a recipe that will have him on his knees." She paused. "You can get fresh mint, yes?"

"I'm sure I can. It's summer here, and there are lots of farms."

"Watch your email. I'll send you the recipe for the *patlican salatasi*—you need very fresh eggplant for that—and my mother's recipe for *lor tatlisi*. It's better than a love potion, never fails. Just make sure you buy the best ricotta cheese you can find." She chuckled. "And promise to save a seat for me at the wedding."

"I think you're getting a little ahead of yourself."

When the recipes arrived, Carly made a shopping list. She wasn't so sure the little lamb raviolis would send Ford to his knees, but it was a fun thought. She checked the Internet hoping to find a Middle Eastern grocery, but no such luck. She was going to have to make do with what she could find at the supermarket and the farmers' markets in and around town. If nothing else, preparing all those tiny dumplings for the *manti* would take her mind off the stress of trying to get the carriage house ready for the opening.

At least the design for the invitations was ready, and with Ellie's approval, she'd photographed *Stolen Moments* to use as the logo for the event. The image on her camera phone wasn't sharp enough, so she borrowed Ellie's good camera and got a great shot. Hopefully, at some point over the next week—when she wasn't cooking—she'd complete the photographic inventory of the paintings.

"Stress? What stress?" she mused as she drove to the market, list in hand. Cooking always did have a calming effect on her, and if nothing else, this dinner would be an adventure.

*   *   *

Ford arrived at Carly's house promptly at six thirty on Wednesday. Instead of wine, he carried a six-pack of MadMac's latest beer—Summer Breeze—and a big bouquet of blue hydrangeas.

"I wasn't sure what you liked," he told her. "But the woman at the flower shop said everyone likes these."

"I do like them. Actually, they're one of my favorites. Bring them on out to the kitchen." She pulled his arm gently to bring him closer, and kissed the side of his mouth. "Thank you."

She searched the cupboards for something that would make a suitable vase, and finally opted for the soup tureen. She hadn't thought to buy a vase when she ordered all of her kitchen goodies online. It had been so long since anyone had brought her flowers, and it was something she rarely thought of doing for herself.

"It smells great in here. Can I help?"

"You can open a beer for me." She slipped an apron over her head. She'd debated for far too long on her clothes for the occasion, and the last thing she wanted was tomato stains or olive-oil splashes on her shirt or her skirt. She'd hesitated on the skirt—she'd had no time to spend on a beach or near a pool this summer, and her legs were pasty white—but in the end, she went for comfort. Pants would have been too hot, shorts too casual. The skirt seemed like a good compromise and, paired with a short-sleeved, button-down shirt, seemed just right.

"Glasses?" he asked.

"Second cabinet on the left." She grabbed a pair of kitchen shears from a drawer and cut the flower stems so they'd fit better in the tureen.

"There. Beautiful." She placed them in the center of the kitchen table. "They make me think of summer days when I was a kid. My mom always had white hydrangeas growing along the side of the garage, and at night, we'd chase fireflies across the lawn and the hydrangeas would stand out in the moonlight."

Ford handed her the glass of beer. "Sure I can't do anything?"

"You can sit right there and keep me company while I cook. If I need an extra pair of hands, I'll let you know."

She placed the plate of *muhammara* on the table next to the flowers, the red of the peppers in bright contrast to the white plate.

"Wow. Look at that." He raised an eyebrow.

"Pita for the dip." She set a small basket of toasted pita wedges, two small plates, and a pile of paper napkins on the table. "Help yourself."

"That's incredible," he said after he'd dipped pita into the dip. "It tastes just like the *muhammara* the last time I was in Turkey. You can taste the walnuts and the . . . what's that spice?"

"Cumin."

"It's delicious," he said as he went back for more.

She checked the flame under the large pot of water that was just starting to bubble. If she kept to her timetable—provided by Elvan—everything should make it to the table at precisely the same time.

"May I ask what you're making? Other than this dip, and something with lamb, of course . . ." He spooned some more dip onto one of the small plates and added a few more pitas.

"Smarty. I *am* making lamb. I'm making *manti*."

She served herself some of the spicy dip. It was excellent, she had to admit. Hopefully everything else would be as good.

"Where'd you find them around here?"

"I said I was *making* them." She couldn't help but add smugly, "From scratch."

"Seriously? All those little-bitty dumplings . . ." His jaw almost hit the table.

"Made them this morning. They just have to be cooked." She turned back to the counter so that he wouldn't see the grin on her face.

"It must have taken you hours."

"All day."

"I am impressed almost beyond words."

"Oh, be impressed. I also made a chickpea salad and *lor tatlisi* for dessert. The only thing I didn't make from scratch is the pita." She turned to him and grinned. "You wanted Turkish, you're getting Turkish."

"When the woman said she could cook, she wasn't kidding." He dipped another pita, ate it, then took another sip of beer. "Did I mention that this was delicious?"

"You did. So now you know how I spent my day. Tell me how you spent yours."

"I made the mistake of telling my mother your suggestion that I interview Lola. She liked the idea so much she started thinking that I should not only interview Lola, but I should plan on an entire series of interviews of some of the other local characters."

"Such as . . . ?" She helped herself to another bit of dip. Yum.

"Such as Captain Walt, and his wife, the lovely Rexana."

"Did I hear right, that she's a former showgirl?" Carly looked over her shoulder at Ford.

He nodded. "The story I heard my dad tell once, old Walt went to California to visit his brother. On the way back, he stopped in Vegas, met Rexana, and that was that. They got married in one of those chapels out there two days after they met and he brought her back to St. Dennis."

"I wonder if it was an Elvis chapel," she mused. "Anyway, so you're going to interview them for the paper. Cute idea. Their restaurant is very popular, so I'm sure the summer people will love to read about them."

"I'll get to them after I talk to Lola. Seems she's headed out on vacation next weekend, so I had to schedule to meet with her tomorrow afternoon."

"That's one interview I will not want to miss."

"At the rate my mother's going, I may never get out of St. Dennis. Not, at least, until she can use her hand again and get around. She's started some modified physical therapy already, though, so there's hope."

"Would that be so bad, if you had to hang around for a while longer?"

"It hasn't been bad so far," he admitted. "I've kind of enjoyed getting reacquainted with my hometown again. Seeing people I used to know, going places I used to go . . ." He sighed. "No, it probably wouldn't be so bad."

He looked surprised to have said it aloud, so Carly let it pass without comment.

A few seconds later, he slapped his hands on his thighs. "I can't sit here like a lump. Give me something to do."

"All right. You can get the salads out of the fridge—

they're already plated—and you can set the table."
She showed him where everything was located. "I'd
have rather eaten in the dining room, but I still have
the notes from the book and the catalog scattered
about in piles. It's like a postpartum reaction. I'm just
not ready to file it all away yet."

"This is fine," he said as he put plates and flatware
on the table. "I like this room. I like the view out the
back there."

"I like it here, too, now that the air conditioner is
working."

She finished preparing the yogurt dressing for the
manti and set it aside, then removed the tray of tiny
dumplings from the fridge and set it on the counter.

"I can't believe you made all those." He shook his
head. "How did you know how?"

"A friend sent me her recipes. Actually, she sent all
of the recipes for everything we're having, so if you
approve, you can send Elvan a thank-you email in the
morning."

The water for the *manti* was starting to boil, so
Carly placed each one of the dumplings carefully into
the pot. Ford had finished setting the table and had
put the salads on top of the dinner plates.

"I think we can go ahead and start on those while
the dumplings cook," Carly said.

They sat across from each other and attacked the
salads: chickpeas, grape tomatoes, thinly sliced red
onion, black olives, feta cheese, tossed in a dressing of
olive oil and lemon juice and spices.

"This is so good," he remarked. "If I close my eyes,
I could imagine we're at one of those rooftop restaurants in Istanbul, overlooking the Bosporus."

"I've been to one where you can see the Hagia Sophia in the distance." She smiled, remembering the last time she was in that city, when Elvan and her relatives had taken her to dinner.

He was even more amazed when she served the *manti*.

"Oh my God, are you kidding?" he exclaimed after he tasted the dish, which she'd artfully prepared exactly as Elvan had instructed: the lamb-filled dumplings on the bottom, the yogurt sauce over them, and the red-pepper-infused olive oil over the yogurt.

She wished she'd taken a picture to send to Elvan before Ford dug in.

"This is amazing." His eyes narrowed and he watched her from the other side of the table. "Fess up. You've done this a thousand times before."

"Nope. First time." She bit into a dumpling and had to admit she'd outdone herself. While she wasn't happy with the fact that she was eating lamb, the little bit of nutmeg she'd ground to add to the mixture seasoned it perfectly.

"I cannot believe you did this for me." He put his fork on his plate, his gaze on her face. "I may have to marry you."

She laughed off the joke, tried to pretend that her heart hadn't just jumped even though she knew he wasn't serious.

"All kidding aside, Carly. You could get a job selling this. It's just as good as anything I ever had in Turkey. The only difference is that the sauce isn't quite as garlicky. But it's just as good," he hastened to add.

She smiled. She'd deliberately cut the amount of

garlic the recipe called for, figuring that you don't overgarlic the sauce when you're planning a big night.

And she was planning a big night. She'd thought over Ellie's words a hundred times since Sunday, and she knew her friend was right. She had been overthinking, overanalyzing whatever it was that was going on between her and Ford. She needed to get out of the way and just let the relationship go where it was going to go. Whichever way that might be, she was ready for it.

But just in case, she'd left most of the garlic out of the yogurt sauce.

They finished the *manti* and Carly served the dessert—round scoops of ricotta topped with a sugary syrup, and while it wasn't authentic, she added a few fresh blueberries to the bowls for color.

"I hope you won't get upset if I'm still sitting here in the morning," Ford said after he'd finished every last bite. "I don't think I'll be able to move until maybe Friday afternoon."

"Too bad. I was thinking a little walk around the block might be in order." She began to clear the table.

"Got a crane or some other piece of heavy equipment to get me out of the chair?"

She laughed and finished her beer. It had been the perfect accompaniment to the dinner.

"Come on." She reached out a hand to pull him up, and he pulled her onto his lap.

"We could just stay right here." He nuzzled her neck.

"I need to walk it off. I'm not used to eating so much at one sitting." She ran her fingers through his dark hair, something she'd wanted to do since the first night she met him. It was thick and silky and felt exactly the way she thought it would.

"All right." His hands on her waist, he lifted her and set her on her feet, then stood. "We'll go for a walk."

He glanced at the stack of dishes, pots, and pans on the counter and in the sink. "Still no dishwasher?"

"Still looking at 'er."

"I'll help you when we get back."

"I'll hold you to it." She tugged at his hand. "In the meantime . . ." She pointed to the door.

They went out through the side porch and, hand in hand, walked together for several blocks, shoulders and elbows occasionally bumping, to the end of Hudson Street. The sun had set and the streetlights had come on and cast a hazy glow at the intersection.

"Did you deliberately choose this route so that you could check up on the carriage house?" He pointed straight ahead.

"No. I thought we were just sort of ambling along."

They turned onto Old St. Mary's Church Road and he headed across the street.

"Ever walk down to the river?" he asked as he led her down the driveway.

"No."

"You mean to tell me you come here every day and you've never sat on the riverbank?"

She shook her head and he said, "Shame on you."

They walked past the carriage house, picking their way carefully in the dark around the back of the building all the way to the river's edge. Ford lowered himself to sit on the ground and pulled her down next to him.

"See what you've been missing?" he asked.

She looked across the river to the woods on the other side, barely visible in the faint moonlight.

"This used to be a favorite place of mine when I was a kid. One time Mr. Enright—Curtis—came to our school and gave us a talk about St. Dennis's history, how before and during the Civil War, there'd been more than one stop on the Underground Railroad. This place used to be one of them. There was a tunnel from an old outbuilding that used to be over there . . ." He pointed across the lawn—to a house that stood at the corner of Hudson. "That house is gone now, and the old shed is, too, but the story made for some powerful images in my head. They used to say that if you were real quiet, at night the ghosts of the runaways would come up the embankment. I used to steal over here sometimes and sit in the dark and wait for the ghosts to show up."

"Did they?" She rested back against him, and he put his arm around her.

"Nope. Still waiting." His smile was wistful. "There are three huge rocks down there right at the riverbank. Those were the landmarks the runaways looked for when they came up the river. Mr. Enright told us how they'd see the rocks, and jump out of whatever boat or barge they were on, hop onto the rocks, and they knew they were safe. I think one of the reasons he gave the property to the town was so that all of it—not just the grand house—but the stories would not be forgotten." He leaned back on one elbow on the grass and stared out at the river, and Carly could imagine him as a young boy coming here, sitting quietly in the grass, hoping to see the ghostly procession from the river to the shed.

She lay down next to him, and he pulled her to him, then kissed her, gently at first. His lips were soft as they grazed against hers, barely touching her. He nipped at her bottom lip, then kissed her again, full mouth to full mouth, his tongue seeking hers as the kiss deepened into a hot duel. She felt her body reach out for his, the longing for him growing with every second. There was no overthinking, no analyzing what to do. She fell onto her back and brought him with her, his weight on her hips. His hands were on her waist, on her face, on her breasts, and she rose with the sensation that flooded through her. His mouth trailed along her throat to the top of her shirt, his breath hot on her skin, his teeth on the top button of her shirt. With one hand, she began to release each button, his mouth following each inch of skin as far as her breasts. He took first one, then the other in his mouth, his tongue slipping under the soft lace of her bra, torturing her until she unfastened the hook at the back. She arched her back to him, silently demanding that he take more as a soft moan escaped her lips.

His hand ran the length of her thigh and up under her skirt, slipped under her panties, and caressed her until she wanted to scream. She tugged at his belt, her hand lowering to feel the length of him.

"Carly . . . ?" he whispered.

"Yes. Yes."

He rose on one elbow, and she heard the crinkling of the foil wrapper that he'd removed from his pocket. A moment later, he was above her, and she wrapped her legs around his, raised her hips, and pulled him closer. She could feel him just there, at the entrance to her body, and wanted only to feel him inside. When he slid into her, she exhaled a moan so soft that even she barely heard it. With her hips setting the rhythm, they moved together in the dark toward an explosion of sensation that left them both rocked to the core.

He lay with his head on her breast, his breathing still erratic, his hands holding hers next to her head. She tried to force a normal amount of air into her lungs, tried to ignore the pounding of her heart. She wondered if he could hear it.

"Your heart is beating like a kettledrum," he whispered.

So okay, he heard it.

"Ummmm" was the best she could do at the moment.

A few moments later, when she felt she could trust her voice, she said, "Tell me that wasn't your boyhood fantasy."

"What, making love with a beautiful woman on a perfect summer night while the stars were twinkling and the river flowed quietly by?" He raised his head and smiled down at her. "Ya think?"

She laughed softly and looked around. "I wonder if they were watching."

"The ghosts?" He glanced over to the spot where the old shed was rumored to have stood. "If they were, they got an eyeful."

She pulled him back to rest against her again, closed her eyes, and listened to the night sounds. A loud group of kids passing by the mansion reminded her that they weren't the only people out and about. She startled and he laughed.

"Relax. We're about two hundred yards from the street, and it's pitch-black out here."

"Two hundred yards? That doesn't sound like much."

"Think the length of two football fields."

Still, she felt uneasy, so he sat up and began to rearrange first her clothes then his own. She watched him try to button her shirt, then laughed and told him, "I'll do it. You take care of your own business."

Carly put herself back together and sat, staring at the pale strips of the river that were outlined by the moon's light. When Ford finished dressing, he held her face in his hands and asked, "What are you thinking?"

"I'm thinking I'm glad I wore a skirt . . ."

They walked back to the house lazily, and once they were back inside, he helped her turn off the lights, lock the doors, and then, without need of discussion, followed her down the hall to her bedroom.

"We lived out one of your fantasies," she told him as she backed into the room and kicked off her sandals. "Now let's try one of mine . . ."

Chapter 22 ⌒

CARLY awoke in the morning, a smile on her face. She glanced over at the beautiful man sleeping next to her, and delicately traced the outline of his jaw where the dark shadow of just the hint of beard was visible. He wrinkled his nose in his sleep but did not wake. She smiled and got out of bed. Where Ford appeared dead to the world, she felt energized. She showered, changed, and was in the kitchen washing dishes from the night before when she heard him come into the room.

"Good morning, sleepyhead." She looked over her shoulder to find him behind her.

He kissed the nape of her neck and made a sound that was somewhere between a groan and a word, and she laughed.

"What was that you said?"

"Coffee."

Carly opened a cupboard in which several boxes of tiny coffee cups were stacked.

"Choose your poison," she told him.

He sorted through the boxes, then handed her one of the cups.

"Extra-bold Sumatra? If you say so . . ." She tucked the cup into the coffeemaker, put a mug on the little platform, and set the machine to brew. When all the coffee had dripped into the mug, she handed it to Ford. "The sugar's in . . ." She pointed to the cupboard, but he shook his head.

"Black. Thanks."

"Now, one would think you had a long night last night," she teased.

"Longest night I've had in . . . oh, maybe forever."

"Me, too."

Her eyes met his, and he set the mug down on the counter. He put his arms around her, and just held on for a long moment before kissing the side of her face and releasing her. He took the mug to the back door and looked out.

"Nice morning," he observed.

"It's even nicer outside," she replied. "Not too hot yet, the humidity's still low, and there's a breeze. Go on out. I'll be out in a minute."

He unlocked the door, and through the window, she saw him standing at the edge of the patio, looking around the yard. She dried her hands, made a second mug of coffee for herself, then joined him.

"It's nice," he said. "Your yard . . ."

"It desperately needs some attention. The grass needs to be cut and the flower beds need to be weeded. I'd thought I'd get out here to tend to some of it, but there just hasn't been time."

"Guess you didn't bring a lawn mower with you from New York."

"Connecticut," she corrected him, then added, "No, I didn't."

"I used to be friends with the kid who grew up next door. Lincoln Calder. We were in the same class from kindergarten through our senior year." He looked over the fence at the scruffy black dog that was chasing its tail in the center of the yard. "Wonder where old Linc is these days."

"Do his parents still live there?"

He shrugged. "I have no idea."

"I bet your mother knows."

"My mother knows everything that goes on in this town." His mouth turned up on one side. "I wouldn't be surprised if she already knows about last night."

"Please don't even put that thought in my head." Carly faked a shiver. "I'd never be able to look her in the eye again."

Ford laughed. "I didn't mean she'd know everything. Just that I'm here."

"How would she know that?"

"One of the family's cars is in the driveway."

"So? You think everyone in St. Dennis knows what the inn's cars look like?"

He nodded.

"Please." She rolled her eyes.

"I will bet you that before the day is over, Grace has something to say about it."

"What's the bet?"

"If you win—if she says nothing—I will cook dinner for you every night for a week."

"You're that good a cook?"

"Are you kidding?" He scoffed. "I can't cook squat. I'm just that sure of my mother."

"You're on." She reached out to shake his hand.

"Now, enough talk about dinner. Let's see about breakfast."

"Good idea." He opened the door and held it for her. "Was there any *manti* left from last night?"

"You wouldn't eat that for breakfast . . ."

"Sure. Why not? It's protein, carbs . . . best way to start the day."

"Ugh. I can't even think of eating lamb at this hour of the morning."

"So tell me what to do and I'll do it."

She followed him into the house and showed him how to heat up the *manti* while she spooned yogurt into a bowl and topped it with honey for herself.

"Oh, there's a hearty breakfast," he commented when he sat down at the table with a plateful of last night's leftovers.

She stuck her tongue out at him and he laughed.

"So somehow last night we forgot about the interview," he noted.

"The interview?"

"You? Me? *The Gazette*?"

"Oh." She nodded. "That interview. I don't know how that could have slipped our minds."

Ford smirked.

"I think this time we're going to announce the Carolina paintings." Carly became all business. "You know, okay, we've found this cache and we're going to introduce the works to the art world as part of the dedication of the art center." She looked at him across the table, not surprised that he wasn't taking notes. He was simply watching her face.

"What?" she asked.

"You are so serious when you talk about Carolina. Even your eyes get serious. They get darker." He leaned forward and rested his elbow on the table, and his chin in his palm. "How do they do that?"

"Are you trying to distract me from the fact that you are not writing down anything that I said?"

"No. I just really like looking at your face."

"I like looking at your face, too, but we have work to do."

"Right." He patted his pockets. "No pen."

In spite of herself, Carly laughed. "How 'bout I write up what I'd like you to say about the exhibit, and the paintings, and you can incorporate it into your article."

"I don't mind if you don't mind."

"I don't. It might be better. That way I can coordinate what goes into the paper with the press release I'll be sending out. I'd like both pieces to go out at the same time."

"You have this all planned."

"Right down to popping the champagne at the opening."

Her cell phone rang, and she jumped. She grabbed it off the counter, and looked at the caller ID.

"Oh my God. Tony." Carly stared at Ford. "I totally forgot about Tony coming today to start putting in the security system."

She answered the call and promised Tony she'd be at the carriage house in fifteen minutes.

"Take your time," he told her. "I think I'm going to run back to that coffee shop I saw up on the main street and grab myself a cup."

She glanced at the wall clock anxiously. If she hadn't been running late, she'd have made coffee, but as it was, she had just enough time to jump into the shower and get dressed.

"Go ahead. Do what you have to do," Ford told her. "I'll clean up here and lock up before I leave."

"Are you sure . . . ?"

"Positive. Tell Tony I'll stop over tomorrow to say hey."

"Don't forget, you're meeting Lola . . . ," she reminded him before she bolted from the room.

"Right. Now go."

She went. Straight to the shower, then into her bedroom to dress, ignoring the rumpled bed and last night's clothes that were kicked here and there. She picked up her underwear and shirt and tossed them into the hamper. She'd look for her skirt later. It had to be there somewhere.

She went into the kitchen and tried to pretend it was the most natural thing in the world for her to have an adorable man washing her dishes, singing along to the playlist on his phone, which was on the table.

"Bruno Mars," she said, recognizing the song and the singer. "I like him, too."

She leaned up to kiss him good-bye, and he turned just enough to catch her mouth full-on.

"Thank you again for cleaning up here." She smiled. "You could be my houseman."

"Houseman? Is that the colloquial for sex slave?"

"In some circles, yes." She tossed her phone into her bag and went out the door, the song he was singing still in her head. *"You're amazing, just the way you are . . ."*

It stayed in her head for most of the morning, even when she and Tony discussed how he would wire and connect each of the paintings to a central motherboard so that removing one from the wall would trigger an alarm.

"We'll get everything else set up," he told her. "Then a few days before you open, I'll come back and I will personally wire each frame. It will be tight to get it all done, but we'll make it work."

"Thank you so much, Tony." Carly sighed and felt one more weight being lifted from her.

She spent several hours meeting at the mansion with residents who brought their favorite works of art for her consideration. She made a list of what she had, and counted how many spaces she still had to fill in the great hall. Most of the works were . . . well, dismal, but their artists were proud of them and she wasn't one to squelch talent or enthusiasm, so she took almost everything that was brought to her. She thought maybe she might find one bright light among them, and when Steffie MacGregor showed up with a portfolio of her mother's work, she knew she'd found that gem she'd been hoping for.

"Your mother did these?" Carly thumbed through the matted watercolors. "They're gorgeous. I can't choose just one of these. Does she have a favorite?"

"Probably, but she doesn't know I brought them. I just thought that they were good and I wanted you to see them, to see what you thought."

"I think she's incredibly talented. She could have

her own showing just about anywhere she wanted."
Carly made her way from the beginning to the end a
second time, marveling in the beauty of the scenes
that were obviously painted in St. Dennis. "Tell her I
will hang whichever painting she wants me to hang.
Any one of these would be an asset to the opening."

"Can I have her call you?"

"Absolutely. Let me give you my cell number."
Carly wrote it down on a card and handed it to her.

"Thanks." Steffie breathed a sigh of relief. "She
didn't want to bring anything for you to look at because she doesn't think she's very good and she said
she didn't want to waste your time. She might kill me,
but I'll make sure she follows up."

That was a pleasant surprise, Carly was thinking as
she went back to the worktable she had in the old
kitchen of Curtis Enright's onetime home. It was quiet
here, and cool in spite of the fact that there was no
central air-conditioning. She worked on the press release she'd be sending out to everyone on the art beat.
She prayed it would generate the kind of interest she
was hoping for.

She called Enrico, and went over a few addresses
that she wasn't sure of, and reminded him that he
was, in fact, invited to the opening.

"Oh, Gawd, I can hardly wait. I'm going to have to
send my navy blazer to the cleaners so I can have that
whole nautical thing goin' on," he told her happily.

She hung up, shaking her head, but loving the guy
who kept her biggest and most important gallery running. A promotion and a raise would be in his future.

Before she knew it, the alarm she'd set on her phone

went off, and she folded up her work and hurried over to the carriage house, making a mental note to tell Ed Lassiter that he'd need to arrange for the mansion to be cleaned before the dedication. One more thing to remember . . .

Tony was packed up and ready to go by the time she arrived next door. He assured her he'd be back in the morning, and to ignore the wires hanging out of the walls and from the ceiling. She locked up and decided to leave, too. She was so tired she could barely keep her eyes open, and found herself wishing she'd walked from home that morning.

She pulled into the driveway and, though she knew Ford would have left, felt a little stab of disappointment when she saw that his car was gone. She dragged her tired self into the house, dropped her keys and bag on the kitchen table, and looked around. Ford had washed, dried, and put away everything that hadn't been cleaned last night. The counters were shiny and the flowers now sat in the middle of the table. There was a note standing in front of the tureen, and she picked it up to read it.

Carly—wasn't sure where you kept things, so I made it up as I went along. Good luck finding everything. F.

She smiled and, leaving the note on the table, went into the living room and crashed on the sofa.

The sound of a lawn mower somewhere nearby woke her. She checked the time—she'd slept for almost three hours. Disoriented, she stood up and looked out the window. There were cars going by, and a few kids on bikes, but no one was out mowing their grass. Still sleepy, she stumbled to the back door and looked out.

She blinked several times.

Ford, dressed in shorts, no shirt, was making his way back and forth across the backyard with a power mower that he'd gotten from . . . where? At one point, he stopped and walked over to the fence, and called to someone on the other side before resuming cutting the grass. She stood and watched through the glass for several minutes, enjoying the sight of his shirtless self.

Ellie's advice had been right on. She needed to go with her gut. Well, she'd done that last night, and with any luck, she'd go with it again tonight, and for however many nights they'd have together.

She opened the back door and waved when he saw her. He followed the mower as far as the patio, then turned it off.

"You didn't have to do this. And where'd you get the mower?"

"Oh, Linc's parents still live next door. I saw his dad out back while I was standing at the sink this morning. So I went out and we talked for a while, and I asked him if he had a lawn mower I could use, and he did." With his right arm, he brushed sweat from his forehead. "Looks pretty good, doesn't it?" He turned to admire his work.

"It looks great. But what about Lola . . . ?"

"Oh, I met with her at the inn. Mom called and said that she was coming by to have lunch, so I should join them. Which I did." He paused. "You owe me dinner again tonight. And tomorrow night, and the night after . . . how many nights did we bet? A full week?"

"She didn't." Carly cringed.

Ford shrugged. "What can I tell you? Grace knows all. She said to tell you that she'd love for the chef to try some of your recipes."

"She didn't know that, too." Carly had heard whispers—none of which she'd repeat to Ford—that Grace had some woo-woo abilities.

"Not until I told her. I described the meal in detail, and I can tell you, Gracie was impressed big-time."

"She's welcome to the recipes," Carly told him, "but as far as tonight is concerned . . . does takeout count?"

He nodded. "Takeout is fine."

"Well, then, why don't you return the neighbor's lawn mower, then come back and take a shower, and we'll try to think of a way I can thank you for the yard work."

He wheeled the mower toward the fence. "I'm sure we'll come up with something . . ."

Carly awoke around three, the bed shaking just enough to rouse her. In his sleep, Ford was agitated, his head moving from side to side, uttering words she couldn't understand, except for one: Anna. Her first inclination was to wake him, but she'd read somewhere that if someone was having a nightmare, it was best to let them sleep through it. But after it had gone on for several more minutes, she touched his shoulder lightly, and he jumped. Startled and obviously unsure of where he was, she spoke softly.

"Ford, you're here with me. Carly. You were having a bad dream."

"What . . . ?" He appeared momentarily confused.

"You were having a nightmare. Do you want me to turn on the light?"

He nodded, and she snapped on the lamp on the bedside table.

He looked at her for a long moment, then said, "I'm sorry I woke you."

"It's okay." She wrapped the sheet around her and sat up. "Do you remember what you were dreaming about?"

"I always have the same dream." He rubbed his hand over his face. "I'm used to it. I'm just sorry that I disturbed you."

"Who's Anna?" she asked, though she wasn't sure she really wanted to know.

He leaned against the headboard, his shoulder touching hers. For a while, she thought he wasn't going to respond.

"It's okay," she said. "I shouldn't have . . ."

"Anna was the first woman I ever fell in love with for real."

Her heart sank. She should have figured there'd be a woman. A man like Ford had to have a woman in his life.

"She was with the Peacekeeping operation in Sudan when I first arrived in Africa, my first assignment with that team. She was a pretty, blond Swiss, very idealistic, so out of place in the brush in that world, and I fell like a ton of bricks." He smiled, thinking, no doubt, of nights he spent with Anna. "So did she. For a while, anyway." He cleared his throat. "We were together for about eight months, and I started thinking about quitting the military and bringing her back to the States with me."

"So what happened?"

"Well, the first thing that happened was Stephano."

"Stephano?"

"Italian guy who joined her group. She took one look at him and it was bye-bye Ford. Within two months, she and Stephano were married."

"You're kidding. She dumped you and moved on to this other guy just like that?" She snapped her fingers.

"Just like that." He snapped his. "But seeing them together, I knew that what they had was the real thing. What she and I had . . . I guess that was more of a fling to her."

"But not to you?"

He shook his head. "I was in love with her. I wasn't happy when she cut me loose, but after a while I realized that it was okay. I still loved her, but it was in a different way. Stephano was quite a guy. I respected him, actually grew to like him. And they were happy together, anyone could see that, so it was a situation I had to accept and adjust to."

"You said 'the first thing.' What else happened?"

"They were both shot and killed, along with two guys from my unit."

Carly's jaw dropped. "How . . . ?"

"The area we were in was in the midst of civil war, I think I might have mentioned that. It got to the point where you couldn't tell the good guys from the bad guys. Both sides raided the villages, both sides recruited the boys who were old enough to carry a gun— 'recruited' being a polite term for kidnapped. Both sides burned the villages to the ground, raped, pillaged— didn't matter, rebel or government forces, they were all the same." He paused. "Still are. Very little has changed."

She'd read about such things, about the horrors

that were going on still in certain countries where the political situation was volatile and things changed from day to day. She'd never met anyone who'd been in those countries, who'd been caught up in the madness, whose life had been changed by it.

"So Anna and Stephano had found a way to 'liberate' a band of nine- and ten-year-olds who'd been abducted by one of the rebel forces. They were leading them to what was thought to be a safe area, where the boys could be put on a plane and taken someplace where they'd be protected till the fighting was over. The kids' families were gone—killed—their homes gone . . .

"Anyway, our assignment was to ensure safe passage for the band of boy soldiers and their UN protectors. Anna and Stephano and the two others went on ahead, and the rest of us had dropped back a bit because the boys were tired and were slowing down, so we stopped to give them a few minutes' rest. Then, without warning, we heard automatic weapons firing for what seemed to be a lifetime. We got the boys to the ground, but we couldn't return the fire for fear that the kids would be found. So after the firing stopped, three of us went through the brush to the edge of the clearing. Anna, Stephano, and the others lay on the ground, shot to pieces, surrounded by thirty or forty rebel soldiers."

"Did you kill them?"

He shook his head. "There were six guys left on my team, including me, and thirty or more of them. We had a group of young boys who needed protection. Engaging the rebels would have put the kids at risk. All we could do was wait until they left the area."

"What about the . . ." She hesitated. "Anna . . ."

"When we met the plane, we secured body bags and went back for them . . . the remains."

"And that's when you decided to leave."

"Yes."

"That is so horrible, all of it," she whispered. "I wish . . ."

"Yeah, me, too."

"And the boys you 'liberated'?"

"They're safe in Capetown, for now."

"There's that, at least. I guess one good thing came out of it."

"Two, actually. Two good things."

"What was the second?"

"The leader of the rebel band that day has been identified. Raymond Nakimbe. He's been trying to unite all the rebel factions so that he can stage a coup, overthrow the current government, and put himself on the ballot in next year's election."

"Who would vote for someone like that?" Carly was horrified.

"You'd be surprised what people will do when someone has a gun to their head."

"Can't he be stopped?"

"If enough support is given to the current president— the legitimate government—then yes, he can be stopped from taking over, but he has to be caught first. He's been very clever in his alliances. He has backing from some tribesmen who are aligned with al Qaeda, among others."

"So if the government captures him . . . ?"

"Game over. Like I said, he's been clever, and he's

elusive, but if the current regime gets their hands on him, it's done. One of the things about making alliances with people who are not generally trustworthy is that, well, you can't trust them. Everyone's playing their own game right now."

"So say he's betrayed by one of these other groups, and they hand him over to the government?"

"A real possibility, which is why he's so hard to find. But in that case, he'll be brought to justice, with or without a trial. Which in that world means executed by whichever means the president wants."

"That would be your first choice."

"Damn right."

"It won't bring back Anna or Stephano or anyone else he murdered."

"No, but it would stop him from murdering more innocent people."

"Could you go back?"

"Anytime I want."

"Would you go back?"

His answer was a long time coming. "I don't know. I left because I'd had enough. I started to think there had to be something more, something better in life. I don't regret where I've been and what I've done, don't misunderstand. But I figured it was time to move on, see what else there is."

"Like interviewing local characters." She tried to lighten the mood.

"Hey, you were one of those characters I was sent to interview." He turned and took her in his arms. "Smartest thing I ever did was say yes when my mom asked me to do a couple of interviews for her paper. Look where we are."

"Where are we?" As soon as the words left her mouth, she regretted them.

"I guess we're on the road to what comes next," he told her, not seeming to mind that she asked. "I guess we're just going to have to see where that road leads . . ." He paused. "You in, Car?"

"Yes." She nodded. "I'm in . . ."

Chapter 23 ～

CARLY was beginning to understand that when Ford made a bet, he meant business.

"What would you have done if you'd lost the bet?" she asked him over dinner several nights later.

"I'd have paid up."

"You would have made dinner for the rest of the week." She rolled her eyes. "Right."

"Of course. That's what a bet is. You lose, well, you pay up."

"Even though you don't know how to cook."

"I can cook a little."

"Like what, eggs and toast? Oatmeal? Please."

"I'd have gone to the chef at the inn and asked him to give me a crash course." He leaned back against the counter. "So what's on the menu tonight, Julia Child?"

"Take-out Thai." She held up the bag unapologetically. "I didn't get to the grocery store."

He got out the plates and set the table without asking, as if it was the most normal thing in the world for him to do. "I think your calling me out on my lack of

cooking ability when you're doing takeout is somewhat, oh, I don't know . . . hypocritical?"

She laughed at his affected sanctimonious air.

"I believe I've already proven myself."

"True. But the bet was to make dinner—not reservations, not orders for takeout," he reminded her.
"However, I'll let it slide this time because I happen to
love Thai."

"So I should consider myself lucky."

"Very. Perhaps better planning on your part will
help avoid this situation in the future."

She rolled up a dish towel and tossed it at him, and
he laughed as he ducked and caught it with one hand.
She watched him move around the kitchen, at ease
with its layout, almost as if he belonged there.

She chastised herself for letting that thought slip in.
She had no idea where he was headed—if he knew, he
was keeping that bit of news to himself. Carly's path,
on the other hand, was pretty clear. There was so
much on her plate, she had little time to think about
anything except making sure that she delivered everything she'd promised.

She had two more weeks in St. Dennis before the gallery would open and she'd be showing off Carolina's
paintings. Who knew what came next? She'd have the
option of taking some of the works back to New York
to sell in her own gallery—if Ellie decided to sell any
of them. So far, she hadn't been able to decide what to
do. She could sell a few or none at all. She could pull
them from the gallery in St. Dennis—aptly dubbed the
Enright Gallery by the town council—and send all or
some of them back to New York with Carly. It seemed
she changed her mind daily. The indecision was mak-

ing Carly so crazy, she found herself avoiding the issue entirely.

The town council had balked at the price of the security system, despite Carly's assurances that eventually the gallery in the carriage house would repay the expense. After the success of the Carolina Ellis exhibit, Carly had explained, other artists would want to show there as well—assuming the security of the works could be guaranteed—thus raising more revenue. But she'd been unable to convince them, so she ended up paying Tony's bill on her own. The system was in, and the test runs had been completed on everything except the wiring on the individual paintings. Tony would be back next week to tend to that, and once that entire system was in place, they'd hang the paintings.

To that end, Ford had accompanied her to Ellie's to measure the paintings that were stored there.

"I still think it's nuts that you'd pay all that money for fancy security at the carriage house while the paintings are in Ellie's attic." He followed her along the walk up to Ellie's front door. "Remind me again what kind of security system she and Cam have?"

Carly's knock on the door was followed by an explosion of barking from inside.

She looked over her shoulder and grinned. "Guard dog."

Ford rolled his eyes, but she saw the glint of humor there and laughed.

Gabi let them in, and they made the obligatory fuss over Dune, who followed them to the second floor, but wouldn't go up the third-floor steps.

"It's just as well," Gabi told them as they ascended

to the attic. "She'd just get into stuff and either chew it or bring it downstairs. Go ahead and do whatever. Ellie said to ask you just to lock the back door when you leave and that she was sorry that she and Cam couldn't wait but they had to get to Dallas's to finish up something at the studio that she wanted done before the weekend. I have to leave for field-hockey camp and I'm really late."

Gabi was halfway down the steps when she called up to Carly. "Could you do me a favor and just walk Dune a little before you leave?"

"Sure thing," Carly called back.

"Thanks! See you guys later . . ."

"So what are we doing?" Ford rubbed the back of his neck and looked around the crowded attic.

"We're going to measure each painting and write down its dimensions. Then I will photograph each one for the catalog."

"I thought you already did that."

"Only with my phone. I need higher quality for the catalog."

"Okay, why don't you measure and I'll take the pictures?" he suggested.

"That's what I had in mind." She unwrapped the paper from the first painting and stood it against the wall, measured it with a tape measure, then wrote down the name of the painting and the dimensions on her smartphone.

"I can see why you like Carolina's work," Ford told her after he'd taken pictures of several of the paintings. "They're pretty and the scenes are all so peaceful. Like this one." He pointed to the one he'd just photographed. "That's right down there on the beach."

"What beach?" She was preparing to rewrap the painting.

"The beach at the end of the road. See there, there's the inlet across the way."

She studied it for a moment. "Wouldn't it be interesting if we had photographs of the places she painted? Sort of a now and then . . ."

"Don't go looking for work," he cautioned. "I think you have enough to do between now and the end of the month."

"True, but it could be wonderful."

"Carly . . ."

"Okay, okay. So maybe not for this exhibit, but maybe for sometime in the future . . ." She liked the idea of Carolina's paintings of places in St. Dennis from her day hanging next to photos of those actual places in today's world.

"You planning on being around to do another exhibit?" he asked casually as he set up the shot on the painting she was unwrapping.

"I hadn't really thought about it till right now. I mean, Ellie and I talked about me taking some of the paintings to my gallery in New York to display and then maybe sell a few, but she can't make up her mind. Which means that the entire collection would still be here, and that means someone's going to have to be in charge of the exhibit."

"Couldn't they hire someone else?"

"I guess." The very thought annoyed her. The exhibit was hers.

"So you'd just turn the whole thing over to someone else?"

When she didn't respond, he continued. "How would you work that out? I mean, if you were to stick around."

"I don't know. I guess I'd think of something."

"Guess you could always stay at the inn."

"I guess. Or at the house, if it's still available."

"How long is your lease for?"

"I took it through the end of the year because the original idea was to have the gallery open for the holiday house tour."

"So you could come back . . ."

"I could."

She wrapped and rewrapped, and he took shot after shot until the job was completed. They were greeted merrily by Dune when they got back to the first floor.

"Oh, I told Gabi I'd take her out before we left." Carly took the dog's leash from its place near the back door and hooked it to her collar. "Want to go to the beach, Dune?"

The dog wagged her tail all the way from the house to the dune that led to the little stretch of beach at the end of Bay View Road. She scampered along the sand sniffing at whatever had washed up overnight, occasionally picking up bits of flotsam that Carly had to take from her.

"See there?" Ford stopped at the water's edge and pointed across the Bay. "There's the inlet I was talking about." He raised the camera that still hung around his neck and took a series of shots. He looked through the viewfinder, nodded his approval, and showed Carly the images in the camera.

"Nice. Oh, that does look like the painting, except the tree line is closer to the water. Damn, it's a shame I don't have time to—"

"You don't."

"But you know what would be really cool?" She tugged on the dog's leash to head back to the house. "A sort of photo essay that would run in the *Gazette*. Yesterday through the eyes of Carolina Ellis—today through the eye of the lens."

She thought he was about to remind her again that she didn't have time for such a project, but he surprised her by falling silent, and she could tell by the look on his face that the idea appealed to him, too. Finally, he said, "That could be interesting."

They returned to the house, where Carly gave Dune fresh water, a biscuit for being a good girl, and one tummy rub before locking the back door behind them.

After Ford dropped her off at the house—not missing an opportunity to cheerfully remind her that her week wasn't over and she still had a bet to pay off— Carly made herself a cup of coffee and went into the dining room to work on the catalog. She printed out the photos from the camera and worked on the placement of each. She wasn't aware of how long she'd been working until her stomach began to growl. She looked for her phone to check the time and found it was well past two o'clock.

There was pad Thai left over from the night before, so she heated up some of that and ate it standing up at the counter. With Ford not there, the house was so quiet it seemed the life had gone out of it. She found herself looking forward to seeing him every day, taking a trip to the market together, talking things over while she prepared dinner and while they ate. They'd gotten into the habit of walking after dinner, and over the past week they'd covered just about all of St. Dennis. He pointed out places that had been significant while he was growing up, and more and more, Carly looked forward to seeing bits and pieces of the boy he'd been as she walked through the town with the man he'd become. She was finding herself falling for the town almost as much as she was falling for him.

And then, he'd stay for the night.

It had taken Carly several days of his leaving in the morning and coming back at night to realize it was as close as she'd ever come to living with someone.

"Did you ever live with someone?" she asked over dessert one night.

"You mean, a woman?" He shook his head. "You ever live with any of your old boyfriends?"

"No."

"Is this your way of telling me that it bothers you that I'm here so much?" He put down his fork.

"Oh, no. No, not at all. I like having you here." Her foot slid out of her sandal and reached for his leg under the table. "It's just a new experience for me, to be around someone so much. I've lived alone since I left school," she explained. "It's just . . . different, that's all."

"I've always had people in my space," he told her. "I went from growing up in the inn to school to the military. So being with one person instead of a crowd, I guess that's different for me, too." He smiled. "I kinda like it."

"Actually, I kind of like it, too."

It occurred to her as she rinsed off her plate that her week was almost up. She'd bet seven days, and now they were down to two. The thought made her uneasy, so she pushed it from her mind and refused to think about what might happen when those two days had come and gone.

Ford called around four to ask her if she knew how to cook fish.

"Of course I can cook fish." She pretended to be insulted. "I can cook anything. Why do you ask?"

"Because I'm down at the marina and the fishing boats are coming in. I ran into a guy I went to high school with—he fishes with his dad now—and he offered me a tuna he caught this morning. I told him I'd have to check first to see if you wanted it."

"Wait, do I have to clean it?"

"Nope. I'll do that part."

"You know how to do that?"

"Please. Bay-boy here." He put his hand over the phone and said something to someone in the background.

"Okay, then, Bay-boy. I will leave that part in your hands."

She hung up and tried to avoid thinking about a time when he wasn't in the house in the morning when she woke up, or when he didn't call to check in during the day. It must have been on Ford's mind, too, because on the seventh night, in her bed and in her arms, he asked, "So, are you ready to lose another bet?" But they couldn't agree on what to bet on, and no bets were made.

He surprised her the next day, when she was still wondering. She's spent the day at the carriage house working with Tony on wiring the individual frames and hanging them. She couldn't wait to get back to the house on Hudson Street to tell Ford how fabulous it all looked, and take him there later to show him.

But there was a knot in her stomach the size of a base-ball, because he'd said nothing that morning about dinner. She pulled into her driveway, thinking about how she wished she'd made that second bet after all.

She went into the quiet house and tossed her bag onto a dining room chair, then headed straight to the kitchen to dump out a bottle of water she'd found on the floor of her car. One look out the window and her heart skipped a beat. There was Ford kneeling by one of the neglected flower beds, a mile-high pile of weeds on the ground. He was shirtless in the afternoon sun, and his back and shoulders gleamed with sweat.

She poured a glass of water, popped some ice into it, and opened the back door.

"Hey," she called as she walked across the yard.

"Hi." He stood and brushed dirt from his hands onto his shorts. She handed him the glass and he took a long drink.

"Look at all the work you've done out here. I can't believe how good everything looks." She went to put her arms around him, and he backed away.

"Sweaty-guy alert," he told her. "You can thank me later."

"And I will. Whatever possessed you to do this?" She was still in shock. Who just showed up in some-one's yard and pulled weeds?

"You mentioned that you wanted it done, and ob-viously you don't have time to do it, but I did." He raised his sunglasses and wiped his face with the back of his hand. "Besides, I thought it would make you smile, and it did. So, time well spent."

"You . . . you . . ." She shook her head, unable to

find the words. His simple, honest response had touched her heart. "Thank you."

"You're welcome." He bent down and kissed the tip of her nose. "More to come after I get a shower . . ."

Dinner that night was takeout—and late.

The next morning, he surprised her again.

"Get up." He stood over the bed, fully dressed, at six thirty.

"Why?" she grumbled.

"Because we have someplace to go." He smacked her lightly on the rump. "Come on. Get your clothes on."

She was still grumbling when she came into the kitchen and headed for the coffee machine.

"Uh-uh," he told her. "Not today."

"What? Are you crazy?"

"Possibly." He took her hand and led her out the door.

"Where are we going?"

"You are playing hooky for a while this morning. Since I walked over yesterday, you're going to have to drive."

"Drive where?"

"To the inn."

"Why?" She unlocked the car and got behind the wheel.

"Because." There was that smug look again.

"All right. But there'd better be coffee . . ."

There was coffee, a thermos of it, fixed the way she liked it, tucked into the picnic basket that waited for them right inside the kitchen door. Ford picked up the basket, shouted his thanks to the chef, and took Carly by the hand. He led her down to the boathouse, where he told her, "This is going to be tricky."

He dragged a double kayak into the water and motioned for her to hand him the basket.

"Get in," he told her.

She took off her flip-flops, waded through the shallow water, tossed in her sandals, and climbed in after them. When she was seated, he passed the basket back to her.

"Don't peek," he told her.

"How am I going to paddle if I'm holding the basket?" she asked.

"I'm paddling. You're going to keep a good grip on that basket. I have it on good authority that there's some pretty good stuff in there."

He walked the kayak farther into the water, got on board, and paddled out into the Bay. It was quiet on the water, and she heard every stroke of the paddle against the gentle waves. She closed her eyes and leaned her head back and let the breeze blow over her. She felt free and happy and knew there was no place in the world she'd rather be at that moment.

"Sure you don't want to trade?" she asked. "You hold the basket and I'll paddle."

"No thanks. I want to get there this morning."

She laughed and dragged one hand in the water as the kayak glided along the coastline.

"Do you actually have a destination in mind, or are you just winging it?"

"Don't you worry about where we're going."

"Are we close?"

"Another five minutes."

She readjusted the basket and was tempted to open

the lid and take out that thermos, but she'd wait. Wherever they were headed, he'd obviously put some thought into it.

Finally, he directed the craft toward a cove, and once he rounded the bend, he asked, "Recognize this place?"

She started to reply, no, she'd never been there before, but the word died on her lips. There was something familiar about the narrow sandy beach, the pine trees.

Loblolly pines . . .

"Oh my God, this looks like . . . ! This is the place!"

"Whoa! Calm down," he told her. "You're going to capsize us."

She couldn't contain her enthusiasm.

"It's the place from *Stolen Moments*."

"Damn, maybe I should have blindfolded you when I had the chance."

"I'm sorry." She laughed. "I'll sit still. It's just that . . . oh, how did you ever find it?"

"It's Sunset Beach." He hopped out and dragged the kayak toward the sand, then helped her out. "I used to come here a lot when I was younger. It was sort of my place."

He set the basket on the beach and opened it.

"In case you were wondering why it was so heavy." He took a blanket out and spread it on the sand. He placed the basket on the blanket and asked, "Are you ready for breakfast? Coffee first?"

"I'm . . . yes, please."

He poured the dark liquid into a mug and handed it to her.

"Ford, this is the coolest, most thoughtful, most wonderful thing anyone has ever done for me."

"I doubt that." He tried to pass off her comment, but she could tell he was pleased by her reaction.

"No. I mean it. I can't believe you planned this."

"I thought it would make you happy," he said simply. "I wanted to make you happy." He leaned over and kissed her. "Because you make me happy. You went along with that stupid bet and you were so good-natured about losing and making me these wonderful dinners every night." He took her hand. "I admit that I thought about saying, 'oh, never mind,' but then I wouldn't have had an excuse to spend so much time with you."

"You didn't need an excuse. I . . ." She caught herself about to say, *I loved every minute of it,* and wondered if that was saying too much. She realized she didn't care. "I loved every minute of it."

"Me, too." He cleared his throat as if surprised by his admission, then turned his attention to the basket. "I thought maybe a breakfast picnic was the way to go. You know, to show you how much I . . ." He appeared to be deliberating. "How much I appreciated that you were such a good sport." He cleared his throat and added, "How much I appreciate you. Being with you."

He opened the lid and started removing dishes. "I told the chef you liked yogurt and fruit in the morning." He passed her a glass bowl covered with a red plastic lid. "And I thought you looked like a croissant kind of girl."

The napkin he gave her held a flaky pastry filled with chocolate.

"Oh my God. My favorite thing in the world to eat."

He beamed and set out the rest of their meal. Three egg-and-sausage sandwiches—two of them for him—a slice of quiche with bacon and Swiss chard, and a small container of raisins and walnuts. "For your yogurt," he told her.

"Ford, this is just . . ." She was almost too touched to eat. "Thank you. I can't think of anything else to say but thank you."

"You're welcome." He tucked a loose strand of her hair behind her ear. "Now drink your coffee, 'cause we both know how crabby you get without caffeine."

"She came here, with him. The man she loved. It doesn't look all that different from the painting."

She couldn't stop chattering. She tried to tell herself to shut up, but the words kept coming. Ford leaned back on one elbow and ate, looking amused. He held up a spoon and handed her the yogurt.

"I'm talking too much." She took the spoon and began to eat.

"You had quite a run on." He nodded.

"I'm just excited. I wish I had my camera."

"We can come back." He finished one of the sandwiches and rolled up the foil it had been wrapped in. "Anytime you want."

"Really?"

"Sure. I come here a lot. At least, I used to. It's always been a quiet place. I've always been able to think here." He unwrapped another sandwich. "When I was younger, especially. There was always so much going on at the inn, I had to find a place where I could just think things through. Like when I screwed up a ball game, or screwed up on a test." He paused. "Or like when my dad died."

"I had a place like that, too, near the house where I grew up. There were woods near the back of our property. There were trees so tall that they formed this huge canopy overhead, so it was always sort of dark there, and it always smelled of pine. Whenever I had to get away by myself for a while, I went there. When we moved from that house, I missed that place more than I missed the house or my friends. It was sort of a refuge. Even now, the scent of pine takes me back to that place, and it always calms me."

"That's how I feel when I hear the water lap onto the sand the way it's doing now." He nodded toward the water's edge. "Sometimes, on a really calm day, at low tide, you can hardly hear it at all."

They finished eating and cleaned up, putting everything back into the basket.

"We should probably be getting back," he said. "I know you're supposed to meet the caterer to talk over the menu for the opening."

"I don't meet with her until two." She lay back on the blanket and pulled him down to kiss him.

From the water came a loud whistle as a rowboat full of kids started into the cove.

"Oh, hey, thanks, guys," Ford called to them, and waved.

"I'm guessing this is a more popular place than we thought."

"I guess." He sat up, but kept his arms around her. He took his phone from his shirt pocket and scrolled through a page, then set the phone on the blanket. She rested against him, watching the waves spill onto the shore, and closed her eyes. A song began to play on the phone, and for a moment, it was just background music. Until she listened and heard the familiar voice.

Kenny Chesney. "You Had Me at Hello."

She turned in his arms and looked up at him.

Ford nodded. "You did. From the first time I saw you in the lobby, you had me."

She held his face in her hands, and kissed him. "You had me, too," she told him. "Let's go home."

"You have that meeting . . ."

She stood and pulled him up. "There's plenty of time between now and then. Hours, actually . . ."

Chapter 24 ~

DEANNA Clark had come highly recommended as the best caterer on the Eastern Shore. Carly hoped her reputation proved true—the RSVPs were already starting to arrive and some of the biggest names in the art world were planning to attend. The press release she'd had Enrico send out on Friday of the week before had done the trick. So far, no one on the VIP list had declined. Carly wanted the reception on Saturday before the gallery was opened to be simple but elegant, and to reflect the Bay.

"I know exactly what you want," Deanna assured her. "Tiny crab cakes, smoked bluefish, seared tuna. Oysters. Some of our fabulous local vegetables—I'll email you a list of my recommendations and you can chose."

"Wonderful. Could I ask you to send it sooner rather than later? Time is getting short . . ."

"You'll have it within the hour. Just look it over, make your selections, and I'll get right on it."

One more big item crossed off, Carly thought, and wasn't she lucky that Deanna had had an event cancel on her right before Carly called, ready to apologize for the late call and prepared to plead with the caterer to take on the event.

She went back over her list. She'd ordered the champagne for the reception and sent invitations to all the local dignitaries. She'd asked several friends to host at the mansion once the doors were opened to the public, just to keep an eye on things, and she had a list of volunteers to take shifts so that they could all check out the main event. She'd included those people—Vanessa, Steffie, Brooke, Sophie, and of course, Ellie and Cam and Gabi—on the guest list. Dallas and Grant had been on the VIP list, inasmuch as he was a member of the town council. Dallas's great-aunt Berry was included because, well, she *was* a true VIP.

Carly had sent Grace an invitation, but was afraid she wasn't going to be able to attend due to her injuries. She mentioned as much to Ford that evening right before she fell asleep.

"It's such a shame your mom can't make it to the opening," she said.

"Who said she wasn't coming?" He yawned.

"Really? You think she'll make it?"

"Really? You think she'd miss it?" He yawned again. "Don't worry. We'll get her here. She's already put out the word."

"Great. I'd hate for her to miss it. She was so instrumental in getting the project off the ground, you know?" When he didn't respond, she turned over to find him sound asleep.

Well, he's been really busy with the paper, she reminded herself. Interviews every day, and all the time he'd started spending at the office. She knew it must please Grace that he was really into the *Gazette* these days. Carly hoped that meant he'd be staying, but she never had the nerve to ask after that one time. Maybe his answer would still be "I don't know." If he were to stay, she'd stay. Well, maybe not every day, but she'd come back on weekends when she could. Maybe sometimes during the week. Maybe she'd keep the lease on the house, or if Hal wanted to sell it, maybe she'd put an offer in. She'd already started to think of it as their house . . .

She fell asleep thinking happy thoughts about the way things could turn out.

And awoke to the sound of a ringing phone, and Ford's voice.

"When? Where?" He got out of bed and grabbed his clothes and started putting them on.

Dreaming, she told herself. Must be dreaming. Why else would he be getting dressed in the middle of the night?

"All right. Yes, by morning. Hold the plane for me. I'll be there."

The next thing she knew, he was leaning over her, calling her name.

"Car? Carly? Wake up, baby."

"What?" She opened her eyes. He was fully dressed. It hadn't been a dream.

"I have to go."

"What do you mean, you have to go?" She looked at the clock. "It's three in the morning."

"I have to leave."

"Where are you going?"

"Raymond Nakimbe has been arrested. I'm going back."

"Wait. You're going to Africa? Now?" She sat up. "I thought you said you were out of the military."

"I am out of the military. I've been asked to go back to give testimony against him about what I know, what I observed. I want to go, Car. I *have* to go."

"For Anna . . ."

"For Anna and for the two guys from my unit. Our old commander has arranged for all of us to go."

"They're going to put him on trial."

"Eventually." He kissed her, long and deep. "I'm sorry, baby."

He kissed her again, and then he was gone.

Carly heard the side door open, then close, heard the engine start in the driveway. She sat still as a stone in the middle of the bed, trying to figure out what had just happened. Finally she lay down on his side of the bed and held on to his pillow while she sobbed.

For Carly, the next twelve days were a blur. *Stolen Moments* went on sale and the first of the reader reviews were glowing, thanks in no small part to Dallas MacGregor making it known that she was dying for the film rights and was hoping to make it her second film. The splash was loud enough that three of the four people who had previously refused to have the Carolina Ellis paintings they owned put on display— including Susan Lane and Ariel Peters—had reconsidered and now wanted in. Unfortunately, Carly had had to tell them there was no space for last-minute additions, but she promised to call them should a subsequent exhibit be planned.

The catalogs had come back from the graphic designer and had to be mailed out immediately to the invitees on the VIP list. The rest would be available at the door on opening day. Ellie and Gabi had offered to help, but Carly had declined. It would take her three times as long, but if her mind was occupied, she'd have less time to think about Ford and where he was and what he was doing and whether or not he was still alive. On more than one occasion, he'd mentioned how dicey, how unsettled and volatile the area was. The country was in the midst of a civil war. What if some of Nakimbe's followers decided to eliminate whoever was going to testify against their leader? What if the government was overthrown while Ford was there? What would happen to him?

She was glued to the TV channels that broadcast mostly news, just in case. She missed him so much it physically hurt.

There were no phone calls, no emails. Nothing but silence. It was almost as if he'd never been there at all.

On the morning of the dedication of the art center and the opening of the gallery, she awoke with an ache in her head and a cramp in her heart. She'd looked forward to this day, meticulously planned every detail. She'd staked her reputation in part on the success of Carolina's works, and was nervous about unveiling them to the rest of the world. What if the buzz wasn't what she'd anticipated? What if the paintings weren't well received? What if no one else saw the genius in the paintings that Carly saw? What if what if what if . . .

The dedication ceremony was scheduled for two in the afternoon, and the reception for the gallery at five. Since she would attend both, she tried to find something in her closet that would be appropriate for the outdoor dedication as well as the cocktail reception. Finally accepting that she owned no such animal, she pulled out the blue dress she'd worn on her first date with Ford. She'd fantasized that he'd arrive at the party, see her in that dress that had done a number on him the last time, and he'd swear to never leave her again.

Her fears about the exhibit had been unfounded. Carolina Ellis's name was on everyone's lips, and Carly was asked to pass along offers to Ellie from art patrons and gallery owners alike.

"I cannot believe how you pulled this off." Ellie hugged her when she arrived. "The paintings all look so much better hanging on these walls than they did standing up in my attic."

Carly laughed. "It's amazing what a good cleaning and some good lighting can do. But you're right. They all look fabulous. It seems that everyone on the VIP list has a favorite that they'd like to buy when you're ready."

"I don't know, Car." Ellie bit her bottom lip. "It's so hard to decide which ones to part with."

"Sweetie, you don't have to part with any of them if you don't want to," Carly assured her. "You can keep them right where they are forever, if you like."

Ellie sighed. "You're right. I shouldn't feel any pressure, even if everyone I meet wants to buy one."

"Go. Bask in the glow of being the owner of all this gloriousness."

"I will. Oh, look, there's Dallas." Ellie leaned in and whispered, "Is she really interested in the film rights, or was that just promotional hype?"

"Go ask her."

"I will." Ellie disappeared into the crowd.

Carly saw her parents at the door and went to greet them.

"Sweetie, we're so proud of you." Carly's mother hugged her before passing her off to her father.

"So proud," her father repeated, giving her an extra squeeze. "We've been following the hype in the *Times*. You really did call out the big PR guns this time."

"Enrico did most of the heavy lifting, but yes." Carly nodded. "I called in every favor I was owed and I'm not ashamed to say it."

"This is an interesting building." Her mother stepped out of the doorway to let the next group of arrivals enter. "Look, Patrick. Open beams. So beach house."

"Go look at the paintings, Mom, Dad." Carly ushered them toward the exhibit. "I have a lot of people to chat up and a short amount of time in which to do it."

"Go do your thing, Carly." Her father patted her on the back. "If we don't catch up later, we'll see you in the morning at brunch."

"You were able to get a room at the inn?" Carly asked.

"We have a lovely suite of rooms," her mother told her. "It even has a name. The Captain Something or Other Suite. Some ancestor of the inn's owner. The views of the Bay are divine. Now go, mingle. We're keeping you from your work."

Carly watched her parents drift toward the exhibit area and exhaled gratefully. So far, everything was going as she'd planned.

"It's all so *gorgois*," Enrico crooned in her ear. "All these fabulous works under this one rustic little roof.

The photos didn't do them justice. Carolina really was a genius, Carly."

"I'm so happy to hear you say that. I was beginning to wonder if maybe my eye had failed me."

"Hush your mouth, girl. Your eye never fails. Everyone is going to be talking about this for the next *forever*. The showing is a howling success and your book is the talk of the town. *Everyone* says they're reading it, and everyone says they want to buy *Stolen Moments* and everyone is thrilled to death that Dallas MacGregor is here. Ellie will be able to name her price for that painting, and she'll get it." He squeezed her arm. "You have hit it so far out of the park, kiddo. I'm so proud of you."

"Thanks, Enrico. I'm proud of you, too." When he raised a questioning eyebrow, she said, "If you weren't doing such a great job in New York, I wouldn't have been able to concentrate on all this the way I have. So in a way, you're as much responsible as I am."

"You are too, too sweet, but I'll take it and bask in it." He kissed her cheek. "Thank you." His eyes drifted toward the door, then he leaned over and asked, "Who's the old lady in the wheelchair?"

"Oh. Grace. That's Grace." She patted Enrico's arm and walked to the door. "I'm so glad you were able to come, Grace. I was hoping—"

"I wouldn't miss this for anything." She turned in the chair and told Dan, who stood behind her, "Just lift the damn thing over the damn threshold."

Carly stifled a laugh, and grabbed two glasses of champagne from a passing waiter and handed one to Grace, and one to Dan, who thanked her and immediately took off for the paintings.

"I met your parents this afternoon," Grace told her. "I just happened to be in the lobby when they were signing in. Lovely people, dear."

"Thank you. I'm really happy they were able to make the trip."

"How are you, Carly?" Grace asked, and Carly knew she wasn't inquiring after her health.

"All right." She nodded. "I'm all right."

Grace wasn't buying it.

"Me, too." She sighed. "Have you heard from him?"

Carly shook her head.

"Neither have I. Honestly, when he came home this time, I thought he'd finally gotten all of that wanderlust nonsense out of his system." Grace took a sip of champagne. "Apparently not."

Carly leaned back against the wall. She didn't want to have this conversation in the middle of the gallery opening with people milling about and trying to get her attention.

"I do not know what's wrong with that boy. He's never been able to stay in one place for very long, and it drives me crazy." Grace's eyes filled with tears. "I thought this time he'd found himself at the paper. It seemed to me that he was starting to come around, and more and more, he seemed to be enjoying it. He's come up with several really wonderful ideas for future features and he's been talking about making some content available online, even ways to beef up the online advertising. And he found you." Grace reached out to take Carly's hand. "I was hoping he would. I knew you were going to be important in his life."

"Apparently not important enough for him to stay, Grace."

"Africa." Grace spoke the word as if she wasn't sure what it meant. "Why in the world would he go to Africa?"

"I'm sure he'll tell you . . ." She stopped before she could add, *When he gets back*. She didn't know if she believed he would or not. This was one of those times her positive attitude was failing her.

Enrico touched Carly's shoulder and said softly, "Excuse me, Carly, Evan Smith from the *Times* wants to talk to you."

"Thank you. Tell him I'll be right there." She turned to Grace. "There are some people I need to talk to. But please go look at the exhibit. It really is a marvel. I hope you enjoy it. Without your help with the town council, none of this might have happened. So, go. Look. Enjoy it. And just for a while, try to put your worries aside."

"Have you, dear? Put them aside?" Grace asked before she wheeled herself away.

No more than you have, Carly could have said. Instead, she merely shook her head, plastered her best smile on her face, and set off to find Evan Smith.

By eleven, it was over. The visitors had all trailed off, most to one of the B&Bs in town where they'd been lucky enough to find a vacancy, others to the inn. Just as had been hoped, most of the people on Carly's VIP list had come to St. Dennis on Friday night and were staying till Sunday. Carly saw out the last of the stragglers with promises to call when such and such a painting became available.

"You could have sold every last one of them," Enrico told her.

"Ellie could find herself a very, very wealthy woman if she decides to sell them."

"She still doesn't know what she's going to do?"

Carly shook her head. "She might not do anything with them for a while, and she shouldn't, at least until she has a strong feeling to either sell or not sell. She doesn't have to sell any of them right now, or ever."

"Good," he said. "Drives up the price the longer they stay off the market."

"True enough."

She turned out the lights and paused at the doorway before arming the alarm. "Ready?"

"I am." He walked past her and she punched in the code, then locked the door.

"Where does a thirsty guy go to get a drink in this little town?" he asked as they walked to their cars, hers in the driveway, his rental a few blocks down the street.

"There's a nice place down by the marina. Captain Walt's. Great seafood and a great bar."

"I'm there." He stopped next to her driver's-side door. "You want to join me?"

"Thanks, but I'm exhausted. I have done nothing but eat, sleep, and drink this exhibit for the past couple of months. I'm going to go back to the house and crash."

"You okay?"

"I'm just tired."

"I guess I'll see you tomorrow. Brunch at the inn where I'm staying, right?"

She nodded. "See you in the morning."

Carly drove home, exhausted and depressed. All of her energy had been poured into making this day, this night, a success, and she'd done that. Still, the evening had lacked the shine, the electricity she'd hoped for. The zip it would have had if Ford had been there with her. For Carly, the paintings and the exhibit were all entwined with Ford, with their days and nights at the house on Hudson Street. Now that he was gone, everything, even Carolina's paintings, had lost their glow.

She pulled into her driveway, got out of the car, and locked it. She was almost to the porch when she saw the figure sitting on the top step.

"How was it?" he asked.

Her heart almost stopped. "It was fine. Ford . . ."

"I'm so sorry. I tried to get home in time. I swear I did. But my plane was late and I—"

She burst into tears. In two strides he was there, holding her, rocking her gently.

"I'm sorry, I really am. I know how much the gallery means to you, how much the exhibit . . ." He swallowed hard. "Baby, I'm sorry I didn't make it. Please stop crying."

"I'm not crying because you weren't there." She gulped between sobs. "I'm crying because you came back. Because you're here."

"Of course I came back." His arms tightened around her. "*You're* here."

"What happened?" she asked.

"Mr. Nakimbe is now a guest of his government. He'll be put on trial soon for war crimes. That is, if he isn't assassinated while he's in prison."

"But you're done with it?"

He nodded. "I gave my testimony. I'm done with it." He took her hand and led her back to the porch. He sat on the top step and pulled her onto his lap.

"Does your mom know that you're back?" she asked.

"There's time to tell her in the morning."

"She's going to want you to stay, you know. To stay and take over the paper."

"That's the plan," he said solemnly.

"Seriously? You want to work for Grace at the paper?"

"I'd rather have her work for me."

Carly laughed. "Like that's going to happen."

"That has to be part of the plan. I'll work for her now, learn the ropes, but she's going to have to ease out at some point and let me take over. She can continue to write features when she wants, she can cover the local events and the weddings and the parades like she has for the past fifty years. But sooner or later, she's going to have to cough up the reins."

"You're going to push her out?" Carly was horrified.

"No. I'm going to make her an offer she can't refuse." He stroked her back while he spoke. "This accident of hers has made me realize a lot of things, like the fact that my mother is mortal. She's worked too hard for too many years, and she deserves to slow down a little. Take life a little easier."

"What if she doesn't want to?"

"That's going to be the deal. I'll stay, I'll take it over, but she has to take more time for herself."

"Would you leave if she refused?"

"Would you go with me, if I did?" He turned her face toward him. "The whole time I was away, all I could think about was you. How much I missed you. How much I need to be with you."

"Don't say you'll stay in St. Dennis just because of

me. If you take over the *Gazette* and your heart isn't in it, you'll end up resenting me and the paper and probably your mother as well."

"That's the thing. I had a lot of time to think, Car. I realized that I *want* to work at the paper. I want to be the one from my generation to keep it going, just like my mom, and like my granddad was in his day. I want to be the one to step up. I always sort of pooh-poohed it, but being here, seeing what that newspaper means to the town, to the people who live here and work here . . . I can't let it end with my mother." He smiled. "Besides, I kind of like doing the features thing. Meeting people, interviewing them, finding out what makes them interesting or special. I've enjoyed it." He tilted her face to his. "I want to stay, Car. I want to stay here with you and see what kind of a life we could build together. If you're interested, that is."

She searched in his pocket for his phone, scrolled through his playlist until she found what she was looking for, made her selection, then stuck the phone back into his pocket as the music began to play.

"You Had Me at Hello."

"That's my line," Ford told her.

"I'm borrowing it." She wrapped her arms around his neck.

"Does that mean you'll stay in St. Dennis, too?"

"That means I'll work out a way to run my businesses from here as much as possible. Ellie's thinking about leaving all of her paintings right where they are, and that means that someone has to be in charge of the exhibit for as long as it's running. No one knows Carolina's work better than I do. Besides, I've had some really good ideas for that gallery, and I'd like to explore them."

"Well, then, it looks like we've both landed in the same place at the same time."

"Looks like." She ran a finger along the side of his face. "So I guess this means you're staying."

"I guess it does. You know what they say: there's no place like home."

She searched her bag for the house keys, stood and pushed open the door, and led him into the darkened house. She wrapped her arms around him, then kicked the door closed with her foot.

"Welcome back, Ford," she whispered. "Welcome home . . ."

Diary—

My mother always used to tell us that in every well-lived life, there should be balance. You know, some sun, some rain.

Well, I'm waiting for the storm to begin because for most of this summer, it's been all sunshine. Yes, yes, there was that business of falling down the steps and breaking a couple of bones. I'm still in the casts and I'm still in the wheelchair, but even so, there's been more sun than rain.

It started when Ford came home. My sweet son has grown up to be everything his father and I could have hoped for. He pitched in when I needed him to, and wonder of wonders, he's been coming up with new and creative ways that the _Gazette_ can serve St. Dennis. My hands are shaking as I write this—and I can hardly believe it myself, but it appears he's planning on sticking around to implement those changes. To say that my prayers have been answered would be an understatement, because not only is Ford starting to believe—as I have all along—that his place is at the helm of the paper, but it appears that he may be thinking of settling down here permanently.

Of course, we have Carly to thank for that—of that I am certain. I knew the first time I met her that she was the one—it just took him a little longer to figure it out.

So he spends much of his time on Hudson Street, and that's just skippy with me. It's plain to see that my boy is in love, and since it's equally obvious that that love is returned, I couldn't be happier.

As for Carly, well, the gallery could not be a greater success than it is: glowing write-ups in the _New Yorker_ and the _New York Times_ and the _Washington Post_! Such a fine spotlight shining on our little town, and of course, on Carolina Ellis. Yes, Carly has done exactly what she said she could do, and St. Dennis is better for it.

And from what I hear from Ford, Carly is planning on sticking around. Dallas apparently has read her book and has made no secret of the fact that she wants to make Carolina's story into a movie to be titled—what else?—_Stolen Moments._ Not only that, but Carly's making plans for another big showing at the gallery. The headliner this time around? Not Carolina, but our own Shirley Wyler, Steffie and Grant's mother. The whole town is positively abuzz! Who even knew she painted?! Ford said with so much going on, Carly's decided to make an offer to buy the house on Hudson Street. It doesn't take a psychic to figure out that she won't be living alone for much longer.

So, all in all, much more sunshine than rain lately. I have

all my children here in St. Dennis—though no longer under my roof, but that's fine. Lucy and Clay are happy and talking about starting a family. Ford has found his heart, and I feel a joy in him that I haven't seen since he was a boy. One could say that two out of three isn't bad—but it's beginning to look as if Dan seems married to the inn these days. I'm afraid he'll spend the rest of his life alone. He's barely looked at another woman for more than a few weeks since Doreen died, and that's been years now. Long enough, certainly, for him to move on. Oh, I don't mean forget—she was the love of his young life, the mother of his children. He never will forget her, nor should he. But perhaps there's another love for him somewhere—maybe the love of the rest of his life. I just wish he'd make some effort to find her.

Cue the heavy sigh . . .

~ Grace ~